The
Black Locust

Ken Mann

First published in 2015 by Ken Mann, Brisbane, Qld, Australia.

ISBN 978-0-9942598-1-3 (eBook)
ISBN 978-0-9942598-0-6 (softback)
ISBN 978-0-9942598-2-0 (softback)

For further information,
you may contact me via the following channels;

www.kenmann.net

or follow me on Facebook at;

www.facebook.com/kenmannauthor

I am grateful to the following services that
assisted me in getting this novel to publication;

Cover Design;
Created by Ken Mann – credit is given to the following
Dreamstime artists whose works contributed to the final cover;
Simon Alvinge
Dwnld777
Mdorottya

Editorial Services;
Red Adept Editing
Thank you to both Lynn and Stefanie
www.redadeptediting.com

Formatting;
Original Edition
Polgarus Studio
www.polgarusstudio.com

Revised Edition
Ken Mann

For Jane, Rachel, Natasha, Tristan, Lorelei and Aidan.

Thank you for your support, patience and love.

Glossary

<u>Gaelic Translations</u>

Aedán – Fiery One (AE dan)

Aes Sidhe - A Faerie race in Gaelic mythology (AYS sheeth uh)

An – The

An Croí – The Heart

An Eisint – The Essence

Artagan – StoneART ug an

Asrai – Water Faerie

Beannaigh – Blessed Be

Bitseach – Bitch

Bogha – Bow

Brat – A Woollen Cloak

Buíochas - Thanks

Cac – Shit

Cac Capaill – Horse Shit

Caladbolg – Gaelic two-handed broadsword

Cál Ceannann – Colcannon

Clurichaun - Night form of Leprechaun

Crann úll - Apple Tree

Crios – Belt – used with Dealg to fasten Brat

Daideó – Grandfather

Dealg – Brooch – used to fasten Brat

Dullahan – Without the head – Gaelic unseelie Faerie –
Headless rider

Duass – Prize

Emain Ablach - Name of a mythical island paradise (Isle
of Apples)

Fear Dearg – Red Man Faerie

Fionghan – Fair-born (FIN uh ghun)

Foraire – Sentries, guards

Fuarán na n-óg – The Fountain of Youth

Grá mo chroí - Love of my heart

Hóra – Hi, Hello

Kaelan - Brave Warrior (KAY el in (Kellen))

Léine – Loose fitting – long sleeved Tunic

Le do thoil – Please

Leprechaun – Gaelic Faerie

Magairle – Balls (testicle)

Maimeó – Grand Mother

Niamh – Radiance (NEAVE)

Oren – Pale   (O ren)

Praghas – Price

Púca – Spirit/Ghost - Shape Shifter Faerie (POO ka)

Rhoswen – White Rose (ROES wen)

Scian – Long dagger

Shillelagh - Gaelic hand weapon, is a wooden walking stick and club or cudgel

Sidhe – Mound

Silas – Of the Forest

Súgach – Merry

Taog – Poet (TOOK)

Taraghlan – White brow (TA ruh ghlan)

Truis – Tight fitting pants

Teagmhaigh – Meet – Meeting

Tuatha Dé Danann – Tribe of Goddess Danu

Ulchabhán – Owl

Upthóg – witch, charm worker

Japanese Translations

Arigatou gozaimasu – Thank you very much

Sayonara – Goodbye

Shitsurei shimasu – Very formal, this greeting is often used to a superior or when you leave someone's presence

1

Jane McKinnon sat cross-legged on the old worn carpet in the sunroom of her Aunt Claire's house, thumbing through her Book of Shadows. It was a day like any other for Jane—she intended on joining her aunt at the shop later to do her fair share of work as she had agreed to earlier over a breakfast of Pennyroyal Tea and lightly buttered toast. The Beltane fires would not burn for another week, and Aunt Claire would need Jane's help to get everything in order for the upcoming ritual. Jane's concentration was broken by the hoot of an owl, and she fleetingly lifted her eyes from her reading. Her Book of Shadows was a hardbound leather book, burgundy with a gold pentagram inlaid on the front cover. The book had been in Jane's possession since she was a little girl. Not long after she first moved in with her aunt, after her mother passed away, Aunt Claire had given it to her.

Jane was a very attractive girl standing five foot eight. Her lightly tanned skin matched with her long straight brunette hair of 'dark chocolate tones,' as her hairdresser would say. Her striking amber eyes possessed a slight russet tint—the family trait skipped every second generation but was said to be a sign of greatness. Her grandfather had told her once that he believed they were blessed with the ability to see into the animal world and utilise the animals" sight to foretell of events to come.

"Like an eagle," she would say.

"Yes, like an eagle," he always replied.

Jane turned towards the eastern wall of the room, which mostly consisted of glass panels that allowed the morning sun through. The simple design helped heat the house during the cold Tasmanian winters. She scanned the landscape in a vain attempt to pinpoint the source of her distraction. The owl's call, unusual for such an early time of day, interrupted the morning sounds of wrens and magpies once more. Her gaze settled on the bird perched in a wooded thicket of a nearby eucalypt.

"Merry Meet to you, my feathered friend," Jane whispered under her breath as the corners of her mouth turned upward. Jane studied the majestic creature for a moment longer before the bird waved her beak in a downward motion and pushed herself forward from the branch. Her wings lifted, and in one smooth motion, she was in the air. She faded into the distance.

Jane murmured to herself briefly before releasing the now-vacant eucalypt from her gaze. She looked down at the handwritten pages in front of her, waiting for her eyes to re-adjust to the words that stared back at her, and sighed. She studied when she found time for herself, to reflect, to find the answer for the problems that life threw at her, or to find solace in the comfort of her written word.

The Book of Shadows was the witches' diary, a collection of thoughts, spells, and rituals. The book was a witch's bible, if you will, containing the lore that a Wiccan lived and practiced.

That day, however, her concentration was flawed. She knew that no matter how hard she tried, she would not be able to find the answers she sought. She closed the book, and the sunlight brought a brief smile to Jane's features as the glow reflected onto her hands from the gold leaf inlay of the pentagram on the cover.

"Tomorrow," she whispered. "Tomorrow, I will find you with the help of Cerridwen and Cernunnos to guide me in my search, this I promise to thee. Until I seek the knowledge of your pages again, blessed be, my friend."

Jane squeezed the book gently then raised the cover to her lips to kiss the Wiccan symbol before returning it to rest upon the top of the Jarrah coffee table to her right. She swung her feet from underneath her, gaining a purchase on the carpet. She stood and surveyed her surroundings. The sunroom was a converted veranda with a solid bottom wall that had been the railing before the room was closed in as a solid tongue-and-groove timber wall. Above the old height of the railings, windows reached the ceiling, allowing plenty of light to enter the room. The walls and timber frame had been painted white a couple of years ago, but Jane could still remember the smell of the fresh paint. The carpet, however, was an old green shag pile that hadn't been in vogue since the seventies. The door at the end of the sunroom led out to the secret garden where Jane loved to read underneath an old apple tree beside the pond. Opposing the door to the garden was an old fireplace constructed from round-edged river stones of pale browns and grey.

"Jane," a voice called from beyond the door to the lounge room. "Are you inside?"

"Yes, I'm here," Jane replied to her Aunt Claire as she stepped into the lounge room.

Claire, Jane's mother's older sister, was very protective of her niece, and she operated a well-respected business in town. At age forty-eight, she'd been practicing Wicca for approximately thirty years and had begun teaching Jane the craft.

"Do you mind going down to the store for me? I've run out of anise, and I need some for tonight's dinner… oh, and a bunch of baby bok choy, as well," Claire said as she poked her head around the corner of the kitchen and into the lounge room.

"Yeah, sure thing. Is that all that you need?"

"Yes, it should be. I'll need some fresh ginger, as well, but I can get that from the greenhouse garden later. There's money in my purse on the bench."

"Okay, thanks. I'll just put something a bit warmer on and go. I might stop by Sophie's and see if she wants to join me. "Jane walked into the hall towards her bedroom.

"That sounds like a good idea. Say hi for me when you see her."

Moments later, Jane hopped back into the kitchen. She propped herself up against the wall as she pulled her shoe over her heel.

"The sun seems to have disappeared early this morning. Make sure that you take your coat with you."

"I will. What time are you heading into the shop?"

"About half an hour or so. I am sure people won't mind if I am ten minutes late," Claire replied with a soft laugh.

"I'm sure they won't. I'll see you in an hour or two."

"Okay, love, see you then."

Claire turned back to the bench where she was checking the ingredients for dinner. Jane stood there for a moment and regarded her aunt. Claire's features were very similar to Jane's mothers, so she could easily imagine what her mum would have looked like. Five foot six inches tall, Claire was a little stockier than Jane's mum had been, according to the pictures Jane had seen. She had brown eyes and a short black bob, which grey hairs were starting to infiltrate. The grey had never bothered Claire, though. She was happy to grow old gracefully in the company of her family, the Gods, and her customers at the shop. Jane loved her and was always thankful that Claire had taken her in. She was a second mother, really, and in moments like that, Jane imagined what her life would have been like if her mum had not passed away. She always loved sitting in the kitchen and talking for hours with Claire or helping prepare the meals, but a part of Jane always longed to know what life would have been like with her mum.

Jane turned to leave the room as Claire dumped the pots onto the bench top. The simple kitchen was a basic rectangle with benches that ran along the east side. The sink was underneath a large bay window, where small pots of assorted herbs flourished in the morning sun. The window also looked out towards the path that led to the front gate. Behind her, a rectangular oak table sat in the middle of the room. It was where everyone ate and caught up on the events happening in their lives and other news about town. The opposite side of the kitchen was occupied by the fridge, stove, and cooktop. A huge walk-in pantry separated the dining room from the kitchen. The room had a very eclectic country feel about it. Many objects decorated the room— cows, chickens, and blackboards where Claire kept many reminders. Amongst all of that were other keepsakes of the alternative lifestyle that they lived—pentagrams, chalices, and the Wiccan Rede that was printed on an old stained parchment and hung in a walnut frame.

Claire had just retrieved the last of the ingredients from the pantry when Jane called out, "Bye, Aunt Claire. I'm going now. I will see you at the shop a little later. Love you."

"Blessed be, angel," Claire replied.

The subtle metal groan of the screen doors" slow swing back to the jamb was familiar to Jane. She started along the path towards the front gate and turned back to wave to Claire, who she knew would be watching at the kitchen window.

Jane loved living at Avalon. The house had been named after the song made famous by Bryan Ferry and Roxy

Music, or so she thought. In fact, she had never asked Aunt Claire why she called the house Avalon, assuming that Aunt Claire had named it. Every time Jane drank in the sight of Avalon, she felt upbeat, dreamy, and blissful. Like the song, the house was one of few things that made her truly happy. The old light-blue double-story weatherboard had white windows and trimmings and a roof of silver corrugated iron. A beautiful country house, unique in its own way, never received visitors at the front door. The house, strangely enough, faced north. However, the road that serviced the property ran along the east side of the property so that the path leading from the front gate past the kitchen actually took visitors to the back door.

Jane turned back towards the house to wave to Aunt Claire as she knew she would be watching through the window. Her aunt reciprocated and mouthed something at her, and Jane assumed that she was wishing her well. Jane made her way along the concrete path bordered by colourful snapdragons, violas, alyssum, and foxglove. Claire planted the border garden just after Ostara in September, and the blooms had exploded into vibrant colours that followed the meandering path. The temperature was starting to warm, as it was mid-October. That meant that the fires of Beltane were not far away. Jane opened the old rusted gate that was bordered by two oak trees. As it swung closed on rusty hinges, the gate's groan interrupted the peace of the garden. As Jane stepped out onto the grassed verge between the house and the street, she turned to Blue Belle, her most prized possession—well, one of them. Blue

Belle was her 1971 Volkswagen Superbug Beetle. She'd bought it when she was only seventeen, using the money she had saved from working in Aunt Claire's shop and a few years of gifted money that she'd tucked away under the mattress.

She did have some money that was held in trust for her, as well, but that was part of an inheritance from her mum's estate. She would not be able to use any of those monies until after she turned twenty-one. Therefore, all of the restoration that went into Blue Belle had to come from money that she had earned herself.

She walked over to the sky-blue Beetle parked on the curb of Delta Road. At the door, she hesitated for a moment. She patted down her pockets, her fingers drawing up and bunching the material of the pocket in her palm that she squeezed to make sure that it was not there. She then checked her bag, fumbling for a moment before retrieving the grocery list Aunt Claire had given her.

"Thought I'd lost you for a moment," she said to herself under her breath. Jane replaced the list back into the centre pocket of her handbag and felt the jingle of the car keys in amongst the lipstick and eyeliner. Normally most people in town did not lock their cars, but the increasing number of tourists who either stayed in or passed through town made Jane uneasy. She wasn't an untrusting person, but she normally didn't park on the curb, and she had invested so much time and money into Blue Belle that she couldn't imagine losing her.

Jane unlocked the door and opened it. She threw her bag in the back and slid in then pulled the door shut behind her. She put the keys into the ignition then sat for a brief moment before taking the stick out of gear. She turned the key as she pressed the accelerator with her right foot. The distinctive hum of the air-cooled engine roared into life. Jane loved the sound, and she identified it her with lifestyle. She was not a hippie by any means. However, she was an environmentalist. She was a green, albeit not a political one, and because she was Wiccan, she felt a responsibility to the environment. The Beetle was economical with fewer emissions than most petrol vehicles, and it spoke volumes about Jane's character.

She let the engine warm for a moment while she turned on the stereo and checked her face and hair in the mirror. She then pushed the clutch and shifted the stick into first. Johnny Mars's upbeat jangle-pop guitar riff introduced The Smiths' *This Charming Man* before Morrissey's whimsical voice took her on a lyrical journey. The engine's hum was lost in the music, and the melody moved through Jane's body. She adjusted the vent and looked one last time at the house before driving off. She had a habit of looking at the windows in the kitchen first, just in case. If Aunt Claire was still watching, she could give one last wave. Then her gaze would follow the path down to the gate and between the two oak trees before settling on the little rectangular iron plate that hung over the white letterbox embossed the name Avalon.

Jane looked over her shoulder for any traffic and slowly pulled away from the curb. She travelled west along Delta Road into town from Avalon, which was situated on the outskirts of town and near Freycinet National Park.

She turned onto Jetty Road and pulled over in front of Sophie's house, a low-set timber cottage. The cream coloured house was accented in heritage green on the gutters, window shutters, and stairs that led to the front door. The gardens were well maintained and showed off a wide variety of flora native to Tasmania.

Jane cut the engine, stored the keys in her handbag, and unclipped the seat belt. She sometimes thought that she would like to put automatic retractable seat belts in Blue Belle as she found it cumbersome to turn to hang the seat belt buckle on the hook above her right shoulder. Then she always suppressed the dream by reminding herself that she was trying to keep Blue Belle as close as possible to factory condition, with the exception of the digital stereo that had been installed last year. She brushed her hair and checked herself in the mirror one last time. When she thought that she was presentable, she opened the door and exited the car. The door shut with a thud as Jane turned to see the curtains in the front window falling back into place.

Jane had only taken three steps towards the house when the front door swung open.

"Hey, gorgeous. How are you?"

"Hey yourself," Jane replied as she reached the bottom of the three steps that led up to the front landing and door. "I'm good, Soph. How are you?"

"Yeah, can't complain."

"Are you busy this morning?" Jane asked.

"Hmm … depends. What are you planning?"

"Oh, nothing much, just going to get some groceries for Aunt Claire that she needs for tonight. I got to work in the store later, but I thought I'd drop in on the way and see how you are."

Sophie leaned forward as Jane approached the door and wrapped her arms around her in a comforting embrace.

"It's good to see you," Sophie said softly into Jane's ear before releasing her. "Where are we going?"

Jane regarded Sophie for a moment before replying.

Sophie Bainbridge was her best friend. They had met in primary school a couple of years before Jane's mum died and they had been practically inseparable since. Sophie was taller at 5"10, with long blonde hair and a fair complexion. She was slim in stature and looked very angelic in appearance. She did not fit into the stereotype that most nineteen-year-olds did yet her appearance was always homely. She mainly wore flats and leggings, normally black, but she would mix it up at times with some prints and on top was something that was always loose—whether that was T-shirts or jumpers, they were always two sizes too big. She was very much like Jane in many ways, but she was not drawn to Wicca the same way Jane was. Sophie had always been interested in knowing more, but she had her own path to follow. Sophie was all about connections, and she had many. Jane aside, Sophie's biggest connection was one that she rarely shared with anyone for fear of being ridiculed.

She was very spiritual and had a strong bond to the spiritual world, so strong that she could sense when spirits were near. She frequently saw apparitions and could channel their thoughts and converse with them. She didn't like to label it, though, and did not like being called a medium. If anyone asked, she gave a broad answer, saying only that she was spiritual. Jane and Sophie respected each other's beliefs, and at times, they complemented each other, especially at certain times of the year, such as Samhain.

"Hello!"

"Sorry," Jane replied as a smile crept onto her face. "I was just thinking."

"Of what?"

"Nothing." Jane paused. "Never mind, it doesn't matter… I was just going down to the shops to grab some things for tonight. Did you want to come? I was thinking about travelling over to Swansea, but I think I'll just stay local. What do you think?"

"Yeah, sounds good. Give me a sec to get changed?"

Jane followed Sophie into the house and sat down on the edge of the lounge. Her eyes scanned the room as Sophie continued down the hall, running her hands along both the timber walls of the hall to her room. Jane always felt as if she had slipped back in time when she came over to Sophie's, which was decorated in '70s retro style. The lounge that she was sitting on was a low-back Jens Risom three-seater sofa from the US. Its teak frame with polished exposed legs had a strawberry-red upholstery that covered the seats with slim cushions. To the left of the lounge, near the hallway, was a four-drawer teak Danish Lovig desk with a brown Stromberg-Carolson rotary telephone on it. Jane had never heard the phone ring, but every time she stopped over, she was tempted to call it on her mobile or pick up the handset to see if it had a dial tone. Opposite sat a huge tube television encased in a brown timber lowboy. The HMV logo of the dog and gramophone always reminded Jane of the old television that had sat in her grandfather's house prior to his death just over ten years before. What always amused her most, though, was the generic framed print of three flying wood ducks that lived on the wall where the lounge room met the dining room. Returning her gaze to the teak coffee table in front of her, Jane saw an old issue of *UK Cosmo* with frayed edges and Isla Fisher on the cover. She picked it up and started flipping through the pages. She normally did not read gossip or fashion magazines, but she knew exactly where to turn to for the readers" forums. Moments later, Sophie bounced down the hall, wearing a short summer dress and pumps accessorised with a small clutch. She stopped at the entry to the room and struck a pose: one knee slightly bent behind the other, one heel lifted off the ground, and arms outstretched with one diagonally above her head and the other pointing towards the ground.

"How do I look?" she asked as a smile beamed across her face.

"You look like you're ready to hit the town. Shopping, that is."

"Yeah, I know, right."

Both girls broke into laughter.

13

Jane stood up from the lounge and tossed the *Cosmo* back onto the table. "I don't know why you read those."

"It's not mine."

"Yeah, sure." Jane grinned.

"No really, it's Natasha's. She has a whole collection in her room."

"You're kidding!"

"Seriously, now let's go mole," Sophie quipped as she walked past Jane and out the door.

Sophie had an older brother, Isaac, and two younger sisters, Natasha and Stacey. Isaac was twenty-two and moved away from Delta just over three years ago, when he'd accepted a position with a bank in Hobart. Both Natasha and Stacey, seventeen and fourteen respectively, were still at home. Both were very different from Sophie, and neither seemed to share Sophie's gift or have any interest in exploring if there was something in them. This disappointed Sophie but she knew that she couldn't live her sister's lives for them. Nevertheless, Sophie did hope that they would come around eventually.

Sophie's parents were still married, which was quite unusual for couples anymore. They were due to celebrate their thirtieth wedding anniversary in December, and the entire family was looking forward to it. Her dad worked the piers down at the local marina as well as the dry dock, looking after all the day-to-day and maintenance issues. He prided himself on his ability to provide for his family while doing a job that he loved. Sophie always used to mock her father at barbeques and other gatherings when he'd talk about responsibility and job satisfaction, saying, *"You can rarely find something in life that you can do and love at the same time. Whereas, most people just settle for what they can get."* In most cases Sophie was somewhere in the background, mouthing along with her father and pulling faces.

Sophie's mum was a homemaker. The liberated woman was very opinionated, and if something or someone wasn't right, she didn't hesitate to let someone know about it. Appearances could be deceiving, though, because from the outside looking in, she seemed a typical 1950s homemaker.

Jane pulled the heavy door shut behind her, tested the handle until it latched into place correctly, and joined Sophie. They strolled down the steps onto the lawn.

"What time do you have to be at the shop?" Sophie asked.

"I'll go in about ten thirty or eleven, I think. I didn't really say a time, just that I'd get the groceries first and then come in."

"Okay, are we just going down the Esplanade?"

"Yep, climb in," Jane said as they reached Blue Belle.

2

The silver Holden Statesman cruised into the car park off the Esplanade and rolled to a stop beside the real estate. The vehicle sat for a minute, then the driver's door opened slowly, releasing a mushrooming cloud of smoke into the atmosphere.

A mysterious red figure exited the car, took two steps, and stopped to take in his surroundings.

He was wearing a pair of black shoes manufactured circa 1758. The style was known as Ligonier's after the British attack on the French Fort Ligonier in present-day Pittsburgh, Pennsylvania. The shoes were dressed with traditional square colonial military brass buckles. Two or three inches of red sock peeked out below black trousers held up by a thick leather belt of the same colour with a huge bright brass square buckle. He wore a black button up shirt beneath a red coat that hung below his knees. His look was completed by a red Paris Beau top hat albeit slightly lighter in shade, with a small silver hat band. The ensemble really stood out against his pale, almost translucent skin tone. He carried a large cane that could have been considered a staff. Finally, there were his eyes. They were pale green, but in certain light, the pupils sometimes appeared to be blood red.

He turned back to the vehicle, closed the driver's door, and walked behind the car, grinding the loose gravel of the car park underfoot. He reached the footpath, stopped, raised his right hand to his mouth, and took a final long drag on his cigarette. He dropped the butt and ground it out on the cement with the sole of the shoe. Looking up, he exhaled the smoke, which the mild breeze carried down the street.

The red man surveyed the street in front of him. All of the buildings were early-century timber-clad structures with covered walkways out the front. The windows of each shop were very large and well-dressed so passers-by could see into the shop to see the wares inside. The shopping precinct looked very similar to a main street that had been transported in time from the eighteen hundreds. The shops in Delta, though, were individually painted in different soft colour palettes with all the fascia, gutters, and railings painted in brilliant white.

Directly across the Esplanade from him was a pale yellow bakery, the all-white butcher, and of course the green greengrocer. The building to his left, the largest on the street, shared a car park with the Hotel Delta. The hotel had a brown-and-white German half-timbered façade that most people mistook as being Tudor in style.

He stepped out onto the pavement and turned right towards the real estate. Few people were out on the

Esplanade that morning. Only the odd car drove past, and the only pedestrians he noticed were on the opposite side of the street. He walked with a hand holding his hat firm on his head and his eyes cast down towards the pavement to avoid making eye contact with anyone. Upon reaching the front window, he shuffled crab-like back and forth along the window, looking at the property listings. A strong breeze blew down the street, picking up papers and other debris. He was oblivious to the small blue Beetle that turned onto the Esplanade from Jetty Road until the hum of the air-cooled motor rose over the sounds of the breeze. He turned to see the car pass by. The driver was a young female with long black hair that was blowing in the wind. He couldn't make out any features of the second person in the car. A smirk touched the red man's features as he turned back to the window.

∞

Carla Ison was just finishing a call when she noticed a gentleman at the front of the shop, looking through the current listings. It had been a quiet day, and she was keen to get any business in that she could.

"Thank you, Mr Ashford. Yes… yes, I will get that invoice out to you today," she said petulantly, her legs bouncing up and down as she watched the man out the front. *I'd better not lose a possible sale today,* she thought.

Carla started to twist in the chair impatiently as she replied, "Yes, of course, Mr Ashford, definitely, today for sure, no problem. Okay, will do. You, too. Thank you. Talk to you soon, Mr Ashford," Carla said as she cradled the phone with a huff.

She dropped her pen onto a pile of new brochures that were due at the letterbox the following day. She checked her makeup and hair in the reflection of the computer monitor. She ran her fingers through her auburn bob then went through her checklist.

"Hair done. Lippy done," she said as she puckered her lips at her reflection. She stood and side shimmied while running her hands down her body, over her figure hugging black dress. "Looking good, girl. Now go get him," she whispered to herself as she stepped around the side of the oak desk.

Carla watched her potential customer on the other side of the glass as she walked from her desk into the foyer of the office. He moved from one listing to the next, reading intently. She noted that he was trying to remain inconspicuous by keeping his head down, and that only made her all the more curious.

Carla tapped the glass, breaking his concentration. He looked up in shock at Carla, apparently realising that his attempts to remain discreet had failed. He looked past the display cards and into the office. She motioned for him to come inside. However, he tilted his head slightly to each side, as if checking to see if he was being watched, then he turned and walked back in the direction of the car park.

"Oh, no, you don't," Carla called out as she sprinted towards the door, struggling to keep her balance on her heels. She pushed open the glass door and looked at where the man had been standing. She caught a fleeting glimpse as he turned the corner at the edge of the building.

"God, why am I having a shit month?" she questioned as she descended the two steps to the pavement. She grabbed the sides of her dress and ran as fast as her ankles would allow. "Wait, sir," she yelled at the empty walkway.

When she reached the corner, she rested her hand on the edge of the timber building while she tried to regain her composure. "Sir," she gasped, trying one last time to get his attention. She knew that her attempts were in vain, as she lifted her head to see a silver vehicle drive past her out the driveway.

"Shit!"

3

Both Sophie and Jane were enjoying the drive into town. The windows were down, and the rush of fresh air filled the car, blowing their hair in all directions. The Smiths CD was still in the player, and when *How Soon is Now* started, Jane reached forward and turned the volume up to eight. She never went louder than that, as the sound lost clarity and started to distort. A heightened sense of anticipation built as the girls sang along. Marr's haunting tremolo guitar riff bounced throughout the car, and then in unison, Jane and Sophie turned to each other as they joined in on Morrissey's famous lyrics. Letting the melody envelop her body, Jane danced her fingers along the top of the steering wheel. She loved the classics of the eighties, especially those by British groups such as The Smiths, Joy Division, OMD, Orange Juice, the Jesus and Mary Chain, Echo and The Bunnymen, New Order, and her all-time favourite, The Cure.

The morning sun was starting to heat up, and its glare bounced off the chrome VW emblem on the hood of the car.

Sophie rested her elbow on the door and dangled her left hand flat outside the window, moving it in fluid motions up and down as she surfed the wind. She turned to Jane with an excited expression on her face. "Hey, we should just totally drop what we are doing today and go to the beach. It's so perfect today, it would be great. What do you think?" Sophie's smile reached from one side of her face to the other.

"Yeah, that would be great, but I promised Aunt Claire that I'd get the shopping done this morning and then help her out in the shop. Why don't we drop in to see her before we go back and see if we can go after lunch?" Jane pushed down the indicator lever to turn.

Sophie changed the CD to a mixed collection of '80s tracks that Jane had in the glove box. "Yeah, okay. Sounds good. I can't wait," Sophie said as she reclined into the seat.

The tick of the indicator was barely audible over Morrissey's *Every Day is Like Sunday*. The two of them rode down Jetty Road for a couple of minutes in silence, just listening to the music, lip-syncing to the lyrics, and taking in the sun while enjoying each other's company.

"You know, I could help out at the store so we could get to the beach earlier," Sophie said.

"Thanks. That would be great." Jane smiled as her hand gave a gentle rub on Sophie's right leg.

They approached the small shopping precinct of Delta known as the Esplanade after the street of the same name.

The Tasmanian Fire Service had a small firehouse on the left beside the local police station on Jetty Road. On the corner was a light pink hairdresser's shop called Little Cuts. Opposite was the Hotel Delta, and beside Little Cuts was Minty Fresh, the local clothing outlet. Many people had thought that a dentist was moving into town when the business name was hung out the front. It would have saved a lot of travel time for those who had to drive to Swansea to get their check-ups. Marilyn, the owner of Minty Fresh told the *Mercury* newspaper that the store was named after the original colour of the building, which got a bit of sprucing up prior to opening day.

Jane turned the corner into the Esplanade, where Aunt Claire's shop was located at the end of the street near Civic Park.

"Hey, look at that guy," Sophie exclaimed with amusement as she pointed across Jane's eye line towards a man outside the real estate.

"What the fudge? Watch what you're doing." Jane twisted to see past Sophie's hand but also to look over her shoulder at what or who had caught her attention.

"Did you see him?"

"No, not really," Jane replied as she straightened herself, questioning Sophie's sanity. "Why what was wrong with him?"

"Nothing, I guess. He was dressed funny. I mean, it was all olden-day stuff but funny colours. Not what you'd expect, especially in Delta."

"What was he wearing?"

"You know, the stuff that pilgrims used to wear—those funny big hats with the buckles on them and the shoes that had the buckles." Sophie paused a moment and seemed to consider what she was saying. "Okay, okay. I got it. Think of a guy dressed in bright red, looking like a cross between a leprechaun and a Pilgrim," Sophie said with a slight comic tone in her voice.

"Are you serious?" Jane asked, thinking the conversation was getting a little bizarre, as she pulled into the supermarket car park.

Then she and Sophie burst into laughter.

"Well, let's get this over and done with, shall we?" Jane said as she turned to look at the front of the store.

"What's on the list? We can take an aisle each," Soph replied as she walked to the back of the car to join her friend.

"Okay, we have to get some anise and baby bok choy."

"Okay, I'll grab that, and you can get to the shop early.

Did you want anything for lunch?" Sophie asked.

"Nah, I'm not really hungry, but I'd love chocolate milk," Jane replied.

"Okay I'll duck in and get it. Meet you in five?"

"Yeah, okay." Jane turned to walk the pavement leading around the end of the cul-de-sac.

Jane stepped onto the covered boardwalk that followed the shopfronts along both sides of the Esplanade. She passed the record store, 33-45-78, and the café, Froth n Stuff, before stopping outside the Silver Moon. As she did every time she arrived, she studied the window dressings.

Satisfied, she opened the door. A brass bell hanging at the top of the door announced her arrival.

Jane stepped into a familiar world that she loved. The shop's external walls were a light mauve colour, and the interior was a mix of purple, black, and silver. She scanned the shop for customers and Aunt Claire. The bookstand near the door displayed all the best known Wiccan authors such as Scott Cunningham, Silver Ravenwolf, Raymond Buckland, and Yasmine Galenorn. The counter that ran the length of the shop held an entire collection of valuable items: crystals, silver and pewter jewellery, swords, and athames, all under lock and key. The other side of the shop had the herbs, altar tools, candles, pentagrams, and incense. At the rear of the store were the music selections and the counter with cash register. Aunt Claire carried such artists as Medwyn Goodall, Loreena McKennitt, and Clannad.

Loreena McKennitt's *The Mummers' Dance* was playing. Jane had fond memories of the song—not only did she love it herself, but Aunt Claire always played it when Beltane was approaching. The lyrics were suggestive of primitive maypoles dressed with ribbon at springtime.

The black curtain separating the shop floor and the rear storage room slid open. A hand pushed the last inch at the top of the tabs to the end of the rod.

"Merry Meet, Jane," Aunt Claire said as she stepped through the doorway.

"Merry Meet, Aunty. Listening to *The Mummers' Dance* again?"

"Of course. You know it's one of my favourites," Claire said with a guilty smile. "Did you get the anise that I asked for?" She walked behind the service counter in the back.

"Soph is getting it at the moment," Jane replied as she turned towards the front of the shop. "She should be back any minute. Has it been busy today?"

"A little. Two people in before ten. Did you want a cuppa?" Claire asked as she sat down behind the counter and picked up a trade catalogue.

They were silent for a couple moments. Claire sipped her coffee as she scanned new items in the supply catalogue. Jane began her routine of checking stock on the shelves, starting with the music. She slowly ambled along the racks, looking at the CDs. She picked up *The Best of Medwyn Goodall*, reviewing the song list as she turned back to Aunt Claire.

"There's a song on here called *Avalon*. Have you heard it before?"

"Yes, I love that one, as well. I can put it on for you when this is finished, if you like?" Claire said.

"Okay, sounds good." Jane walked over to the counter and rested her elbows atop the counter. "Has your house always been called Avalon?"

Claire tilted forward, placing her mug down in front of her. She regarded Jane for a moment before answering. "For as long as I can remember," she finally said. "Did you know that your mother named it? Your Daideó and Maimeó couldn't ever decide on a name. Each had a favourite, but never could they meet on a decision."

Jane could see the memories flooding Claire's mind as a smile flicked the corners of her lips, and her eyes seemed to be distant for a moment before clarity returned. "You know, your Daideó used to tell us stories of Arthurian legends. We would sit and listen to him for hours with pillows and blankets wrapped around us. One of us was always sure to nod off before he finished," Claire added with a chuckle.

"What are the Arthurian legends?

"King Arthur and the Knights of the Round Table," Claire replied.

"That doesn't sound very interesting," Jane said in a disappointed tone. "It sounds very boyish if you ask me."

"Luckily, I didn't ask." Claire laughed before adding, "Your Daideó was a very good storyteller—the best, I think. Your mum loved it when he spoke of Morgan le Fay, a sorceress. She was King Arthur's antagonist and the leader of nine sisters who lived on Avalon." "On Avalon?" Jane asked.

"Yes, on Avalon—it was an island. It was said that the great sword Excalibur was forged there and that King Arthur was taken there to recover after fighting Mordred in the Battle of Camlann. The Welsh called it Ynys Afallon. The Angles called it Avalon, and the commoners called it the Fortunate Isle or the Island of Apples. No matter who was calling it what and in what tongue it was said, it all meant the same thing."

"What was that?"

"Apples silly," Claire replied with a big grin. "And I'll

tell you what," she continued, "that tree that you sit under back at home out in the garden—your mum planted that tree when we were little girls, and she did it because of the stories that used to tell us. We used to sit out there and tell our own stories, creating our own memories as if it was our own little island, and that's how the house got its name."

"Cool. So it was after the stories that Daideó told?"

"Yes but mostly after the apple tree. The stories were part of the inspiration, but being under the tree made your mum and me happy, and when Daideó and Maimeó saw that, they agreed to call the house Avalon after the apple tree."

"I've always felt at home under the tree, as well," Jane said with a smile. "It must be the connection that we all have."

"Yes." Claire reached forward and took Jane's hand. "And maybe it could be your mum looking over you, as well."

A warm rush flooded over Jane, followed by an emotional sigh. "Thanks, Aunty Claire," she replied with a smile as she stood, shedding a tear. She leaned in across the counter to give her aunt a hug, then the bell at the door broke the moment.

Sophie bounced into the shop with a bag of shopping in her right hand and flavoured milk in her left.

"Hi, guys," she said as she let the front door close behind her. "Did you miss me?" she asked as she walked towards the counter at the back of the shop. "You know how hard it…" Sophie trailed off as she seemed to realise that she had come in at the wrong time. "I'm sorry. Should I go and come back later?"

"No, don't be silly," Jane responded with a sniffle as she wiped away the tears welling in her eyes.

"Are you sure?"

"Yes, we are sure. Now come over here," she said, motioning with her hand.

"Merry Meet, Sophie. How are you going?" Aunt Claire asked as she got up from her chair to give Sophie a hug.

"I'm well. Thank you for asking. How are you?"

"Good, busy but good. You're looking well. I hear that you volunteered to do some shopping for me this morning. Did you have any trouble getting the anise or bok choy? I find the store doesn't always have it when I want it, which can be annoying."

"It was no trouble at all. They only had the bottled anise, though, nothing fresh. Is that okay?" Sophie asked.

"Yes, that's okay, dear. Thank you."

Claire took the bag from Sophie and asked if Jane didn't mind taking it home with her when she left the shop.

"Sure thing," Jane said as she got herself composed. "Okay, now what can we do to help today, Aunty Claire?"

Claire turned towards the storeroom at the back. "I've had some boxes of ritual herbs delivered that are out in the back. Do you mind getting them and putting them in the display racks, please?"

"Yeah, okay," Jane replied. "Are you ready?" she asked Sophie.

"Sure am. Let's get to it."

The two girls walked through the black curtain and into the back room.

"Is it this box near the fire extinguisher?" called Jane.

"Yes, that's it. Just make sure to put the new ones to the rear of the existing stock, please," Claire replied as she walked to the front of the shop to check street and pedestrian traffic. She had a habit of doing that several times throughout the day. The shop was doing well, and Claire made a good living. However, business was rather slow during the week. Things picked up on Saturdays when tourists and other folk drifted through town, usually on their way to get-back-to-nature treks into Freycinet National Park. The holiday season in summer was the busiest time of year, and things were just starting to pick up as Beltane and the end of October approached.

"There's not many people about town today," Claire called out to towards the back room.

"No, there's not," Jane replied as she and Sophie carried the boxes of herbs back out to the front of the shop. "Although Soph saw an interesting character before in front of the real estate as we got here."

"Really?" Claire enquired. "What was so interesting?"

"He just looked out of place, that's all. He was wearing some weird red outfit straight from some old movie or something," Sophie said as both she and Jane dropped the boxes to the floor and began sorting the bags of herbs into alphabetical order.

Claire decided to go out to grab something to eat for lunch while the girls finished stocking the display racks. "I'll be back in a moment. Are you sure I can't get either of you anything?"

"No thanks," they both replied at the same time.

"Jinx," they yelled simultaneously then broke into laughter.

"You know, I am a little hungry," Sophie said after Claire had left for the Froth n Stuff.

"Yeah, so am I, but we'll be done soon. Aunt Claire will be back, and we can grab something to eat on our way to the beach."

Fifteen minutes later, the entry bell jingled, and Claire returned from the café with a caramel latte and lamington fingers.

"Who wants some lamingtons?" she asked as she held up the bag, gently shaking it as she walked to the back counter.

"Yes, please," they both replied.

"Help yourselves when you're ready," Claire said as she put the bag on the counter.

"Cool thanks," Soph replied. The girls both got up from the floor and helped themselves to a lamington, cupping one of their hands underneath the cake to catch any of the desiccated coconut that fell off as they bit into them.

"We're just about finished," Jane said in a muffled voice, holding her hand to her mouth as she spoke with a mouthful of food. "We're thinking about going down to the beach this afternoon. Is there anything else that we can do before we go?" Jane asked.

"No, that's okay, dear. I'll be fine. Thank you for your help."

Jane returned the empty boxes to the back room. "Did you want the boxes in here, Aunty Claire?" she called out. "I can put them out the back in the industrial bin if you prefer."

"No, just out there is fine. I'll find a use for them," she replied as she walked to the doorway and pushed the black curtain aside.

Jane stretched her back after she placed the boxes in the corner then let out a slight yawn. "Okay, then, we'll make a move so I can be back early for dinner. Did you want me to start anything if I'm home before you?"

Claire seemed to pout for a moment as she thought before replying, "The pork shoulder has been thawing in the fridge today, so would you mind taking it out and cutting it for me, please?"

"Sounds interesting. What are you cooking?" Sophie asked, showing renewed interest in the conversation.

"It's going to be braised pork with anise and ginger," Claire replied. "Would you like to stay over for some?"

Sophie's smile disappeared as the realisation came over her. "I'd love to, but I have to babysit Natasha and Stacey tonight," she said in a sad tone.

Claire stepped over to Sophie, put her arms around her, and moved her mouth to her ear. "I'll save you some," she whispered then smiled.

"Great, thanks so much, Aunt Claire," Sophie said with a huge grin.

"Okay, grab your stuff, Soph," Jane said as she picked up her bag from behind the counter, "Let's get to the beach before we lose all of the sun."

"I'm right behind you."

"Blessed be, girls."

"Bye, Claire."

"Blessed be, Aunty Claire."

4

Jane waved to Sophie as she waited at the curb outside her house. Sophie ascended the three steps and put her bag and towel on the setting outside the door. She turned to see Jane waving then leaned over the railing.

"Bye," she yelled while swinging her hand in the air above her head with her feet perched on the bottom rail.

The engine's raspy burble picked up tempo as Jane shifted into first and released the clutch. She honked twice as she pulled away from the curb, her right arm outside the window, trying to wave over the top of the roof as she drove away.

She drove a short distance then did a U-turn and drove back past Sophie's house. No one was outside for her to acknowledge, but she beeped the horn twice anyway.

At just past five in the afternoon, she drove back towards home. The setting sun created an orange glow across the sky. There was probably less than forty-five minutes of daylight left when Jane turned right onto Delta Road. The remaining couple of kilometres to Avalon were uneventful; her only distraction was singing along to The

Cure's *Just like Heaven* she remembered dressing like the band from their earlier days, circa 1984. She'd worn all black, white foundation, and red lipstick and teased her hair into an unruly mess. That had been only five years ago, and everyone used to ask if her look was goth or emo. *"Neither,"* she would always reply. *"I'm just me, dressing like The Cure."* In time, she'd accepted people calling her goth, although she knew from previous interviews that Robert Smith never considered the band to be goth.

As she identified more with her Wiccan roots, she began to wear more free-flowing dresses made from natural materials, let her hair down or tied it back, and wore less make-up. She stopped making any effort to conceal the pentagram that hung around her neck. She still wore black on occasion, but she'd started going to the beach again and getting out in the sun in general. The deathly white skin tones of the goth world no longer mattered to her. Nonetheless, those same people who had called her goth referred to her as a witch once she changed her look. That description was true in every sense of the word, but it was still a label with an inaccurate connotation.

Blue Belle's brake lights illuminated the darkening silhouettes on the side of the road as the car slowed to a gentle speed. Avalon was just ahead; Jane navigated the crossover and stopped the V-Dub in front of the large gate that denied access to the driveway. She unclicked the seat belt and opened the door. Leaving it ajar, she to unbolt the gate latch. A slow grinding screech escaped the hinges while Jane pushed the heavy wrought-iron gate open to rest against the pine sleeper that separated the drive from the garden. She walked back to Blue Belle, hopped in, closed the door, and drove up the drive to park in front of the back outhouses. Sitting stationary in the drive, Jane turned off the stereo then shut down the engine. She sat there for a moment, happy with life, reflecting on the day in the shop, the beach, and her time with Claire and Sophie. A smile lifted the corners of her lips as the heightened sense of joy snapped her back to reality. She grabbed her bag then exited and locked her car. Looking back down the drive, she decided to leave the gate open for Aunt Claire. She walked the first ten metres of the twenty metre gravel path then looked up into the blackening sky, her attention caught by the Goddess.

"Merry Meet, my Lady," she said, looking at the waxing moon while pressing her pentagram against her chest with her left hand. "It's a beautiful night," she continued as she started along the path again. She cocked her head briefly and stopped, hearing a subtle whooshing noise approach. She held her ground as a rush of air passed over her. She caught a flash of white, tan, and brown. Her eyes followed the low-flying object as it came to rest in a tree beside the house. It took a moment to settle then made a loud rasping screech and returned Jane's stare.

"Well, hello and Merry Meet to you, my friend," she said as she walked closer to the tree where the southern boobook owl had perched. "Aren't you a magnificent creature? So beautiful and stunning. Is there something I could do for you?" she asked.

The owl screeched again, silently took flight again, and was gone.

"Hmm, maybe not." Jane shrugged and turned back towards the house. The moon was in front of her again, and she looked towards the silvery pearl suspended in the sky, "Thank you, my Lady," she whispered and walked on.

The screen door squealed as she opened it and rested it against her shoulder while she unlatched the lock of the wooden door. Stepping inside, she flicked on the light switch. The incandescent bulbs lit the kitchen with a warm white glow that gave the accents and hues of the room an inviting atmosphere.

Jane glided over to the table, still on a high after her chance meeting with the owl, as the screen door closed behind her. She dropped her bag on the table and stretched her arms high above her head.

"Okay, where to start?" she said to herself as she scanned the kitchen benches. "The pork," she continued, moseying to the fridge. She retrieved the thawed shoulder and laid it on the table behind her.

Jane searched for the recipe amongst Aunt Claire's cut outs and recipe cards, which she kept in one of Maimeó's old wooden recipe boxes. "It's never there when you need it. Braised autumn vegies, braised swede and leek, braised orange with fennel, braised skirt steak, braised pork with star anise and—here it is!" She took the card over to the empty countertop beside the sink and leaned it against a ceramic cookie jar. She scanned the card. "Okay, twenty minutes prep and fifty-five minutes cooking. I'd better get a crack on if I'm going to get it on before Aunt Claire gets home."

Jane turned to look at the clock above the entry as she stepped over to the table to retrieve the pork shoulder. She proceeded to cut the pork into thin strips. She was in a good rhythm when a set of headlights slowed down in front of the house. Jane looked up and watched the lights curiously. She thought it was her aunt at first but realised that the headlights were square, not the rectangular shape of Claire's Mitsubishi Magna. A very long, nervous ten seconds that seemed like a minute passed, then the vehicle continued past the house. A sense of relief enveloped Jane's body. She didn't know why she was so tense—she'd always felt safe at Avalon. It was her bastion and her rock, and she'd never felt compromised there. Maybe she was just insecure about being alone at night. Jane shook away the nerves, picked up the carving knife again, and got on with the job at hand.

She was returning from the pantry with the matches to light the gas element on the stove when a second set of lights outside caught her attention. A car slowed down again, and Jane's heart skipped a beat as she held her breath while watching the vehicle. She sighed, and a warm flush came over her body as the car turned into the drive and she recognised the shape of the headlights. She put the matches down on the table and went to turn the outside light on for Aunt Claire.

Jane returned to the bench to continue cooking while listening to the familiar sounds of Claire's car coming to a stationary position beside Blue Belle. The engine noise was replaced by the brief muffled sound of an unrecognisable song on the stereo, which was interrupted by silence. A door opened then closed and was quickly followed by footsteps and the clinking of keys. Jane's anticipation rose as the footsteps got louder and closer. The squeak of the screen door announced Aunt Claire's arrival home.

"Merry Meet, my sweetheart," she said as she stepped into the house, her handbag slung over her left shoulder and a carry bag in the other.

"Merry Meet, Aunty," Jane replied as she wiped her hands on a tea towel. She turned to face Claire with her arms open for a hug.

Claire released the embrace by gently pushing back with her hands on Jane's shoulders and paused. "It's only been five hours since I saw you, but you still amaze me how you seem to have grown just that little bit more every time I see you."

"Oh, stop it. I do not," Jane retorted with an exaggerated laugh. "But thank you for saying."

"I see that you've got most of dinner done already."

"I was trying to get it on before you got home."

"I'll just put my bags away and get changed, then I'll be out to help you," Claire said as she moved into the lounge room on her way to her bedroom.

"Sure thing. I'll be here," called Jane as she continued with the meal preparation. "Now what was I doing?" she whispered to herself as she looked about the room. Releasing a sigh as her eyes darted back to the oak table, Jane recalled that she had left the matches on the far end of the table when she'd turned on the outside light. She walked over to retrieve them and turned off the light.

She returned to the bench, opening the matchbox. She took out a single match and struck it against the flint strip on the side of the box. She turned on the gas element and lowered the match. With a small whoosh of light, the gas ignited. Jane turned down the gas and reached over for the pan to place it on the hob. She could hear the muffled sounds of Aunt Claire changing down the hall and decided that they both might enjoy wine with dinner. The pork and carrots started to sizzle and brown, and Claire had not come out from the bedroom, so Jane emptied the pan onto a plate and put it aside.

Just as the second batch of pork and carrots started to brown off, Claire appeared in the entry of the kitchen. "Okay, I'm back. What can I do to help?" "I thought you were going to change?"

"I did," Claire replied. "I put my bag in my room and kicked off the shoes and *voila*! I'm ready to relax and help with dinner."

"I was thinking of some wine with dinner. What do you think?"

"Sounds great. Have you got any out yet?"

"No, I couldn't decide between the Crouchen Riesling and a Moscato. What do you feel like tonight?"

"Mmm." Claire paused in thought. "I like the Crouchen, but I do feel like something a little bit sweeter tonight," she said with a little mix of conviction and doubt.

"Are you sure?"

"Yes. Moscato it is, and I think we'll have the Rosé over the white tonight. Do you agree?" Claire asked as she walked to the pantry.

"Yes. I'm quite looking forward to it, actually. It's been a while since we've had a wine with dinner."

"A whole week, I think." Claire opened the door to the pantry door, which was actually bigger than it looked from the kitchen. It was fully shelved on both sides and the rear, and it conveniently hid a small wine fridge at the rear. Claire walked in and reached up to pull the cord for the overhanging light. The click was followed by a flood of light.

"Well, I got the Moscato," Claire said as she appeared back in the kitchen a few moments later. "All I need now is a bottle opener."

"They're the screw-top bottles, aren't they?" Jane queried.

"Ah, yes, you're right. I'll grab the glasses and pour some for us." Claire took the bottle over to the white kitchen hutch behind the oak table.

Jane loved the two-piece hutch that sat atop the sideboard; its vertical timber panelling gave it an unmistakable country feel. In fact, it was very similar in style to the interior walls of Avalon. Sophie had once commented that she'd seen very similar furniture at IKEA in Melbourne. She'd said it was called a Liadorp or Liatorp—she could not remember exactly, but Jane never really had a look on the Internet. She wondered how a mass-produced piece of furniture could be as beautiful as Claire's hutch.

Claire retrieved two wine glasses from behind the hutch's glass doors. The clanging of the glasses mixed with the sizzling sound of the ginger and garlic that Jane had thrown into the hot pan.

"Would you like yours over there?" Claire smiled as she motioned to the wine with a tilt of a glass in Jane's direction.

"No, I'll have mine at the table. I just have to add the stock and bring to the boil, then simmer for about forty minutes. Then dinner will nearly be done," Jane said as the last of the anise entered the pan. She watched the stock, waiting for it to boil. "Tell me something. Did you plan this all along?"

"Plan what?" Claire asked with a bemused, almost pained expression on her face.

"Getting home this late? You knew I'd start dinner, and now you're kicking back, sipping on the wine," Jane quipped sternly.

Silence fell on the kitchen for a moment. Claire was seemingly uncertain whether her niece was being serious or not.

Then Jane burst into laughter. "Gotcha there. You should have seen your face."

"Yes, I could imagine," Claire replied with a disenchanted tone. She managed a smile but quickly put the glass back to her mouth.

"Aw, come on. I was just joking," Jane pleaded as she twisted back to the pan, her attention drawn to the sound of the boiling stock, which she brought back to a simmer. "Okay, just another forty minutes to go on simmer, and we'll be ready."

Jane turned to Claire, who was sitting at the table in the centre of the kitchen, and regarded her for a moment.

She took in a deep breath and stepped towards the table.

"Must be time for that wine now." She picked up the glass as she dragged the chair out from underneath the table. "How was the afternoon? Did it pick at all?" Jane enquired, sitting opposite Aunt Claire.

"A little. Five separate people came through after you left the store. A couple of browsers and small purchasers, but Constance Wagner came in with a big purchase— nearly five hundred dollars, which was fantastic."

"Constance Wagner," Jane repeated, perplexed. "I can't put a face to the name."

"She comes in a few times a year to restock on supplies. Herbs, burners, and the like. She has long brunette hair. About, um, late forties, I'd say. She's a solitary, has a property up near Bicheno. I'm sure you've met her before."

"Yeah, she's starting to sound familiar."

"Her homestead was broken into last week when she was out. Nothing much of value was taken. They made more of a mess than anything, but they did take her athame. The police think that they would have used it in other crimes before discarding it somewhere." Claire's face was pained as she told the story. "It makes you wonder. You'd never hear about crime down this way. Only in Hobart or Launceston, maybe sometimes in Swansea, but nowhere else. It just goes to show the direction in which the world is going. Everything is going black. I just hope that they didn't use the athame to hurt anyone." Claire met Jane's stare. "It just makes me feel uncomfortable for the future."

"That's terrible," Jane said, dropping her tone to match the sombre moment. "But the gods were protecting her that day. She wasn't harmed. That's a blessing, isn't it?" Jane reached forward and took Claire's hand in hers.

"There is that," Claire acknowledged with a nod as she took another sip of wine. She returned the glass to the table with a small sniffle while composing herself before adding, "Dinner is starting to smell good. Is there long to go?"

"No, not really. The timer will go off soon, and I just need to add a few more ingredients and cook the rice, and then it's done."

Jane retrieved the greens from the fridge and returned to the bench. She trimmed the bok choy leaves, sliced the shallots, washed them, and added them to the pan. She put the rice in the microwave and turned back to Claire. "The rice is supposed to be steamed, but I'm just going to do in the microwave. Is that okay with you?"

"I don't mind."

Jane roughly chopped a little coriander, threw it into the pot with a sprinkle of ground salt and pepper, and stirred it. A moment later, the microwave pinged and stopped its dull hum.

"Looks like everything is ready. I'll just plate up. It smells great. I can't wait. Do you mind pouring me another wine?"

Jane served the braised pork on bone-white dinner plates atop a blue-and-white gingham tablecloth at the end of the table, where they would dine.

Claire breathed deeply through her nose. "You're right. It does smell great. I'm sure it'll taste even better," she said as the plate passed her face on its way to the table.

"I'll give thanks for tonight's meal." Claire put both hands flat, palms down on the table in front of her, her elbows tucked against her side. Claire closed her eyes while Jane imitated her aunt's actions and waited.

"From forest and river;
From mountain and field;
From the fertile earth's nutritious yield;
I now consume celestial energy;
May it lend health, strength, and love to thee;
O, Cerridwen and Cernunnos,
Blessed Be."

"Blessed be," Jane repeated as she opened her eyes, reaching for the fork.

The two of them enjoyed the meal in relative silence; however, rather than an awkward silence, an understanding existed between them. Claire and Jane had built a strong and close bond since Grace's death. They could both have their mouths full, and through body language—a shrug, a head turn, or eye winks—they would know what the other was trying to convey, which was always acknowledged with a smile and a nod.

After fifteen minutes and each had drunk another glass of wine, their meal was finished. After wiping the corners of her mouth with a napkin, Jane pushed her plate forward then put the napkin aside and her utensils on the plate.

"That was good, even if I say so myself," she said with a smile. "Compliments to the chef."

"I agree. Here, here," Claire replied as she raised her glass to her niece. "I should have brought some desert home."

"Never mind. We've still got chocolate ice cream in the freezer, if you'd like," Jane said as she got up.

"No, it's okay, love. I still have this wine to finish. Did you want another one with me? I really shouldn't finish it by myself." Claire grinned.

Jane returned to her seat. "Okay, one for the road, hey?"

"Why? Where are you going?" Claire replied with a bemused expression.

"Oh, nowhere. Just a figure of speech. I might pop outside and sit in the garden for a while tonight. Do you have any plans?"

"I have to go over arrangements for Beltane, and I'll probably watch a little television, but that's about it."

"How are the plans coming along?"

"Yeah, not too bad. Everything's organised for the store, which is a relief. We are planning to spend the evening out at Freya. Are you coming out, or are you going to do something yourself?" Claire looked at Jane with anticipation.

"Of course I'll be coming out to Freya. I wouldn't be away from family and friends on a sabbat," Jane replied, slightly astonished that Claire would even ask such a question.

"I know, but you know I will always check rather than assume about anything that you do. You are your own person, you know?"

"I know, Aunt Claire."

Claire consumed the last of the wine from her glass, pushed the chair back from the table, and stood. "I'll get the dishes done tonight," she said as she started to clear the table. "You did a brilliant job with dinner. Thank you. Now go grab your book or whatever you are going to take out into the garden and relax."

"Thanks, Aunt Claire, I will." Jane stood with her glass in hand. She leaned over the table, retrieved the empty Moscato bottle, and walked to the sink. Placing the bottle on the bench, she finished the remaining wine from her glass and sat it down beside the bottle. "I'm just going to freshen up. I might have a shower and then do some reading out in the garden." Jane turned from the sink to see Claire picking up the last of the plates from the table, then she walked to the doorway that led into the lounge room.

"Blessed be, Aunt Claire."

"Blessed be, my love."

Jane walked through the lounge room and towards her bedroom, which was at the end of the hall. The hallway walls were painted a soft blue about two to three shades lighter than the outside of the house. The floors were polished hardwood, the same as the rest of the house, with white colonial baseboard. The doors to the bedrooms were also white; each had a pentagram centred below the top jamb. A few framed pictures of family members hung between the doors. Jane's favourite was of her mum, Grace. It hung outside her bedroom between the door and the stairs that led to the attic. Jane rarely ventured upstairs unless Aunt Claire was with her, as it contained a lot of ritual items and stock that did not sell or overstock from the store. Jane was sure that most of it would never make it to the shop anyway because neither of them really went up there. Jane called it a black hole, where things went never to be seen again.

Jane picked up her pyjamas from her bed as well as her Book of Shadows and the latest Steven King novel she was reading. She ventured back down the hall, through the lounge room, and into the second hallway that wrapped around the east side of the house. Both Claire and Jane generally spent most of their time in the west side of the house, where the kitchen, lounge, and sunroom were. Two hallways led from the lounge room. The top hallway led to the three bedrooms and the attic stairs. The bottom hallway followed the southern perimeter of the house, where the bathroom was located. It continued along the corner of the house and turned, running past the study on the left and an outside-access sliding-glass door on the right. Farther along to the left was a third smaller hallway leading to the altar room, the sacred heart of the house. The hallway ended at the laundry, which also had a toilet attached to the rear of the room.

In the bathroom, Jane closed the door and put her items on the bench underneath the large vanity mirror. She turned on the hot water in the shower and allowed the room to steam up while she undressed. Jane heard Claire sit down on the old brown-leather recliner. It was a little batted around the bottom edges with scuffmarks and the like. Jane called it the Nanna chair as it had a multi-coloured knitted throw rug over the back. The kind that you would associate with the Country Women's Association or a quilting group. Once in the chair, Claire reached to her right side, grasped the brown wooden lever, and pulled it back. The springs of the chair grinded into motion and the bottom foot rest sprung out, taking Claire's feet with it and coming to rest about two foot off the ground. She retrieved some paperwork that sat on the coffee table beside her as well as her reading glasses. She positioned the frames on her face; she then found the remote control for television and pressed the on button. The almost silent atmosphere was broken by a commercial as the television burst into life.

"Damn ads, they're always louder than the show," she said to herself as she shuffled through the documents in front of her while partially looking over the frames at the television at the same time.

After showering, Jane strolled into the lounge room, where Claire was sitting in her old brown leather recliner. She was shuffling through paperwork and glancing at the television over her glasses frames. She noticed the time on the PVR's LED display said just past eight o'clock.

"All settled in for the night, Aunt Claire," Jane stated rather than asked.

"Yes, dear. Enjoy the evening. Do you have a jumper with you? It may be cold out there," she said raising her voice.

"Yes, Aunty," she replied as she marched closer to the wooden door. Jane was telling tales, though, as all she had in her possession were the Book of Shadows and her copy of Stephen King's *Just After Sunset*.

Jane stopped at the door to go through the little ritual that she did every time she visited the garden. She held her breath for a moment in anticipation of going to her favourite place in the house. She grasped the doorknob then slowly released her breath as she turned the handle and swung the door open. Complete darkness lay in front of her, but she'd been expecting that. Jane drew another breath, closed her eyes, and felt for the light switch on the wall. She flicked the lever at the door, exhaled, and opened her eyes. Before her was a short tunnel with a line of fairy lights that provided a dim but spectacular entrance to the garden. Beyond that, she could see more light, and shadows bounced off the different structures in the garden at the end of the tunnel. She walked slowly, holding her books in her right arm and running her left hand through the leaves of the jasmine vines that created the walls of the tunnel. The fairy lights were intertwined with the jasmine in no particular pattern. The jasmine and fairy lights hung down from the tunnel roof, and some of the vines touched her hair or brushed her shoulders and she passed underneath. Jane thought that the random was not so random but purposeful, as if it was meant to be in the grand scheme of things. She always imagined that the fairy lights were little fireflies playing amongst the vines and lighting her way towards the garden. The outside structure of the garden walls were large white lattice sheets and posts that were completely covered by the jasmine vines—there was no seeing in or seeing out. Past the entrance tunnel, the walls veered off to both left and right then met the opposite side of the garden, creating a precise circle that was approximately fifty metres in diameter. Jane drew long and deep into her nose, and the smell drifting through the air filled her nostrils and excited her senses. Releasing the scent and focusing on the lights, she walked the two metres to the end of the entrance, where the garden opened up. As she always did before she went in, she stood there for a moment, admiring the garden. The garden's mystical and enchanting aura was a living testament to Daideó, Maimeó, her mum, and Aunt Claire, and that was why it was her favourite place in the house.

She surveyed the garden from left to right; it could have been straight out of *Alice in Wonderland*. A line of garden lamps followed the outline of the circular garden walls, providing a soft light to the back of the wall and outer garden. To her left was a small gazebo with white posts and an open-frame natural-coloured roof that supported a mass of mauve Chinese Wisteria racemes that hung like perfumed lanterns. A path made from compacted red crusher dust continued from the sunroom door and meandered between the gazebo and a large grassy knoll, leading to a rock pond in the centre of the garden. Daideó had built the pond twenty years ago, a year or so after he first built the garden. It was certainly the centrepiece of the garden but by no means the focal point. Jane did not like singling out any particular feature of the garden as the best or the focal point—the garden itself was the focal point of Avalon. The pond, though, certainly was the tranquil point of the garden. The shape of a kidney, it was elevated a foot and a half above ground level and made of sandstone. The topside of the pond wall was flat, probably ten inches across, and sometimes doubled as a seat. The water was filtered and heated by being pumped through a black poly pipe to a network of coiling pipes on the roof of a nearby shed outside the garden. The sun would warm the water before it flowed back into the main body of water, over a small waterfall near the apple tree.

The pond was alive with colour during the day as most of the surface area was covered by the viviparous bronze green leaves of the water lilies that had either white or purple starflowers with deep-yellow stamens in the centre. At one end of the pond, clumping dwarf cattails looked like needles of green with the odd flower spike that was like a sausage on a skewer. Beside the cattails grew variegated spider lilies that looked similar to mother-in law's tongue. It had strap-like leaves of green and cream, and it bloomed at night with a very fragrant cluster of white star-shaped

52

blooms. Japanese Koi lived amongst the foliage in the pond. The path turned to small brown, tan, and cream river stones as it approached the pond and encircled its perimeter. Behind the pond, the earth rose up into a sizeable embankment dwarfed by the majestic Winesap apple tree positioned on the very top. This is where Jane would relax—sitting on the knoll with her back against the tree.

When possible, she spent hours out there, reading, sleeping, and enjoying the tranquil sounds of the waterfall, the buzz of the insects, and the chirping of the birds that knew of the garden's existence. Most of all, it made her feel close to her departed kin. She knew, at times, that they were with her in the garden. Even alone, she sensed a closeness that was so dear to her.

As Jane walked around the pond, the gravel crunched under her feet until she stepped onto the grass. Beneath the apple tree was a worn patch of grass where Jane normally sat. The temperature had started to drop outside, and a film of dew had begun to form on the grass. Jane steadied her feet on the wet grass as she approached her favourite posy. She guided her posterior down onto the worn patch then looked to the items that she carried with her. She decided to pick up where she'd left off in *Just After Sunset*. After placing the Book of Shadows on the ground, she clasped the novel with both hands. Sighing, she swotted over the cover art for a brief moment before thumbing her way through the pages to find her place.

"Chapter five," she said under her breath. "Ah, there you are. I really should get bookmark."

A smile touched the corners of her mouth as she scanned the page before her. Jane settled in, her back pressed against the apple tree. She suddenly noticed the eerie silence of the garden—an absolute deathly stillness. The birds had left, and the shadows along the garden walls had grown long.

An uncomfortable numbness pervaded Jane's bum, so she shifted her hips to the right and pulled her legs to the right side of her body. She tucked her ankles almost underneath her. The numbness gave way for the tingling sensation of pins and needles. She put the book aside and rubbed her glutes, to relieve the tingles and get the blood flowing again. She was happy and relaxed, maybe too relaxed, as she tilted her head skyward to look at the Winesap branches above her. A rush of warmth came over her, and she released a long slow yawn, wanting to stretch. She was a captive of her body's desire to shut down and sleep. Her eyes glazed over and closed as the yawn came to a finish.

"Hmm," she mumbled as her body slowly came to rest on the ground, the novel lying behind her back. Resting her head on her outstretched hands, she drifted far away.

The shadows of the night danced upon the walls and structures of the garden, swaying back and forth as if to a slow old-time melody. All held time in movement, except for one. A black shadow darted from branch to branch of the Winesap, clapping hooves upon the bark, spraying splinters.

Jane twitched at the sensation of something hitting her cheeks, her lips, and nose. Another object connected with her closed eyelids. She stirred, blindly touching her face.

"Ouch." She sat up, and a small but sharp pain travelled along her right index finger. Opening her eyes, she studied her hand and fingers—and saw nothing. She held her hand up higher to catch the light reflecting off the pond. The changing light hampered her scrutiny, although she did become acutely aware of the lines on her hands.

"I should try and moisturise more often," she said to herself as her attention was drawn to a small grey object embedded in the side of her index finger. "Ugh."

Jane tried in vain to remove the splinter, but it was too small, and her efforts seemed to only make the intruder entrench itself deeper. Another and another piece fell onto the top of Jane's hands.

She brushed them aside. "What the hell?"

Jane twisted her upper body, crooking her neck to look skyward, squinting to protect her eyes from any further falling objects.

She scanned the lowest branches then deeper into the tree. Mid-way up the tree, towards the outer extremities, a spot was strangely void of anything of substance. Grimacing, she turned to get a better view then pulled her bum up towards the trunk of the tree. She looked back towards the curious area that had caught her attention.

She had lost its position briefly but found it again after scanning the branches.

"There you are, I think," she said in a cautious tone. "Or should I say what you are or what it is? No, that doesn't sound right—oh, stop blabbering." Squinting, Jane concentrated on the area. She was just about to give up and turn her head when she could have sworn that the void moved, albeit just a little. With renewed interest, she fixated on the area, certain that something wasn't right. Her back pressed against the trunk, she rose slowly, her eyes still trained on the object. Jane sallied from the shaft of the tree, closing the distance between her and her fascination.

Without warning, the darkness shot off to the other side of the tree. It stopped for probably two seconds then raced through the branches, weaving in and out, avoiding collisions while building speed. A black tail similar to that of a comet's tail grew in length as the unidentified object travelled faster and faster through the tree. Jane's eyes darted back and forth, as if she were watching a pinball. The darkness reached the top of the tree then hung at the top for maybe ten seconds before launching itself. Jane swallowed in fear, but her throat was dry. She opened her mouth to scream, but only a faint resemblance of a sound escaped. The darkness was closing in quickly; Jane registered only two orange glowing dots at its front. Jane tried to roll but only managed to collapse to the ground. She looked up as the thing closed in—three metres then two metres. She put her head in her arms and braced for impact.

Tense, teeth clenched, lying in a foetal position and holding her head, she waited… and waited. Nothing. Why was there nothing? Jane slowly twisted her head towards the tree, releasing her arms. Tears of fear on her face, she sniffled to clear her nose.

"Aye, now that wasn't very ladylike now, was it?"

Jane pulled herself back to a sitting position. "Who said that?"

"Why, I did, of course."

"Where are you?"

"I'm just a wee yonder above your head, of course."

Jane eyes rolled upwards as her head gently tilted back. "What in the Gods" names is going on?" Jane said to herself under her breath.

"I'm glad you asked. Allow me to enlighten and release you of that burden."

"Burden? What burden?" Jane asked as her searching gaze came to rest on a horse standing on a low-hanging branch just above her head.

"Why, the burden of your current dilemma, dearie."

Jane's eyes widened in disbelief. "I-I'm sorry. I don't know what you are talking about." Jane hesitated before continuing. "I'm-I'm Jane." She got to her feet and brushed herself off. "I mean my name is Jane, Merry Meet." She held out a hand. "*What am I doing?*" she thought as she realised that she was offering her hand to a horse. "Umm, I'm sorry." She withdrew her hand in embarrassment.

"That's all right, dearie," the horse replied with a laugh.

"I know who you are, Jane Grace McKinnon. It is you that

I seek."

"Why?"

"To give you a warning, dearie, but first, allow me to complete the pleasantries and introduce myself. My name is Aedán, and I am pleased to make your acquaintance.

"W-what are you, and how do you know my name?" Jane asked apprehensively.

"I am *púca*, a being from another realm called Emain Ablach. *Púcas* look like horses. However, I can take any form I wish. And yes, we can talk. A lot of people consider me to be a shape-shifter. That may be true, but first and foremost, I am Fey."

"You're Faerie?"

"There are so many terms. However, we prefer Fey."

"We—I thought…" Jane hesitated as she looked up into Aedán' fiery eyes. "Oh, never mind. It doesn't matter." Jane's voice trailed off as her gaze dropped towards her own feet.

"What you were expecting? A pale little person with pointy ears and wings?"

"Um—well, yes. I guess so. I mean you grow up hearing and telling stories of fairies, and you just get this image that stays with you."

Jane lifted her head towards Aedán again.

He stood proudly on the branch above her. His eyes shone like deep crimson rubies, and his black coat reflected the light from the surface of the pond below. He caught her stare in his and brought the conversation back to the matter at hand. "Yes, well, dearie, that will have to be a chinwag best kept for another time perhaps. I am here with the gravest of warnings," Aedán said sternly.

"Why? What's wrong? What's going to happen?" Jane responded with trepidation, understanding that the answer would not be a positive one.

Aedán lowered his muzzle. "Aye, the claws of darkness has dragged itself into this realm in search of a pureness, an essence. Be very careful, dearie, of who your path crosses with," he said in mysterious yet authoritative tone while striking at the branch with his front left hoof. A spray of fine bark splinters fell onto Jane's face and shoulders.

"Pah, pah," Jane sputtered, spitting the tiny pieces of wood out of her mouth. "What do you mean, 'Darkness'?" Jane asked, filled with anxiety.

Aedán just stood there, not responding to Jane's plea for more information, motionless except for his mane that blew in the wind. His red eyes stood out like warning beacons against the black of his body and the night sky.

Staring, just staring down at her, he gave her nothing.

Anger had replaced her apprehension. Jane's voice took on its own fiery tone. "Aedán, answer me now. What is this darkness?"

Aedán' features had set to stone as if he had cast his own eyes upon Medusa herself. Moments passed, and Aedán' mane still floated away from his neck on the winds around him. Jane could not take any more; she slumped down onto the ground in despair as tears rolled down her cheeks.

"Why? Why won't you tell me, Aedán?" she sobbed. "Please, I need to know," Jane murmured between her shallow breaths. "Tell me. I need to know. Why won't you tell me, Aedán?"

Jane rocked back and forth on the grass in a foetal position, her hands clenched and pressed against her chest, her voice a little raspy and faint. "Why?"

Jane as she released her hands to find purchase on the ground. "Aedán," she mumbled. She raised her head, stretched her neck, and got up into a sitting position. She paused for a moment, dazed.

"Aedán?" She looked up into the branches of the Winesap. "He was just there. Where did he go?" Jane scanned the branches, searching for the void, the darkness, and the fiery red eyes, but she saw only branches, leaves, and a few scattered stars shining through the canopy.

"Aedán," she called. "Aedán!" Jane waited, but there was no reply. "Surely, he was here—I couldn't have just imagined him." Jane rose to her feet, wiping the grass from her bottom. She turned a full three hundred sixty degrees but did not see him. "Am I going mad?" she asked herself as she clasped her pentagram hanging around her neck. She closed her eyes, holding the pentagram in front of her face.

"O mighty Cerridwen, O mighty Cernunnos,

I seek your guidance. Please make me clear of head and sharp of thought.

Cast a guiding light towards Aedán *the Púca, for he is the object that is sought.*

Blessed be," she recited as she bent forward and kissed the pentagram. She opened her eyes and squinted to adjust her vision.

The night sky seemed a lot brighter than it had been she'd closed her eyes. She held a flat hand above her forehead to shield her vision from the light. She could see shapes again and could make that the light was near the tree. She stepped backwards towards the pond, where the light was not as severe and her eyes could focus. A bright orb of light hovered in the middle of the Winesap, near the trunk. Jane could only stare at the orb, and moments later, the light was gone. "What the? What does that mean?" she asked herself. "Aedán is in the tree? Aedán *is* the tree. Did I just dream the whole thing?"

Jane sat at the edge of the pond and just stared at the tree, fixated on the Winesap as if she were in a trance. Minutes passed, and a frog jumping from a lily pad and splashed into the water. A single droplet of water flew through the air, arching over the side of the pond, and landed on Jane's left forearm. The small wet tap on her arm was enough to break her trance and bring her back into reality.

"What the heck?" she exclaimed with a jolt as she jumped sideways, looking at her arm. The water droplet pooled into a little bead between the fine hairs. Jane moved her elbow upwards; the droplet broke free of the two strands and rolled towards her hand. Jane watched the droplet's journey, as it got smaller and smaller, just leaving behind a wet trail down her arm.

Jane's thoughts returned to the apple tree and Aedán as she struggled to understand the warning she'd been given. "*Realm?* What do you mean "another realm"?" she pleaded with the tree. "And what do you mean "a purity"? And who I cross paths with. What's that mean?" she asked with a hapless tone. "What does that mean? Am I the purity? Am I in danger? Aedán, where are you?"

Jane stood in front of the tree, her arms slumped to her sides. The sounds of the night returned—the crickets and the frogs. The moths flew around the garden lights, and the Winesap's branches stilled. A tingle travelled down Jane's spine, and she sensed she was being watched. She had never felt uneasy at Avalon before—and for the first time, she did not feel safe.

Jane rushed forward to gather her books from beneath the apple tree. She turned back towards the path. She swiftly walked back to the tunnel, half-expecting to see someone— or something—in the garden, watching her. She entered the small jasmine tunnel, reached the door of the sunroom, and turned the handle. The door groaned and grinded as she opened and closed it. A sense of relief flooded over her as she locked the door. She made her way to her bedroom, still shaken but happy that she was inside the house. After putting her books on the side table, Jane removed her shoes and slid into bed. She lay there for a moment then finally took her pentagram in her hand and recited her bedtime chant.

Jane, comforted by the walls of her bedroom, drew the pentagram towards her and kissed it. "Blessed Be." A sense of calm descended upon her, and a small smile tugged at the corners of her mouth as she rolled onto her side and fell asleep.

5

The sun's warming morning rays crept up the side of the house, pushing back the silhouettes of the night, and entered the window of Jane's bedroom. Outside, the Superb Fairy-wrens were up early, bounding around and searching the lawn for hoppers and other small insects while a boobook owl watched from the heights of a nearby eucalypt. The crowing of Avalon's resident cockerel periodically interrupted the melodic sounds of the morning. The dew glistened on the grass. The obscurity of night retreated as the sun filled the room with light. Dawn held the promise of another beautiful Tasmanian day.

Jane's room was like most rooms of girls her age. The window, draped by floral tab-style curtains, let an abundance of light and air into the room. Jane kept the room fresh by leaving the window slightly ajar so the salubrious oxygen always circulated into the room. Jane loved the fresh airy feel that her room always had. Its crispness always hit her as soon as she walked in the door, like the smell of the air after rain

Her cream-coloured melamine desk was quite tidy, harbouring only a laptop, which was continuously on, a small inkjet printer, a wireless mouse, and pair of speakers. The dresser, however, was never tidy, and the clear lacquered pine surface rarely saw the light of day. Clothes were always strewn across the floor around it or hanging from the round knobs on the drawers. The top was decorated with an incense burner and two trinket boxes—one held Jane's runes, and the other was for her jewellery. Framed photos of Jane as a small child, Aunt Claire, Daideó and Maimeó, and her first dog were scattered atop the dresser. Sam, Jane's black-and-tan standard dachshund had passed away when she was fifteen. Though witches stereotypically had cats, Jane had always been a dog lover at heart. And she was never one for stereotypes. They were just like rules—some were meant to be broken. The centre of the dresser was reserved for one photo only, and that was of her mother. The photo had been taken a couple of months before her death in a car accident. Looking back over her shoulder, Grace was wearing an emerald-green summer dress with shoestring straps. Her long blonde hair was straight with a slight wave that swept off her forehead. It caught the light in the photo and had a shimmer of health. She looked very happy—her beaming smile revealed her perfect pearly whites and the greenest of green eyes that had drawn people to her.

Jane's bed, a large white four-post single with a sheer linen canopy, was centred on the adjoining wall between the door and window.

Jane rolled over and yawned as she blinked a number of times, trying to focus on the clock that hung on the wall near the door.

"Aww, seven o'clock. I feel like I haven't slept at all." She threw the doona back off her body and swung her legs around to the left side of the bed then planted them firmly on the floor. She stood and threw her arms skyward, releasing another big yawn. The smell of breakfast wafted into the room, and she heard the faint sound of the television. Jane kicked about the floor, searching for her slippers. She found them under the bed, dragged them out, and put them on.

Jane teetered down the hall towards the lounge room, staggering between consciousness and sleep, occasionally bumping into the wall as the sound of Aunt Claire's morning shows grew louder.

"Good morning, sleepy head," Aunt Claire hollered with a smirk as Jane entered the room. "How did you sleep? Or should I say that you should still be asleep?"

"Hmm," Jane grunted, peering at her aunt through squinting eyes. "Good morning."

"There's tea in the pot and bread in the basket near the toaster if you're hungry."

"Thanks." Jane shuffled through the lounge room and turned towards the kitchen. "I feel like"—Jane yawned—

"like I haven't slept at all."

Jane trundled through the doorway and scanned the kitchen. The teapot, along with her cup and saucer, were waiting for her on the table. She walked towards the table.

The scent of mint was in the air, and the last remnants of steam were trying to escape the cup. The old white-bone china setting had belonged to Maimeó, whose mother had handed it down to her. Claire treasured the set, and though it would fetch a pretty penny on the market—the "Chelsea Sprig" manufactured by Adderley's of England was antique—she cherished its sentimental value. Aunt Claire loved antiques, but they still had to serve a purpose and not just collect dust.

Jane pulled the chair out from the table and sat down. She raised the cup to her mouth. The vapours and heat lapped at her nostrils, and she drew in a deep breath, savouring the aroma as she it put the edge of the cup against her lips.

"What did you get up to last night?" Aunt Claire asked as she followed Jane into the kitchen.

"Mmm," Jane murmured, her mouth full of tea. "Um, it was good, I think." Jane paused before continuing. "I don't know. I went out into the garden to read, and I think I fell asleep. I cannot remember for how long, but I woke up underneath the apple tree. It was so strange. I… I… it's hard to explain. I had a strange dream, I think," Jane said as she turned to look at Aunt Claire.

"What was the dream about, do you remember?

Just tell her, surely, she won't think you're totally nuts – will she?

"Yes, I remember. The bizarre thing is, though, I don't think it was a dream." Jane cleared her throat.

"Tell me what happened, love." Claire took a seat beside Jane and reached for her hand.

"Oh, it's silly," she said with a shrug. "Probably nothing."

"Well, you know—a problem shared."

Jane proceeded to explain what she recalled of last night's events. "I sat underneath the tree to read my book, and after some time—I can't remember how long—I noticed that there was something landing on me. It was wood, and I looked up into the tree. I noticed something moving back and forth, all over the place like a pinball."

Claire leaned in closer, and her grip on Jane's hand tightened. "What was it? It didn't hurt you, did it?"

Jane hesitated briefly, trying to comprehend what had happened so she could answer. "Um, yes. Oh, no, no… it was okay. I didn't get hurt at all. He was very friendly."

"He? Friendly? Who is he? Jane Grace McKinnon, you know the rules. Strangers are forbidden in the secret garden," Claire said sternly.

"No, no. It wasn't like that. It wasn't a boy."

"So who was he then?"

"Aedán."

"Aedán? I've never heard of Aedán. It sounds either Irish or Scottish. Anyway, that's beside the point." Claire looked puzzled. "Who is he, and where is he from?"

"He, Aunt Claire, was a *púca,* and he is from a place called Emain Ablach—it's Gaelic," Jane replied with confidence as she met Aunt Claire's gaze. *What is she thinking? Does she think I'm mad?*

"No, I don't think you're going crazy." Claire smiled, confirming her understanding as she read Jane's facial expressions. "I've known you all your life, love, and I know that sometimes, things can be farfetched, but there is always an explanation for everything that exists. I don't know what a *púca* is or where Emain Ablach is, but I'm going to find out."

"Oh, I know what a *púca* is, and I know where Emain Ablach is. Well, at least I think I do. Aedán is Fey, and he is a horse, black as the darkest night with eyes of fire."

"Okay, now I'm starting to get a little worried. A talking horse?" Claire raised her eyebrows. "There is no doubting that there is a faerie world but one that travels in the form of a horse? This could be danger. I'm going to have to consult with the books and the Gods to get guidance."

"He was okay. I don't think he would hurt me at all. He just made some vague comments about darkness, and then before I knew it, he was gone. But it didn't make any sense, and then I woke up. I looked for him everywhere, but I couldn't find him," Jane said.

"Okay, so you were asleep. It could have been a dream, dear."

"That's what I thought…" Jane squeezed Claire's hand. "But I sought guidance from Cerridwen and Cernunnos, and they lit the tree when I asked for help to find Aedán."

"So Aedán is the tree?"

"No, he is not the tree. I mean, I don't *think* he is. I know what I saw—it couldn't have been a dream, could it?" Jane asked.

"No, I'm sure it wasn't, but you do still look very tired. Why don't you go back to bed and catch up on some sleep," Claire suggested as she started to run her fingers through Jane's hair.

"I can't. I have to get ready to come in and help you in the shop."

"Jane McKinnon, I insist that you listen to your aunt. Now go and get yourself back to bed at once," Claire ordered as she pushed the chair back. She stood and pulled Jane to her feet. "Now get some sleep, love, and you can come into the shop later in the morning."

Claire looked into her niece's eyes while running her hands along Jane's arms to her shoulders. She pulled her into her bosom and gave her a reassuring embrace. "Now get back to your room and get some sleep."

Jane was tired and knew she needed to catch up on sleep, so Claire did not have to press her case too much before Jane gave in.

"Okay, Aunt Claire, I'll get a couple of hours of sleep and then come into the shop. If it's all right with you, I might get Soph over to go over last night's events and see if she can make any sense of it," Jane said as they stepped back from each other.

"Sure, love, you do that."

Jane walked into her room and let out a frustrated sigh as she pushed the door closed behind her. She questioned her sanity again.

"Surely it did happen. I couldn't have dreamt the whole thing." Jane paused, looking at the photograph of her mum. "Was it a dream, Mum? Is Aedán real?"

The onset of a yawn broke the moment. She went to her laptop and pushed the home button. The computer sprang to life. A couple of clicks later, the media player opened, and the screen was an array of colours spinning around in a mosaic pattern. The Pixies drowned out the laptop's hum, and as *Where is My Mind* pulsated from the speakers, Jane sang along, her voice echoing in the room.

Jane lost her place in the song and let the music envelop her as she sauntered over to the bed. She could feel the invisible sheet of sleep already wrapping itself around her. Kicking her slippers off, she turned to sit down and yawned as soon as her bum touched the mattress. Sizing up the pillow, Jane settled into her usual position, but this time, a small but sharp pain in her hand caused her to jump. She sat up and looked at the hand, seeing nothing. Upon closer inspection of her fingers, she found a small button of blood on her index fingertip.

"What's that?" she said to herself. She turned to look at her pillow. To her amazement, she found little pieces of wood all over her pillow, and like a bolt from the skies, the memory of the previous night's visit returned.

Suddenly, Jane had a renewed vitality—she had proof to reinforce that Aedán wasn't a dream. Her smile stretched from ear to ear, and she kicked about the floor, looking for her slippers once again. "Last night did happen! Aedán is real, and I'm not crazy."

Her elation soured a bit when she recalled Aedán' warning about the darkness. "I have to call Sophie."

∞

Jane turned away from Aunt Claire and walked back out of the kitchen towards her room. After a moment, Claire released a breath that she wasn't even aware that she was holding as she looked at the palm of her hand. She poked at a small brown object that she'd plucked from Jane's hair. It was a splinter of wood that looked as if it had been produced by something blunt.

"Looks like I've got some research to do today," she said to herself as she put her hand into her pocket. She rubbed her thumb over the palm of her hand until she could no longer feel the shard of wood. Taking her hand from her pocket, she surveyed the table for a minute then left the kitchen.

6

"Okay, babe. I'll see you soon. Blessed be, Sophie." Jane smiled and set the handset back on the cradle. She sat in the sofa chair for a moment and pondered what she was about to tell her friend. *How will I explain it? Will she believe me?* Perplexed, she sighed.

"Well, there's only one way to find out," she said aloud for the house to hear as she rose from the chair.

She was clad in a long white cotton summer dress with gold-leather chappals on her feet, and she'd accessorised with her gold-and-blue stone-encrusted pentagram and a gold-and-pearl chain headpiece. She pulled paper and a pen from the drawer on the side table just inside the lounge room. She wrote a note for Aunt Claire:

Aunt Claire,

It was real. I realise that now. I'm okay; I've gone over to Sophie's to talk to her. Will be back soon. Love you.

Blessed be,

Jane

Jane walked into the kitchen and rested the note upright against the fruit bowl in the centre of the table so it would be in Claire's line of sight if she entered through the back door. Jane picked up her phone and checked the time on the display. She checked her bag and removed her keys.

Pulling the door shut, Jane locked it and yanked at the door twice to check that the lock had engaged. A couple of steps down the path, as she was zipping her bag, she detected something abnormal about the morning. Jane stopped; a sense of the uncertainty came over her. She looked around. Something was different, wrong, yet it all looked the same.

"Okay, pull yourself together. It must be coincidence."

Jane stretched her neck and looked over both shoulders one last time. She walked across the drive to Blue Belle and unlocked the door. She threw her bag across to the passenger seat, put the key into the ignition, and took a seat. She had a particular ritual that she followed when she got into Blue Belle, and she'd deviated from it only once—when she'd had to rush to hospital when Maimeó was sick.

Jane buckled the chrome seat belt and turned the ignition key. The engine sprang to life, and the raspy hum of the air-cooled motor filled the air.

"Merry Meet, Belle," Jane said as she caressed the sides of the steering wheel. "Let's have a safe trip today."

Jane leaned over to the glove box and chose a CD. "This one will do."

The jewel case clipped back into place, and Jane threw it onto the seat beside her. She fed the disc into the receiver and scanned to the second song: *The Whole of the Moon* from The Waterboys' album *This is the Sea*. She loved the album's spiritually uplifting mix of Celtic influences and rock themes.

Jane pulled out onto the street. She drove off, fingers tapping the top of the steering wheel. The ill feelings that had disturbed her at Avalon slipped from her thoughts as the melody took over.

Sophie was waiting on the front porch when Jane arrived. She stood from her seat and descended the steps from the landing to the footpath. She waved to Jane as she walked towards the curb. She skipped joyfully then stopped when she seemed to catch herself. Her smile, however, was infectious. Jane pulled Blue Belle to a stop, returning Sophie's lively smile.

"Hey, babe. How are you?" Sophie asked as she leaned across the hand brake to kiss Jane on the cheek.

"Merry Meet, Soph," Jane replied.

"You're looking good today. Got a date?" she asked, tongue in cheek. "So what's up? You sounded—oh, I don't know—sort of excited but apprehensive at the same time."

"You're looking pretty good yourself," Jane added as she checked the rear-vision mirror then pulled out.

Sophie was wearing her favourite blue jeans, white sneakers, and a white linen peasant top with red-ribbon trim around the arms and collar.

"Thanks, but I wear this all the time. Stop avoiding the question." Sophie tilted her head to one side, making a mischievous expression.

A moment of silence passed between them, then Sophie lightly pushed Jane's shoulder. "Come on, spill. Do we have a new man?"

"No—nothing like that. Can it wait until we get back to Avalon? I want to show you something as well as tell you what happened last night."

"Hmm, okay. You've got my curiosity running riot at the moment," Sophie said with a smile that turned into a small giggle. "It's not something in your room, is it?"

Jane tried to give Sophie a stern glare, but as soon as they made eye contact, both were consumed with laughter. A comfortable quiet fell between the two friends. Sophie stared out the window at the properties as they passed, and Jane concentrated on the road.

"What's this?" Sophie gestured to the stereo, which was playing The Waterboys' *Be My Enemy*. "It's a bit deep, isn't it?"

"Yeah, it's a fantastic album. It's The Waterboys'. Do you remember them? They were big in the mid-eighties. The music is very uplifting, but this would be the darkest song, I think. I love the fiddle and keyboards in most of the songs. It makes me very dreamy, and I just want to close my eyes and float with every note as if I was lying in a big white, fluffy cloud."

"I don't know about a cloud, but you're definitely on something this morning." Sophie turned to look at Jane, her snicker turning into a rapturous laugh. "Yeah, maybe so, but you wait and see."

Jane turned into the drive then parked in front of the garage. The two girls exited the vehicle and strolled up the path towards the house. Sophie looked intrigued when Jane stopped before reaching the door.

"What is it?"

"What do you mean?" Sophie looked from the garden, east of the path that led to the front gate, and back towards the car and the garage, surveying the immediate area as if she were searching for something while delaying her answer.

"What's up? I know that look. Do you sense someone or something?"

"I don't know… I sense something, not a person, but there is definitely something out here," she said grimly.

"Okay, now I'm getting a little freaked out," whispered Jane as she reached for Sophie's hand. "Let's get inside quick."

"Okay, now you're starting to freak me out."

Jane opened the door, and they spilled into the kitchen as the door closed behind them. Jane let out a sigh of relief and turned to Sophie.

"What do you think is out there?" she asked.

"I don't know. I'm a spirit whisperer, not a clairvoyant or whoever they are, but whatever it is—and I definitely sensed something—it's nothing that I've sensed before.

Still, I can say with utmost certainty that it's no spirit." Leaning against the kitchen table, Sophie turned to Jane.

She seemed confused, and her body language was defensive, her arms crossed, her gaze scanning the room.

"Hey, Soph, I felt it this morning when I left. When I closed the door and turned towards the path, I knew something wasn't just right. I could not pick it, though. It felt as though I was being watched, but it felt magickal. Do you know what I mean? I'll have to talk to Aunt Claire about it, and hopefully, she has sensed it, too."

"Is that what you wanted to show me?" Sophie asked as she uncrossed her arms.

"No, actually, it's not. Like I said, I didn't know about whatever it is outside until I locked up to come over to your place this morning," Jane replied as she walked towards the doorway and motioned to Sophie to follow her. "I wanted you to come over to show and tell you about what happened last night."

Sophie followed a couple of steps behind Jane as she explained, although she was still trying to come to terms with what had happened. They walked through the sunroom and out towards the garden. Every ten paces or so, Jane turned to look at Sophie as she spoke.

"So I came out here and sat under the apple tree to read my book when…" Jane's voice trailed off when she turned to look at Sophie. "Are you okay? You seem a bit… err, like a deer caught in headlights, I guess." Jane watched Sophie's face contort in the light.

Sophie turned her back to the sun and paused a moment, blinking rapidly. Her back still to Jane, she held out a hand.

"I won't be a sec," she replied as she stood upright, still blinking.

"Okay, I'm right now," Sophie said as she twisted around, "I just had to… whoa, what is this place?"

Jane glanced back at Sophie for a moment. Her face was awestruck, her jaw open as she turned to take in the full scenery of the garden.

"I forget that you haven't seen it before. It's magnificent, isn't it?"

"Magnificent? It's fucking awesome!" Sophie exclaimed, her eyes wide with excitement. "Wow. How long have you had this?" She took a few steps forward then stopped. "Hey, how come you've never told me about this before?" Sophie frowned. "Nah, I don't care. I know now. Do you come out here often?"

"At least once a day," Jane replied, smiling.

"Do you meditate out here?"

"Sometimes. It's a place of tranquillity and relaxation, but mainly, I come out here to read."

"And you kept it a secret from me," Sophie said with a slight scowl, seeming just a tad betrayed.

"Well, it *is* the *secret* garden. Daideó, my mum, and Aunt Claire made it many years ago."

"The secret garden, huh? As in the movie? So what else aren't you telling me?"

"Yeah, sort of, I guess. I don't actually think I've seen it, and no, there is nothing… else that I'm not telling you.

Really, now let's go," Jane exclaimed, motioning with her hand. "I'll show you what I was talking about."

"Okay," Sophie responded with large eyes and a pout, "but if I find out that you're not telling me something, I will—" Sophie pointed her index finger at sharply at Jane.

Jane turned around. "You will what?" Jane replied sternly, crossing her arms. They both stood there for a moment, caught in time like a photograph, staring at each other, waiting for the other to respond. Then as if on cue, they both broke into a fit of laughter.

Minutes later, after they composed themselves and caught their breath, Jane proposed that they continue so she could show Sophie what she had originally called about.

"Okay, lead the way."

Jane walked Sophie past the gazebo and grassy knoll, along the path towards the pond. The mid-morning sun had risen high enough to spill over the walls of the garden, bringing the flowers and insects to life. The jasmine and wisteria were teaming with bees collecting pollen, and the faint hum of their work filled the garden.

"We're nearly there," Jane said. "Just past the pond towards the apple tree."

Sophie paused a moment at the wall of the pond, drinking in her surroundings. The Japanese koi swam below the surface in a small school between the lily pads, occasionally breaking the mirrored plane to catch an unsuspecting insect. Dragonflies dived at the face of the water, flying perilously between the stems of the spider lilies and cattails, performing a chaotic yet mesmerising dance.

Jane stood for a moment and watched Sophie take in the splendour of the garden. Her mouth was agape in wonder, and her smile reached her eyes.

"You look like a child in a candy store," Jane said, grabbing Sophie's attention.

"This is absolutely brilliant. I'm so in love with this place—it's so surreal. I still can't believe that you kept this a secret."

Jane laughed joyfully, glad she could finally share the magick of the garden, the same feelings that she felt every time she came out here. The moment was priceless for both of them and would surely strengthen their bond.

"And that's why it's magick," Jane said as she composed herself again. "The tree is just here behind the pond." She turned, stepping onto the grassed area of the garden behind the pond.

Sophie looked up at the Winesap standing just as an apple fell from the top of the tree. It hit the ground with a dull thud and rolled down to the pond wall.

Sophie walked around the pond to join Jane at the base of the tree, where they both sat down and looked out over pond.

"Okay, so last night, I had this very strange experience," Jane started as she shifted herself to be able to face Sophie better.

"I think the last day has been strange, full stop."

"Yeah, well, that's true, and this may make it a little stranger, but I want to ask for a favour or your advice on something."

"Sure thing, whatever you want." Sophie leaned in, placing her hand on Jane's wrist reassuringly.

"I'm going to tell you what happened to me here last night—well, the abridged version anyway—and then I want to ask you if you can to use your gift to sense what you may feel about this place, the tree, or the garden. Is that all right?"

"Yeah sure, babe. What happened?"

Jane took a deep breath. "Now, this may sound a bit farfetched, but stay with me."

Sophie listened intently to Jane's story, interjecting when she had questions.

"So Aedán is a *púca*?" Sophie hesitated for a moment before continuing, "A speaking black horse with fiery-red eyes that is Fey."

"Yes, that's right."

"Were you frightened? Did he hurt you at all?"

"I was at first. I didn't know what was happening. This thing was speeding through the tree like a bullet in a pinball machine, and then it turns out to be a talking horse. I thought the Gods had put me in a Hitchcock version of *Mr Ed*."

"What's *Mr Ed*?"

"It's a sixties show from... oh, never mind. If it's ever on television, I'll point it out to you."

"Oh, okay then, so what happened next?"

Jane repeated Aedán' warning for Sophie: "Darkness has dragged itself into this realm in search of a pureness, an essence. Be very careful of who my path crosses with." She looked up at branches above them. "I pleaded with him to tell me more, but he divulged no more," she said softly.

"What do you think he meant? Was he talking about you? What are you going to do? Sorry, but all this does is create more questions."

"Yeah, I know. I think he may be talking about me," Jane replied as her head dropped. A moment of silence past, Jane lifted her head and continued. "Well, it has to be about me, doesn't it? He wouldn't have come to me if it weren't about me. He'd have gone somewhere else or alluded that it was about someone else. At least that's what I'm telling myself. I thought I was going insane this morning before I called you, you know." Jane's eyes settled back on Sophie's face. "It took me a while to think things over, get things straight in my own mind. Do you know what I mean?"

Sophie swallowed then cleared her throat. Something dropped from the tree, passing by right in front of her face. Startled, she blinked and jumped back towards the trunk. The object thumped to the ground in front of them then rolled down the knoll, coming to rest beside the pond.

"It's okay," Jane said. "It's just an apple. We've picked most of them, but there are some at the top of tree that we can't get to. We leave them to just fall off when they want to."

"Geez, that was close. It scared the shit out of me after I listened to your story, but I know what you mean—something like this does not happen to you every day. Are you sure that one of those apples didn't hit you in the head?" Sophie grinned.

Jane returned her friend's smile as she leaned in and gave her a push on the shoulder. They both laughed together, their bodies falling to the grass.

"You know, you might just be insane," Sophie said between moments of laughter as they rolled about.

"But that's just it," Jane said, pushing herself back up to a seated position. "When he didn't answer my questions about the darkness, I was pleading and pleading, and then it was like I just woke up. I was on the ground as we are now. I experienced the cloudiness of sleep when I got up, but I remembered everything so clearly. So clearly that I couldn't be asleep, so I got up and I searched—there had to be some evidence, something to support that what had happened."

"It was just a joke, babe. I don't think you're insane," Sophie added quickly.

"Yeah, I know. But I did question it myself for some time until this morning."

"Why, what happened."

Jane walked around in a tight circle in front of Sophie, her arms crossed. Sophie watched her intently.

Her thoughts battling with logic, Jane propped, turned back to Sophie, and pointed towards the tree. "This is it."

"This is what? The tree?" she asked.

"That's what I think. Last night, I searched everywhere for Aedán. I could not find him, yet I could not have dreamt the whole thing. It was too clear—there was too much detail. I turned to Cerridwen and Cernunnos for guidance. They presented me with an orb."

"What do you mean "an orb"?"

"A ball of glowing light. I asked for them to show me where Aedán was and the orb appeared in the tree. It was like a crystal ball that a gypsy or a fortune teller might have, and the light that came from it was the whitest of whites. I think if I looked directly at it, I could have gone blind."

"And did it show you?"

"That's just it," Jane exclaimed as she bent down a little closer to Sophie. "It didn't move. It appeared in the tree, and it stayed there until it faded back to black and disappeared. I didn't get it at first—I thought he had to be in the tree. I searched the branches as best I could. I walked around the tree, but I couldn't find anything. That's when I got a little freaked out and decided to come inside."

"That was probably a good idea," Sophie added.

"In the morning, I woke up, and I really doubted myself. I went downstairs and spoke to Aunt Claire, who took it quite well. She listened to what I had to say, said that she believed me, and suggested that I go to bed and catch up on some sleep as I looked tired."

"Do you think she was being nice and sent you back to bed to get sleep because she didn't believe you?"

"No, she wouldn't do that," Jane answered. "She would

be honest with me. She always has been in the past. Anyway, I went back to bed, I put the Pixies on and went to lie down—and there it was," Jane said with an excited timbre voice.

"There was what?"

"Wood, splinters of wood," Jane replied

"I don't understand," Sophie said, looking up at her through squinted eyes.

"The wood was from Aedán. That's how I knew at first that something was above me. Little splinters or shavings of wood were falling on me. When I went back to bed, there were the same pieces of wood on my pillow. The same ones that were falling on me last night, and there must have still been some in my hair." Jane sat down beside Sophie, tapping her feet and bouncing a little where she sat. "I was so excited that I ran down and called you. I knew I wasn't insane," she said as she spoke a little louder and rose to her feet again.

Jane held out both arms, spun around, and repeated herself with a guffaw, "I'm not insane." She stopped when her twist came around to face Sophie, and her arms fell to her side. She gave her a huge grin. "But this is where things get interesting."

"This is where you want me to do something?" Sophie asked with just a hint of hesitation in her voice.

"I want you to see if you can sense anything—a being, a spirit a presence, something."

"You want me to see if I can find Aedán?" she asked nervously.

"That would be great if you could," Jane replied, clasping her hands together, her voice pitched with hope and anticipation. "Oh, I can go if you want to be on your own, if it helps," she added.

"No, it's all right. I'll see what I can do, but as I said before, I'm not a conjurer of otherworldly beings, just spirits. I can feel that this is a special place already," she offered.

"Yes, but don't—"

"Jane," Sophie snapped, turning to her friend as she got up from the grass, "don't tell me what to do. You asked for my help, and I'm here as your friend to help. Just let me do my thing and see what we can find. Okay?"

"Yes, I'm sorry, Soph. I didn't mean to be rude. I'll sit by the pond and let you get to it," Jane said, holding her arms outstretched.

Sophie walked over and engaged the hug; they kissed each other on the cheek.

"It's okay," Sophie whispered. "You've been stressed out."

They both squeezed a little harder then released the embrace. Sophie stepped back a pace, and Jane turned to walk down the incline to the wall of the pond, stopping to pick up an apple. She sat down, benefiting from a morning snack courtesy of the tree.

Sophie sat back down, cross-legged under the tree, eyes closed and arms outstretched. Resting her palms upwards upon her legs, she sat in silence for a moment.

Must be clearing her thoughts, Jane thought.

Moments later, Sophie murmured a brief chant. She rose to her feet and brushed her backside.

Jane got to her feet as well, a smile on her face. *Surely, she can't be done yet.*

Sophie looked down at her and shook her head, holding out both hands with a downwards motion.

"Oops, excuse me," Jane said at a volume that only she would hear and sat back down.

Sophie began to walk to perimeter of the garden, starting at the back point behind the Winesap. She walked slowly past the gazebo towards the arbour that held the jasmine tunnel in place. She crossed the path, circled the back of the grassy knoll, and came back towards the tree. When she completed her circuit, she mumbled something to herself.

Moments later, she was on the move again—down the centre of the garden and toward the main path back to the house. When she reached the jasmine, she stopped and traversed back along the path towards the pond, passing Jane. She walked back up to the tree and stopped. She closed her eyes, clasped her hands together, and stood motionless for what Jane felt was an eternity although it may have only been a minute or two.

Okay, this is taking a bit longer than I expected.

Sophie circled the tree. On the first pass, Jane did not notice anything unusual about her friend, although her impatience was clouding her own awareness of what was happening around her.

Sophie made a second pass—this time Jane did see, and her jaw dropped. Sophie stepped in a slow, purposeful way, like a bride walking down the aisle. The rest of her body was bolt upright, her hands clenched. But her face surprised Jane the most. Jane has seen plenty of magick before, but this was no magick. This was a morph that Sophie had done herself. Her skin tone had become paler, and her eyes had become saucer like, rounder and larger than normal. She had no pupils or white of the eyes. Her eyes were pale blue, like an ocean that shimmered with ice. Jane was aghast at the sight. Leaning forward from the wall of the pond, she waited while Sophie made her third pass of the tree. Sophie didn't blink, as if she had no eyelids at all.

Sophie stopped and turned towards the tree. She began to chant, and her arms rose towards the branches of the tree; she held them for a moment, her hands shaking. The chant became a little faster, like the crescendo of a suspense movie. Then, without warning, it ceased, and Sophie's arms dropped back to her sides.

Silence fell upon the garden as Sophie stood still, caught in a trance, for a long, long moment.

"Okay, she should have turned around by now," Jane said to herself as she searched around, looking for the best spot to gain a purchase on the rocks. She got to her feet, looked down at the wall to make sure that she hadn't left anything behind, and began to walk up the incline towards Sophie while keeping her eye on the pond wall.

"Interesting," a loud voice said from beside Jane. Startled, she hadn't realised anyone else was in the garden.

Turning quickly, she saw the outline of someone right in front of her. She jumped back, releasing a yelp. *Did I just yelp like a dog? God, I hope no one heard that.*

"Sorry. Did I scare you?"

Jane steadied herself; she recognised the voice and turned herself to face the person who owned it.

The moment clarified and focussed, and she recognised Sophie was only a couple of steps away.

"I scared you, didn't I?" she said then laughed at Jane's misfortune.

"Hey, Soph. I didn't expect you to be right there in front of me. How did it go? Did you find anything out?

Did I just sound like a real girly girl then?" Jane asked.

She laughed. "Yep, you sure did."

Sophie replied, "like a big girl." She calmed down a little and continued, "It was certainly an interesting read." "What did you find?" Jane asked, still for the answer.

"Well, the garden certainly does have its share of spiritual presences. Your Daideó and Grace have strong connections to the garden. You know you should probably talk to them more often."

"I do. I talk to my mum all the time."

"I know you do, but I mean with me, use me as a medium," Sophie suggested, pausing a second as she watched Jane process what she was saying. "Now that I know about the garden, we could do it and make contact with Grace. It should be relatively easy—anyway, think about it and let me know." She smiled.

Jane was excited about the prospect of speaking to her mum again but found the offer a little too overwhelming. "Okay, great. Sounds great. I'll consider it. I mean, I'd like to do it. I'd just have to prepare myself to speak to her, communicate with her, I mean."

"Hey, no rush. It's an offer. Let me know." Sophie reached out to place her hand on Jane's shoulder in a gesture of support.

"Yeah, okay. I will, thanks." Jane smiled as she placed her hand upon Sophie's. "Now, what else did you find out?"

Sophie became really animated as she started to explain what she'd found. "What, apart from finding your mum and grandfather? Oh, nothing too much, just that your place seems to be a spiritual portal."

"What do you mean a portal? A portal for what?" Jane asked. "Emain Albach, where Aedán is from? I'm confused."

"A portal to Emain Albach, I guess, but it could also be a portal to somewhere else. I don't know." Sophie seemed to have a flash of inspiration. "That's it!" she said excitedly.

"That's what?"

"Okay, imagine that you're in a pitch-black room, and there is nothing except a bright light in the distance. I like to imagine an old-century London lamppost, a green one with the brightest of lights. Maybe I've seen this in a movie I can't remember. Anyway, the light is connected to other lights, creating a spiritual network, and each light is a possible destination."

"Okay," Jane replied as she protracted the word with an uneasy tone.

"Well, what I'm trying to say is if you were in the room, you would go to the light. Would you not?"

"Yeah, I'd say so."

"What I'm trying to say is that the garden is like the streetlamp shining bright in a dark spot. Spirits, otherworldly beings, and whatever else is out there that may be able to see it will be attracted to it and so maybe able to enter our world via the garden."

"So you're saying that the garden is like a doorway?"

"Sort of," Sophie replied as she stepped past Jane to sit on the pond wall. "The interesting thing is, though, that it's not the garden itself, but spirits may use it as a safe haven or stop over, if you like. The tree is the streetlamp," she said enthusiastically while making a sweeping motion with her arm towards the Winesap.

"So things can use the tree as an entrance point to the house?" Jane asked, feeling quite uncomfortable about the information.

"Yeah, I'd say so." Sophie paused a moment before continuing, "I would have thought that you'd find this more exciting, being a witch."

"I do—don't get me wrong. It's quite thrilling, and I do appreciate what you've done, but this is in my house. This is Avalon. It's always been a safe place, and to now know that anyone or anything can come and go as it pleases is kinda freaky. I think I need to go inside to think about this for a while." She turned back towards the path. "I'll also have to speak to Aunt Claire about this, as well."

∞

Jane turned away and walked back through the garden towards the house. Sophie watched her friend leave, believing she had created more questions than answers. She felt for her friend but thought that she would give her a couple of minutes to herself before going in.

She looked up at the tree and regarded it for a moment, thinking of different stories that she'd heard of since she was a young girl about ghosts, goblins, and elves. She pictured various scenes playing in the branches of the tree.

A shiver ran up her spine causing her to twitch her shoulders.

"What do you want here? With Jane, with the house?" she pleaded to the apple tree. "What is the danger? I demand that you show yourself and explain the ramblings of last night."

She didn't expect anything from her ultimatum, and after a minute, her stare retreated from the tree and back to the ground near her feet. Then a black object moved quickly from the lower branches towards the top in her peripheral vision. She jerked her head upwards to catch a better view, but there was nothing. She knew she had seen something, but whatever it was, it was gone now. She scanned the tree repeatedly but saw nothing.

Shit, I'm starting to imagine things myself. She stretched her eyebrows and rubbed her temples before reiterating her demands to whatever she had seen to show itself.

Sophie waited but got no response. Only the sound of the Koi piercing the pond surface to catch an insect broke the deafening silence of the garden. She could sense that she was not alone. Knowing she was being watched triggered a cold tingle that ran through her body. She rose to her feet, acknowledged the tree while scanning its branches and the garden behind it, turned, and scampered back to the house.

7

The radial tyres slid for a couple of metres on the verge of Delta Road, flicking stones and dirt into the Statesman's wheel bays before coming to a complete stop. The V8 engine gurgled and sputtered as the chassis vibrated up and down. The driver of the car sat motionless for some time, surveying the houses visible from the road. Smoke from his pipe escaped out the open window into the morning air.

The driver sat for approximately ten minutes, scribbling notes in a pad, counting the vehicles and pedestrians that passed. He noted the different items in people's yards: dogs, cars, trees, children's playgrounds and the like—anything he considered possibly useful for the future. He observed little activity from most of the properties, which ranged from five-acre to twenty-acre lots. He had noticed a large green-and-white for-rent out the front of the property opposite him.

Finishing the pipe, he leaned forward to rest it in the dashboard ashtray. He took one more look around, scanning the properties from left to right. Then he checked the rear view mirror and opened the door. As he stepped out, the sun shimmered on the brass buckles of his boots. He turned back to retrieve the pipe and tapped it against the heel of his right boot. Its dark and burned contents emptied onto the ground, then he placed the pipe in his inside coat pocket. He checked the car for anything that he may need and pushed the door shut in a subdued manner so he did not attract any unwanted attention.

A particular property just ahead was of the utmost interest to him. It held a certain prize that he craved. He had tracked it for some time, but he knew he was getting closer, much closer, than he had been in years.

"The *grá mo chroí* was wise to conceal *an croí* from me for all of these years. However, it is time that I collect what is rightfully mine," said the Red Man as he walked along the side of the road, crunching gravel underfoot. He walked for two hundred metres down the side of the road, the tension building within him, as he knew what was expected of him. His dream would soon to be within his grasp, like an apple waiting to be picked from the tree. He walked another twenty paces then stopped; he looked up and down the road, but something was drastically wrong.

"This should be the house, but I do not feel anything. This is not what was foretold by the Gods," he cursed. "I shall have my *duass* before the fires of Beltane smoulder." He swore as he kicked at the loose stones beneath him.

Turning back, he walked towards the car, passing a blue-and-white timber house surrounded by gardens at the front. He stopped for a moment as he reached the white iron front gate, sensing for a brief moment that his *duass* was there.

Did he have the wrong house? He surveyed his options, observing the oak trees guarding the gate, where the path beyond led to the house.

"Avalon," he whispered to himself, reading the name of the property from the iron plate above the letterbox. "This has to be the residence of my quarry, although my senses are faint, but I know there is something here."

The gate was secured by only a D-type gate latch. He reached over the gate, lifted the latch, and pushed open the gate. It swung all the way open with a barely audible groan until it came to rest against the sleeper of the garden behind the letterbox. Looking up the path, he planned his next moves. *I'll knock on the door, see if anyone is home, and have a discussion. I'm a traveller, and I've broken down and need to call for help. Name—I need a name. David—no, no, no. Let me see… Sean. Ah yes, Sean, a good Irish name, it is.*

He was just about to step past the gate when he heard a sudden swoosh of air. He turned his head just in time to see a greyish-tan creature with a large wingspan and piercing eyes crash, talons first, into the side of his head, jolting him sideways and knocking his red Paris Beau hat from his head. He stumbled and fell awkwardly, landing on his right hip and elbow. The hot twinge that travelled up his trunk culminated in an anguished shriek. His thoughts of the task diminished for the moment as the subconscious need for self-preservation took over. The dust kicked into the air hadn't even settled when the Red Man rolled to his left side, looking skywards for signs of his attacker. He could hear the swish of flapping wings as the assailant gained altitude and speed. He watched his aggressor leave the scene, its profile getting smaller as it put distance between itself and the Red Man.

When the figure was no longer visible, the Red Man attempted to move. His muscles were sore and probably bruised. However, his immediate action was to put his left hand on his head near his temple. He felt a sting and winced. He took his hand away, and his palm was covered with a smear of blood.

"Damn you, *ulchabhán*. I will see you plucked and tarnished and use your hide to carry my trinkets," he vowed with a threatening tone. "Neither you nor any other talisman will keep me from *an praghas*." He blew strands of ginger hair out of his face.

The Red Man got to his feet. Hearing the sound of an approaching vehicle, he stood facing the letterbox. A black sedan sped past, its driver seemingly unaware of the Red Man's presence. He then vigorously brushed himself down. However, his red jacket bore the signs of his entanglement with the owl: dirt scuffs were ground into the elbows and hip of the jacket. He walked back towards the gate, still cursing the owl under his breath when he paused again at its entrance. He focussed his eyes with determination, found his mindset, and stepped through the gate.

His knee hit something that bounced his leg right back, nearly toppling him. He let out a growl of frustration, huffed, leaned forward, and marched through the gate— only to be repelled once again.

"This cannot be happening. This is some kind of trick." He looked towards the house, half expecting an answer.

This time, he approached the gate with caution. He studied it carefully; there were no barriers beyond the opening, there was nothing on the footpath itself, and there was nothing to explain why he could not walk up to the house. He reached out with his right hand and felt nothing. He stepped closer, his arm outstretched, until he could feel some resistance. Still, he saw nothing to explain it. His hand stopped just inside the gate, where he could feel something spongy, something pushing back. The more he pushed, the stronger the resistance got.

"This cannot be possible," he said to himself as he stepped back from the entrance, "I must retrieve my trinkets at once," he exclaimed as he turned to hurry back to his vehicle.

Moments later, he returned from the vehicle with a bag fashioned from the hide of a stoat. He stood once again at Avalon's front gate, no longer concerned with remaining inconspicuous. Kneeling, he swept the ground in front of him with his free hand, untied the leather strap on the bag, and emptied its contents onto the ground. He placed a small bowl beside of the rest of the items, his eyes searching over of the remaining objects until he found his scrying stone, a flattish piece of clear crystal quartz. He placed the crystal into the bowl then took a flask of water from his coat. He poured just enough water into the bowl to cover the stone.

"Step one, purification," he whispered as he washed the stone. He dried it on his stoat pelt that hung from his belt. "Step two, look into the house."

Placing the stone upright on the fencepost beside the gate, he stepped back three paces, closed his eyes, and got down on his knees. Channelling all of his concentration, he began to recite. "Stone of light, I seek your help, your wisdom, and insight. Show to me what keeps my task at stay, so that I may remove thy blockage and be on my way."

Opening his eyes, he watched the stone, willing it to do something. Ten seconds past, nothing. Twenty seconds…

"Come on, you piece of *cac capaill*," he cursed at the stone just as the face started to cloud and swirl in a brownish-grey mist. "Yes, yes, show it to me," he said excitedly as he moved closer to view the image.

The mist cleared, revealing a silvery blue that rippled in the light.

"What is this?" he asked, frustrated by the cryptic image in front of him. "Is this water? Show me more," he pleaded with the stone.

The image swirled to grey again and sharpened to reveal Avalon with a silvery-blue, almost-transparent dome over it.

"Ah, this explains it." He rose and walked to the pathway. He reached his hand forward, flat palm facing outwards until it could go no more. He could feel resistance when he tried to push closer to the house.

He laughed heartily. He pulled back slightly until he could feel his hand sitting upon the dome that the stone had revealed to him. He paused a moment, his hand flat in front of him, and with a concentrated effort, he moved his flat palm quickly across the surface. Standing back, he could see the surface of silver and blue shimmer in the light. Ripples moved away from where he ran his hand across it, like waves on water. He walked a hundred metres down the fence line to the boundary of the next property. He pushed his arm across the fence line and felt no resistance. Taking three steps back, he tried again and met the same resistance as he had at the gate.

He walked back to the gate, assuming that the left corner boundary would return the same conclusion. Bending down to collect his trinkets, he returned them to the stoat hide bag. Last was the scrying stone from the fencepost. "*Buíochas,* my friend, for you have uncovered the work of witches. A protection spell may stop me today, but it will be only a hiccup in the grand scheme of things," he said as he returned the crystal the bag.

The Red Man returned to the car and sat there for a while, watching Avalon. He visualised the protective dome over the property, scheming and hatching a plan B to get in to get his *duass*. A red pick-up drove past; the wind trailing it rocked the chassis while he packed his tobacco pipe. Looking up from the pipe, he caught sight of the green-and-white real estate sign opposite.

"Stunning five-acre property for rent, three bedrooms, three bay garage, large kitchen, and entertaining area with decked pool area out the back. Set up for horses, the property is fenced into four paddocks all sharing one dam.

Contact Carla Ison, Delta Realty, the Esplanade, Delta. 9989 1100."

The sign also had a picture of the agent, whom he assumed was Carla Ison. She was pretty, with short brown hair and dressed professionally in a white blouse, navy jacket, and red scarf. After retrieving his notebook and a pencil from the glove box, he jotted down the details from the sign and threw the notepad onto the passenger seat.

The engine roared as he turned the ignition key and depressed the gas pedal. Placing the pipe into the open ashtray, he checked the mirrors then headed back into town.

Ten minutes later, the Red Man pulled the vehicle to a stop in the car park between the pub and the real estate. He locked the door behind him and turned to walk out to the footpath. A brass bell suspended above the entry rang announcing his presence in the shop when he opened the door. He stood for a moment, scanning the room. To his left were a number of seats bordered by large pots of golden cane palms. The reception desk immediately in front of him seemed empty, and the desks to his right he assumed belonged to the agents working there. He sensed movement from behind one of them then heard papers shuffling and the clearing of a throat. A face appeared above the desk divider, and a woman walked around the desk and into the foyer area to meet him.

"Good morning—or should I say good afternoon?— my name is Carla, Carla Ison. How can I help you?" She held out her hand to engage in the pleasantries of a handshake.

"I know who you are, Miss Ison," he replied abruptly. "I have seen your picture on a sign."

"You have? Great. Where was the sign?"

"A rental out on Delta Road on the way to Freycinet," the Red Man replied.

"Yes, I know the one. Horses?" Carla replied with a quizzical expression.

"I beg your pardon, madam," he said, bemused but watching her every move.

"Horses—do you have horses? It's a great property for it. I know the neighbours of the property. I had to agist my own horse with them two seasons ago. There's plenty of rain, so I didn't have to take much feed as the paddocks always had ample feed." She moved back behind the reception desk to locate information about the property. "Here it is—the dossier on the property. You're lucky; It's only been listed a couple of days. Shall we drive out and inspect the house?" She picked up car keys off her desk.

"No, that's okay. I'm sure it's more than what I require."

"Are you sure?"

"Yes I'm sure. When can I get a key and move in?" His tone reflected his heightening impatience.

"Okay, we'll get the paperwork done for you. I'll need some identification and a bond of five hundred dollars."

Carla shuffled through some paperwork from the desk drawers before turning to the computer.

The Red Man watched her for a moment before intruding on her concentration. "The rent for the property—how much is it?"

"It's currently listed at two hundred and forty per week on a minimum six-month contract."

"A contract, Miss Ison. Surely you can help me with that, can't you?" he said sternly while moving closer to the reception desk to lean his arms upon the top of the hutch.

"I'm sorry, sir, I didn't catch your name." Carla looked to meet the Red Man's gaze.

"That's because I didn't give it to you, Miss Ison." A wry smile touched the corners of his lips as he looked up at a framed print of a local landscape on the wall behind the desk. He looked back at her.

"No, I guess you didn't, but the owner does insist on a minimum six-month contract. Otherwise we cannot let the property."

"Look…" He sighed with some exaggeration. "I'm sure we can come to some arrangement, and it's O'Fihelly."

"What's that?"

"It's my surname, O'Fihelly."

"Oh, I know that. I meant what's the arrangement that you're suggesting?" Carla asked with interest.

"I will give you eight thousand dollars for the use of the property. That should cover six months" rent, bond, and a little extra for any incidentals. However, I do insist there be no paperwork." He reached into his coat to retrieve a bundle of green notes.

"That's certainly an intriguing offer. However, I will have to run it past the owners first. I'm certain that they'll find the offer quite tempting," Carla said with a cheeky smile as she reached for the bundle of notes, "I would be remiss, though, if I did not enquire as to the purpose of your short stay. I'm positive that the owners will make their own enquiries, and as their agent, it's my duty to know everything in relation to tenants" activities and the welfare of the properties under my care."

"I understand. Let's just say I'm here on a short business trip. Now you run it past the owners and meet me out at the property at five this afternoon. If they agree, bring the keys only. Do you understand, Miss Ison?"

"Yes, understood. I will contact them now, and with any luck, I'll be seeing you again this afternoon, Mr O'Fihelly."

Carla took the money, placed it in a calico bag, and wrapped it with a rubber band.

The Red Man gave her a parting smile and a tip of his hat as he turned to exit the office.

"Until then, Miss Ison, I bid farewell and trust I'll see you at five with good news."

He opened the door, and the brass bell rang above his head as he walked out.

"Until then," Carla called out to the Red Man as the door closed behind him.

8

Jane pulled her V-Dub to the curb outside Sophie's house. Sophie opened the passenger door but sat in the car to chat for a moment before going.

"Are you sure you don't want to come down to the shop with me, Soph?"

"No, it's okay. I want to take some time to clear my head. It's been a bizarre day, and besides, I think you need some time to talk to Claire about what's been going on."

"Yeah, you're probably right." Jane turned away from Sophie and paused a moment.

"What's wrong?"

"Nothing, I just haven't made up my mind if I'll talk to her today or wait until dinner tonight."

"Yeah, big call. Anyway, babe, I'm going to head inside. I'm sure you'll figure it out, but I might pop down to the shop later." Sophie reached over and touched Jane's thigh.

"Okay, thanks." Jane smiled.

"Love you," Sophie said as she leaned forward, pressing her weight against Jane as she kissed her cheek.

"Love you, too, Soph, and thanks for today. I really appreciate it."

"No worries, hon, I'll talk to you later," Sophie said as she swung her legs out of Blue Belle and planted her feet on the ground.

"Okay, talk to you later… Oh, Soph," Jane called.

"Yeah, hon," She leaned back in through the open door.

"When you were channelling today—" Jane paused briefly to choose her words carefully. "Have you ever seen yourself do it?"

"Um no. Why?" Sophie asked.

"Just curious, that's all. Your eyes changed. I was just curious if you knew."

"What do you mean they change?" Sophie asked.

"They change to blue," Jane said, "and I mean like the whole eye, not just the iris, and they were rounded, as well. In a good way, though. I mean I liked it," Jane said with a mix of excitement and trepidation.

"Cool. I do enter a trance-like state when I'm channelling, but I didn't know that they changed. I might have to get a photo next time," she joked. "Okay, then I'll speak to you later." Sophie smiled and closed the door as she stepped back from the curb.

Jane put Blue Belle into gear, indicated and pulled away from the curb, tooting the horn as she left. Looking in the rear-vision mirror, she saw Sophie waving. She turned onto the Esplanade at just after noon, and Jane thought that she would grab some lunch for Aunt Claire from Froth "n" Stuff before she called in at the shop.

She skirted the diners seated outside the café on the boardwalk and entered the shop. It had a real café atmosphere about it. The alluring smell of freshly ground and brewed coffee drew in the wanting. The tinkle of a cuppa being stirred mingled with the clatter of glasses and plates from behind the counter while mixing with the beats of soft-rock classics that Abigail played all day. Abigail Grey, the owner, was a gorgeous twentysomething, five foot four with brunette hair that turned outwards at the shoulder, hazel eyes, full lips, and a perfect figure. Fiercely proud of her business and her achievements, she was a local through and through and loved Delta and its residents. Surprisingly, though, for all her good looks and success, she was still single, albeit she was very active in the local singles scene.

Jane stood back a moment and read the blackboard menu on the back wall.

"Hi, Jane. How are you?"

"Oh, Hi, Abby." Jane looked down from the menu board to see Abigail waiting at the counter. "I'm good. How are you?"

"Good, busy as usual, but can't complain. How's Claire?"

"She's well, busy like yourself," Jane replied.

"Good to hear," Abby said through a beaming smile. "Now what can I get you, love?"

"Um, I'll get two hamburgers with beetroot and two caramel lattes, single shots please," Jane asked, her purse at the ready in her hands.

Tapping at the buttons on the register, Abby replied, "Sure, that'll be sixteen ninety, please."

Jane paid and stepped back from the counter to wait while her order was prepared, checking her mobile phone and watching the other diners and passers-by. Approximately five minutes, Abby called, "Jane, your order's up. Have a great day and say hi to Claire for me, as well, won't you?"

Jane took the two white paper bags holding the burgers in her left hand and managed to slide her right hand under the brown cardboard tray that carried the coffee.

"Thanks, Abby," Jane replied, smiling as she left the shop.

Jane walked into the Silver Moon and went straight to the back of the shop, passing by two women standing near the herb racks talking to each other. Aunt Claire was seated behind the counter, preoccupied with a magazine. She looked up only when she heard movement near the counter.

"Merry Meet, my dear. I see you come bearing gifts," she said warmly as she stood up to greet her niece.

"Yes, I thought you'd be hungry by now, and I know that you wouldn't get out to get anything yourself."

"Yes, that's true, but I did bring in something from home."

Jane giggled. "Yes, but an apple and a punnet of bean sprouts is not substantial enough to get you through the day, is it?"

"I guess not." She smiled. "Thank you. It smells great. What did you get?"

"Hamburgers and caramel lattes, so I hope you're hungry." Jane placed the food down on the only empty space she could find on the counter. "Abby next door said to say hi, as well. She always seems to be very busy over there."

"Yeah, she always is. I might have her over for dinner one night when she has time. Anyway, so how are you? You didn't seem yourself this morning." She reached for one of the lattes from the tray.

"I'm feeling good now," Jane replied as she drew back the curtain to the backroom. She dragged a chair back out of the counter area. "I went back to bed and then got up again soon after, went over to Sophie's, and brought her home. We chatted for a while. It was eye opening, that's for sure. You know how when you want to find something out and when you do, you just have more questions than answers?"

"Yes, I do," Claire replied, putting down her coffee. "You've got my attention. What's happened?" she asked, reaching over to comfort Jane.

"I'm okay, I think. Everything is just so cryptic at the moment." Jane heard footsteps behind her and turned to see the two customers had walked over to the counter to make a purchase.

Claire excused herself and stood up to serve her customers. "Merry meet, ladies. How are you both this afternoon?"

"We are good, thank you. I'd like this bag of dragon's tears and the fresh pennyroyal, if I may," said the older of the two women, handing them over to Claire.

"Certainly, I haven't seen you in here before. Are you passing through or new to the area?"

"Oh, we're passing through," the younger of the two replied. "Doing a trip from Launceston. My dad gets many stomach complaints, and we find that pennyroyal tea is the best thing to settle his complaints. We saw the dragon's tears on the rack, as well, and it looks cool. What can I use it for?"

Claire rang up the sale and placed the goods into a brown paper bag for them as she replied, "The pennyroyal is a great way to start the day and perfect for settling upset stomachs. Just be careful not to overdo it, though. Stick to one a day and do not exceed five days" use in succession. Otherwise, there may be some side effects that can be nasty."

"Okay, it wasn't explained to us by our naturopath that there could be side effects," she said, sounding worried. "What can happen?"

"Well, if you use it sporadically, everything should be okay, and there are many other benefits other than fixing upset stomachs. But continual or excess use can lead to kidney and liver damage. So at times, you'll need to balance this with other forms of relief or medication, but if all else fails, there is always the GP," Claire offered with a smile.

"I didn't think that there could be a danger," the older woman added.

"Yes, take care with herbal remedies just as with other medications," Claire stated as she looked from one to the other.

"And the dragon's tears?" the younger one asked again.

"Oh, yes, the dragon's tears. Again, a very useful herb, it's not actually from dragon's blood. It's a resin from the cinnabar tree that is dried into bright-red tear shapes, hence the name. It's used in a lot of spell work for witches and pagans for protection, power, and good fortune. In a powdered form, it can be burnt as an incense, or it can be made into an ink that a lot of folk use to write their spell work." Claire turned towards the younger of the two and leant forward. "I'll tell you a secret—the red lipstick that you're wearing might contain the same resin that this is made from."

Claire stood back up and offered the bag to them by placing it on their side of the counter. "That'll be twelve fifty, please."

"Okay," she replied reaching for her purse before the older of the two interrupted her.

"Do you need the dragon's tears?" she asked, "I don't think you'll use them."

"You're probably right, but they do look cool."

"You can also use them to clean your floors," Claire added. "Dilute them with boiling water and add some vinegar and wash away."

"Okay, I've troubled you too much this afternoon. I'll take both," she replied as she offered fifteen dollars to Claire.

Claire counted the change back into the customer's hand. "Have a great afternoon and safe travels. Blessed be." "Thank you. You, too," she said as they turned to leave.

Claire turned back to Jane and took her seat again. "The hamburger smells great. Hopefully, it's not too cold now. Thanks for bringing it all in, love. I really appreciate it."

"It's okay, Aunt Claire," Jane replied with a smile while swallowing her food.

The two of them sat there in relative silence while they ate, listening to the background music that Claire had playing in the shop. Most of the time, Jane didn't mind their silences. However, on this occasion, she was feeling a little anxious about discussing last night's events with her aunt. She was second-guessing what her reaction would be, and Jane always tended to lean towards the worst-case scenario when dealing with the unknown.

Aunt Claire put the last of the burger in her mouth, picked up the napkin, and wiped around her lips. "That was what I needed. Thanks, love." She threw the napkin back in the white bag as she reached for the coffee cup. "Now what was it that you wanted discuss? You were saying something about something being cryptic," she said, looking somewhat puzzled from what she could recall about the previous conversation.

Jane put her coffee on the counter and lounged back into the chair. "I wasn't sure whether to speak to you about this now or later when you got home. I didn't want to cause any alarm or worry you."

"That very sentence has me concerned already. I'll be beside myself if you don't tell me what's on your mind, and besides, if you don't, I'll come over that side of the counter and shake it out of you." She smiled weakly.

"Okay, I'll tell you," Jane started with a sigh. *What the hell am I supposed to say? I don't want to scare her, but what if she already knows?*

Jane looked down at her aunt's hand holding the coffee cup. "I felt a strange sensation last night when I was out in the garden. It was like I was being… watched, but I wasn't." She continued quickly, attempting to reassure her aunt, "I checked, and I checked again. I walked around the garden, and I couldn't see anyone or anything at all, but it was bugging me, you know! Then after you left this morning, I felt something strange again, when I went outside. I went and picked Sophie up and brought her back to the house, and she said that something made her feel weird when she was outside, as well. It's only been in the last day or so, and I don't know what it is. I didn't want to alarm you, but something's different about the house."

"Okay, okay, that is definitely concerning and something that we should not take too lightly. It's only been in the last day, you say?"

"Yes, that's right," Jane replied. "Do you know what's going on?" She leant forward towards the counter, expecting to hear her aunt impart with a great wisdom that explained everything—well, at least everything that she had cared to divulge.

"I'm thinking that we go home and investigate this. What do you say? The shop's been a little quiet today anyway," Claire said.

"What?" Jane spat with surprised horror. Closing the shop early was unheard of. "Are you serious? I cannot let you do that. You've never done that!" She stood from her chair to walk a few paces to digest what Claire was suggesting. She turned back to her aunt. "I know that you're making this overture with the best of intentions. However, I cannot and will not let you close the shop, not for my benefit. I can't stress this enough." She pressed her right palm pressed against her forehead, the other on her hip. Claire never took sick days. She'd even had the doors open during a flood five years ago, although she didn't sell anything.

"Okay, we'll keep the store open for another two hours, but you must do something for me."

"What's that?"

"Go out back into the store room and grab a couple of hours" sleep. I think you need it," she proposed with a smile. "Oh, and I think a hug is in order, as well."

Jane agreed with the raise of an eyebrow and a smile. She stepped towards the counter and embraced Claire, who came around to meet her.

"Now go get some sleep. I'll wake you when it's time to close up, and then we can go home for dinner, or we might grab some take-out. Okay?"

"Okay, Aunt Claire. Blessed be." Jane turned away and walked out the back through the draped curtain.

"Blessed be, love, and sweet dreams."

9

The silver sedan pulled onto the verge, coming to a complete stop just past the real estate sign on Delta Road. It parked the wrong way, facing oncoming traffic. The time was quarter to five in the afternoon, and everything seemed to be going to plan. The Red Man sat in the car for a moment, staring into the rear-view mirror, waiting for Ms Ison.

He started to think she might not show, so he picked up some possessions and stepped out of the car. Walking around the front of the car, he perched his butt against the hood, where he could watch Avalon down the road. He reached into his tobacco pouch and retrieved his corn pipe and a large pinch of rum-dipped tobacco. He puffed the smoke, drawing the flame to burn the tobacco. He exhaled a chain of five mushroom-shaped clouds until he was satisfied that the pipe was well alight.

The light was starting to fail as the blues gave way to greys and blacks. However, he could see the white of the gate and the outline of the roof of Avalon just over the tops of the trees when a set of approaching headlights drew his attention. An amber flash indicated that the approaching vehicle was pulling over to the left-hand verge of the road. Slowing, it gently rolled past where the Red Man was parked. The green Ford hatch completed a quick U-turn to park facing the silver Holden. The driver's door opened, and he could hear a continuous ping sounding from the vehicle until the driver exited and closed the door behind her.

"Good afternoon, Mr O'Fihelly. Thank you for meeting me," Ms Ison said as she approached him, holding her right hand out to engage a handshake.

However, the Red Man did not reciprocate the gesture. "Good day, Ms Ison, I trust you have a satisfactory answer to my proposal," he said as he exhaled a mouthful of smoke.

Carla watched the smoke spiral into the air, a white haze against a backdrop of the dark sky. "I think you'll be very pleased, Mr O'Fihelly." She smiled as she leaned against the car beside him, dropping her handbag to the ground beside her heels. "The owners have agreed to your proposal, and while we find it very peculiar, they believe the financial reward to be very generous."

Carla turned towards the Red Man, flicking her hair from one shoulder to the other, and placed her right hand on the Red Man's upper left thigh. "They were very interested, as you could understand. Particularly as to why you'd make such a proposal with no contract. I was instructed to find out what it was that you intended to do on the property, as they want to indemnify themselves against any obligation of disclosure to their insurance company. In short, they don't want any activities that you do to leave them in any compromising positions."

The Red Man glared with disdain at the woman, but he knew he needed her services to get what he desired, so he made the decision not to terminate their relation there and then.

"I'm grateful that we could find an accord on this matter, Ms Ison," he said as he picked up her hand and placed it back on her tailored skirt. "However—"

Carla was quick to react—she grabbed the Red Man's hand and placed it between her legs. "I can sense that you're a shrewd businessman, Mr O'Fihelly. I could sense that when I first met you. In fact, I recall seeing you yesterday out the front of the shop. I know you do your research and that you probably always get what you want, and I'm no different. You may not be upfront with me now. However, the deal will not proceed unless if you disclose the purpose of your stay. If you do, you will find that I will be very open and accommodating to ensure that your business with me is very satisfactory," she said in a very flirtatious tone as she released his hand.

"I'm not sure that I would conduct my business in that way, Ms Ison," he retorted as he pushed himself away from both her and the vehicle to walk a couple of paces towards her car. "So they want to know my business, do they?" he asked as he turned to face her once again.

"Yes, as do I, Mr O'Fihelly."

"Then I suggest we continue our discussion as you show me through the property, Ms Ison."

"Yes, great idea. I have the keys," she said as she pulled a key ring off the clipboard inside her handbag. "Shall we leave the cars here and walk up?"

"Lead the way, Ms Ison." He bowed and swept his arm towards the path to the house.

"Carla, please… call me Carla." She walked past him and stepped onto the path.

He could make out little of the yard and the house in the poor light. However, he remembered the white-and grey two-storey property with a hedge at the front of the property. He followed Ms Ison's clicking heels along the cement path, listening to their cadence until he broke the pattern with a question.

"Do you know how old the property is, Ms I…" he cleared his throat, "Carla?"

"It's about twenty years old, but it has recently been renovated and painted throughout. The current owners have had the property about five years, I think. Watch your step up here. Stay close behind. The path bends a little here," she said as she held a hand back, reaching for the Red Man, but he avoided her touch.

"The trees aren't as high as I would have thought for a property so old."

"No, they're not. The previous owners used to run a lot of horses on the property. The new owners, not so much. They've kept the paddocks as they are, so there is plenty of space at the rear of the property for grazing animals.

However, this front paddock has been turned into an orchard, so the trees here can't be any older than four years,

I'd say. Watch your head here," she said with a strained voice as she ducked under a low-hanging branch. "Some might be starting to fruit if you're lucky. The weather is certainly starting to warm up as summer approaches. It'll be Christmas before you know it," she said with a nervous laugh.

"I don't celebrate Christmas."

"Oh, I'm sorry. I didn't mean to offend."

"I did not take offence… the path is longer than I realised."

"It can be very deceiving, especially from the road, but we are nearly there. Looks like the moon will offer some light tonight—there's not much cloud cover."

The Red Man looked skyward for a brief moment. "Pfff…" He returned his gaze to the darkening silhouette of the woman in front of him and the looming presence of the house as it grew larger and larger with each step.

"You don't say very much," Carla said as she carefully navigated the path a step at a time, not game enough to look behind at her companion.

"What's to say? I have to keep focussed, keep my mind on the job. I do not have time for pleasantries with the opposite sex."

"Okay, but it would make it more comfortable for both of us if we talked some more."

"You can talk all you want if you like. It doesn't mean that I'm going to listen. Are we there yet?" he snapped, feeling a little anxious.

"Well, it's right here in front of us, silly. Only another twenty metres or so, and we'll be at the front door."

He was looking forward to his new base of operations.

"We've reached the steps to the landing; there are three steps up with side rails on each side. Would you like some assistance?" she asked holding out a hand to the void behind her.

"No thank you." He brushed past her shoulder, almost knocking her off balance.

"I apologise for getting in your way, Mr O'Fihelly. I didn't realise that you were that close behind me," she said sarcastically.

The ground had a little more give than the path they traversed from the cars did. His each footstep echoed and creaked.

"The landing is a hardwood deck, a great place to relax and look out over the orchard on a lazy Sunday afternoon," Carla said, fumbling with the keys in front of the main entry door. "The door opens to a foyer that is bound by a utilities room on the left and the hall that services all of the other ground floor rooms on the right."

She turned the key, making an audible click. The door chafed the jamb as Carla pushed it open, then a rush of stale air escaped past them into the night. While she felt around the corner of the opening for a light switch, headlights drew the Red Man's attention to two vehicles a kilometre down the road.

"Come in," Carla said, waving an arm. Her voice echoed off the walls in the small entry way.

The Red Man turned away from the lights of the approaching cars, back towards her voice, and as he did, a flood of light rushed out of the door and slapped him in the face, making him turn away for his eyes to adjust.

He stepped into the house, stopping on a brown bristled mat to wipe his feet. The entry was a small square room with a picture rail run around its circumference. The walls were painted a light grey under the picture rail and off white above it. To the left, Carla had opened a white door to the utilities room and flicked the switch, revealing an array of old brooms, mops, and buckets as well as paint tins and brushes leftover from the renovation.

"Storage is on your left, and plenty of it, may I add," Carla declared as she stepped out of the way and past the mirror that hung on the opposing wall to the entry door. Along the length of the frame were black iron hooks to accommodate hats, scarfs, and the like. The Red Man checked his appearance in the mirror when he turned from the utilities room, adjusting his collar and sleeves.

"It's a great mirror, isn't it?"

"What?"

"The mirror—I wish I had one at home. I love colonial furnishings like that piece. Don't worry. You look good," Carla said. "Now if you'll follow me into the hall, we'll view the rest of the property." She stepped through the open doorway on the right of the foyer into the hallway.

"This hall services all of the rooms on the lower level. To our right is the sitting room." Carla opened the doors of each room and turned the lights on so that her client could see all the features of each room as they went. "Next is the lounge room, which is quite spacious. Do you have much furniture yourself, Mr O'Fihelly?" Carla enquired with interest.

"No, it's just me. No furniture," the Red Man said. He was getting weary of the predicament that He'd found himself in. "I don't care too much about the rooms down here. What's upstairs? Take me upstairs at once," he demanded waving his hand about, pointing in Carla's direction.

"Sure thing, Mr O'Fihelly. Follow me down the hall." Carla shuddered once she'd turned her back to him. "You know I didn't mean any disrespect in relation to the furniture. There is some furniture here, albeit sparse. The owners didn't intend on letting a fully furnished house, but you if don't want to bring furniture in then, well, that's okay, isn't it? You can do as you want." She turned back to check that he was following her. "The laundry is on your left, as is the dining room here, and on your right is the engine room of the house, the kitchen." "Upstairs," he barked.

"Yes, upstairs, the stairs are in the left corner at the rear of the house," she said without a moment's hesitation, "Would you like me to—"

"No." He pushed past her, knocking her off kilter. "You stay down here," he demanded as he found the stairs, which he bounded up two at a time.

∞

What an arsehole! Carla walked into the kitchen and turned on the light. There was no fridge, only a cob, oven, bench top, and sink. Carla sauntered over to the table, pulled out a chair, and collapsed into it, releasing an exaggerated sigh. *"I don't deserve this crap."*

Ten or fifteen minutes later, Carla sat at the table, bouncing her legs nervously like a schoolgirl on her first day and tapping the table with her fingers. Every now and again, she heard footsteps on the wooden floors above, pacing back and forth.

"What the fuck is he doing up there?" she grumbled as she got up from the wooden chair. She reached for her mobile phone to check the time. It was nearly six o'clock. "Okay, we're going into my time now," she muttered as she put the phone back into the inside pocket of her blazer. Walking over to the stairs, she noticed that there was no light filtering down from the upstairs.

That's odd. She grasped the handrail and slowly navigated up the straight wooden staircase. The steps groaned under her weight, which didn't reflect her petit athletic body.

Might have to go to Gym after this.

It was pitch black at the summit of the stairs. She looked down the hall to the front of the building but could not make out anything. There was no noise. She moved into the hall, trying to be as light-footed as possible. However, the creaking floorboards weren't forgiving.

"Shit! Mr O'Fihelly?" she whispered into the darkness. "Are you there?" She shook with nerves, feeling like Shaggy and Scooby looking for the rest of the gang while all the time waiting for something to jump out at them. She kicked off her heels to reduce the noise as she walked down the hall.

"Mr O'Fihelly, are you there?" she whispered again as she tip-toed farther down the hall, running her fingers along the walls, feeling for a light switch as she went. She passed two rooms; no noticeable light protruded from underneath the closed doors. The hallway was becoming lighter the farther she ventured along the narrow passageway.

Her gullet was dry, her muscles taut. She felt as if a giant had a hold of her throat and was squeezing like a vice. She tried to call out again.

"Mist…" The words didn't come; she swallowed repeatedly and moved her tongue about in her mouth in an attempt to lubricate her lips and vocal cords.

"Mr O…" The words failed her again, then she had a light-bulb moment. She retrieved her mobile phone from her jacket. It vibrated in her hand, slipping a little from her grip when she pressed the power button on the side of the device to wake it up. She quickly swiped her finger across the screen to activate the home screen, but her haste and sweaty hands caused the phone to fall to the floor. She could not believe the turn of events that were transpiring and was on the brink of screaming when she managed to contain the swelling feeling in the pit of her stomach that yearned to be released at a hundred decibels. She looked down the passageway. Her eyes had adjusted, and she could definitely see some light coming from a room. She stripped off her jacket and dropped it where she stood before getting down on all fours to feel around to locate the phone.

Her fingers were spread wide as she padded the floor for the phone. Her shallow breathing was getting faster by the moment the more flustered she became. She crawled a few steps, sweeping the floor with her arms.

A creaking floorboard stopped her dead in her tracks.

"What the fuck was that?" She froze, listening for more sounds, but the harder she concentrated, the louder and clearer the cicadas became.

Creak!

"Mr O'Fihelly?" she whispered as she felt her body tense up with fear again. She fell silent, lying on her stomach on the floor, waiting and listening.

Creak… creak… creak. She turned her head towards the noise but couldn't see anything. The noise grew louder and closer; her heartbeat grew faster, like a steam train gathering speed.

"I'm… I'm going to die," she sobbed to herself. She started picturing her family—her mum, her dad, and her sister, Rachel—and the fun times they'd had while she was growing up in Delta.

Creak… creak…

The sound of present danger, the march of impending doom resonated in her mind; it got closer and closer… then stopped.

"What?"

She waited for the noise to recommence, waiting for something. She felt as if she were at the edge of a cliff, her arms flailing around trying to keep her balance, knowing she was only seconds from death. She felt pressure on her left shoulder like a pinch followed by a dead weight. Her body contorted slightly as she was going to grab at it. Then her brain computed the sensations, and she realised someone had a hold of her.

"Ms Ison."

She heard her name, but an animal from within took control of her body, pushing its way from the depths of her loins, gaining momentum as it passed each of her organs, expanding her lungs, shooting up her throat.

"Aaarrrrrrrrgggggggghhhhhh," she screamed, a primitive urge spawned deep within as her body went into full defensive mode.

"Carla… Carla… shhhh. It's okay. It's me, Mr O'Fihelly."

She twisted sideways, flipping from her stomach to her back in one motion and crawling backwards a couple of metres commando style while yelling at her assailant, whom she hadn't recognised.

"Who are you? What do you want… what do you want?" she screamed at the dark figure that crouching before her.

"It's me. It's Mr O'Fihelly. We're here to look at the property to rent… remember?" he asked in an awkward tone. "It's okay," he reassured her again, "I won't hurt you. Give me your hand, and I'll help you up."

Carla hesitated then offered her hand cautiously in a slow movement, jerking back each time she sobbed. She recognised his voice but could not make out his features in the dark due to her tears.

He took her hand in his and, with a firm but gentle grip, pulled her close into his embrace, her face coming to rest in the crook of his neck.

"It's okay, Carla. There is nothing here that will hurt you, just an old dark empty house," he reassured her in a calm, soothing voice.

She composed herself as best as she could, although the odd whimper and involuntary chest compression remained.

"Thank you, Mr O'Fihelly. Thank you for finding me." She sniffled as she squeezed him tight in appreciation of his good deed.

"Silas, my name is Silas," he said as he pulled her to her feet. "Why were you up here in the dark? Didn't I tell you to remain downstairs?" His short moment of being nice ended. He waited for answer, but all she could do was snivel before him.

"Do you have nothing to say?" he demanded.

"I do," she said finally after clearing her throat. "I was looking for you. Don't ask me why after the way you treated me downstairs," she bellowed as she started to gather courage to stand up for herself. "You were an arsehole, but I waited like I always do. Something to do with ethics and 'the customer's always right' and having to close the sale, and all that shit. That's why I stayed, and for what? To be treated like a doormat that you could walk all over? I don't think so. I'm a real person with real feelings," she roared, her anger turning to frustration as she paced around in front of him, her right hand pressed against her forehead.

The sound of breaking glass rose from the floor.

He reached past her right shoulder and flicked the light switch, illuminating the hallway. The decoration was the same upstairs as it was downstairs.

"Calm yourself down, Carla. I told you to stay downstairs for your own good, but you think what you want. Your opinion of me is not of my concern." He turned away from her and walked towards the end of the hall.

"Where do you think you're going?" she yelled at his back, "You're being an arsehole again, Silas… what kind of name is that anyway?" She followed him, stepping over the broken phone, doubting her every action while her anger swept aside all rational thoughts.

"Of the forest," he replied without paying her the courtesy of turning to face her.

He reached the end of the hall and turned into the last room on the right. The light switch remained off, as the drapes were open allowing the moonlight to filter into the room. Carla reached the door of the room, propped her weight against the doorframe and took deep breaths to pacify herself.

"What do you mean "of the forest"? Were your parents hippies?"

"That's none of your concern." He turned to look at her briefly, exposing the teeth behind his devilish smile. "What is your business, Ms Ison, is that we return to discussing the property." He muffled a snicker while surveying the landscape beyond his grasp. "Ms Ison… Carla, you may consider the deal done. I have found what I am looking for."

Carla stood firm on both feet in the doorway. "I don't understand what it is that you've found, nor do I consider the deal done, Mr O'Fihelly. I still need paperwork and answers to disclose to the owners such as what your business with their property is." She stepped into the room, her confidence and control returning to her like an ally on the battlefield of business that is property management. She stopped five paces from him and surveyed the room in the moonlight; she could see the outline of a bed and dresser against the far wall.

"If you think that discussing business in the bedroom will close the deal, you're sadly mistaken. That ship has already sailed, Silas."

"Is that so, Ms Ison? Well, now that could be a problem," he responded as he turned and stepped towards her. "You see, I don't do paperwork, and I don't have to disclose what my intentions are. In fact, I believe I have made an attractive offer—eight thousand dollars attractive. But in hindsight, Ms Ison, I would be remiss if I didn't look after you in the deal." He stepped closer, his hands out in front of him, rocking back and forth slowly, gesturing his understanding.

Carla tried to swallow without success as the man approached her. She'd lost all the saliva in her mouth, and her muscles reacted by tensing up as an overwhelming sense of danger plunged through her body again.

"Are you okay, Carla?"

"Um… yes," she replied as she stepped back away from him.

"Why do you step away from me? Do I scare you?" he asked.

"Yes, please stop." She held her hands out towards him as she continued her retreat.

"But, Carla, you haven't heard my offer yet. Would you like to hear my offer?"

"Yes," she replied, her voice quavering with uncertainty.

"That's a good girl. You see, you are a part of a bigger plan, Carla, and although you are not to know what that plan is, I shall reward you for your part." He retrieved a roll of cash from his pocket.

"O… o…okay." She trembled as she felt the back of her legs press the mattress. She couldn't only go forward or escape was across the bed. She looked towards the door quickly then back to Mr O'Fihelly.

"There's two thousand dollars here, Carla, and It's all for you." He held the money out to her. "Take it. Go on. It's all for you."

"No," she screamed, knocking the money from his hand. She turned to climb over the bed. However, he anticipated her reaction and quickly moved to prevent her escape by grabbing her ankles and pulling her back across the mattress towards him. She clung to the far edge, straining to remain steadfast as he tugged at her legs.

"Let go of me!" she howled, kicking out at her attacker.

He lurched forward and hauled her backwards with great force; her hold on the bed broke as her body crashed into his legs.

"Don't fight me, Carla. You know this is a good business deal, and besides, you put it on the table," he quipped with much jubilance as he tossed her onto her back, forcing his hand up her skirt and inner thigh.

10

Aunt Claire pulled down the shop's security shutter above the entry. The rattle of the metal tracks and thud of the roller door hitting the floor sent a shudder up Jane's back. It was just after five, and Jane had been asleep for the last two hours while Claire kept things going in the shop.

"Did you park opposite?" Claire asked as she rifled through her handbag, searching for her car keys.

"Yeah." Jane yawned, stretching her back and rolling her shoulders. "Near the supermarket."

"Okay, I'm in the usual spot at the park. I'll walk you to the corner and follow you home." Claire looked concerned.

"Yeah, I'll be okay, just need to wake up some more. A coffee would have been great, but I'll put the window down and the music up." She grinned at Claire.

"See you at home. Blessed be," she called as she turned to follow the path that led to the small car park in Civic Park.

"Sure thing," Jane replied with a wave. "Blessed be."

Jane unlocked Blue Belle and slid into the driver's seat. She pushed the key into the ignition, shut the door, fastened her seatbelt, and started the car. She for a second then sighed, staring out the windscreen.

"I feel like I could sleep for a thousand years," she said to herself. "Okay, I need some happy tunes for the way home." She reached into the box and replaced The Waterboys with The Cure and skipped straight to *Inbetween Days*. It always brightened her mood, although the album as a whole did that, as well.

The song was well into the second verse when Jane decided that she'd better stop singing along and get onto the road as Aunt Claire would be waiting for her. She started out onto the Esplanade. Over her left shoulder, she could see the headlights of Claire's Mitsi leave Civic Park behind her. She turned onto Jetty Road, smiling as she looked in the rear-vision mirror to see her aunt in the vehicle behind her; she turned right to make the trip back to Avalon. The unique dulcet tones of Robert Smith and the rest of The Cure kept her company, and she tapped along with the melody, singing every word in time with the lyrics. Smiling as she sang along, awash with joy, she forgot temporarily why she had gone to see her aunt in the first place.

The trip home was completed in less than fifteen minutes when Jane pulled to a stop on the drive in front of the gate. Claire slowed to rest on the verge behind Blue Belle. The headlights of both cars illuminated the front of the property with white light that intermittently turned to orange from the blinking of the indicators. Jane unlatched the chain that secured the gate to the post, pushing it open to allow access; she turned back towards the cars, shielding her eyes with her hand.

She drove in with Claire following slowly then parked in front of the garage. Jane swung open the door to the sound of dusk time animals and insects. After exiting Blue Belle, she stood beside the open door, listening for the silent approach of yesterday's visitor, to feel the rush of broken air just above her head. A smile graced her lips as the memory of her encounter flooded back, but alas, that visitor did not return. However, Jane felt that the curious creature was not too far away, which was a comforting thought.

The slam of a door and rattle of keys slapped Jane back to the present. Claire was walking towards her as she put the keys into her handbag.

"Did you see the two cars parked opposite? We might be getting a new neighbours. What do you think?" Claire asked as she walked around the front of the V-Dub, brushing her leg against the chrome bumper, her attention still in her handbag.

"Yeah, I saw them when we went past. The lights were on in the house, and it was Carla's car out front. I haven't seen the other one around before. Maybe Carla is just doing some of her own entertaining again." She closed the car door.

Claire looked up from her bag. "Did you really say that?"

At first, Jane did not know if Aunt Claire was serious and thought she may be in trouble. However, she never shied away from saying what was on her mind.

"Yep, I sure did," Jane replied as she waited for a reaction. Claire studied her niece for a moment, then they both burst into laughter.

"Oh, that was a good one," Claire said she started towards the backdoor, "Are you coming?" she called out.

Jane waited that one moment longer to allow her special friend to make an appearance, but still, there was nothing. She scanned the tree, gently kicked the ground, and turned towards the house to follow Claire inside.

"I'm going to make dinner tonight. You can have a shower or get changed and relax if you like."

"Really?"

"You sound surprised!"

"Well, yes. I guess I thought we could talk about, you know, what did not feel right with the house," Jane managed.

"Yes, and we will. I might open a bottle of Moscato, and we can discuss everything over dinner." "Okay, what are you making?

"Something quick and easy. Nothing special," She added, "Now go take a load off."

"Okay, I might run a bath, if that's all right?"

"Yes definitely. See you soon, love."

Jane ran a hot bath and soaked until her skin had become wrinkled like an old prune and whiter than fresh snow. *Time to get out*. She felt a bit lightheaded from the heat in the small enclosed room. She towelled herself down, dressed in an old pair of Supergirl pyjamas, and went to the kitchen.

"Mmm, smells great. What have you made?"

"It's just an old curried sausage recipe that I whipped up. Your wine is on the table," she said, motioning with her hand. "You weren't in the bath long. Do you feel refreshed?"

"Not long? I was in there about thirty minutes, wasn't I?"

"No it was about ten to fifteen, actually."

"You're kidding? I could have sworn it was a lot longer," Jane said in disbelief.

"Are you feeling okay?"

"Yes, I'm fine. Just got a little dizzy from the humidity in the bathroom, that's all. I might go out into the garden again tonight for some fresh air and relaxation—you know, clear my head so I can get a good night's sleep."

"Did you want me to go out with you to check that there is no one out there?"

"No, it's okay. I can do that. I think I just overreacted a little last night. That's all," she offered with some confidence. *With any luck, I will see* Aedán *again.* She walked over to the cutlery draw. "I'll set the table."

"Great thanks, love. Dinner will be another five minutes."

"Thanks, Aunt Claire. You're too good to me, you know," she said with a big smile that confirmed her affection towards her aunt.

Minutes later, they were both seated at the table, enjoying the curry served with basmati rice and poppadums while sipping their Moscato.

"Did you feel it today?" Jane asked, abruptly putting an end to the silence that they both enjoyed while they ate. "When we got home, did you?"

"Yes, I did."

"What do you think? It feels weird, hey! What are we going to do?"

"Do?" Claire raised an eyebrow as she paused, fork suspended midway to her mouth. "We are not going to *do* anything."

"What do you mean? Do you know what it is?"

"Yes, and it is nothing to be scared or suspicious of, trust me." Claire consumed another forkful of curry.

Jane placed her cutlery down on the table, and the ting of the steel against the ceramic plate echoed fleetingly around the room.

"Well?" Jane said, begging to be indulged with an explanation. "Are you going to tell me?"

"Yes, it was—or should I say it is—a protection spell. What you can feel is the spell that I cast that is protecting the house."

"Oh, okay, that makes sense." Jane nodded as if the whole commotion of the issue suddenly weren't so big after all. "I've never been on the other side of a protection spell before. Normally, I've enchanted a totem or talisman to keep with me, but this was different. It was like the atmosphere had changed, like I was stepping from one climate into another."

"Well, in theory, you are," Claire stated, seemingly enjoying the discussion on the matter. "It's like a dome over the house, protecting it from intruders that mean us harm."

"Okay, but why would you do that?" Jane asked with some concern.

"You were not yourself. You seemed shaken this morning when you came down from your room, and so before I went into the shop, I cast the spell, just as a precaution. You know what they say—prevention is better than…"

"A cure," they both said simultaneously, grinning.

Jane studied her goblet. She swished the last morsel of her second glass, creating a mini-whirlpool. Her mind travelled back to last night and Aedán. *Will I ever see him again?* Thinking of water, liquid always reminded her of the pond in the secret garden.

"Don't fall in," Claire warned. "You're getting quite lost in the glass."

"Huh? Oh, sorry. I was daydreaming again, wasn't I?" She raised the glass to her lips and swallowed its sweet contents. "Fancy another bottle?"

"I'd love one, hon, but tomorrow is another work day, and I'll need my wits about me to get through it rather than fall asleep at my desk."

"Okay, then, we'll save it for another night. I'll clear the dishes tonight. Can't have you doing everything, and besides, your shows are about to start." Jane pushed the chair back and rose to her feet.

"Thanks, love."

Claire finished her wine, dabbed the corners of her mouth with her napkin, and dropped it back on the table. The chair grated along the wooden floor as she stood up. "Sure you don't need a hand, love?"

"No, I'm fine," Jane replied over her shoulder as she walked to the basin.

Claire turned and walked towards the doorway, peering up at the clock on the wall. "Fifteen minutes to kill until *Grimm* starts," she said to herself. "I might have a shower before I sit down. I won't be long," Aunt Claire muttered wearily as she trudged down the hallway.

Jane was just finishing up with the dishes when her phone vibrated and the intro to The Cure's *Catch* spilt out from her pocket. She reached for the phone and swiped the screen to activate the received message.

19.21

Hey U, WYD 2morrow. Catchup?

Soph xoxo

Jane grinned as she tapped away at the screen, typing her reply.

19.22

Ur on. Call rfter bfast xoxo

She returned the phone back to her pocket and leaned back against the counter, biting at her bottom lip as she thought of Aedán again. She stood there for maybe five minutes, when Claire walked past the doorway, disrupting her concentration. She looked to the wall clock: 7:27. She leaned backwards towards the window, nearly breaking her back to peruse the night sky.

Looks like a great night, she thought as she straightened up. *Time to go out to the garden again.*

She walked into the sunroom. "Just going out to the garden for a while. No need to wait up if I'm not in when you go to bed," she called.

"Okay, dear. Just make sure that you're warm enough," Claire replied, being the responsible parent that she'd promised Grace she would be.

Jane reached the door that led out to the secret garden. She flicked the switch on the wall and could see the garden light up through gaps in the jasmine. She paused, her hand on the doorknob. She closed her eyes, inhaled a few deep breaths to clear her mind and relax her body. Although she could hear the faint sounds of the theme song to *Grimm* coming from the lounge room, it did not break her concentration as she prepared a chant to gather courage before she entered the garden.

O mighty Cernunnos,
O mighty Cerridwen,
With hope and trust, I seek your power
To be blessed upon me for an hour
To make me strong when I feel weak
To grant me the wisdom that I seek
To fill me with courage so I do not flee

Blessed be upon you, so mote it be!

Jane took one last deep breath, held it for a moment and slowly exhaled, blowing the air from her mouth through puckered lips. She opened her eyes, turning the door handle. The groaning hinges drowned out the noise from the television. She stepped out into the jasmine tunnel, and the rich sweet aromas of the blooms enveloped her, heightening her senses and pleasuring her mind.

The screen slammed back against the jamb, shaking Jane from the moment's peace that had flowed through her. The lights, blurry at first, danced around in her head until her eyes adjusted to the limited light. She carefully stepped through the tunnel and into the open garden, surveying every feature in the hope that she might see Aedán waiting somewhere in the shadows. However, there was nothing to be seen, just the moths and other insects attracted to the garden lighting. Satisfied, albeit disappointed, that she was alone, Jane strolled towards the pond and apple tree.

She drew a long deep breath through her nose—the air was so unbelievably crisp and fresh for a spring evening that vapour condensed when she exhaled. Normally, the temperature didn't drop so far for another four to five months, at least, but Jane was learning that not everything was normal at Avalon, especially not in the secret garden.

Jane walked along the path with a stutter step almost like wedding march, her arms swinging by her side while she was seemingly entranced in a daydream. She sat on the edge of the pond, her hands planted firmly on the wall, holding her weight as she shifted to look at the tops of the Winesap.

She turned back to the pond as movement in her peripheral vision grabbed her attention. Green tree frogs sat around the aquatic environment, between the reeds and rocks, waiting, hunting, for a quarry to satisfy their need for sustenance.

She sat for some time, just taking in the ambience of the garden. She stretched her legs, her clenched hands firmly wedged between her limbs. Sometimes noticing the steaming exhale of her breath, she would shuffle her feet to prevent the onset of pins and needles.

"What are you doing?" she asked herself. "Waiting in the cold for a ghost, a spirit, an apparition? I don't know—maybe I am going crazy."

"You're not crazy."

"Yes, thank you. You see? I'm not crazy, but I'm a witch—I deal in things that most don't believe in and given a chance to interact with someone that most would think was fantasy, and I'm dismissing it myself without regard, fact or reason. I know it is not me but…" She sighed. "I'm rambling again. Wait… isn't talking to yourself a sign that you are going crazy?"

Jane stood up, shook herself down, and looked at the Winesap, smiling as thoughts of her mum returned to her. She recalled Aunt Claire's story of how her mum and Claire had planted the tree many years before. "I feel your presence in the garden, Mum. I feel you protecting me like how the apple tree protects the garden and Avalon. You created a dream, a beautiful garden, an escape, a utopia, and for that, I am thankful. The tree is certainly Avalon's talisman."

"You know, some might say the same about you, dearie," a strange yet somewhat-familiar voice said above her.

"Aedán, is that you? I mean is that really you?" she implored, running around the end of the pond wall to the base of the tree while looking up into the branches to catch a glimpse of him.

"Aye, it is me, but I am not that popular to be causing a fuss over."

"Where are you? I can't see you."

"Why, I am right here, dearie."

Jane looked expectantly to her left and right before turning back to the pond, and as she did, the reflection of the garden lights rebounded off the surface of the pond water and onto Aedán' shiny black coat. His eyes were a darker colour tonight—a grey slate colour. However, Jane could still make out a faint pulsating glow of red deep within them. He was just how she remembered him, and his presence rein stilled her faith within herself.

"How are you, Aedán? It's good to see you. I wasn't sure that I'd see you again or if I had seen you at all."

"As I said before, dearie—you are not crazy."

"There was a moment this morning when I didn't believe that, so I sought the assistance of the Gods to guide—well, give me courage." Jane walked over to Aedán and sat on the pond wall beside him.

She studied him up close for the first time. His nostrils flared slightly when he breathed, and both his mane and tail were long and well groomed. The light reflecting from the pond showed off his tight and well-defined muscle tone in his chest, haunches, and gaskins. But for all that, her attention was drawn back to his eyes. The fiery-red flames that lay behind a slate-grey facade, like a burning fire that lay beneath a sheet of tinted glass, commanded her recognition.

"Have you heeded my warning, Jane McKinnon?"

Jane smiled and swallowed hard. "I heard your warning and took it on board, but it was cryptic, and I didn't know exactly what it meant."

"Well, then, we do not have much time, for he is here, and he is looking for you." Aedán raised a front hoof and struck the sandstone capping of the pond wall.

"But what does that mean? Who is here? And why is he looking for me?" Jane pleaded, as she looked from side to side, half expecting someone to jump out and lynch her.

"But I already told you, dearie—darkness is coming for you."

Playing out the worst possible scenarios in her mind, Jane sat crossed-armed, her legs bouncing up and down with a nervous twitch. She didn't know what to do or say. Aedán just stood there, watching her, awaiting her response, his mane and tail blowing to exaggeration in an almost non-existent wind.

Jane stood up from the wall and commenced pacing between Aedán and the Winesap. She felt helpless; she tried to recall from her years of experience what she could do. *A binding spell—no, that won't work, and I don't even know who the darkness is. A protection spell for me personally? Oh, I don't know. Think, Jane… think! What would Aunt Claire or Mum do? That's easy—they would consult their Book of Shadows or convene the coven, but I can't do either.*

"Do you need some help, dearie?" Aedán asked as he looked on.

"No no, it's all right. I have this one."

Jane continued pacing for a couple of minutes, her hand swapping from her brow to her hips, growing more anxious with every passing moment.

"He may be here soon if you don't hurry." "Okay, okay, don't rush me," she barked.

For a fleeting moment, Jane lost her poise as she turned back towards the pond and took two awkward steps sideways. She managed to recover her balance, yet her world had started to spin. Her equilibrium was off kilter, and her sense of time was speeding up dramatically.

"Aedán, are you there?" She flung her arms outwards, feeling, searching. "I can't see you."

Jane's vision became blurry. She was losing focus and became more unstable with each step. "What's happening?" she screamed. "Aedán!"

"Step towards me. dearie."

"I can't. I can't see you… everything's…"

"Follow my voice."

"I can't," she pleaded with open arms as her body flailed. She crashed heavily to one knee. Beads of sweat gathered on her brow, and tears welled in her eyes. Her consciousness faded in and out. She wanted to get up, but the thought, the desire, and lack of energy made her spiral. "You can do it."

"I… I… It's spinning… I ca—" She fell to both knees. Time braked suddenly. Slow motion replaced the fast head spins, and the ground was quickly approaching. Closer— green thud! Black.

11

A groan born in the depths of Jane's diaphragm spewed out as she began to stir. She opened her eyes and pulled herself up to a seated position at the end of the bed. "Where am I?" she managed, her tongue sticking to the roof of her dry mouth. "Why is it so dark in here?" she asked what she believed was the outline of a person seated in a chair in front of her.

She rubbed her eyes, trying to adjust to the muted light as shapes of the room slowly came into focus.

She could see shadows frolicking in the dim light of the oil lantern on the grey weather-boarded walls of the room. The small space was humid because of the constant drip of water from the ceiling in an empty corner. Moss was thriving, slowly growing up the walls, hidden in the relative darkness of the enclosed dwelling, and the pooling water escaped into the sodden patches of bare earth. She found herself on a wooden single-frame bed against the farthest wall from the only door that she could see. Beside the door, an oil lantern was perched on a small shelf. A nightstand beside her bore the weight of a single brown leather bound book with a gold inlay inscription of an ancient text and a plain round white animal bone plate that held a quart of water.

Muffled voices from another part of the lodging were audible between the drips of water that pooled on the rotten floorboards and the creak of the chair as it rocked back and forth. Her attention was drawn back to the strange-looking bedfellow who was perched in the rocking chair before her. It was a woman, but Jane did not recognise her. The sitter moved forward from the chair, reaching for the cloth from the bed stand to comfort her.

"Who are you?" Jane screamed as panic gripped her chest. Her breathing was shallow as her senses could not process the sights and sounds she was experiencing. Her head become light, and she could feel the room starting to spin.

Her sitter grasped the cloth from the bone plate and sat on the bed, wrapping an arm around Jane's shoulders. She patted her brow. She rocked both of them slowly and whispered, "Aye, you'll be fine, dear. A days" rest will see you bright eyed and running with the elk—you'll see."

"Who are you?" she sobbed through jerked breaths and teary eyes. The pit of her stomach churned, and an acid taste swelled in her throat. The unfamiliar room continued to gyrate, but before her caretaker could answer, a black shroud fell over her again.

∞

Moments later, the heavy round-top wooden door swung open, the hinges groaning, calling for a drop of oil. Rhoswen cocked her head towards the opening door and light that infiltrated the small room.

"There's no need on coming in. The wee lass is taking another kip," she said to the silhouette standing at the door.

"Come out and have something to eat. Aedán can look in on her from time to time," the strong confident male voice said.

"Aye, my love. I'll be right out." She stood from the chair and stepped over to the bed to check on her patient before joining the others in the adjoining room.

"Soon enough, you'll be over the travel illness, and when you are, we'll break some bread and tell tales together," she whispered as she pulled a sheet up to Jane's chin. She cleaned up some gag that was dripping from the corner of her mouth, returned the cloth to the bone plate, and then left the room.

"Rhoswen, Rhoswen, come join us," Aedán sang out as she ambled through the open door to the living quarters, the heart of the home. She paused to take in the festivities at the table as the door closed behind her.

"Oh, come on. Don't be shy, dearie."

She smiled as she looked from Aedán to Kaelan and Oren.

The three of them were seated at a large rectangular oak table—the surface and most edges were smooth from many years of use. Although parts were rough, the odd splinter was a common injury for those partaking in a warm meal, exuberant conversations, and other assorted frivolities. That evening, they were enjoying a meal of cál ceannann and spiced honey mead.

Boards ran length ways from post to post that were approximately five yards apart, circling the round room. The posts supported large beams that curved along the ceiling, and each one met in the middle of the room to rest upon one large supporting post. This post bore many inscriptions that served as reminders of celebrations, victories, and defeats. Except for the moss-covered parts, the timber structure was natural and faded to a soft grey, despite the heat generated by the fireplace on the southern side of the room. A number of lit oil lanterns were also scattered around the room, complementing the burning candles that sat on the oak table.

Rhoswen prepared the meals beside the fireplace in a crude kitchen area that consisted of a small table, a large ceramic bowl used for washing food, and the wooden plates that the food was served on. Under the table were small wooden crates that housed the blades and other cooking utensils as well as dried herbs and other ingredients that were ready for use. Suspended by a chain across the front of the hearth was an old bronze cauldron, where Rhoswen cooked all the food. It was a heavy cumbersome pot with two opposing handles that the chains were attached to. She never really removed the lid because of the weight of it; she would instead move it to one side so she could get ingredients in and the cooked meal out. When she did require it to be removed, she normally got Kaelan to do it for her.

Between the hearth and the main table, a variety of rosemary, sage, thyme, and small game animals were strung up from the beams to dry before the fire. The walls of the room were also used for storage: large hooks protruding from the wooden boards bore the weight of assorted men's and women's clothing and tools such as shovels, picks, and hoes. A saddle and stirrups, collars, and harnesses hung there, still exhibiting the dirt of previous day's work and travels, next to various weapons from slings, bows, axes, and the weapon of choice—the caladbolg, a heavy two-handed sword. Long spears also rested vertically against the wall. Other miscellaneous items of the house that required stowing, such as leather strap drinking horns, would eventually find their way to a hook in the round room.

Rhoswen strolled to the table, pulled a chair out from the table and took a seat. She reached for the ewer of mead, which trebled as the water vessel and milk jug, and an empty chalice that lay on its side on the table. Tipping the ewer, she sensed that her three companions were watching her. "Never seen a lady drink before?" she asked as she lowered the mead back to the table.

"Aye, we've seen you drink before, but a lady you're not." Oren guffawed as he rocked back on his chair then came forward and slapped the table.

Aedán chuckled a little; however, both Rhoswen and Kaelan only stared back at Oren.

"What? It was funny."

Aedán sensed that his hosts were not happy and returned his mouth to his mead while Oren, who was a little less accommodating of anyone's feelings, continued to smile proudly and sip his ale.

Kaelan, obviously far from impressed with his cohort, watched intently for Rhoswen's reaction from across the table. She pouted as she thought, and as she was about to rebut Oren, Kaelan swiftly intervened.

"Oren, my friend," Kaelan said as he turned to face his companion, "am I not a man of values?"

"Aye, that you are," Oren replied with a tip of his head, raising his chalice.

"Am I not an admirer of all things beautiful?"

Oren tilted his head towards Kaelan, a wry smile on his face. "I'd be careful, Rhoswen," he said as his expression shifted to a grin. "I think your Kaelan may be taking a liking to me." He laughed.

"Be careful of words that part your lips, Oren, as they may cost you your tongue," Kaelan said sternly in an attempt to rein in his companion's crude remarks.

"Kaelan, Rhoswen, my apologies. I did not mean to speak ill or imply a false reputation. I was merely making jest of the situation and did not mean any harm," Oren pleaded, his eyes filled with remorse as he looked from Kaelan to the Man's betrothed and back again.

"Oren," Rhoswen said sharply, "I don't care for your jokes and humour. If I had my own way, you'd lose your tongue for such comments. However, you are my husband's friend, companion, and kinsman, which makes you my kin and companion, but there are times when I will stop short of calling you a friend. Now is that time."

"Aye," Oren said as his head slumped downwards, his chin resting against his chest.

"We have a visitor, an important visitor. When she is well, she will require our help, our guidance, and maybe our swords. Therefore, as kin, we shall act united and put this moment behind us as there may be some difficult days ahead. We must keep our wits and skills sharp. The Red Man will be back soon enough in search of his quarry. It is up to us to protect her while she is a guest in our lands."

"Aye."

"Aye, kin," Kaelan shouted as he stood, his chalice raised towards the ceiling in his right hand. Droplets of mead escaped its vessel as he raised the toast, and they landed on the table like a sparse shower.

"Oren, fetch the pipes and play us a tune. Aedán," Rhoswen said as she turned from Oren to their equine acquaintance, "are you up for a verse or two? Let us all celebrate tonight and drink to our kinship, as tomorrow we may face the troubles that curse this girl."

Oren stood up from his chair and retrieved the uilleann pipes hanging on the wall. He pulled his seat clear from the table to give himself sufficient room to play. Strapping a piece of worn leather called a popping strap to his right knee, he took a seat. He placed the black-leather bellows between his right hip and elbow and the bag between the opposing hip and arm then tucked the regulators and drones on his lap. He looked around the table at his companions as he drew a long, slow deep breath. He closed his eyes and placed the chanter on his right knee on top of the popping strap and positioned his fingers above four of the eight finger holes. His three fans watched in anticipation as Oren readied himself. He released his breath, flapping his right elbow on the bellows. The drone hummed, and he began to finger the holes of the chanter. The melodic resonances of the uilleann filled the round room with cheer and warmth. Kaelan, Rhoswen, and Aedán burst into song as they held their chalices high. They rejoiced, forgetting for the moment the challenges and perils that will soon be at their reckoning.

∞

Jane stirred; the sounds of pipes filled her head as she opened her eyes and blinked rapidly to adjust to the low light in the room. She turned her head towards the source of the melodic tunes and could see the faint yellow-gold glow of light that entered the room between the cracks around the door jamb.

A half-muffled moan escaped her mouth as she stretched her jaw. *Is that Celtic music I can hear?* She turned her head back to face the ceiling. A thought struck her like an alarm: someone had been in the room with her before everything went black.

"A woman!" She sat bolt upright. A dull pain shot through her head, interrupting the sound of the pipes like a bang on a drum, and she fell back. Her arms went limp as she crashed back to the mattress underneath her, but she remained conscious. The throbbing pain was a slow, constant beat in her temple lobe; she rubbed both sides of her head with her index and middle fingers to relieve some pain, but it was only temporary. She lay there for some minutes, rubbing her head, controlling her breathing, and stretching her eyes and jaw. The sounds of the pipes became more dominant in her mind again. This time, she could hear singing. She listened for a moment; the soothing melody reminded her of a CD her aunt had purchased back in the early nineties at a *Riverdance* performance.

She shifted her weight on her hips and moved both legs simultaneously off the side of the bed to find purchase on the earthy floor. She sat there, contemplating her next move. Should she stay put and hide until someone walked in? And if so, would she hide and make a run for it or take her chances to overcome them?

Her eyes had adjusted to the dark, and she could clearly see the outline of objects in the room, especially the now-empty chair in the centre of the room. After two songs, the idle chatter of voices in the next room, with the odd laugh breaking up the conversation, replaced the pipes. Jane looked from the door of the room to the hip pocket of her jeans; she could feel the outline of her phone as she pushed her two fingers in either side of the phone to retrieve it. She turned it over; the screen was black, so she pressed the on button, thinking it was in sleep mode. "Come on!" she yelled at the phone when it didn't respond. She froze, suddenly realising what she'd just done. "Shit!" she said under her breath as she quickly placed the phone under the pillow and flipped herself onto her back to lie flat on the bed, facing at the ceiling, her eyes clenched shut. She waited and listened, anticipating that whoever was in the room would rush in to investigate the commotion. She lay as still as she could, telling herself to relax, to look natural, as if she were asleep. Minutes passed, and still no one had come, so she rolled to one side to face the door.

"They had to hear me," she whispered to herself. She could hear the faint sound of footsteps, and her body tensed up. Cussing to herself, she froze. *They must be on the other side of the room.*

Her anxiety heightened as she listened more intently. The steps got steadily louder and faster. Jane closed her eyes and tried to control her breathing, counting to herself. *One, step, two, step, three, step, four, step...* The longer she counted, she realised that a pattern was forming. She ceased counting and concentrated on the steps: *one, two, three, and four.*

"You idiot, It's your heart," Jane said to herself as she released a big sigh of relief. But she was not convinced that she was out of the woods just yet. Lying there, Jane started to hum to clear her head—just a simple tune at first that she made up spontaneously to pass time. Then she heard another burst of laughter from the other room. Her mind wandered as she tried to visualize an action plan, her fingers twisting and interlocking with each other while resting on her torso. She replaced the humming with a muted rendition of Depeche Mode's *Enjoy the Silence.*

The door to the room remained shut; only light trespassed from the other room. Jane focussed on the door as her performance came to an end. She knew that the song went for over four minutes, and that if her captor were going to make an appearance, they would have done so already. Still, she kept a silent vigil for the next couple of minutes.

The voices on the other side had become quiet. *It's time.* She pushed herself up to a sitting position and leaned towards the door, listening for a sign of life. Hearing nothing, she leaned in closer from the bed, her posterior resting right on the edge of the frame. She could make out what she thought was talking between two people—there was definitely a male voice, and the other was a female voice.

"Darn it, speak a little louder," she whispered as she edged closer to the door. Then she lost her balance. She slipped and fell a foot and a half to the hard floor below, landing on her butt, her back coming to rest on the side of the bed.

"Ouch." She grimaced.

She sat there for half a minute, massaging her sore backside before she remembered her phone was still under the pillow. Using her elbows on the side of the bed, she propped herself up to her knees and reached across the mattress. The phone's screen was as black as it had been before. Jane pressed and held the power button—nothing. Rolling her eyes and cursing under her breath, she removed the back cover to check the battery. It didn't look damaged, so she shook the phone and listened for any broken parts— nothing. It just wouldn't work.

"For the love of the Gods." Jane seethed as she was tempted to throw it away. "What else can go…" She felt her chest for her pentagram. "What the fuck? This can't be happening." She gasped in disbelief. "Okay, okay, get a hold of yourself. The Gods haven't abandoned me yet," she reassured herself as she searched the bed and side table in case it had fallen off while she was sleeping, but she didn't find it anywhere.

"Okay, centre yourself, Jane. You can overcome this." She looked around the room for anything she could use. The room was scarce of items apart from the empty chair, the oil lamp, the bone plate and cloth.

I have to seek clarity. I need to cast a circle—quietly.

She rose from the bed and walked around the room to find anything that could be used in place of her athame, wand, or candles. With the realisation that the room was certainly empty, she picked up the chair in both hands, holding the diagonal opposite legs. Leaning the chair to one side, she pushed the bottom leg into the earth with a subdued grunt. She looked towards the door and listened for any activity, but nothing was forthcoming.

Maybe they had gone for a walk or something. She tilted on her back hip, grimaced, and dragged the chair backwards, walking deosil in a circle as the earth parted under the weight of the chair leg. She stopped when she completed a full circle and the shape was complete in the earth before her. Unaware of her location, Jane could not with any authority know where the cardinal points of north, east, south and west were in respect to her circle. So she could not invoke the guardians of the watchtowers. On this occasion, though, she used the opportunity to seek guidance within the comforts and protection of the circle.

Jane walked the circle a second time in the same direction, chanting silently, *I cast this circle to protect me from all negative energies that may do me harm. I draw into this circle only the energies that are right for me and my work.*

Jane stopped at the completion of her second circle and turned inwards to the centre of the circle. She did not have the right tools or an altar at her disposal, so she positioned the chair at the centre of the circle, facing the door. She returned to the edge of the circle and quietly commenced a third and final walk of the circle. *I create a sacred space. So mote it be.*

Jane returned to the chair, turned her back to the seat to face the door, and extended her right arm with her index finger outstretched. "I shall use my own body as my tool, my finger in place of my athame."

Jane expelled a long slow breath, lowering her finger towards the earth before her and traced a pentagram as she began another chant:

"O Mighty Cerridwen,

Queen of the Gods,

Lady of the Moon,

The architect of all that is natural and free.

Mother of man and woman,

Lover of the Horned God and protector of all Wicca.

Descend upon my circle,

So mote it be."

Jane paused and drew another long breath then traced another pentagram towards the earth before her and chanted quietly:

'O Mighty Cernunnos,

King of the Gods,

Lord of the Sun,

Dominant of all that is natural and free.

Father of man and woman,

Lover of the Moon Goddess and protector of all Wicca.

Descend upon my circle,

So mote it be."

Upon completion of the invocations of the God and Goddess, Jane stole a quick glance at the door in front of her. She could hear voices on the other side again, and she knew she risked being caught. However, she had to press on as the circle was cast—the Gods had been invoked, and the disturbance to the universe if the circle was not closed could be catastrophic.

She lowered herself onto the chair, trusting that it had not moved during the invocations. Closing her eyes, she visualised the circle around her. In her mind, she could see the circle as a shimmering bluish-purple flaming dome of light encompassing her, protecting her.

"O Mighty Cernunnos,

O Mighty Cerridwen,

It is Asrai's circle with whose presence you grace.

I seek your wisdom and guidance to deliver me back to

Avalon;

To leave this location with unwavering haste.

I call for your aid by hurried antiphon.

O Mighty Cernunnos,

O Mighty Cerridwen,

Provide me with safe passage home.

Blessed be."

Jane sat on the chair for a moment in silence, contemplating her next action. Normally, she would complete a spell, give thanks, and make an offering, but this was not her ground, not her altar, not her sacred site. She did not have the right tools to complete her desired spell to travel back to Avalon safely. She was without a stone, a yellow candle, a censor, lavender oil, or paints, but she knew the spell well. Yet it seemed pointless to recite the chant without the ritual, but she still had hope. She still had belief. She believed that Cernunnos and Cerridwen would grant her divine intervention and guide her home.

Jane stood and walked to the edge of the circle. She had tested her luck against her captors thus far, but she knew her luck could not last forever. She did have a better chance with the aid of the Gods, but to ensure that she did get their aid, she had to close the circle.

"O Mighty Cernunnos,

O Mighty Cerridwen,

I thank thee for gracing my circle with your presence.

Blessed be."

Jane outstretched her right arm, her index finger pointing towards the edge of the circle. She used herself in place of her athame again, this time to close the circle. Jane closed her eyes. Starting at the edge closest to the door, she could see her finger penetrating the inner edge of the flaming bluish dome around her. She took in and exhaled a long deep breath. Her visualization of her finger dragging through the sphere made tiny shimmering waves ripple over the entire surface of the dome.

On her next breath, Jane opened her eyes and took her first step in a widdershins direction.

"I send this circle into the cosmos to do my bidding.

The circle is undone but not broken.

Blessed be."

"Well, I guess that's it." She turned back towards the empty chair in the middle of the circle. "I'm feeling a bit outta sorts after that," she said to nobody. "I don't have to do anything. There's nothing to clean up!"

Jane sat for a moment to contemplate what she was going to do next. A sigh not of relief or weariness but of frustration and trepidation escaped her as she stared at the door.

"I could just bust through and fight my way out, or maybe I could sneak out when everyone is asleep or maybe…"

"Or maybe what, dearie?" Aedán interjected, to Jane's surprise.

She jumped from the chair, almost landing on her hip on the earth below. She saved herself from embarrassment only due to the sturdiness of the chair beside her, "Were you hatching some kind of plan to escape – Asrai?" he asked with a bemused if not quizzical tone.

"Aedán, it is you? Is it really you? Where am I? Am I a prisoner? Am I—"

"Hey, steady on, dearie. One question at a time. I have trouble keeping up with my own thoughts at times. I can't be answering a hundred at once, and besides if you are my prisoner, I wouldn't be answering any of them, now would I?"

"I… I guess not," she replied nervously, "so what's going to happen to me now?"

"Absolutely nothing, dearie."

"What do you mean? I'm not a prisoner?"

"No, dearie. You're a guest," Aedán said as he walked over to Jane to reassure her that he was her friend. "Now tell me, is your name Jane, or is it Asrai?"

"It's Jane, and it's Asrai," she said. "It's both!"

"It's both?"

"Yes and no. Oh, don't confuse me. Jane is my worldly name that everyone knows me by, but Asrai is my magickal name, the one I took when I was initiated. It's the name that the God and Goddess know me by."

"Interesting," Aedán said with a widened eye and nod of his head. "Interesting because it is an old name that carries great meaning and power. Do you know its true meaning?"

"I chose it because I read that it means siren or mermaid, like the "the Lorelei" from the Rhine in Germany that would call to sailors who would be captivated by her singing only to drown when their ships smashed on the rocks below her."

"Sirens, yes, and maybe selkies and morgens, as well. Have you heard of them?"

"I think so. I'm not sure. Maybe in mythology at school?"

"Mythology?" Aedán laughed. "Now you're being funny, Jane McKinnon—Asrai, dearie. A mermaid, I think not. You see, a mermaid has a tail, whereas an Asrai has webbed fingers and toes, but a part of mythology they are not. Would you like to meet one?"

"Meet one?" Jane's tone pitched higher than normal in disbelief.

"You seem shocked. They do exist, although they are very timid, and it may take some time to convince them to talk to you. And remember, if that sounds a bit farfetched, just remind yourself that you are speaking to a talking horse, dearie." He tittered.

"Yes, well, there is that, and I do try to keep an open mind."

"The Asrai, dearie, are a small race of water faerie. They stand only about three feet tall, yet they are beautiful creatures, striking like young maidens of fair hair and skin with large wings, but they are also an ancient race, individually living for hundreds of years. It is said, though, that if a mortal man sees an Asrai that the desire to have her will drive him to capture her at all costs. The Asrai, however, are very afraid of mortals and the sun, as well, for that fact, but if an Asrai is captured or if a ray of sunlight touches them, they will die and turn into a pool of water. Interestingly, though, if you are touched by an Asrai, the area of your skin that receives the touch will forever feel cold and unable to be warmed regardless of what one does to warm it. I do digress somewhat, though. My meaning is that you are not a captive. Therefore, you did not turn to water," Aedán finished with a chuckle.

"No, I didn't, but then I am only Asrai by name, not by being."

"Aye, this is true," Aedán agreed while looking Jane up and down. "You look like you do need something to eat and drink, though. Are you hungry?"

"I would love something to drink," she replied with a smile.

"Excellent. Come out and meet everyone," Aedán responded, nodding towards the door.

"Are they friendly?" Jane asked hesitantly, pausing after taking just one step away from the chair.

"You are our guest, and yes, they are friendly—as I am, am I not. Besides, you are my friend. Therefore, they are your friends, as well."

"Okay, I think that made sense," she said to herself as she stepped towards Aedán. "Actually you haven't said where here is. Where am I?"

"Let's partake in some mead first, dearie, and then I'll tell you everything you need to know."

12

Aedán pushed open the door to a much larger room. A flood of light burst in, illuminating Jane with golden hues. She squinted briefly, turning her head away to give her eyes an opportunity to adjust. Turning back, her gaze momentarily came to rest on Aedán. She didn't know much about him, and she had not known him long, but the warmth she felt when she was with him made her feel secure.

"Are you ready, dearie?"

Jane smiled. "Yes."

"Okay, then, make a move, dearie," Aedán insisted with a nod of his head to usher her through the door.

Jane stepped into the room. The first thing to strike her was the enormousness of the space before her—it was larger than she had imagined from the small dark hovel that she just departed. The glint of light reflecting off metal drew her to what she recognised as armour and weapons hanging from hooks on the far wall. A bizarre sensation rushed through her—a sense of déjà vu. She didn't feel as if she had been there before, but she felt as if she had seen it before—she just couldn't place where that was.

"Come along, take a seat," Aedán said as he tried to shepherd her over to the table. "Here dearie, you sit here," he said as he pushed a chair out from underneath the table with his nose.

Jane sat down and pulled her chair in, her attention still captivated by the items that hung around the room. "It's very Viking, isn't," she said turning back to Aedán. "I mean, I know it's not Viking, being that they had long houses and this one is round, but it has the same feel to what I've seen in movies."

"Ha!" he bellowed. "Movies! Let me tell you, dearie, what you would see around here you will never see in any movie. The folk in this land are not the same as those that you're used to and let—"

"Aedán!" a voice snapped from a darkened crook of the room.

Jane turned to see the figure of a woman approach from the shadows of the room. She was not of great height, maybe four and a half feet tall, but her wings—she had striking large forewings that added another foot in height above her head. They were long and transparent with a swirl pattern that pulsated like veins. The leading edges of the wings were harder and thicker but had a silvery sparkle as if they were covered with glitter. Under her hips were the two hindwings, which were much smaller than the forewings but similarly shaped.

Slim and fair, she was very beautiful. She wore a loose fitting blue *léine*, a linen tunic that was fastened by a *crios* and *dealg* under her full curvaceous breasts. Her long blonde hair was braided and tied just above her hairline with a fine piece of gold ribbon that Jane thought at first glance resembled a crown. The remaining strands flowed over her pointed ears and fell past her shoulders. Her eyes were a crystal light blue that sparkled in the light like cut topaz, round in shape and slightly larger in size than Jane was used to seeing. She was mesmerized by this vision of beauty—she had never laid eyes on anyone as attractive as this strange woman standing in front of her. Every aspect of her drew Jane's attention towards her.

"Hóra, my dear, don't pay too much mind to Aedán, as sincere as he is. At times, his mouth can run," she said in a calming dulcet tone. "My name is Rhoswen, and I welcome you to my *sidhe* and to Emain Albach."

"Emain Albach!" Jane exclaimed in disbelief as she turned back to Aedán. "You're from Emain Albach. This is your home, too?"

"Aye, but I do not live here, dearie. Let's just say I'm visiting for a while."

"So if you're Fey," she said to Aedán, "then you're Fey, as well?" Jane asked hesitantly, turning back to Rhoswen.

"Yes, dear, I am, as is every other being in Emain Albach. Here, we are all faerie of some description or another. Aedán is *púca,* and I am known as *Aes Sidhe* of the *Tuatha Dé Danann* tribe, the people of the mounds or "fair folk," as we live inside mounds that we call *sidhe.*"

"A *sidhe* is your home, that's a mound?"

"That's right. On the outside, the *sidhe* looks like a large mound of earth that has a covering of grass or small bushes growing on it," Rhoswen replied.

"I'm not dreaming, am I, Aedán?" Jane asked. "This must be how Alice felt when she arrived in Wonderland," she continued, not waiting for Aedán to reply.

"Who is this Alice that you refer to?" Rhoswen asked with a curious smile.

"Oh, sorry. I was thinking out loud. Alice is a fictional character in a story who falls down a rabbit hole and finds herself in a strange new fantasy world. In the beginning, she felt quite disorientated and didn't know where she was, and well, I rather feel the same."

"Well, that's understandable, dear. You've made your first crossover, which can be daunting by itself. However, Aedán did say that you were unconscious when he brought you across."

"Unconscious? Well, that explains the throbbing in my head," Jane replied with a half-hearted laugh that sounded more like a harrumph. "Aedán! What happened? How come I was unconscious?"

"Well, dearie, I asked you about my warning and advised that he was getting closer—" "The darkness," Jane interrupted.

"Yes, the darkness. You became anxious and starting pace back and forth under the apple tree, thinking out loud about what you could do to protect yourself, and I think it became all too much for you as one minute, you were up.

The next, you were on the ground. There was no help about, and I felt the only option for your own safety was to bring you back to Emain Albach with myself. It wasn't easy you know getting you onto my back."

"Thank you, Aedán. I appreciate it," Jane replied with a smile as she reached out to place a hand upon his mane.

"You're welcome, Jane McKinnon. Now let's celebrate your safe passage with a chalice of mead and discuss what we do from here."

"I'll get the mead." Rhoswen turned to collect the jug from the bench top of the table beside the hearth. She returned to the table with the jug and three chalices.

"What's it like being a witch?" she asked Jane as she placed the mead and drinking vessels on the table.

"A witch? I never said I was a witch."

"So you're not a witch?"

Jane felt a sudden wave of anxiety wash over her. She was not ashamed of being Wiccan, but the term *witch* normally drew with it negative connotations from those who did not understand it. As she prepared her answer in her mind, she looked over to Rhoswen, who was seated at the end of the oak table. Watching Jane, awaiting her reply. She took in her features again and found herself being drawn into her crystal-blue eyes.

"Jane McKinnon," Aedán said, startling Jane back to the present.

"Oh, sorry. A witch, yes. I am, but I tend to use the term Wiccan. I enjoy it very much—it's my chosen path.

Why?" she asked with a tone of resentment.

"I do not ask to cause offence," Rhoswen stated, trying to dowse any inflammation that her question had caused. "We do not get many witches around these parts. In fact, it's been nearly eleven turns of the wheel since we had one pass through. Her name was Eerin. It was not a name that I had heard before, and of course, not one that I've forgotten, either. She said it was native to a foreign land in your own world, but it's that part where my memory does fail me, unfortunately."

Jane decided not to debate about being offended and thought it best to move on for everyone's sake. "Eerin, that's a nice name, but I can't say that I've heard of it, either. What was she doing here?"

"Just travelling through. She didn't say too much about her business, but she was very nice and treated everyone she met with respect, so we didn't question her motives a great deal. Kaelan, my betrothed, may be able to tell you some more when he returns."

"The wheel that you talk about—how long is a turn?" Jane asked with enthusiasm, thinking that it may be similar to her own year wheel.

"The wheel is based on seasons that is split into four seasons or quarters that make up one turn of the wheel."

"That sounds very similar to a yearly calendar in my world, summer, autumn, winter, and spring. In Wicca, we have a year wheel that is split into eight sabbats, but that is mainly centred on the celebration of environmental seasons and harvests."

"Interesting, you'll have to tell me more about that sometime."

The main door to the round room swung open, hitting the wall with a dampened thud that echoed through the room. A rush of cold wind blew in, carrying a swirl of leaves and other small plant matter. The wind was followed by two men of stocky build. They were the same height as Rhoswen, and Jane assumed straight away that one of them was Kaelan. They rushed in, carrying a load of wood in both arms. The second stopped a few steps in to turn and push the door shut with his leg. They both walked over to the hearth, dropped the wood to the floor, and allowed it to land and roll where it pleased.

"It couldn't possibly be any colder out there without snow," the darker of the two stated as he turned towards the table, rubbing his hands together. "I see that our guest has recovered from her travel sickness. Looks quite spritely, better than I imagined," he said jokingly as he stepped closer to the table.

"Jane, this is Oren. He is a blithe character, or so he thinks, but clever with his hands and a sword, might I add. Behind him is Kaelan, whom you have heard Rhoswen mention. He is the master of the house and a leader in our village. He will be able to talk to you about Eerin, but only when he has rested and finished a mead," Aedán announced.

Jane studied both of the men sitting at the table before her. Oren was fair skinned like Rhoswen. Kaelan's skin, however, was slightly darker in complexion. Both Oren and

Kaelan were taller than Rhoswen by half a foot; however, it was quite noticeable that the men did not have wings as Rhoswen did.

Oren was solid in build, with strawberry-blonde hair; the orange tinge was more evident in the flickering light of the fireplace. He also wore braids in his hair that hung from between his ears and temple lobes on both sides of his head and were decorated with hollow golden balls that hung an inch away from the end of the braids. The remainder of his hair flowed past his pointed ears and over his shoulders to reach the midpoint of his back. He wore an open heavy brown *brat*, a woollen cloak over an off white *léine* that finished at his knees. The *brat* was secured by a leather *crois* and a bronze *dealg* over the shoulder with the pin up. Jane noticed that none of her hosts were wearing any form of footwear, and she wondered how they would fair out in the cold, especially at winter time, assuming that it snowed in Emain Albach.

Kaelan was very similar in look and dress to Oren, but his blonde hair was almost as white as snow. Gold ribbon was threaded through the long braids that hung just in front of his pointed ears. Kaelan's attire was much more colourful than Oren's. His *brat* was a deep blue with gold trimming on the edges, his *léine* was a bone colour, and the brown leather of the *crois* was inlayed with gold patterns that looked similar to the swirl of veins in Rhoswen's wings. He also wore a pair of tight-fitting black linen-covered hose called *truis* that finished just above the ankles and was secured by a garter on both legs under the knee. Kaelan wore a sheathed caladbolg.

"I see our guest has awoken from her sleep. How do you feel, child? Aedán tells me that your travel here wasn't the most conventional," Kaelan said with a wry smile as he picked up a piece of bread from a plate in the middle of the table. He tore it in half.

"Pleased to make your acquaintance, Kaelan," Jane said nervously, half rising from her seat as she second-guessed what was customary when addressing someone of importance in this land. "And I thank you for your hospitality in advance, but I must apologise for my ignorance. Aedán has told me that I was unconscious when I travelled here, and that I'm in Emain Albach and something about a darkness that I had to be careful about, but aside from that, I do not know too much else. Rhoswen was telling me about a person who travelled through these parts eleven wheels ago named Eerin and that you could tell me more about her. Any information that you could enlighten me with would be greatly appreciated," Jane said, finishing with a deep breath as she rushed through her little speech to Kaelan.

Kaelan's boisterous laugh echoed around the *sidhe* as he raised the chalice to his mouth to wash down the bread with mead.

"Aedán tells me you're a witch."

Jane sighed before answering, "Yes I'm a witch," she replied, not bothering to correct his terminology.

"Do you not want to be a witch?"

"Yes, I do," Jane snapped back before drawing a deep breath to calm herself down as Kaelan watched her. "Look, I'm sorry. I'm just a little on edge at the moment. I feel like I'm in the dark about what's going on, and I need to know why I'm really here."

"Well, all you need to do, child, is ask."

"Haven't I been doing that already?" Jane replied through clenched teeth.

"Yes, you have," Aedán said. "Allow me to answer her question, Kaelan," Aedán said, looking to Kaelan for approval.

Kaelan nodded.

"There is a connection between your world and this one. There are many, to be exact, but your house is a portal to Emain Albach. All the portals have a common thread—trees."

"The Winesap in the secret garden," Jane chimed in with anticipation as her excitement level grew.

"Yes, the apple tree in your garden. Emain Albach means "the fortress of apples," but Avalon means ""the island"—"

""Of apples,"" Jane finished with a feverish enthusiasm in her tone. "Yes, yes, I have heard of it. My Aunt Claire was telling me about the tales of Arthurian legend that my Daideó used to tell to her and my mum when they were little girls." She told them of the secret garden and how the house got its name.

"Very insightful of them, although I wonder if luck played a part in that decision," Kaelan said.

"I would think not but rather destiny is more the case when you think about it," Jane retorted.

"Coincidence, fate, destiny—all the stars must have aligned on such a day to allow the portal to be formed. You told me, dearie, that your gift is not unique to yourself but flows through your family, therefore I salute your Daideó, as he must have great knowledge and power to create the garden. He must have known that there would be a good possibility that our worlds may connect via his creation, so I say that the portal is not coincidence but destined to be created." Aedán confirmed Jane's supposition.

Jane was thrilled to hear Aedán' and to discover that the garden she loved so dearly was also a portal to another realm. "So if the tree is a portal between Avalon and Emain Albach, then why haven't I slipped into it?" Jane asked.

All she received in return was silence and looks of confusion.

"You know, like a door? Was it something that I could open or accidentally go through without trying cross over?"

An uncomfortable period of silence passed, then on cue, everybody, including Jane, burst into laughter.

"Okay, okay, stop. I know that sounded sort of stupid, but really how does one cross over from one realm to the other?"

"Well, that's quite easy, dearie," Aedán replied. "All you need is a silver bough."

"A silver what?"

"Bough," Rhoswen repeated. "It's a tree branch." "To be used like a wand," Oren said.

"It is said to be a tale, a myth, and a legend, but I tell you with no uncertainty, dearie, that it is very real. The silver bough is said to be from a mystical apple tree that could be used as a doorway to other lands. The tree itself grows right here in this part of Emain Albach, and although the stories of its history say that it is a branch of silver, truth be known, any part of the tree can be used to aid travel."

"But that still doesn't tell me how it works, Aedán."

"Patience, dearie. I'm getting to that part. The secret to crossing the realms is to have a silver bough from the mystic tree—perhaps it was said to be silver due to the colour of the bark—but as long as you have a piece and the knowledge to use it, you'll be able to cross over."

"Don't forget about the portal itself," Kaelan said.

"Yes, the portal is always an apple tree, but not just any apple tree. It must be an heirloom variety, and that's why your Daideó chose a Winesap—because of its lineage. Many trees in your world are grafts of one variety onto another's rootstock, which may provide a plentiful harvest to the farmer to take to market, but it is not a true apple. Like most things in your world, everything is so diluted that the truth of the simple things in life—the healings, the pleasures, the tastes, and smells—are being lost forever."

"I'm aware of that. It's one of the reasons why I chose to follow a Wiccan path."

"I'm pleased, dearie, but to travel through the portal, one must be in the tree and place the bough against the trunk and recite:

"Reconnect the bough to the mystic tree

And seek safe passage to…

This, I request of thee."

"You state where you want to go such as Emain Albach or Avalon, and only after you've recited the whole chant, a crystal-white light will illuminate underneath the bough, and not a moment later, the tree will open and draw the traveller into the belly of its trunk to then appear in the tree at your destination. You can now understand the difficulty I had getting you here when you were asleep."

"I guess you did, but I do thank you for not leaving me."

"Aye. Well, what else could I do?"

Jane sat there, thinking about what she had just learnt while Rhoswen stood and refilled those chalices with mead.

"Appreciation, my darling," Kaelan said as he waited for the last drop to fall from the lip of the jug. "How long will I stay here?" Jane asked.

"This will only be a short stay. As I said before, it was necessary to bring you here to get you out of harm's way. We shall return soon. Otherwise your absence may raise suspicion back at Avalon."

"Why did you find me, though? Why me, and what danger am I in from the darkness that you refer to," Jane asked grimly as she looked from Aedán to each of the others one by one, finishing with Kaelan.

"The darkness is also known as the Red Man," Oren blurted as he leaned forward against the table.

"Oren, that's enough," Rhoswen snapped. "It's not your story to tell."

"Agreed," Kaelan added. "It's Aedán' responsibility." A cry resonated throughout the room.

Jane's head bobbed up. "Is that a baby?"

"Yes, excuse me." Rhoswen stood and walked towards the room opposite to the one Jane emerged from earlier.

The table temporarily fell silent; the only sounds that graced their ears were the faint cries and Rhoswen's soothing voice, which emanated over the cracking of the fire and shuffling of feet under the table. A couple of minutes passed, then Aedán cleared his throat with three shallow coughs to get everyone's attention.

"Jane McKinnon," Aedán intonated rapidly, "I will tell you now of the darkness that is seeking you out." He paused. "Well, as much as I can."

"Okay," Jane said nervously in a protracted fashion.

"The darkness—or "the Red Man" as he is known—is from both this realm and yours."

"How is that possible?"

"He is born of a human mother and a Fey father, a *fear dearg*, to be precise."

"A *fear dearg*? Well, that explains how she got pregnant," Oren joked as he slammed his chalice onto the table.

Jane looked from Aedán to Oren and back, a sick pit of anxiety in her stomach.

"Have you ever heard of a leprechaun?" Aedán asked with a raise of his eyebrows while looking at Jane.

"Yes, I think everyone has heard of leprechauns. They're Irish myth, are they not? Saint Patrick's Day, pots of gold, that sort of stuff," Jane replied as her demeanour became somewhat upbeat upon hearing something that she recognised.

"Yes, well, there's something to be said about that perception, but they are real, all the same, as real as the sun will rise in the morning and set in the evening. Leprechauns are Fey as I am and live here in Emain Albach. They do not protect pots of gold, though. Think of them more as workers like bees in a hive. They do the majority of the manual labour work within the villages of the *Tuatha Dé Danann* tribes. Now *fear deargs* are cousins of and look similar to leprechauns but are always dressed in a red coat and hat and busy themselves with gruesome jokes and deeds. They are the Fey responsible for going to your world and stealing human babies and leaving behind changelings in their place," Aedán explained.

"Aye, nasty creatures, that lot," added Kaelan as he listened intently.

"I don't think I'd like to come across one of them." Jane quivered as her mood started to change again. *I wish I were at home, warm and safe in my own bed away from this madness.*

"Aye, not pleasant at all," Aedán agreed, "and in this case, the Red Man can be considered even viler, as he is part changeling himself."

"Like a shapeshifter?" Jane asked gingerly.

"No, he was not born with that power, thankfully. The *púca* are the only shape changers in these parts of Emain Albach," Aedán explained with a touch of smugness in his voice. "A changeling is a Fey child that is swapped in the middle of the night with a stolen human child. Normally, any child born with a defect of any description will be branded as suitable to be a changeling, and in the Red Man's case, being a half breed was reason enough to the *fear deargs*."

"That's awful. What happens to the children?" The thought of the young ones being taken weighed heavily on her mind.

"The changelings left with humans normally grow to lead a good life—well, those ones that look like humans. My determination, however, is that the vast majority of them would be shunned by human culture to live in the shadows of your cities and towns."

"Well, that would certainly explain many of the myths and urban legends that you hear of from time to time, but what of the human children?"

"They lead a full and happy life in Emain Albach with the families that they were given to."

"But how? How can they? They don't look the same. I don't look the same. Surely they would know that they are different when they're old enough to understand!"

"No, they don't," Kaelan replied. "Those that do find out, find out not by their own doing but by the tongue of someone else. Great steps are taken to ensure that the changelings that come to Emain Albach grow up thinking they are Fey. Their ears are shaped, their growth is stunted, both sexes are sterilised, and females grow up being told that their wings have been removed for their own health."

"But that's not right. They'd be a shell of their former selves," she implored, but she knew she was pushing a case for human rights in a world that she didn't know anything about and whose inhabitants were protecting her against a resident evil.

Rhoswen came back to the table, nursing a youngling at the breast. Jane could not see the child as it was wrapped tightly in a colourful linen fabric, but she was curious to have a look.

"Have you told her yet?" Rhoswen asked as she sat back at the table.

"Aye, nearly done."

"Oh, you have your own child," Jane lilted as she sat straight in the chair, straining her neck to steal a glimpse of the child. "Boy or a girl?"

"A girl. Niamh is her name. Would you like to have a look?"

"Yes, please." Jane got up and walked around to stand behind Rhoswen. "She's beautiful, Rhoswen. How old is she?"

"Three full moons," she replied with a smile as she looked up at Jane.

"Wow, okay, three months. Her wings are larger than I'd expect for her size," Jane observed as she pulled aside a corner of the wrap with her finger to get a better view. "Do they get in the way?"

"No, that's normal. When the *Aes Sidhe* is in the womb, the child is encased by the wings, which are wrapped tight around the foetus as it grows. After birth, they will sit at the back of the child as mine do."

"Not the male children, though," Oren added.

"What?"

"The majority of male children have their wings removed at birth," Kaelan explained, finishing the statement Oren had started. "About one in ten will keep their wings. However, they will grow to be aerial soldiers in the army."

"What or who determines if they keep their wings or not?"

"The lineage of the family," Kaelan replied. "This maybe by blood or proved in battle by his ancestors."

"Then why remove the wings at all?"

"All *Aes Sidhe* males are required to fight if the battle calls for them. However, to swing such weapons as the caladbolg, one must have clear shoulders to draw full thrust against the enemy. The wings merely get in the way."

Things certainly are different here compared to what I'm used to. "Do you war here often?"

"Only when it is forced upon us," Kaelan said dourly.

Aedán cleared his throat loudly to get the attention of all at the table. One by one, they turned to him, and he finished his explanation after another mouthful of mead to wet the tonsils. "Thank you. Now, as I was saying, the Red Man is a changeling sent into the human world, but being a half-breed served his purposes well to survive as he was able to grow and mix within your society, learn your ways, your customs. He followed a dark path and learnt of his origins back to Emain Albach, and before long, he found a way to travel here, where he now lives. He has become very powerful by using dark magick and backs it up with a horde of displaced Fey that are now loyal to him." Aedán swallowed another mouthful of mead.

The lull in the conversation gave Jane a moment to take in what she'd heard, and although the Red Man sounded frightening, she was she perplexed as to how or why he would want to harm her. A lump in her throat tightened as she gathered the courage to ask the most important question. "What does he want with me?" She shuddered.

The table remained quiet. Aedán removed the chalice from his mouth and returned it slowly to the table. All eyes turned back to him, awaiting his answer.

"Well, it has been heard that he is falling ill, his Achilles heel is that the human part of him is aging, and he must replenish himself if he is to survive. To do this, he has to take the life force of another, younger human, preferably female and pure. Our sources have indicated that he is after you."

Jane gasped in horror. Dire thoughts of mad men, demons, and hatchet men chasing her down and killing her in cold blood filled her mind with sickening images of her own demise. "Why—why me? What does he want with me? I don't understand," she snivelled.

"We don't know exactly know why he is targeting you, but you're here with us now, as we have vowed to protect you. You have an inner power, a clarity that is strong within you, and you're a witch who knows powerful magick. Maybe that is what he desires," Rhoswen said. "There must be a link in the chain that is drawing him to you. I can only guess, but we will do our best to protect you," Rhoswen reassured her while lightly bouncing Niamh in her arms.

"It'll be a balancing act, though," Kaelan warned. "You cannot be away from Avalon for too long or family may worry, and if the Red Man is following you, he will grow suspicious if you are absent for any length of time that can't be explained."

"Do you really think he could be watching me?" she asked despondently, her eyes widening as she looked back at Kaelan, almost pleading for an answer that she knew she would not want to hear.

"Avalon is the best place for you at the moment," Aedán said, trying to reassure her. "Think of it as your fortress, your safe haven, as the Red Man obviously does not know that he could portal directly into your garden."

"And the best defence at the moment is to keep the portal a secret for as long as possible," Rhoswen added.

"Why can't I stay here?"

"Because the Red Man lives here. If he senses that you're here—and he will—nothing will stop him at attempting to get you," Kaelan stressed.

Jane got up from her chair and paced back and forth between the hearth and the table. All eyes were watching her every move, seemingly awaiting for her response.

"The Red Man hasn't met the edges of our swords yet, Jane. Do not worry as much as you do," Oren said. "We will watch over you."

"And how are you going to do that?" she cried out, twisting violently to face Oren, her watery eyes staring him down. "How—how are you going to do that?" she wailed as she broke into tears. She stood there, motionless, arms limp by her side, tears streaming from her eyes, staring at the fire as its light danced with shadows. Her hosts sat mouths agape at Jane's reaction.

Rhoswen leaned into the table. "Oren," she said quietly, but no response was forthcoming. "Oren," she repeated a little louder through clenched teeth.

"What?"

Rhoswen nodded in Jane's direction, "Go on. Go to her and give her comfort."

"What?"

"Go on."

"Aye," he replied with a heavy sigh. He got up from his chair and walked towards Jane, mumbling under his breath. Oren put his arms around her and squeezed gently.

"It's going to be all right, Jane McKinnon. You'll see," he offered awkwardly as she released the hug, wiping the tears from her eyes.

Rhoswen got up and walked over to them.

"He is right. You'll be okay," she said, standing in front of them, cradling Niamh and rocking her back to sleep after her feed. "You're a witch who's yet to tap into her magickal strengths like those that have been before you. You must have clarity of mind and determination, and together, we will defeat the Red Man. Trust in us and your family, but most of all, trust in yourself," Rhoswen declared confidently. "We will see this through to the end."

"I wish I had your confidence." Jane sniffled as she put a hand on Rhoswen's shoulder.

"It will grow."

"I hope so." Jane remembered something Aunt Claire had told her before she went out into the garden. "Oh, I just remembered," she said excitedly as she stepped back from Rhoswen and Oren. "There's been so much going through my mind since I woke up that I forgot what Aunt Claire said to me after dinner."

"What's that, dearie?" Aedán asked as he joined them in the middle of the room.

"She said that she felt something was amiss earlier this morning before she left to go to the shop. You know, like something wasn't right, so she cast a protection spell over Avalon so that only we or any invited guest could enter the property. I feel so happy remembering that and safer. That should keep the Red Man from getting me!" "What's a shop?" Oren asked.

"Oren." Rhoswen groaned as she elbowed him in the ribs.

"A protection spell will be effective against him but only for so long, Jane," Kaelan warned as he joined them. "He will use his own magick to overcome it, so take heed—do not venture out on your own. Take any measures you have to protect yourself, and here—take this." He held out his hand, offering something long and rigid.

"What's that?"

"A bough. You'll need this if you are going to cross over." He placed it in her hand.

"Do you remember the chant?" Aedán asked.

"Um, connect the bough to the tree. Safe passage, I ask of thee—oh, Aedán, I'm sorry. What was it again?"

"Reconnect the bough to the mystic tree and seek safe passage to Avalon. This, I request of thee."

"Now, say it five times so that you don't forget, and the bough must be touching the trunk of the tree while you recite the chant. Don't forget that," emphasised Aedán. "Those new to travelling always forget that part."

"It's time for you to return to Avalon, Jane McKinnon, for those that love you will worry if your absence is noticed." Kaelan held out a hand to her as a gesture inviting a handshake.

"Really, it's time to go already?"

"Aye, dearie, it is. Remember I only brought you here on this occasion as a measure of safety."

"Yes, and I thank you, but how will you know if I'm in trouble? How do I call you?" She looked to the others, wanting to find solace in an answer.

"We will know, but if you wish, just go into the garden to your apple tree and call our names. Otherwise, you have the bough," Kaelan instructed. "Now go, be with your kind. We will take care of things here. Aedán will see you home safely."

"Okay, but before I go, I'm missing something—my pentagram. It was on a chain around my neck when I was in the garden."

"Does it have blue stones?" Rhoswen asked.

"Yes, it does. Have you seen it?"

"Aye, we have. It's a very interesting talisman. Does it bring you much luck?"

"It is a sacred Wiccan symbol that is very dear to all witches. Where is it?"

"You were wearing it when Aedán brought you here. We didn't know what alloy it was made of, so we took great care to remove it from you," Rhoswen replied.

"Why would you do that?"

"We had to make sure that it was not made of iron."

"Why would anyone have jewellery made of iron?" Jane asked, a little dumbfounded. "Okay, I'm sure it's a pewter base. Why?"

"Forgive me. I didn't mean to cause offence. The talisman is lovely and is of no danger to yourself or anyone else with human blood, but to someone that is Fey, the object may be very dangerous—that is, if it is made of iron."

"Really, you're having me on, surely?" Jane smiled.

"No. I'm serious. Cold iron is toxic to Fey. It can kill us. Ironically, though, the cold iron will actually burn us."

"Oh, I can see why you would be cautious then. I have heard that before somewhere, I think. Strange how you think of such things as fairy tales and nonsense, not giving it a second thought. But you're saying that it's actually true! Wow, that's so bizarre, no offence."

"None taken."

"So can I have it back then, the pentagram?"

"I won't be a moment, Oren," Rhoswen called as she turned to Oren and Kaelan, "Can you get it for me? It's on table food table beside the hearth. In a small pot," she added as Oren walked over to the table.

"In here," he said as he held up a small clay-fired bowl. "*Le do thoil.*"

Oren walked back, smiling to Jane as he placed the bowl into Rhoswen's awaiting hands. She drew the talisman out of the bowl, reluctantly at first it seemed, still wary of the metal object, but she managed a smile when she presented the chain, the pentagram dangling below her outstretched arm.

"*Buíochas,*" Rhoswen said to Oren as he took the bowl back to the table.

Jane took the chain and placed it around her neck again. "That feels a lot better. I was almost naked without it," she joked but her meaning seemed lost in translation.

They all stood in an uncomfortable silence for a moment, the crackle of the fire providing the only noise until Aedán suggested that they make a move. Jane hugged each of them and thanked them for their hospitality before turning back to Aedán.

"Okay, I'm ready to go. Thank you, everyone. I feel a lot safer knowing that everyone is looking out for me and that Avalon has a protection spell, as well. I'll take good care of the bough, and I'll see all of you really soon," Jane said graciously, feeling upbeat at the prospect of being home again, comfortable in her normal surrounds.

Oren opened the door to the *sidhe* as the group meandered along behind him. A cold wind forced its way in, creating a swirling effect that made the fire leap and dance about sporadically. Small pieces of parchment and cloth were blown about the room by the invisible intruder while the small group of occupants held their collective breaths and clothes as they took step after step into the relentless breeze towards the door. The group stopped at the door. Jane, closest to the opening and taking the brunt of the wind, turned back to thank everyone again before braving the conditions outside and venturing with Aedán back to the mystic tree.

Kaelan grasped Jane by the shoulders and pulled her towards him. He kissed her on both cheeks before taking a step back. "Be safe, Jane McKinnon."

"Yes, take care and remember that we are available whenever you need us," Rhoswen offered. "Just remember to use bough when you need to." smiled Rhoswen smiled and pulled Jane into a tight hug.

"What happens if the Red Man comes back here looking for me?" Jane asked, concerned that her presence could put her new friends in danger, as well.

"Don't worry about us. When he comes back to Emain Albach, we'll deal with him and put to rest any danger that he may present to you," Kaelan said sternly as he patted the hilt of his sword.

"Aye, we'll take care of him," Oren added with a wry smile, "and be safe on your trip back to Avalon." He gave her a final nod.

With her departing pleasantries complete Jane turned to Aedán, her arms wrapped around her trunk to keep in what warmth she could, her teeth chattering as the wind penetrated her clothing chilling her to the core. "Are you ready?" Jane asked as she turned back to the open doorway and stepped outside. *Shit, this is cold.*

"Aye, dearie, ready as the day I was born," he replied as he followed her out. "I'll see you lot but in the warmth of the *sidhe's* belly, soon." He laughed.

Jane studied the surroundings of the sidhe as she waited for Aedán to catch up with her. The day was grey and gloomy; clouds hung low overhead, hiding the peaks of the hilltops on the horizon. The air was moist from previous rains that made the galling winds all that more chilling. It seemed to have a life of its own as it whipped around the *sidhe's* in the village, pushing against Jane's face and body creating a wet film on her skin and dampened clothes while swirling around her legs. From the outside, the *sidhe* was as Rhoswen had described—a large dome or igloo-shaped house crafted from the earth itself covered in a mixture of grasses and moss. The odd little yellowy-pink field flower sprung up randomly on the mounds" surface.

The path twisting its way from the house was bare earth created from many years of the grass being trodden away. On this evening, it was soft and slushy with small pools of muddy water due to the inclement weather. She could see about ten *sidhes,* all with plumes of white smoke escaping the black stacks atop the mounds and being blown away into the darker grey clouds above. The houses were positioned around a clearing that she supposed was the middle of the village. There may have been more on the other side of the clearing, but she couldn't see due to the tree in the centre. Standing on the path, cross-armed and rubbing her triceps to generate heat, she heard Aedán walk up behind her.

"How far is it to the mystic tree?" Jane yelled over the winds.

"Not far, just a little way." He trotted around her to lead the way. "Come on. Try to keep up, dearie. You don't want to get lost."

"You're not going to keep that pace into the wind, are you?"

He slowed to a walk about ten paces in front of her. She gritted her teeth, and with her face pointed towards the ground, she pushed on at a quicker tempo to catch up with Aedán. The path turned to the right towards the clearing in the centre of the village. Jane struggled to keep her balance in the crosswind while trying to avoid the large puddles that dotted the path. The wind's power was lessened somewhat when they walked past a *sidhe* that acted as a natural barrier, giving them some relief where they could relax their bodies. The chilling winds would pick up again, rushing between the large gaps between the mounds, forcing Jane to concentrate her weight on the right side of her body to keep balance.

As they passed each of the *sidhe's* in the village, Jane noticed that no one was outside; in fact, there wasn't much outside any of the homes at all. In Delta, she was used to seeing shoes, brooms, children's toys, and pets. In fact, she imagined that if not for the smoke rising from each of the mounds, at a distance, the village would look just like a group of grassy mounds in a clearing amongst the trees, nothing particularly interesting, really. Then her mind went back to the smoke, which led to the fire, and the warmth she would feel if she were inside one of the *sidhes*. The thought sent a warm flush through her body as she temporarily forgot about the howl and sting of the wind. A droplet of moisture blown from her hair into her eye shunted her back into reality.

Jane pushed up on Aedán' right side to use him as a windbreak to take some pressure off her knees.

"This wind won't let up. Is it always like this here?" she yelled.

"It can be. After all, Emain Albach is an island," he shouted over his right shoulder. "It's mostly calm, though. The winds are a lot gentler just easing through the valleys and between the *sidhes*. Today, it's as erratic as deer running from the hunt."

"Is it a bi—" Jane shrieked as she fell to the ground mid-sentence, a broken red object shooting out from underneath her shoe. "Ouch, my foot," she cried as she grabbed at her ankle, rubbing with her fingers either side of the bone. She looked up at Aedán, her mouth open to call him back, but nothing came out. She just sat there in awe at the sight in front of her, the wind still pushing against her, blowing her hair in all directions, the seat of her pants absorbing the moisture of the wet grass. She forgot about the throbbing pain.

"Jane McKinnon," Aedán roared, snapping her out of her trance.

"What?" Jane replied, drawing out her response as she turned her head towards Aedán. Her eyes were the last to move towards him as her vision was held by a dotted sea of red underneath a towering tree before her.

"It's beautiful, the mystic tree. This is it, isn't it?" she asked.

"I did say it wasn't far."

Jane twisted her back to look over her shoulder at the path they had travelled to get there. "It's odd that we've only walked maybe a couple of minutes from the *sidhe*, but the tree didn't look this impressive from where I stood. Yet now," she said as she pushed herself up from the ground, wincing as the pain from her ankle reminded her of her fall, "it looks like It's more than trebled in size, like fifty foot or more." She limped over to Aedán and stood beside him, favouring her right leg over the other. "Do you mind if I lean against you, Aedán?"

"It's no bother, but you mustn't dilly-dally, dearie, for the mystic tree and Avalon awaits you."

"Trying to get rid of me, are you?" she joked, grimacing through the pain.

"Do you not want to return?" he asked with a sideways tilt of his head. "Your foot will be fine when you return."

"How so?"

"The tree and portal are powerful, so powerful that any ailment you may be unfortunate enough to garner in one realm will be mended while you crossover to the next."

"Really!"

"Aye, but you still must have your wits about you as you can still meet your demise. There is no coming back from that," he added, turning back to the tree.

"Okay, stay alive—got it. Sounds simple enough," Jane replied as she stared into the depths of the trees network of branches.

"Any questions before you make your journey, Jane McKinnon?"

"Do you eat the apples from the mystic tree, or do you let them drop and rot on the ground?"

"Aye, sometimes and sometimes not. It's a complicated answer that's probably best to wait until we next meet."

"And when will that be, Aedán?"

"Soon enough, you'll see. Now move your way to the tree, make a good purchase on the trunk, and climb until you reach the first major fork," he instructed as he reared up on his hind legs and pointed to the divergence with his right hoof. "This is where you'll travel. Have the bough ready to strike the tree, and clear your mind of all but the chant. Now go, Jane McKinnon. Go back to Avalon and be safe, as long as the protection spell holds and the Red Man does not discover the portal to the secret garden, you'll not be in danger. But heed Kaelan's advice. If you need us, go to the tree and call our names or use the bough to come back to Emain Albach."

Jane reached across her companion, wrapping her left arm around Aedán' neck, "Thank you, thank you so much for looking after me," she said as she gave him a gentle squeeze.

"It was Rhoswen who looked after you. I just brought you out of harm's way."

"You know what I mean. Thank everyone for me again, Aedán, will you?

"Aye."

Jane approached the tree with bough in hand. The tree was immense, and she wondered if its size was an optical illusion. "Surely an apple tree can't be this big…" She looked up. "What the?"

Jane walked to the base of the trunk, she could see a glittery shimmer on the bark. It was everywhere. Taking two steps back, she witnessed an awe-inspiring sight— flecks of light bounced off the tree as if the bark were diamond encrusted. At that moment, Jane felt a tiny tremor pulsating through her right hand. She looked down to behold the same phenomenon in the bough; its bark turned a sparkly silver. Jane turned to look back to Aedán for guidance.

"Aye, it's normal. Not a real masculine event, I grant you, but it is part of the tree's mystique. It is gathering its power to send you home as it can sense that you have a bough with you."

"But how does it know where I want to go?" Jane called back over the blowing a gale between them.

"It doesn't. It just senses the bough, and you have to tell the tree where to send you as part of the chant!" "Oh, yeah," Jane said sheepishly.

"Now climb to the first fork!"

"Okay," Jane said to herself as she turned back to the glittering tree. "Where's the best place to start?" she murmured as she looked around the base of the trunk.

When she found the perfect spot, Jane turned back to Aedán one last time to wave good-bye before putting the bough in her mouth and making a foothold on the trunk. Reaching high with her right hand, she pulled herself up the outside of the tree. At that moment, Jane stopped to gaze in astonishment at the bark underneath and surrounding each part of her body. Everything connected to the tree glowed with a magnificent, almost-blinding white light. Then she heard Aedán's voice again in her head telling her to keep going. A smile and a shake of her head later, she reached up with her left hand and pulled herself farther into the tree. Jane blinked a couple of times, thinking that her eyes had deceived her, as her vision seemed sharper. Her hearing was amplified. An apple fell from the tree on the other side of the trunk. The separating of the stork from the branch sounded like a piece of timber cracking under pressure, and her peripheral vision caught a red object falling. She turned quickly, her focus adjusting as she did. She could see the whole apple turning as it fell. It seemed to take an eternity, but the apple passed the lowest branch and hit the ground with the sound similar to an explosion. Then the apple just rolled away.

Jane suddenly realised she could no longer hear or feel the wind; the leaves didn't seem to be moving.

"Weird," she said and turned her attention skywards again. The first major fork was only a few feet above her head. She could not see Aedán anymore but wondered if he could see her progress by the illuminating bark as she went along.

She reached out with her right hand, grasping the top of the branch at the fork. "You got this. One good pull, come on," she said. With a rock back and forth, Jane gave an almighty effort. Pulling herself up and over the branch, she came to rest straddling its girth.

She carefully inched her buttocks slowly towards the fork where the main branches met. Taking the bough from her mouth, she reached for the pentagram and held it tight while she asked the Gods to protect her in her journey.

"Okay, this is it." She took the bough in both hands above her head. She paused fleetingly to practise the chant in her head, and when she was sure she wouldn't stuff it up, she took one deep breath and slowly exhaled to calm her nerves.

"Okay, let's go home," Jane said as she brought the bough down to connect to the fork of the tree. A strike of white light shot skywards from the end of the bough as it vibrated and jumped violently in her hands. She gritted her teeth, swallowed her fear, and began the chant. "Reconnect the bough to the mystic tree and seek safe passage to Avalon.

This, I request of thee."

The passing of the final word from Jane's mouth started an amazing chain of events. The light emanating from the bough reversed in on itself, penetrating the bark of the tree. Then a gush of wind flowed upwards, swirling above Jane's head. The groaning ache of timber being ripped apart reverberated in her head as the two sides of the fork began to split apart. She could see into the depths of the tree—a brown-black hole with specks of white light like fireflies in a dark tunnel. The opening reached a diameter a foot wide, and the churning winds above her head pulled downwards without warning. Jane was sucked feet first into the hole as if it were a giant vacuum. Her mind felt light, almost as if she were unconscious as the wind hurried around her, creating a funnel. She could see the light bluish-grey lines of the wind pass her face. She started to spin and stretch as her hips were suctioned through the opening. Pain receptors signalled her brain that something was wrong. Her body was contorting in ways that it shouldn't, and she screeched at the peak of her lung capacity, yet she could not hear her voice. Her ears were filled with the rushing wind, and in her head, a dull but constant thump beat louder and louder. She tried to scream again, but her jaw was stretched away from her face. As her torso and back followed, she could hear the pop of each vertebrae as if she were being tortured on a medieval rack.

The image in her mind conjured thoughts that she wouldn't survive the journey. She could hear Aedán' voice warning her that she didn't want to meet her own demise in this realm as it was very real. She saw her mum, Aunt Claire, Sophie, and Blue Belle. She screamed again, the shrill of her own voice in her head was low but grew louder as it pushed from the depths of her stomach. Her body stretched further still, and the scream travelled up her diaphragm, getting louder and louder, like a bullet spinning through the barrel of a gun. The scream filled her mouth, and the pressure at her lower extremities pulled her hips through the opening of the fork.

Bang! A thunderclap sounded all around her. She could not feel anything holding onto her anymore. All was black, except for an occasional spark that lit the tunnel. It was hard to breathe in the thick, moist air. Then she saw a distant orange light. She started to spin violently; the light grew larger as she whirled closer and closer. She closed her eyes and waited for impact.

13

The sensation of freefalling melted away. Jane still had her eyes squeezed, shut but the anticipated impact never came. In its place was a familiarity that comforted her. She did not want to open her eyes to find that she was dead or dreaming. Instead, the smells that had excited her senses seemed too good to be real, but were they? Noises filled the air, accompanied by memories of fairy wrens jumping, leaving trails in the dew-covered grass in the secret garden early in the morning, catching caterpillars and singing sweet melodic little tunes. Koi jumped after the low-flying dragonflies, splashing on the surface of the pond. She heard the waterfall trickle down the sandstone rocks into the pond. A smile touched Jane's features, and she felt dreamy, as if she were floating on a cloud.

"Wait," she blurted, startling herself from her visions of the past. "This is all too familiar. I can't be dreaming, can I?" She nervously dared to slowly open one eye, revealing a scene that lay before her—a picture-perfect copy of the secret garden. She looked beyond the pond, and the path led her eye past the grassy knolls, the wisteria-draped gazebo, and the jasmine tunnel. Then there it was. A rush of excitement washed over her as she opened her other eye and focussed her sight on Avalon.

"I'm here. I'm home. Yes!" She made a small fist pump and noticed that she was holding something that looked like a branch. "The bough." She paused. "I-it wasn't a dream!" She was about to push herself off the branch when she realised that she was about five feet off the ground.

"I'm in the tree, and I've got a bough. It was real." She laughed. "I've got to tell Aunt Claire." She pushed herself off the branch, remembering she had an injured ankle. She descended feet first, managing to shift her weight to her right side so that when she landed, she rolled over her right shoulder, alleviating any further injury to her left ankle. Tumbling to a sitting position, she grabbed at her ankle, anticipating the pain. But there was nothing. She removed her shoe and rolled her foot repeatedly. Still she felt no pain.

"Aedán was right," she yelled jubilantly.

Jane rose to her feet, amazed that the pain of twisting her ankle had gone just as Aedan said it would, but she wanted to be sure. She bounced up and down on her ankle. "Just like new!"

Excited to be back, she skirted the pond at a quick step, skipping halfway along the path. When she heard a hoot from her right side, she stopped to look for its source.

Hoot! Hoot!

She heard it again as she scanned the top of the lattice barriers at the sides of the garden until she saw the boobook owl perched on the top corner, closest to her, of the gazebo.

"Merry meet, my friend. It's so good to see you again on this fine morning," Jane said, greeting the bird with a bow as she continued on her way towards the house.

"Aunt Claire?" Jane called over the groan of the screen door as she opened it. She entered the sunroom. "Aunt Claire?"

"Merry Meet, my darling," Claire replied as she walked in from the kitchen. "I didn't hear you get up this morning. Have you been in the garden long?"

"No, not too long," she replied. "Why? What is the time?"

"Nearly seven thirty. Did you have something to eat? I can get you something if you're hungry?"

Jane hadn't actually eaten in the *sidhe*. There had been bread on the table. She'd only had the mead. "Which wasn't too bad, either," she said aloud without thinking.

"What was that? Wasn't too bad? What's that?

"Oh, never mind. I was thinking about something else, but yes, I'd love something to eat, please. Is it too late for a waffle with honey?" She walked over to Claire, who was standing in the doorway, and gave her a big embrace.

"Oh!" She laughed. "It's never too late for breakfast, and why the hug?"

"I just missed you. That's all."

"Okay, it's only been nine or ten hours. Did you sleep okay? You didn't have a bad dream, did you?"

"Actually, I didn't get much sleep at all, but I'm okay. Curiously, I feel quite refreshed, but I did want to speak to you about something else if you have time before you go to the shop."

"Sure, dear. Let's go into the kitchen. You can talk on the way if you wish."

"I'll go to the toilet first, and I'll see you in there," Jane said as she stepped past her aunt. "I won't be long," she called back as she walked down the hallway.

Claire had two waffles in the toaster, a place set on the table with margarine, honey, and a glass of orange juice when Jane walked into the kitchen. She paused at her chair and drew in the aromas that filled the room.

"Did you want a coffee with breakfast, as well?" Claire asked as the toaster switch clicked and waffles jumped out.

"No thanks. The juice is fine."

Claire put the waffles on Jane's plate and returned to the counter to collect her own coffee before re-joining her niece at the table.

"Now what was it that you wanted to talk about?" She pulled the chair in underneath her.

"Okay, now this is going to sound very weird, but I need you to have an open mind. Okay?" Jane searching her aunt's face for understanding.

"You know I don't like to judge," she reassured Jane as she reached over, taking hold of her wrist. "Are you in some sort of trouble?"

"Yes, well, you could say that, but to what degree, I don't know yet."

"I'm not sure I know what you mean."

"Well, you know how I told you about Aedán and him being a faerie and all?"

"Yes, a fairy. I know. I've spoken to many people who have had interactions with the fair folk. I, unfortunately, have not, although Daideó used to tell many stories about them. That is not to say that I do not believe that they exist, though. I just haven't met one yet," she explained with a gentle squeeze of Jane's hand.

"Well, anyway, remember how he told me that I was in danger and there was a darkness that was searching for me?"

"Yes, the cryptic message, but we still don't know what he means by the darkness." She looked down at her coffee, untouched and probably getting too cold for her to drink.

"Did you want to heat it again?"

"What?"

"The coffee—it's probably gone cold by now." Jane nodded towards the cup.

"No, don't be silly. It can wait. Tell me more about this *púca* and what he said."

"Well, he didn't say why the darkness is after me exactly, but…" She thought about what her fate would be if the Red Man did catch up with her. She stared at the table.

"But… but what?" Claire demanded, shaking Jane's hand.

"Oh, sorry," Jane said. She turned back to face Claire. "Sorry, just a little pre-occupied, but he did say that it's a good thing that you put the protection spell on Avalon."

"That's good, but…" Claire paused. "Hang on, he came back again last night? Did he say why the darkness wants you?"

"They didn't say."

"They? Who's they? Is there more than one?" Claire probed.

"No, no, there was only Aedán, but he didn't say because he doesn't know why. Honestly, that's what he said." Jane sobbed as tears started to well in her eyes.

"Then what is it, sweetheart? What did he tell you that's upsetting you so much?"

Jane pushed the chair and stood, turning away from the table towards the doorway to the lounge room.

"Jane McKinnon, don't you walk away from me. Something is wrong, and I want to know what is going on," Claire appealed with tone as she also stood from her chair.

Jane checked her exit and stood still. She could feel a pressure rising in her. She wanted to remain positive so much, but she felt like just falling to the floor at the thought of being murdered. Her chest tightened. It became harder to swallow, and she could feel the tears beckoning to be released.

"Me—he wants me," she bellowed as the tears came like a dam bursting its banks.

She turned to Claire, who rushed to her niece, taking her in a loving embrace.

"It's okay. No one is going to get you. We're protected

in the house, in Avalon," she reassured her as she stroked her back. "I will protect you, but I need to know why. Did this Aedán say what it was that this man wants from you?"

"He said that he wants my essence, my purity," she managed through the tears and exaggerated breaths.

"Your life essence. That means…" Claire seemed to realise the gravity of the situation.

She held onto Jane for another couple of minutes, tightening her embrace and nestling into the crook of her neck. "Everything is going to be all right," Claire said in a reassuring tone as she took one step back from Jane to be able to look at her while she spoke. "I'm going to speak to some old friends today, you know, to get some advice. Will you be okay?"

"Yeah, I'll be okay. I'm sorry for crying on your shoulder," Jane sobbed as she tried to control her tears as she looked around the kitchen for the box of tissues.

"Don't be silly. We just have to remain strong. We'll get through this. We always do!"

"Yeah, that's true," Jane replied as she tried to manage a smile to demonstrate that she was trying.

"Did you want to see if Sophie can keep you company today?"

"Yeah, I think so. I might have a shower, get changed, and then give her a call."

"That sounds like a good idea. While you're doing that, I'll get my things together," Claire said as she turned to walk out of the kitchen.

"Wait, Aunt Claire," Jane called.

"Yes, sweetheart?"

"What about the shop? Who are you going to get to open for you?"

"No one. The—"

"But," Jane interrupted.

"But nothing. This is more important, and we can afford to not open the shop every now and again if something important comes up. This *is* pretty important, don't you think?" Claire responded with raised eyebrows and a goofy smile.

Jane smiled and embraced Claire one more time. "Thanks, Aunt Claire. You're the best ever," she said before she pushed herself away to look at her aunt. "Who are you going to speak to, and do you think they will be able to help?"

"Just an old friend, and I hope so," Claire replied. "Now go get in the shower while I get my things together. I won't leave until you're out."

"Okay, I will," Jane said, feeling a little more secure knowing that Aunt Claire was on her side. She was pleased and grateful that her aunt hadn't questioned her sanity and had taken the situation on face. "Aunt Claire," she called out as Claire was about to exit the kitchen for the lounge room.

"Yes, sweetheart."

"The Red Man."

"What?"

"The darkness, Aedán also called him the Red Man."

"The Red Man," Claire repeated, her expression crestfallen as she looked away from Jane.

"What's the matter? Have you heard of him?" she asked as she took an expectant step towards her.

"Um, no," Claire replied. She paused briefly then turned back to Jane. "No, I haven't heard of the Red Man, Now, you get in that shower. I've got a call to make."

"Yep, going now." She smiled as she walked into the lounge room towards the hall and her bedroom.

Jane closed the bedroom door behind her and decided to put on a song while she was getting her things ready. She pushed the ejected the Pixies CD and replaced it with The Jesus and Mary Chain's *Psychocandy* album. She skipped to *Some Candy Talking* written by William Reid. The bonus track on the 1986 CD release didn't appear on the vinyl or cassette versions. Jane hunted through her drawers and retrieved a clean pair of jeans, underwear, and a black-linen peasant top.

She walked back down the hall, looking in on the lounge room as she passed, but she didn't see Aunt Claire. Thinking she was in the sunroom or kitchen, Jane continued down the hall to the bathroom.

∞

The altar room was located on the ground floor, surrounded by other rooms so that no natural light entered it. The inside was decorated with all things Wiccan, most of which Claire had brought from the shop over the years.

The altar stood within a large pentagram marked out on the wooden floor. The purple cloth draped over the front edge of the wooden altar displayed a small gold inlayed pentagram. Tools of the craft—a pentacle, chalice, candle, and athame—rested atop it. The remainder of the room was quite sparse in comparison to other rooms in the house. The storage cupboard at the opposite end of the room contained all of Claire's other ritual tools and supplies. A light hung in the centre of the room, but Claire rarely used it. The shelf running the circumference of the walls was adorned with candles that Claire used to light the dark room.

Claire heard the water of the shower through the wall—that was her cue. Claire looked at the phone and punched in a number as she walked to the opposite wall near the cupboard. She could hear the ringing tone as she placed the cordless handset to her ear.

"Hello," a female voice answered.

"Merry meet, Gwendolyn. It's Claire."

"Merry meet, Claire. A call in the morning from you," she exclaimed. "Shouldn't you be opening the shop about now?"

"Yes, I should, but today is different."

"Different? How's that?"

"Eerin," she said grimly with a monotone voice.

"Eerin? Are you sure?"

"Yes."

"Okay, you'd better come over."

"Will do. Give me half an hour or so. Jane is getting ready to go over to Sophie's, so I'll leave once she's gone."

"Sure. I'll see you then. Blessed be."

"Blessed be." Claire pressed the end call button on the phone, her attention drawn to the wall behind the altar as she heard the water to the shower stop.

14

Jane walked through the lounge towards her bedroom, having forgotten to take her clothes with her. She had her white towel wrapped around her body under her arms with a second one wrapped around her head, absorbing the water from her hair. She still couldn't see Aunt Claire, although she was sure that she could hear noises coming from the laundry when she walked out.

She entered the room, closing the door behind her. The Jesus and Mary Chain album was still playing, and Jane immediately let the music wash over her. She stood in the centre of the room, her arms raised over her shoulders, gently massaging her scalp to dry her hair quicker. Still half in a daze, her eyes came to rest on the photograph of her mum on the dresser. A smile quickly formed.

"Hi, Mum." She walked over to the dresser and picked up the frame then turned to sit on the bed. "There's so much to say, but I'll get straight to the point—I'm scared, Mum. I met some new people, and they've warned me about a danger. A man they believe will try and kill me." A tear rolled down her cheek. "I'm trying to be strong as they've said they will protect me and Aunt Claire. Oh, she's looking out for me, too, although I haven't been entirely truthful with her." Jane despondently caressed the photograph with her thumb as if she were straightening her mum's emerald dress. She managed to smile through the tears as she spoke to Grace. "You see, the people that are protecting me are Fey, Faerie from a place called Emain Albach." Her voice trailed off as her attention turned briefly towards the window and the singing wrens outside. "I love you, Mum. Look over me and protect me," she whispered to the image in her hands. "I wish you were here." She sobbed as she kissed a finger and pressed it against Grace's face beneath the glass.

Moments later, after staring forlornly at the photograph, wishing that her mum was still with her to comfort and protect her, she wished her spirit well and returned the frame to its place atop the dresser. Turning back to the bed, Jane picked up her clothes and started getting dressed. Then someone knocked at the door.

"Jane, are you in there, love?" Aunt Claire asked. "I thought I heard some crying."

"I'm okay." She sniffled as she pushed her arms through the peasant top and over her head. "I was just talking to Mum and got a little bit emotional, but I'm okay now. I'm getting dressed. I'll be out shortly."

"Okay, love. I'll leave you to it, but you know you can always come to me if you want to have a chat," she offered in a loving, supportive tone. "I mean, I know that you already know that and do it, but this time, I mean it, okay? I really mean it!"

"I know, Aunt Claire, and I will. Trust me, you'll be the first to know," she reassured her as she buttoned the top of her jeans. "I'll be out in a tick. I'm just going to give Soph a call to make sure she's okay if I drop over."

"Okay, I'll be out in the sunroom," Claire replied as she turned and walked away from the bedroom. "I don't think she or do any of her Fey friends have any idea who she's dealing with here. I pray the Gods will assist us to vanquish this threat that has been cast upon us."

"Gods will assist us to do what, Aunt Claire?" Jane asked.

"Oh, nothing. I was just talking to myself."

Jane picked up the mobile lying on the bed beside her and swiped the screen to activate it. She read the notifications awaiting her attention. She had a couple of emails, a new follower on Twitter, update notification from Google Play, and a text message from Sophie.

"Mmm, Rob Schwimmer. What's he up to?" she said as she closed the Twitter screen and opened the incoming messages.

08.13

Hey U, WYD 2day. Wanna come over? Soph xoxo

Jane laughed to herself as she typed a reply then read it back to herself before sending.

08.27

Hey U, I was just saying to AC that I'd cu 2day.

Just about ready to come over. Say 20 mins LU xoxo Jane

Jane tossed the phone back to the mattress and bent down to the floor to put on her black pumps. Then she collected the phone, bag, and keys from the computer desk, closed the lid of the laptop, and pulled the door shut behind her as she walked out into the hallway.

"Aunt Claire," she said announcing her presence as she walked into the sunroom, "I've just spoken to Soph, and she's free today, so I'm going over for a visit to clear the head if that's all right with you?"

"Yes, dear, that's okay, but please be safe. You can't be too careful at the best of times, but you—sorry, I mean we must take these warnings very seriously."

"Yes, I'm taking them seriously, but I've you and Aedán both looking out for me, and I'm not going to be alone. I don't think Soph would let anything happen to me, either." Jane bent down to kiss Claire on the cheek. "Blessed be."

"Blessed be, my dear, and please be careful."

"Will do, bye."

Jane exited the room, turning an immediate left into the kitchen, where she walked to the table in the centre of the room. She paused to take stock of the situation, thinking that something just wasn't quite right, but she couldn't place what it was.

There's something Aunt Claire isn't telling me. Was she being too accepting of the situation? Was it the fact she was acting a little more protective than usual, or was it a contradiction that she was allowing Jane to go outside of the house, outside of the protection of her spell?

"Say hello to Sophie for me," Claire called out, intruding into Jane's distraction.

"Okay, will do, Aunty Claire. Have a great day," she replied as she exited out the screen door to the pebble driveway beyond.

The screen returned to the jamb with a creaking thump when she was halfway to Blue Belle. The weather was shaping up to be a beautiful day. However, Jane couldn't help but scan her surrounds for signs of danger. Anything that moved caught her attention—shadows on the fence line, animals amongst the shrubs and trees, birds in flight. It all seemed a bit much, but Jane was confident that her time wasn't up just yet. The jangle of her car keys did have a calming effect on her nerves when she retrieved them from her hip pocket as she reached the driver's door of the vehicle.

"Merry meet, Belle. How are you today?" she asked as she unlocked the door.

The engine turned over, and the familiar sounds of the air-cooled Volkswagen motor filled the air, and joy filled Jane's heart every time she heard the sweet sounds of Blue Belle. Pushing down on the stick and pulling back, Jane found the reverse gear. Claire watched her niece from the bay window of the kitchen as the blue V-Dub backed out of the drive and turned onto the road. Jane pushed the stick forward into first as she released the clutch, while keeping an eye on the road for oncoming traffic. Jane fumbled about the glove box for a CD that she hadn't listened to for a while. She retrieved *Seven Days in Sammystown* by Wall of Voodoo, a 1985 release under new front man Andy Prieboy after former singer Stan Ridgway left the band. The Kenwood unit sucked the CD in then hummed slightly as it read the disc. The intro to the first song started up—a mix of keyboard, drums, and a western-like bass riff that made the single one of Jane's favourites on the album.

She was happy that no one around her knew she was afraid. She was scared to death of the unknown, but not knowing why she was being targeted was most terrifying. The music was simply a distraction to keep her mind at ease as she drove down Delta Road.

∞

Claire watched the blue car pulled away from the front of the house. She turned away from the window and sighed as if she carried the weight of the world on her shoulders as she looked at the time on the clock. 8.35 a.m.

She stood there for a moment, replaying the events of the morning in her mind while slowly shaking her head in disbelief. "This can't really be happening—can it? After all these years, and we're going to battle it out again?"

As she lowered her head, the change in visual texture from the wall to the floor must have prompted an alarm bell to awaken Claire from her deep consternations.

"Right, I can't stand around here all day, just waiting for something to happen. We have to get prepared."

She went to the altar room and opened the cabinet. She rifled through the loose items that sat in an unruly order at the bottom of the wooden unit. She set aside paper book after paper book covered with handwritten entries detailing spells, enchantments, and other findings. The notes were untested works that Claire had worked on over the years. Only once she had perfected a spell both in theory and practice did it find a place in her Book of Shadows. She sat on her knees, her body prone in a forward position, leaning entirely into the cupboard itself. She tossed aside books that were of no interest to her. She kept at it for a couple of minutes, and the pile of books behind her grew.

"I got!" she shouted gleefully as she rose to her feet, flicking the pages of a book. "I can't believe it's still here after all these years."

She turned from the cupboard, ignoring the books that lay beneath her feet as she tried to navigate her way out of the room safely. She hurried to her bedroom. The room was not a bold statement from a design sense, but it was comfortable for Claire. Jane could not stand being in there, saying the sterile white walls and furnishings gave her a headache.

Claire retrieved a brown gym bag from the cupboard and threw it onto her bed, along with the book. She grabbed other items from her drawers and shoved them into the bag then placed the book on top. "I'm sure I have everything," she said to herself as she picked up the bag and left the room, closing the white door behind her.

She tapped away at the screen of her mobile phone as she walked back down the hall to the kitchen. 8.48

Merry Meet Gwendolyn. About to leave now. Have the book with me. Should be there in ten minutes.

Blessed be. Claire

8.49

See you soon. Drive safe

Blessed be. Gwen

Claire pulled the wooden door to the kitchen shut behind her and allowed the screen to close with a thud that echoed around the clearing where the sheds and garage were located. She sensed a strange lingering vibration in the atmosphere; she paused to take in the eerie feeling that made the hairs stand up on the back of her neck. She sensed the danger—a predator, a foe, an old friend. They had not crossed paths for a long time. He'd been defeated then, but that had been over a decade ago. She feared that he had taken the time to refine and hone his skills. Defeating him had been a group effort last time round, but she was quite sure it would take a lot more to rid themselves of him again. His presence was strong, and although she felt safe under the protection spell, she knew he was near, waiting for the right opportunity. She hurried out to the white Mitsubishi and opened the driver's-side back door. She threw the bag onto the seat and closed the door in one motion. She looked up and took one last scan of her surrounds before belting herself into the seat and starting the motor. She checked the rear-view mirror, reversed out the drive, and slammed on the brakes as a four-wheel-drive towing a caravan cruised past the house.

Dust thrown up from the loose gravel formed a cloud that slowly drifted over the bonnet of the car as Claire, shaken but not hurt by the near miss, watched the caravan travel down the road to the sounds of a fading horn. She sat there for a moment, composing herself with a few deep breaths, then checked herself in the mirror while gathering the courage to attempt her outing again.

The white Mitsubishi increased in speed as it drove past the stationary green Ford hatch that was still parked on the verge outside of the Lambert's property opposite Avalon.

"Must have stayed the night," Claire said to herself with a wry smile as the car confirmed exactly what she and Jane had assumed last night. "That girl will get herself into trouble one of these days."

15

Jane pulled to a stop outside of Sophie's house. She honked the horn twice and sat there, the engine idling, waiting for her friend to join her. She surfed through the radio stations while she waited. Then Jane realised that the buzz and crackle of the airwaves were gone. Only silence reigned between the stations. *Must be a digital thing.* She could remember the crackle on Daideó's wireless when he and Maimeó listened to the big bands out in the garden or when he listened to a sports broadcast. Her ears pricked up a little as a familiar sound rocked out of the speakers. She released the scan button. The music wasn't generally her cup of tea, but it was Australian. And she loved all things Australian, especially its music. The song was *Soul Eater* by the Clouds circa 1991. They broke up in 1997 although they had some small reunion gigs here and there, but Jane had heard that one of the two front women of the band was actually living in Tasmania. She sat there, lost in nostalgia, tapping on the steering wheel, singing to the occasional passing car.

The click of the door release startled her, and a dark figure in the corner of her eye entered the vehicle. She jumped nervously into the door beside her, hitting her hip on the door pull while shouting and raising her hands at the intruder.

"Hey, settle down, babe. It's just me," Sophie said with her hands out in a non-threatening way as she leaned back against the window behind her.

"Shit, Soph, you scared the crap out of me." Jane quivered, wide eyed and ready to defend herself.

"Are you okay? You seem a little jumpy."

"Yeah, I'm okay," she replied as she wiggled her bum back into the seat. "No, actually I'm not. I need to talk if that's okay." She needed to get a different perspective on what was happening.

"Yeah, sure. Did you want to go inside?"

Jane took a deep breath and released it slowly before answering. "No I'd like to take a drive out into Freycinet if that's okay. Do you mind?" She'd asked only to be polite, as she didn't expect the answer would be no.

"That's okay. Is everything all right?" she enquired grimly. "Aunt Claire hasn't been hurt, has she?"

"No, everything is okay. Aunt Claire's fine." The thought of her aunt produced a small smile that temporarily hid her dour demeanour.

"It's me," she said abruptly as she indicated and performed a U-turn after a passing truck. "I'll tell you more when we get there. Do you mind if we listen to the radio for a while?"

"Umm, yeah, sure," Sophie replied. "You did say radio, didn't you?"

"Yeah," she replied as she turned the volume up a little.

"Okay, I don't have any idea about what's up with you at the moment, but we absolutely need to speak about you listening to commercial radio. Cause something has definitely hit the fan if you're not listening to The Cure or some other post-punk gothic English band from the eighties." Sophie laughed.

An awkward silence fell between them as Jane drove out on Delta Road past Avalon towards Freycinet National Park. She slowed as the car passed the visitor reception area just inside the entrance to the park. Activities within Freycinet were starting to get busier as the weather warmed; numerous people had stopped at the centre to collect information on the park for camping, hiking, beaches, and tours. Jane, however, drove slowly past, venturing deeper within its boundaries. She followed the road as far as possible, until she found herself at the Wineglass Bay car park about eight kilometres past the centre.

She crawled to a stop within the lines of the parking bay, and the brakes squealed as they bit down on the discs. The sun was high in the sky as the morning hours passed and marched towards the midday hour. Heat penetrated the windscreen and warmed the interior quickly as the stationary vehicle did not have wind coming into the cab to regulate the temperature via the vent windows. Jane turned the key, cutting the engine, and released a sigh that sounded as if it carried the weight of a thousand troubles with it.

"You know, for someone that lives so close, I should get out here more often," Sophie said as she exited the vehicle, her arms up in the air at a full stretch, pirouetting to absorb the resplendent scenery.

"Yeah, we all should," Jane replied.

"Are you feeling okay?" Sophie asked again as she walked around the rear of Blue Belle.

"Yes and no," Jane replied with a shrug. "I'm hoping that I can clear my head and find some solace here at Freya."

"Sounds good to me." Sophie threw her right arm around Jane's shoulders and pulled her close. "So where are we off to?"

"There's a place nearby, a sacred place where the old coven used to worship," Jane said as she led the way out of the car park and onto a gravel walking track.

"Is it far?"

"Probably ten to fifteen minutes" walk. This is the track that goes past the lookout and onto Wineglass Bay. However, we don't follow it all the way. We'll probably only stay on it for about five minutes or so, then we'll turn south towards the Hazards and Mount Mayson."

"Do they still use it? The sacred site, I mean!"

"I think so, but I'm not sure. Both my mum and Aunt Claire used to be in the coven, but she turned solitary when my mum died. I do know that other members are

still in the area, so It's possible."

227

They had walked for almost a kilometre along the gritty track when a tree caught Jane's attention. Trudging a few more metres, Jane stopped abruptly, Sophie almost treading on Jane's feet in her failure to halt alongside her friend.

"This is it," Jane declared, pointing towards an old fallen she-oak trunk with a red marker spray painted on it: a cross with drip lines stretching from its corners.

"What? A marked tree? There doesn't seem to be much else here," Sophie remarked with an undertone of attitude and cheek.

Jane looked up and down the track to make sure that no one was around to see them. "Follow me … quick," she said, grabbing Sophie's arm as she stepped off the track and into the bush towards the tree. The undergrowth was thicker than she remembered it, but it had been over ten years since her mum had brought her there.

"It wasn't as bad a decade ago, but I guess there wasn't as many visitors to the park either, so it didn't have to be as concealed. Not like this." She grimaced as she navigated around small white kunzeas that scratched the skin and larger banksias.

"Doesn't look like the coven has been here, either," Sophie offered as she followed closely behind Jane, receiving the occasional slap across the legs from a flung branch.

The she-oak was still partly attached to the base of the trunk and lay diagonal to the ground, which created a triangular space underneath its girth while thick scrub grew beyond it.

"We need to crawl under the trunk to get to the sacred site."

"Really? There doesn't look to be a way past the undergrowth beyond the tree," Sophie said despondently as she laid a hand on the trunk to support her weight while looking over the large obstacle.

"Yes, there is," Jane replied, a little frustrated with Sophie's questioning. She turned back to her friend, a smile creeping from the corners of her mouth. "Do you trust me?"

"Of course I do, silly." Sophie giggled.

"Come on then," she called to Sophie as she got on all fours and crawled under the trunk.

∞

Sophie watched Jane crawl under the log and heard her name being called. Then Jane's voice repeated her name, but it grew quieter each time. She bent down and could see a figure still on all fours but maybe a couple of metres away.

"I'm coming," she hollered and as she bent down to commence her crawl, hearing her own voice echo: "I'm coming."

That can't be right, she thought as she paused. "Jane, can you hear me?" she cried. Perplexed and confused, she waited.

"Jane, can you hear me?" she heard come back to her.

Shocked, she jumped to her feet. "It's an echo." She leaned over the trunk again to look at the ground beyond it. She couldn't see any signs of a clearing, no evidence of any passable ground at all and no evidence of Jane, either. "This can't be!" She gasped as she turned away from the tree.

"Are you coming?" she heard coming from the space underneath the tree. She bent down and tried to peer in as far as she could while controlling her breathing and gathering courage.

"She did it," she said and started to crawl.

The space was dark, uninviting, and a little damp. It seemed longer than it should have been, and as Sophie started to doubt herself, she could see light at the end of the tunnel.

She continued to crawl towards the light.

Reaching the end, she poked her head out into the sunshine that awaited, causing her to blink madly to adjust to the brightness as glowing spots that obstructed her vision.

"What took you so long?" Jane asked from somewhere on Sophie's right side. "Here, take my hand."

"I can't see properly. I've got sunspot. Where are you?"

"Just here, my hand is in front of you now."

Sophie reached forward. She could make out the shape of a dark silhouetted figure in front of her, but appendages were different. They were too small for her to see clearly.

Grasping lucklessly at the air in front her, she gave up.

"Here, let me," Jane offered as she grabbed Sophie's arm just above the elbow and assisting her to her feet. "There we go," she huffed as Sophie tried to find her feet. "Steady up, just stand for a moment until your sight returns.

We're not in a hurry as we are here already," Jane finished gleefully, her mood swinging back to a state of elation as if the placebo effect of the sacred site had washed away her fears and replaced them with the memories of her mother, love, and bonds long lost.

Sophie blinked a little more, her distorted vision getting sharper crisper by the second. She could hear Jane speaking to her, and she could see the outline of her face, then her nose and mouth, followed by her amber eyes, her lips, and her smile. Her whole face was smiling.

"I can see again," she chirped gaily, "and I can see your smile, as well. I wasn't sure if I was going to see it at all today, but more than that, I can see all of you smile. And that makes me happy."

"Yes, I am, aren't I?" she replied with a pirouette, her expression suddenly bursting with exhilaration as if she were a child getting a long-awaited gift. However, she stopped instantly as reality swiftly returned. "Oh, Soph, I've wanted to tell you of this place for such a long time, but it's off limits to those who are not dedicated and initiated to the coven. I mean, I—we—could be in some serious trouble if they found out that we were here."

"It's okay. I'm not upset that you've never brought me here before. You have now, and…" Sophie took in the sights that were bestowed upon her.

"I haven't been here for over ten years myself, and even then, I think my mum had some explaining to do," Jane offered apologetically.

"It's okay," Sophie replied as she took a few quick steps past Jane before halting. She looked from side to side then up to the canopy of the trees and the breach above their heads while walking a tight circle. "Oh my God, this place is absolutely amazing," she blurted in stunned awe. "It can't be the same place, surely?"

"It is the same place. It just looks a little different to the rest of the park."

"No, it can't be," Sophie protested. "I looked over the log. There was only dense poverty bushes. Freycinet is filled with granite outcrops, banksias, she-oaks, eucalyptus, and smaller native shrubs. This place"—Sophie waved her hands in the air to emphasise the grandeur of what she was trying to explain—"It's like being in a cathedral with towering pillars on all sides. Moss-covered Huon pines and eucalypts, and over here"—she pointed—"this strange looking tree in front of us that I don't recognise. It could be the altar that some priest would deliver his sermon from."

"That, Soph, is a black locust. It was planted here decades ago by the coven, and it contains many magickal properties that they used to harvest."

"A black locust. I haven't heard of it before. Is it a native?"

"I don't think so. North America, I think."

The girls separated, walking around the sacred site, exploring by themselves, each drinking in the sublime and majestic surrounds. Sophie walked to the edge of the tree line, traversing the perimeter of the clearing. Fallen twigs, leaves, and other plant matter crunched underfoot as she went. She could hear sounds that invoked memories of a family holiday that the Bainbridge's had taken to North Queensland many years ago when she was just eleven years old. Sounds greeted her like long-lost friends: croaking of frogs, a couple of shrike thrushes whistling melodious phrases to each other, the buzz of dragonflies, and a rather distinctive sound that Sophie had always held close to her heart from the family holiday.

"Did you hear that?" Sophie shouted across the clearing to Jane, who was standing between the stone altar and the massive stone pentagram that lay in the middle of the sacred site.

"What's that?" Jane asked nonchalantly, her attention elsewhere.

"A whip bird." She waited. "There it goes again," she bellowed enthusiastically as the long-drawn crescendo of the whip bird suddenly cracked a like a whip breaking the sound barrier.

"Yeah, I heard it."

"We're not here. We're somewhere else. We travelled to, um, Queensland, maybe. I don't know," Sophie riddled to her friend.

Jane finally broke her concentration to engage the conversation. "What are you talking about?"

"The whip bird, the frogs…"

"Yes?"

"These are all animals from the rainforests of North Queensland, not Tasmania, and how do you explain that I couldn't see the trees over the top of the fallen log. It's impossible. I can't explain it, but suffice to say these animals would not survive in our climate."

"Maybe not, but did you not say before that the trees before you are Huon pines?"

"Yes."

"And if I'm not mistaken, Huon pines are only located in Tasmania. Mainly around the Huon River, are they not?" Jane replied with raised eyebrows and a sarcastic tone.

"Okay, you can drop the bitch routine."

"What now? No, now, how about now? Shall I continue?" she asked as a smile broadened across her face.

"Not yet, wait, okay, now," Sophie replied as they both burst into laughter while Sophie slowly made her way over to where Jane was standing. "Okay, seriously, how do you think it all happens?"

"Soph, you think too much. Some things can't be explained. Sometimes the God and Goddess put things on this earth that can't be enlightened, things that defy common logic, but the closer you look, the more you delve, the more magickal they become and then the more sense they will make."

"I should have known that this place would be a keeper of magick, intrigue, and marvel. Now it's me that feels enlightened, and for some reason, it just makes sense. But why?"

"Because it just does. All you have to do is believe."

"Are you trying to convert me, Jane McKinnon?"

Sophie asked as she turned to stroll over to the black locust tree behind the stone altar.

"Subtly." She laughed. "Why? Is it working?" "Maybe, you never know," she called back.

∞

Jane was standing between the pentagram and the altar. Each was made of rounded rocks taken from rivers whose rushing water over many thousands of years had created beautiful symmetrical shapes whose presence complemented the harmony of rainforest that they had come to reside in. The rocks were placed beside each other creating the star within the circle while the altar was perhaps just over four feet in height with a large flat stone at its apex. When Jane closed her eyes, she could sense the energy of the coven and the many witches who had been there before, but she felt Grace's presence most, especially near the altar. She did not know why she was drawn to it apart from her mother's essence, but it felt right. Maybe she was destined to be a high priestess of a coven. She had tinkered with the idea of joining a coven, but her aunt wouldn't approve—at least she didn't think she would; she'd never asked. A smile grew, and a great sense of belonging overwhelmed her.

She turned to Sophie, who was walking around the black locust, dragging her fingertips across the rough bark while admiring its elegant yet unruly shape. Shards of the bark had been cut away, and the wounds had healed over time, thus proving that no rituals had taken place there for some time.

"Black locust," she whispered as she peered up to its summit. "I shall learn more about you when I get home."

"Be careful of the bark," Jane warned.

"Why?"

"The black locust is poisonous. You can touch it, but you can't digest it any part of it. Otherwise, you will be very sick within an hour."

Sophie walked back to Jane, rubbing her hands together, then wiped them on the sides of her waist. "What can it do?"

"I've been told that anyone who consumes any part of the tree will get signs of nausea, vomiting, and diarrhoea within an hour of consumption, followed possibly by delirium, seizures, coma, and death," she said hesitantly as she watched her companion.

Sophie looked at her hands then glanced at Jane. "Oh, babe, I didn't consume any. I'll be perfectly okay, honestly," she reassured her as she placed an arm around Jane's waist. "Now what was it that you wanted to discuss? It must be of great importance if you needed to be here amongst the relics of the old coven."

"Yes and no. It wasn't so much the coven or the place but rather my mum's presence that I sought the comfort of and yours, as well." She smiled. "But it is serious. I've been warned that I could be in danger from a person referred to as the Red Man but for reasons unknown."

"How do you know this?"

"Aedán told me."

"Jane," Sophie said as she took her hand, "Can you really trust him? I mean you've only known him for such a short while, and, um, he's a talking horse," she teased.

"Yeah, I know how it looks, but there's more to it than that."

The pair sat and discussed the warning and Jane's safety over the next half hour before deciding to trek back to the car and depart for Avalon. Jane was quite open about all that had happened, with the exception of divulging her travels to Emain Albach or meeting any of the other faerie. She didn't feel comfortable trying to explain or possibly defend her actions, not to Sophie, Aunt Claire, or anyone for that matter.

The trip home was uneventful, and the two of them occasionally engaged in small talk when they were not singing along with the songs that happened to be on the radio. Blue Belle slowed as she approached the driveway of Avalon. Turning the wheel, Jane caught a glimpse of someone at the far end of the property walking along the verge of the road towards the driveway, but the figure stopped as the Beetle pulled into the drive. Jane slowed the car as she navigated past the gate. She did not recognise the person, but she could make out a distinctive red jacket and strange hat.

"Did you see that person walking towards us?" Jane asked, keeping an eye on the rear vision mirror as she drove up the drive towards the garage.

"No, I was off in another world. Who was it?"

"I couldn't make out who it was," Jane said anxiously, "but it was someone in a red jacket or coat and a strange hat. You don't think it could be the Red Man, do you?"

"It could be," Sophie said as she opened the door to exit while the car was still moving. "It could be the same guy that we saw down at the Esplanade. I'm going to find out," she finished, shouting back at the car as she ran down the driveway towards the road.

"Wait. Stop, Sophie. Come back," she pleaded, but her companion didn't hear.

Jane watched in the mirror as Sophie ran towards the road, where she slid to a stop, causing a small cloud of dirt to rise from under her feet. Then to Jane's dismay, she turned, ran down the verge, and disappeared.

16

Marching up and down the hall between the main bedroom and the stairs that led to the lower level, the Red Man paced while deep in thought, muttering to himself as he devised his next plan of attack.

"The girl is gone. Claire is gone. This presents another opportunity to get into the house. I must—I must get in, but then what? Wait until they get home? No, no, no, there has to be a better way. Where would they have gone?" he asked himself, walking back into the bedroom. He drew the curtains as far as they would go. A burst of light flooded the room, forcing him to turn his head as if He'd been slapped in the face. Disoriented, he stepped back, lurching towards the bed, where he found purchase to sit while his eyes adjusted. He sat there, rocking back and forth. Every passing moment of inaction agitated him further as he struggled within himself to come to a conclusion. Then he suddenly burst out of his skin like a shell being fired from a cannon. He quickly stepped to the window and surveyed the grounds of Avalon, his mind ticking over at a thousand miles per hour.

"Tribulations be swept from my mind," he declared. "I can sense that the protection cast upon that dwelling is still present. The whereabouts of Claire and that wretched child, unknown. I cannot fail in my quest but concede that I may require the services of the Tainted Ones to succeed."

He sauntered downstairs, retrieved the keys to the car from the kitchen table, and proceeded outside to fetch his stoat-pelt bag of tricks. He had moved the car from the verge and stored it undercover beside the house prior to daybreak to keep it away from prying eyes. However, He'd run out of time to move Carla's vehicle. Re-entering the house, he sat at the table and rifled through the bags until he retrieved a black suede shoestring bag. He untied the binds that kept the bag secured then tipped out seven candles, a skull, a smudge stick, incense, a dish, and a variety of gemstones.

To achieve clarity for the ritual, he closed his eyes and cleared his mind with three slow deep breaths that he held fleetingly before releasing. His goal was to use necromancy to achieve the assistance of the Tainted Ones to call upon a higher beast that roamed the lands of Emain Albach. The Tainted Ones were sullied spirits that looked like shadows, black in colour with crystal-white eyes. They took human form only when still, though when flying, their lower halves stretched to give the impression of a jet stream. They roamed the Wild Lands, a place of the unknown, for no living being had ever returned to tell the tale of their journey there. They, however, could crossover to any realm without using portals or creating wormholes.

He began arranging the candles in a slight semi-circle. His hand moving slowly yet with great purpose, he laid the candles in a strict order and position. The curve of the arrangement had the middle candle at the farthest point away from him. The first colour was black, followed by blue and green. The middle candle was white. This pattern continued in reverse to the end of the semi-circle. He placed the skull in front of the white candle and the spirit incense in front of that. He sat before the arrangement for a minute, his eyes closed, controlling his breathing while lowering his heart rate, concentrating on the task at hand so that he was completely immersed in the moment. Ready to proceed, he picked up the smudge stick, a tightly rolled stick of dried sage and sweet grass tied with natural fibre string. He lit the end with a match that He'd retrieved from his coat pocket. A small flame took hold and quickly doubled in size. He allowed it to burn for a moment before blowing out the flame. The orange embers of the smouldering tip produced a pungent greyish-white smoke that the Red Man waved around the table, over the ritual pieces in random jerky movements. A concentration of smoke gathered above the table and lingered.

He placed the smouldering stick into the dish beside the spirit incense and returned to a still meditative state in front of the candles while the sage and sweet grass smoke settled. When he felt the time to proceed was nigh, he retrieved another match and proceeded to light the candles, beginning with black at the extremities of the circle, moving toward the centre, finishing with the white candle. The Red

Man then lit the spirit incense and placed the assorted gemstones of Amethyst, Celestite, and Rose Quartz around the skull while beginning his chant in Latin.

He meditated while waiting for signs of the Tainted Ones" arrival. A minute passed, and no sign presented itself, yet he did not allow the setback to unsettle his resolve. He repeated the chant.

The passing of the final word from his lips heralded the arrival of the spirits that he sought. First, wind rushed in from the outside the building. Strong and fierce, it whipped around the structure, uprooting trees and throwing loose furnishings in its path as it searched for an entry point. The front door was thrust open, smashing against the wall with such force that the top hinge snapped, the door buckled, and the far bottom edge dropped to the floor. The wind pressed its way into the house and travelled towards the kitchen. The Red Man recognised the success of the ritual then proceeded with the last part of the chant:

The flames on each candle flickered violently as the wind swirled around the table, creating a funnel similar to a tornado. He could make out dark figures with piercing white eyes being swept around him by the squall, yet he remained calm in the eye of the storm, calling for the Tainted Ones to come forward.

"Show yourselves," he yelled towards the vortex, grasping the table to keep himself upright as the churning winds that surrounded him pulled at his limbs. "Show yourselves now," he commanded.

The greyish swirling cloud moved away from the table, dragging unsecured objects deeper into the kitchen. The Red Man could make out the images of two Tainted Ones being whipped around the funnel of the cloud, then one glided out as casual as could be, making a mockery of the dangers of the climatic event from which it was spawned.

The Tainted One approached the table and hovered in front of the Red Man, awaiting instruction from the one who had summoned them.

"Greetings, my ancient friend. Firstly, allow me to thank you for responding to my call," the Red Man said with a bow of his head.

The Tainted One did not respond, as they never spoke but were very adept at reading minds. Their craft had sent many Fey and men to their untimely demises, as their thoughts had revealed their double-crossing ways while they were trying to bargain for the Tainted Ones" services. It was said that anyone unfortunate enough to realise this fate that the Tainted One entered their bodies through the mouth or nose and travel to their lungs. Their chests would balloon in size until they pressed against the rib cage and could grow no more. The pain was said to be so immense that the wretched soul would reel about in agony while the Tainted One continued to press on until the bones crack and splinter. The chest cavity would explode, leaving a fatal wound so deep that the backbone was usually visible. Blood and entrails would litter the surrounds of the body, and the Tainted One would gently rise into the air and hover a moment to appreciate its work.

The Red Man was frank with his possible accomplice. "I am hunting a girl, a girl that is very valuable to me, but she is protected by witches who've cast a protection spell around the property. I have called upon you to travel to Emain Albach to track down the *dullahan*. I request his presence in this realm to travel beyond the walls of the dome that protects the girl's house and bring her to me," he stated in a loud clear voice.

The Tainted One regarded the conjurer briefly then turned to re-join his own kind in the spinning vortex.

The two sets of eyes shining like beacons in rough seas spun faster and faster, the wind picked up wrappers, cups, and anything else that wasn't secured in the kitchen and threw it about. Suddenly, a flash of brilliant-white light exploded in front of him, forming a diamond shape that expanded to at least six feet. It held its shape for two seconds then rapidly closed in on itself to the size of a pinhead. Then it vanished. The vortex and the Tainted Ones were gone. In their place was a mess of scattered objects lying on the bench tops and floor and a grin of anticipation of a plan that was coming together.

He sat for a while, the smoke from the smudge stick and the incense still smouldering on the table as he thought of the end—the end to his search, the end of the plan, the end of his suffering, and a new beginning. He stood from the table with a renewed determination; the anticipation of finally getting his quarry overwhelmed him so much that the prospect of waiting for the *dullahan*'s arrival was unbearable. He paced from one end of the table to the other.

"Damn it." He turned towards the objects on the table. "Just one look."

He extinguished the candles then rose to his feet with a new spring in his step. The Red Man walked to the front door, retrieving his cane as he passed the unhinged door. It was just after midday, two days before Beltane. The October sun was beating down on the bayside community. The sky was blue with nominal clouds accompanied by a mild cooling sea breeze.

"Aye, you wouldn't know a tornado could happen on a day like today." He chuckled to himself while he walked down the drive towards Delta Road.

He reached the verge, being very cautious as he proceeded, as he did not want to draw unnecessary attention to himself. Carla's green vehicle was still parked to the left of the drive, near the advertising sign, which reminded him to move it later in the day. There was no traffic coming in either direction, so he proceeded to cross the road to the corner boundary of Avalon. Once in front of the property, he could sense that the spell was still protecting the house, so he lifted his left hand carefully, palm open and flat. He lowered his appendage slowly until he was sure that he could feel the sheet of magick that prevented his trespass. Suddenly, he ripped his hand through the air. The silvery blue shimmer of the dome rippled as his hand passed over the surface.

He was walking along the fence line towards the gate when he heard the familiar sound of an air-cooled engine in the distance approaching him from the east. He froze.

Should I run? The car got closer and closer.

"There has to be more than one of those cars in this town, surely," he said trying to convince himself. He stood motionless, facing the oncoming sound of the vehicle. "This could be the opportunity I need to get in—if I'm not discovered."

The hum of the V-Dub grew louder and louder. He stood still, fists clenched, wishing himself to be as small as possible then the blue car became visible over the rise half a kilometre down the road. He recognised the car as Jane's, and while remaining steadfast, he turned his face from the vehicle.

Hearing the high-pitched squeal of the brakes, he tilted his head to one side to see the car in his peripheral vision slowing at the entry to the property. He saw two females in the vehicle. The passenger had not seen him, yet he could feel the burning glare of the driver as the vehicle slowed to a crawl before driving up the gravel driveway.

"*Cac,* my presence has been compromised." As the words parted his lips, he heard a female shouting, "Come back!"

The crunching of footsteps running on gravel was his cue to make a quick getaway as he turned towards the road. His foot slipped underneath on the loose ground as he tried to run, his cane tucked into the pit of his arm. He did not look for approaching traffic as he retreated across the asphalt, keeping an eye over his left shoulder as he ran towards Carla's car. His right hip struck the rear fender as he threw himself to the ground, taking cover behind the vehicle. He winced as a dull throb coursed through his side. It intensified when he stretched on his haunches to peer through the glass windows of the vehicle. He saw a young female with blonde hair appear from the driveway. She slid to a stop while changing direction then proceeded to run down the verge along the fence line to where the Red Man was standing. He watched her with great curiosity. *Who is this girl? Could I use her to barter for the other girl?* New contingency plans were hatching in his mind.

The Red Man saw his opportunity and stood bent at the hip behind the car, waiting for the girl to turn her back to him. He moved slowly around the vehicle, keeping it between himself and her to obscure any line of sight that she may have. He focused everything on that moment. Adrenaline surged through his veins, and a heightened sense of euphoria released endorphins into his body. He tracked her movements closely, sensing that she was lacking physically as she was bent over trying to catch her breath.

She stood and pirouetted, her back to him. She muttered something inaudible and took her first step back towards the house. His stare was fixated on her when he straightened his spine to step out from behind the vehicle. He felt a rush of wind on the back of his neck, his flesh being pierced, deep into his shoulder blades that sent a rush pain to the receptors in his brain. He flailed backwards, the red Paris Beau falling from his head as he contorted his body, twisting, arms trying to slap at his attacker. Immense pain washed over him, forcing a loud shrill to bust from his lungs. He stumbled, rolling his ankle on the uneven ground as he fell behind the vehicle.

The Red Man struggled to roll onto his back; something had attached itself to him. Its claws gouged into his flesh while tearing at his neck and ears. Veins popped in his temple as he garnered all his strength to put the accoster between himself and the ground. He could feel the resistance of the body underneath him as he pushed down repeatedly. The relentless pressure triggered a release of the claws that tore at his flesh. An immediate discharge of pressure came over him, allowing the Red Man to roll towards the vehicle as a cloud of feathers levitated in the space that they just occupied. He recognised his attacker as the same *ulchabhán* that had swooped him the previous day. It sat on the ground, its large black pupils surrounded by a fiery ring of yellow brimming with contempt as its stare pierced him.

Rage thundered through his body. Warm blood oozed from his wounds, soaking the black shirt under his coat.

He salivated at the prospect of plucking the feathers from the *ulchabhán* one by one then snapping its neck and watching its essence drain from its eyes as it died in his hands. He was on knees when he came face to face with the owl. He could see that it was injured from the struggle. He also realised that this was his time to eliminate this feathered adversary. Slowly, he lifted himself to his feet, his hands extended and ready to grab his prey. The owl hopped away, keeping the same distance between the Red Man and itself.

"I'm going to get you, you bastard," he cursed as he prepared himself.

The owl screeched an angry hoot back. The Red Man dove at the owl, arms outstretched and aiming for the animal's throat. The owl hopped to one side then lifted itself into the air as a flurry of feathers were cast into flight. The displaced air swirled, creating lift as its wings stretched outwards and pushed down. The Red Man felt as if he were reaching in slow motion above his despairing dive to catch a handful of feathers in his right hand as he crashed into dirt and gravel of the verge.

"Fuck you, *ulchabhán*."

17

The white Magna eased to a stop outside a grey-weatherboard single-story cottage on Reserve Road. It was one of the smaller, quieter tree-lined streets in town. Claire gathered her bag and exited the vehicle, stopping on the footpath to admire the property that stood before her. It had the cliché picket fence, although this one had never been painted. The grey timber was weathered, worn, and aged with the odd paling missing from the rails. A path constructed of fading red pavers meandered from the curb to the front gate and beyond. Beside the gate was a white letterbox that bore a gold pentagram and the number eight. The property as a whole was decorated in all forms of eccentric paraphernalia.

The front courtyard beyond the gate was a recreation of an English cottage garden. Massed planted colour took up most of the garden around a large pond and wishing well on the left of the path. The garden was dotted with garden figurines hidden amongst the snapdragons, bellflowers, columbine, coral-bells, daisies, dianthus, irises, and foxgloves. Dozens of little statues of fairies and pixies frolicked in permanent cement poses. On the right of the garden was an old apple tree—she didn't recognise the variety, but it was smaller than the one back at Avalon. Underneath the tree was an old bronze cauldron tipped on its side with ash spilling from its mouth. Claire was in awe of the landscape in front of her. It was picture perfect, right down to the array of trinkets hanging from the bottom branches of the tree. Smudge sticks, wands, pentagrams, charcoal burners—she even saw an old athame. Any amount of anxiety Claire felt when she walked through the gate was immediately replaced with serenity.

She stepped up to the landing and pulled an old rope that sounded three times on the timeworn brass bell. The house belonged to Gwendolyn Ismay. An elder of the Weathered Stone coven, she was a close friend of both Grace and Claire. She'd became the high priestess of the coven after Grace's death. After Grace's death, the coven existed only in secrecy, thriving and meeting at different locations within Delta and out at Freya for special rituals and sabbats. Claire could hear footsteps on a wooden floor getting louder as they approached the door. Then they stopped, and metal clicked as the tumbler in the lock switched open. The large wooden door was pulled open. A tall slender woman wearing a high-tea floral dress with flowing ginger hair that fell over the shoulder answered the door.

"Merry Meet, Claire," Gwen said as she stood behind the open door.

"Merry Meet, Gwen. Thank you for seeing me at such short notice."

"Yes, yes. No problem at all. Come in please," she said, motioning her left hand. "Is everything okay?"

"I think we have a problem, Gwen," Claire said dourly as she walked through the front door and into the sitting room.

"Eerin."

"Yes."

"How do you know?"

"Jane had a visit the other night, from a Fai…" She paused, thinking that maybe it was best to keep some things secret before continuing. "From a fellow who warned that she was in danger from the Red Man."

"No, who was this person?" she asked curiously. "Oh, Claire, how rude of me—please take a seat. You were saying who he was."

Claire sat down in a recliner upholstered in an old print of red garden roses. A smell of musk wafted up from the cushion when her weight pressed against it. The smell reminded her of her own grandparents.

"I don't know. She hadn't met him before that encounter," Claire said, trying to keep a blank expression so as to not give away that she wasn't being entirely truthful.

"What exactly did he say? You know the warning!"

"He said that darkness has dragged itself into this realm in search of a pureness, an essence. He later referred to that darkness as the Red Man."

"How very bizarre, and he meant that that pureness was Jane? Do you think that it's credible?"

"I think so, as Jane also mentioned that both she and Sophie had seen a man about town in a strange red outfit. They hadn't seen him before, and we both know who wears that type of apparel."

"Yes, you're right, but I thought we'd banished him for good."

"So did I, but we are also responsible for making him powerful, as well."

"But we weren't to know that when we initiated him into the coven, were we?"

"No, I guess we weren't," Claire lamented.

"Do you have a plan?" Gwen asked.

"Mmm, I'm not sure. I've already cast a protection spell over Avalon, but I wanted to seek your counsel and perhaps that of the coven before I proceed."

"Very good, you've done the right thing, but the protection spell won't keep him at bay for long, nor do I think that we need to consult the coven just yet," Gwen said confidently as she stood from her seat. "I think we need to consult my Book of Shadows first. Would you like a drink while I'm up?" she asked.

"Um, just water if you don't mind. Thanks."

"Sure thing," Gwen replied as she turned to depart the room.

As Jane watched her leave, she sat back further into the chair. Once she relaxed, the framed artwork hanging around the room drew her eyes. There were many canvases, both oil and colour sketches, all depicting Wiccan scenes of sabbats, circle castings, Gods, and Goddesses. Her favourite was an oil painting of the Goddess, naked, her long blonde hair draped over her left shoulder, covering one breast while she sat upon a full moon, her legs tucked under her and hands spread out as she cast silvery rays of light out into the universe.

"Okay, I think we have an option, Claire," Gwen said as she marched back into the room, her Book of Shadows open in the palms of both hands. "Have a read of this while I'll go back into the kitchen and get you a water."

"Are you sure?" she asked, looking up at her, wide eyed. "Your BOS is such a personal thing."

Gwen laughed. "Of course I'm sure. Look, normally I'd agree, the Book of Shadows is a personal account, record, and diary of a witch, but in this case, lives are at stake. Besides, the world isn't going to come crashing down if you read a page or two."

"Well, under the circumstances…" Claire reached forward awkwardly to take the large book.

"Take your time. I'll get that drink."

"Okay, thanks."

Gwen turned and exited the room again as Claire scanned the open pages before her. Gwen's Book of Shadows was larger than most, and each page was the equivalent of an A3 piece of paper. The dark brown leather-bound book had two lighter-toned straps sewn onto the outside to secure the cover. The sepia pages were relatively thicker than she was used to while the words themselves seemed to flow effortlessly across the page, written with black ink in an older formal style font that reminded her of French script.

She began reading the description of the pages contents; it was a combination of a binding and banishing spell in one. The spell came with a warning.

If you have the need to cast this spell,
Be pure of heart or time will tell.
Banish all evil, dark ones to quell.
If not, law by thrice will be hell.

She continued to read on—the explanation, items required, how to cast the spell, innovations to be made. It was an involved spell that required many items, including one more essential than the others. Gwen returned to the room with a large glass of water and biscuits on a white porcelain tray, which she put down on the side table between hers and Claire's chair.

"Thanks for that," Claire said as she looked up from the book. "Are you not having a drink?"

"No. I just finished a tea before you arrived. What do you think? It's not a spell that is used lightly, hence the warning, but it is an effective one."

"Have you used it yourself?"

"Well, no. Not exactly, but I've been told that it is quite good by an acquaintance over in the States down Georgia way."

Claire sat silently for a moment, contemplating her options before she answered. "This is a dangerous spell to cast, Gwen. I don't want it to come back to me threefold, you know."

"I understand, Claire. We can keep looking for other options if you like," she offered.

"No, I don't think we have the luxury of time in this matter, but if it was you…" She paused to take a moment to prevent herself from getting into a tizz. "Do you trust them?"

"Well, put it this way. If I was over there and needed help, she would probably be the first person I'd turn to in a crisis."

"Okay, that's all I need to hear. Any other advice?"

"Right. Yeah, I was just coming to that." Gwen hesitated as she looked Claire in the eye. "I have complete faith in you—you know that, right?"

"Yeah," Claire replied cautiously. "There's a catch coming, isn't there?"

"Well sort of. The trick to the spell being successful is that it has to be delivered orally."

"You're kidding me, right? How am I supposed to do that? Get him to say "Arrr" and hope that he swallows it?"

"That part I can't help with, but if you let your intuition and natural gift for the craft guide you, then you'll be successful in your endeavours."

"Thanks for the vote of confidence. Did you want to join me for the ritual?"

"I'd love to, Claire, but I have to travel to Swansea this afternoon. I do apologise," Gwen replied sincerely.

"That's okay. I probably should do it myself anyway."

"So you know everything that you have to do?"

"Yes, I have it all committed to memory. I think I'll stop by home and grab a few supplies and then head out to Freya."

"Sounds good. I will have my mobile with me if you need me."

"I should be all right, but thanks anyway," Claire replied politely with a smile as she reached for the glass of water to quench her dry throat. "I wanted to say that your house is simply marvellous, as well. Just a little different from when I was here last."

"Thanks. Yes, I've been pottering about, fixing this and changing that, but I'm happy. That's the main thing, right? My sanctuary." Gwen chuckled with outstretched arms.

"We all need our sacred place to retreat to, don't we?" Claire returned the glass to rest on the porcelain tray. "But I'd best be on my way. There's so much to prepare and so little time."

Claire got up from the chair and turned to Gwen. "Thank you so much for seeing me, Gwen. I'm hoping that this spell is a real success."

"We all are, Claire. Just remember to do the full ritual. The Gods will ensure that the intent of the spell is realised," she replied as she leant in to hug her friend. "I'll call you tonight to check in and make sure that everything is okay, but don't be afraid to call me if you need help. You have my number." She rubbed Claire's back prior to releasing her hold.

"I sure will. Blessed be, Gwen," Claire replied as she opened the front door.

"Blessed be, Claire, and favourable castings."

"Thank you, Gwen. I'll speak to you later about Beltane, as well," she called as she reached the gate.

Gwen stood at the open door, waving to Claire as she stepped into the vehicle. She tarried there for a minute, going over the spell in her mind, organising what she had to do and what she had to get. She decided that since she was already in town, she would drive back to the shop and grab the required items for her ritual there and drive straight out to Freya without calling back into Avalon.

She started the ignition and pulled away from the curb. Claire guided the car into the stop at Civic Park and cut the engine as she released her seatbelt. From the glove box, she retrieved a pad and pencil. One by one, she created the list while the items were still fresh in her min: athame, incense, charcoal burner, black candles, plain paper, and pencil. Reading it aloud, she wrote them down. Satisfied that she had everything she needed, she exited the car and walked briskly towards the shop.

"Hey, Claire. I thought you weren't going to open today," Abigail called out as she saw her friend approach.

"I'm not. Just need to get a few things." Claire hurried past Abigail, who was wiping down the outside tables.

"Oh, is everything okay? Can I do something to help?"

"No, it's okay. Thanks for asking, though." She fumbled with her keys outside the locked door to the Silver Moon, "I'm only going to be a couple of minutes, and then I'll be on my way, but I'll be open tomorrow. So I'll see you then," she offered with a smile.

"All right, then have a good night."

"Will do, Abby. Blessed be," Claire replied as the barrel of the lock turned. She pushed the roller door open, allowing the light to flood through the glass door and into the darkened space behind.

She flicked the light switch and walked straight to the counter at the back of the shop, where she retrieved a bag from under the desk. She marked off items on her list as she placed them in the bag: calico charm bag, string, cauldron, matches, chalice, and knife.

"Altar clothes—where have they gone?" She rifled through an assortment of pentagram-inlayed garments used for both ritual and home decoration. She was beginning to get agitated, cussing as each turn didn't reveal their location. She tossed items aside haphazardly in her attempt to get in and out as quickly as possible.

"It's got to be here." She stopped, hands still on the garments in front of her, and surveyed the shop. Then the penny dropped. "I was out of stock, but the new order came in three days ago and is still boxed up in storage out the back. Where is my mind today?" She walked through the curtain to the back storeroom.

Satisfied that she had acquired everything required to perform the spell, Claire retreated from the shop, closing and locking the door behind her.

"That was quick," a voice said behind her as she shook the door to check that it was properly secured. Claire turned to see Abby standing there, cleaning cloth in hand and a broad smile upon her face.

"I did say I'd only be a couple of minutes."

"And true to your word, as always." She giggled. "Have a good night then, Claire."

"You, too, Abby," Claire replied as Abby walked back into the Froth n Stuff. "Oh, Abby. Abby—" she called as she realised she'd forgotten something.

"Yes."

"I forgot to ask if you have any cake that I could buy."

"I sure do. You have a choice of chocolate or carrot. Which do you fancy?"

"Oh, my two favourites. I haven't had a good carrot cake in some time, but I'll stick to chocolate today, but maybe next time."

"Yeah, sure. I'll go get it for you. Just the one slice?"

"Yes, thanks. Oh, and Abby," she called again, "sorry to be a bother, but do you have any wine, as well?

"Yeah, I think there is a bottle of Sav in the kitchen that we use for cooking."

"Do you mind if I get a glass?"

"You can have the bottle if you want," she offered. "What's the occasion?"

"Oh, nothing really. Just can't be fussed going into the pub. That's all," Claire explained.

"I'll go get them for you, but you'll have to hide the wine as I'm not licensed and can't afford to be caught supplying liquor."

"Of course."

Abby returned moments later with the cake packaged in a small takeaway box and the wine concealed in a shopping bag. "There you go," she said as she offered the items to Claire.

"Thanks a bunch, Abby. I'll replace the wine for you."

"Don't think anything of it. Just tell me the story one day."

"The story?" Claire asked.

"You know, the new man." She smirked with a wink.

Claire convulsed as her body reacted by trying to laugh and choke on air at the same time at the surprise of hearing such a statement. "A man? No, I don't think so," she managed.

"You don't shut the store and get cake and wine for no reason, but I'm patient. You'll tell me sooner or later."

"You're evil, Abby," Claire replied cheerfully. "Thanks for this, as well. Have a great afternoon," she called as she turned to walk back to the car.

"Have a good one!"

"Blessed be."

Claire started the car and looked over her left shoulder to make sure that her inventory sat safely on the rear seat as she clicked the seatbelt into position. Feeling reassured, she put the vehicle into gear and drove off down the Esplanade on her way to Freycinet.

After twenty minutes and an uneventful trip, Claire pulled into the Wineglass Bay car park. All was quiet with the exception of an elderly couple walking back to their car. *Must have been on a morning stroll.* Claire reached behind her to gather the bags and cake. After they had departed, Claire exited the car and locked the door behind her. The sun was suspended high in the sky, and it was a mild twenty degrees Celsius with a soft breeze blowing across the carpark. Claire, bags in hand and sunglasses on, walked towards the trail that led to Wineglass Bay. She played out the ritual in her mind as she went, until she reached the fallen tree with the red cross painted on its trunk.

She could hear voices approaching from around the bend—Asian of some description. She decided not to risk being seen walking off the track and kept walking towards the voices. She rounded the bend in the track, and to her shock, she nearly walked into a man of Asian descent dressed in jeans, a dark blue polo shirt, and a baseball cap.

"Oh, sorry, excuse me," she apologised, embarrassed that she had nearly knocked the man over.

He just smiled at her then bowed.

Claire attempted to return the bow with an awkward smile and realized that she was surrounded by a tourist group. *Must be Japanese.* She straightened her back.

"*Sayonara,*" the tourist said as he stepped around her and continued along the track with the rest of the group.

Claire watched them disappear around the bend and thought that she might keep walking for a minute or two before doubling back to the log. She started off and got only ten metres when the sounds of the birds and wind rustling through the trees were interrupted by someone with a foreign accent calling out, "Wait wait!"

Claire froze as a twinkling of dread overwhelmed her. *What do they want? Did I look that suspicious?*

Footsteps approached her from behind. She took a deep breath and turned slowly to see the same man jogging back to her, holding something in his right hand, which he held out front of him as he approached, breathing heavily. *He mustn't be very fit.*

"*Shitsurei shimasu,*" he said between breaths.

She didn't know what he was saying as her Japanese was very limited, and she couldn't read his expressions.

He pushed the object forward at her.

Following his eye along his arm to his hand, she recognised the charcoal burner as hers. "Oh!"

She reached forward and took it from him, "Thank you. Thank you so much," she said, offering a bow.

He smiled fervently, reciprocating the bow while Claire tried to remember the little Japanese she knew.

Stuttering at first, she struggled with the pronunciation. "*A… ari… arigatou gozaimasu.*"

The man looked at her with an infectious smile and bowed one last time before he turned and disappeared around the corner to re-join his party. *That was nice of him.*

She looked at the burner, flipping it from side to side in her hand as she inspected it.

In that moment, it dawned upon her to question how He'd come to have it. *It must have fallen out of the bag.* "Shit!" she blurted as she pulled the bag from the ground to inspect its integrity. The left side was okay. She turned the bag over to see a rip that was at least five inches across. "Bugger!" she cursed as she ransacked the bag, counting her tools, making sure that nothing else had fallen out.

In the time it took her to check her inventory, the tourist group had travelled far away. The sounds of the bush had returned, and Claire found herself alone again on the track, the sun's touch warm against her skin. She was annoyed that the bag had a hole in it, but her encounter with the Japanese man had reaffirmed her faith in the sincerity of people amidst the turmoil that her family found itself in. She looked at the sky, drinking in the rays of light and allowing its energies to reinvigorate her soul and freshen her outlook on the task. A sense of joy and purpose overcame her as she held the bag to her chest and marched around the bend, back down the track towards the fallen tree.

Claire trudged along, looking down the straights of the track before her. She couldn't see the carpark, but she saw no one else on the track when she arrived at the fallen tree. She stopped, checked behind her one last time, and stepped off the track. Pushing the white kunzeas aside, Claire crouched down on all fours, shoved the bags along the ground in front of her, and crawled underneath the log. On the other side, she rose to her feet, dusting the dirt and debris from her knees. The clearing in front of her was like an old friend, and each time they met, Claire felt as if she'd come home. She stood, absorbing the beauty and ambience of the sacred place before her, filling her lungs with the cool crisp air of the rainforest.

"Merry Meet, Freya," she called as she greeted the tree from across the ritual site. "I trust you'll look over me today," she said with an adoring smile as she moved towards the stone altar.

Claire placed the bags on the ground and began the preparations for the ritual. She took the knife from the bag and approached the tree. She examined the trunk, moving around its girth until she found a piece of bark that suited the spells requirements. She held the knife against the bark, the blade's edge facing the underside of Claire's grip as she leaned into the trunk, tilting her head slightly so that she could whisper into her ear. Not until she had sought permission and explained the purpose for taking the bark did she begin the cut. She sliced away three suitably sized pieces of bark then thanked Freya for her contribution and returned to the altar, where she unpacked the bags.

When everything was laid out, Claire began the task of placing everything where it needed to be. The altar was inside the northern cardinal and high point of the pentagram. She laid the altar cloth over the stone construction then placed black candles at the cardinal points and put the cauldron in the centre, where she would cast the circle.

Claire stood up and stepped ten paces towards the tree line on the edge of the clearing. She looked back upon the magick, the vessel that she believed would protect and save Jane from the Red Man. She closed her eyes and prepared herself by controlling her breathing and visualizing what she needed to do. Mentally prepared, she strode forward to begin the rite.

She knelt in front of the items laid out on the ground, picked up the water bottle, and emptied a large amount of its contents into the silver chalice—her first task was to consecrate the water. She held the filled chalice aloft in both hands at eye level and recited:

"Blessings upon thee, O creature of water,

I cast out from thee all impurities and uncleanliness of the spirits of phantasm,

Confusion, or any other influence not for the free will of all."

She placed the chalice to one side and reached for the dish and salt. After pouring the latter into the dish, she held it at eye level.

"Blessings be upon this creature of salt,

Let all malignity and hindrance be cast forth hence from, and let all good enter therein.

Wherefore, I bless thee and invoke thee, that thou mayst aid me."

Claire lowered her arms then took the dish in her left hand as she picked up the chalice again with her right. She poured a small amount of water from the silver chalice into the dish holding the salt and swirled the base of the dish in her hand to gently mix the ingredients.

"I take this salt of the earth,

blessed with the will of fire;

I take this water of spirit,

exorcised with mind of merit.

I mix them with words of power,

Dedicated to every tower.

By the power of spirit, earth, and sea,

God and Goddess are part of one,

As I will, so mote it be!"

Claire set the dish and chalice on the ground in front of her and rose to her feet in silence. The forest sang around her as she bent to pick up the chalice and walked to the tree line, where a snapped branch on the lower reaches of a Huon pine, perhaps broken many years before, made for a good clothes hook. Claire put the chalice down once again and began to remove her clothing, one piece at a time, hanging it on the tree. The activity of the creatures that called the clearing home suddenly became louder; the energy of the place heightened as if reacting to the natural beauty of the naked body as Claire, with chalice in both hands, walked slowly to the base of the black locust. Claire's body was in great shape for her age, and the rays of light that broke into the clearing through the canopy above accented her beauty. Claire stood facing Freya; she had one last thing to consecrate—herself. She began to pour the blessed water from the silver chalice over her skyclad body, washing away all impurities.

Claire re-entered the ritual site, beads of water sliding down the length of her body, others being dislodged as she moved. She picked up the matches and lit each of the black candles at the four cardinals. Claire was ready and about to begin the most important and dangerous spell she had ever attempted, yet she would have the assistance of the towers as they guarded her circle during the rite and the presence and blessing of the God and Goddess through the ritual process. She was battling her nerves because of the importance of her spell, yet her confidence and determination to protect her niece kept the jitters at bay. Claire picked up the athame and stood facing the stone altar draped with the pentagram-inlayed cloth. She unsheathed the tool and saluted both the sky and earth before walking to the black candle that marked the east cardinal. There, she raised her athame and called out:

"Summoning, Guardians of the Watchtowers of the East,

Element of Air!
I invoke you, I demand you,
Aquila of the Dawn,
Night Glider,
Tornado,
Rising Sun, Approach,
Send forth your radiance,
Be here now!"

As Claire summoned the watchtower to guard the circle, she traced an invoking pentagram in the air with the athame. The symbolism of the act was so intense that Claire saw the pentagram like a glowing pale blue flame suspended in front her. It opened at the centre, allowing a rush of wind to pass through, pushing against her, drying her skin, and creating a tangled mess of her hair. She breathed in deeply, drawing in the power, and then she earthed the force within her through the athame, which she pointed at the ground. She walked towards the south cardinal, tracing a curved line from the eastern to southern points as she began to cast her circle. Once there, Claire stopped, faced the black candle marking the cardinal, and called out:

"Summoning, Guardians of the Watchtower of the South,

Element of Fire!

I invoke you, I demand you, Snake of the Midday heat, Glowing One!

Midsummer's warmth,

Ember of life, Approach,

Send forth your spark,

Be here now!"

Her athame still earthed to the ground before her, she continued to trace the circle on the ground as she proceeded to the candle marking the west cardinal point.

"Summoning, Guardians of the Watchtower of the West, Element of Water!

I invoke you, I demand you,

Water Dragon,

Bringer of rain,

Slater of Day,

Morning Star, Approach,

Send forth your swell,

Be here now!"

Claire, unfaltering in her practice, kept tracing the circle to the last of the cardinal points. She stopped in front of the last black candle, which marked the northern point of the circle.

"Summoning, Guardians of the Watchtower of the North,

Element of Earth,

Foundation of all Influence

I invoke you, I demand you,

Lady of the Devine,

Mask of Darkness,

Guiding Star,

Soaring Mountain,

Bountiful Pasture, Approach,

Send forth your strength,

Be here now!"

Claire continued to follow the curvature of the circle, her athame still pointed at the earth as she traced the line from the north to the east cardinal to complete the circle.

"Wherefore do I bless thee and consecrate thee, in the names of

Cernunnos and Cerridwen."

Claire gently placed the athame on the ground at the east cardinal in front of the burning black candle. Turning to the altar, she retrieved the dish holding the mixture of consecrated salt and water. She held this in her left hand, and standing inside the circle at the cardinal, she took a pinch with her right thumb and index finger and began to seal the circle by sprinkling the salt along its circumference while reciting aloud:

"By brew of earth and water, I seal the sacred circle, Joining air and fire!

By brew of earth and air, I seal the sacred circle,

Joining fire with water!

By brew of earth, air, and fire, I seal the sacred circle,

Joining water with the earth!

As the four directions are brought to merge,

Let influence of the powerful ones converge!"

Tracing her previous steps, Claire, with great concentration, completed the sealing of the circle when she finished back at the east cardinal, but her casting was not yet complete. Placing the dish back at the altar, she picked up the incense and matches to seal the circle with a censer. She returned to the cardinal, holding the incense while cupping the matches as she struck the first match against the flint. She could have lit the incense from the existing flame that flickered back and forth on the black candle; however, Claire did not want to risk disturbing the Watchtower. The flame caught, and she quickly moved the end of the incense into the flame and let it be consumed. She held it in the orange-and-blue flame for twenty seconds until she was satisfied that it was well lit. She separated the two, extinguishing the match then the flame at the end of the incense.

The spirit incense released a fragrant greyish smoke into the air. When it was smouldering to her satisfaction, she commenced tracing the circle again, starting at the east cardinal, and travelled in a deosil fashion while chanting aloud:

"With incense and the power of mind,

East to South, I do bind!

With incense and the power of mind,

South to West, I do bind!

With incense and the power of mind,

West to North, I do bind!

With incense and the power of mind,

North to East, completion I find!"

Claire's impatience swelled—she was eager to start the spell and have it cast, but she had the power within her to suppress such feelings, to put the greater good before her own needs, and get the job done with faltering. She turned to the altar for the third time, this time, to retrieve the white candle. Cupping her hands around the wick, she struck the match and lit the candle, which was far easier to light than the incense. She commenced the last of her sealing rites for the circle as she positioned herself to walk clockwise again from the east point.

"With the fire of emotion and will,

East to South, our dedication fulfil! With the fire of veneration and will,

South to West, our allegiance fulfil!

With the fire of devotion and will,

West to North, our consecration fulfil!

With the fire of commitment and will,

From North to East, this inscription fulfil!

Within the circle, all wills be free.

The circle is sealed, so mote it be!"

Claire returned the candle to the altar, placing it on the ground, still alight. Its flame danced to the sounds of the forest that surrounded it while the smoke from the incense rose in the air to kiss the underbelly of the canopy above. She picked up the athame, saluted the sky and earth one more time, and turned to the cauldron in the centre of the circle. Touching the lip of its mouth with the tip of the athame, she announced aloud for the creatures of the forest to hear:

"The circle is cast. I am between the worlds. Beyond the bounds of time, where night and day, birth and death, joy and sorrow meet as one."

Claire stood beside the cauldron, the athame still in hand at her side. A faint shimmer of the blue flame into the air above the circle. Claire finally felt safe from the world, protected within the circle as she was surrounded by a sense of calm and a definitive silence. Everything was shut out; even the sounds of the forest were completely gone. Though she stood there naked, she felt anything but vulnerable. She turned from the cauldron to the altar, placed the athame back into it sheath, and laid it the ground with the other tools.

Claire ticked each task off a mental list that she visualized between each chant. It was time for her to invoke the God and Goddess and request their presence at the circle. She drew a couple of deep breaths to centre herself then began the invocation:

"O Mighty Cerridwen,

Queen of the Gods,

Beacon of the Night,

Maker of all that is natural and free,

Mother of man and woman,

Lover of the Horned God

Descend, I pray,

With your lunar ray of power,

upon my circle here!

O Mighty Cernunnos,

King of the Gods,

Lord of the Sun,

Dominant of all that is natural and free,

Lover of the Moon Goddess,

Descend, I pray,

with your solar ray of power,

upon my circle here!"

Satisfied that she could feel the warmth of their presence within the circle, Claire smiled. The further into the ritual she got, the more confident she grew that its outcome would be a success and that Jane's safety would be reassured. With this in mind, Claire proceeded with the spell itself to bind and banish the Red Man for good. She gathered the charcoal burner, paper, pencil, matches, calico bag, string, and bark, arranging them in front of her. On the paper, she wrote the name of the person she wanted to banish then held it out in front of her.

"Silas O'Fihelly, I cast you out.

I send you forth.

Let no one protect.

Let no one defend. Your rule of force, Is no more.

So mote it be…"

She then placed the piece of paper on the charcoal burner and took the matches. She struck one against the flint, cupping the match in her hands until the flame was well alight. Her concentration did not waver as she dropped the match onto the paper. The flame ignited the paper at its edge and was ablaze within a couple of seconds. Growing, the flame advanced in an arc as Claire watched it consume the written name upon the paper. The blue-and-orange flare left a trail that turned black and crumbled until it burnt out, leaving ash and a plume of smoke in its wake. She then picked up the three portions of bark, broke them into smaller fragments, dropped them into the burner to mix with the ash, and tipped the entire contents into the calico bag. The bag was very small, about the size of a teabag, and Claire tied it off while reciting the final chant.

"I hold the means of your dismay

Until your cruelty goes away.

As you are cruel,

In Locust I bind.

Your fate in bark, you shall find.

So mote it be…"

It was done. A sense of relief washed over Claire as she placed the bag on top of the burner. She took a moment to look around her—everything was silent within the circle, but beyond the blue haze, the branches of the trees moved back and forth gently. A lizard scurried between the circle and the black locust tree, disappearing into the undergrowth of the far tree line. Claire grabbed the cake and wine. She unwrapped the takeaway box to look upon a moist piece of chocolate cake. She uncorked the wine and poured half a glass into the empty chalice. It was customary to thank and make an offering to the Gods when they were called to a circle. It was also a great time to reflect on the spell that had been cast, to contemplate the powers of the universe at work, ensuring that her spell work would be fruitful. Claire held the chalice to the sky.

"Gracious Goddess of Abundance,

Bless this wine and immerse it with your love.

In your names, Cernunnos and Cerridwen,

I bless this wine."

She took a sip of wine and placed the chalice on the ground; she then took the cake from the box and held it aloft.

"Powerful God of the Harvest,

Bless these cakes and immerse them with your love.

In your names, Cernunnos and Cerridwen,

I bless this cake."

Claire broke a piece of cake from the corner and dug a hole in the earth before her. When it was an inch deep, she placed the corner of cake into the hole and poured a small amount of the red wine over it. She covered them both with the displaced earth.

"O Mighty Cernunnos,

O Mighty Cerridwen,

I thank thee for thy presence

Receive my humble offering of cake and wine.

With kindness of heart and athame in hand,

I conclude the circle, drawing back the power from Earth and sand.

Blessed be."

Claire felt a soft breeze against her skin the moment the circle was released. She looked up at Freya, who stood proudly in front of her, and the blue haze of the circle that was protecting her was no longer visible while the sounds of the forest returned to her ears. Claire sat at peace with the world in that moment and consumed the remainder of the cake then washed it down with the rest of the wine.

After fifteen minutes of reflection, Claire decided that it was time to pack up. She returned to the tree line to put her clothes on before turning around to put all of the ritual tools back in the bags from which they had come. The last item that she picked up was the calico bag, or "charm" as she referred to it. This would remain in her hand, as it was too precious to be trusted to a bag that could spring a leak.

"Thank you for allowing me to practice beneath your gaze today," she said to Freya with a bow prior to turning her back on the tree.

18

Jane turned the key, killing Blue Belle's engine as she pulled the car to a stop and jumped out the driver's-side door in what seemed to be one formulated movement. She ran down the drive, calling after Sophie, but she got no response.

"Oh, Soph, where are you?" she managed in pained anguish between deep gasps of air, but there was no answer. Sophie wasn't waiting for her at the end of the drive. Jane drew a last deep breath as she reached the gate and held it as she convinced herself to turn the corner to leave the protection of Avalon. Was it the Red Man she had seen? *Where is Sophie? Has he hurt her?*

"Am I imagining the whole thing?" she asked herself as she closed her eyes and turned the corner, not knowing what to expect.

"Hey, you," Sophie called.

Jane opened her eyes. "Soph, what the hell were you thinking?" she yelled as she raised an open hand to her. "You scared the shit out of me. What if it was the Red Man?

You could have been hurt!" she reprimanded her friend as a tear rolled down her right cheek.

"Geez, babe, I didn't think, but whoever it was, they're gone now," Sophie replied, seeming aloof to Jane's feelings.

"I'm not happy, Soph."

"Yeah, I know, and I'm sorry. I was just trying to protect you. That's all."

Jane sensed the sincerity in Sophie's voice and sighed. "Oh, Soph, I'm sorry that I snapped at you. I was just agonized that you could have been hurt or possibly worse!" "Well, I wasn't, so it ended well." She laughed.

"Yeah." Jane smiled. "Let's go back up to the house, where it's safe."

"Sounds good. Race you," Soph yelled as she sprung into a trot.

"You win," Jane replied as she walked behind. She had no intention of running. "I've already had my exercise today!"

They both went inside and sat at the kitchen table, talking candidly about throwaway topics—like boyfriends, going out, and shopping—while enjoying a pizza and garlic bread that Jane had taken from the freezer and cooked fifteen minutes earlier.

"We should have put on some music as background noise while we chatted."

"Yeah, that would have been good," Sophie added. "Where was Aunt Claire today?" she asked as she started on the last piece of pizza.

"She was off to see a friend."

"Okay, that's nice," she replied quickly.

"She should be home soon, actually," Jane continued. "Did you want the last garlic bread?"

"No, that's okay."

Minutes later, the white Mitsubishi Magna turned into the driveway and eased to a stop beside Blue Belle. Claire cut the engine and opened the door. She released the seatbelt while looking over her shoulder at the bags of tools on the backseat; however, her attention returned to the charm bag that rode shotgun.

"I'll get you later," she said to herself looking towards the backseat one last time before getting out.

She didn't forget the charm bag, though. Holding it tightly in her left hand, she walked at a quick pace towards the door. Inside, Jane was sitting at the table by herself.

"Merry Meet, Aunt Claire," Jane said as she looked from her plate while picking off the last pieces of cheese that remained.

"Merry Meet. I'm glad you're here." She walked towards the table. "I've got something to give to you," she said as she saw a dark object move into her peripheral vision.

"Hi, Claire. How are you?" Sophie said as she walked into the room. Suspecting Sophie was at the house, Claire continued, the charm bag still in her left hand. "I'll give it to you tonight after dinner," she finished with a raise of the eyebrows. "Merry Meet, Sophie. I'm good, and you?"

"Okay, I'll wait," Jane interrupted.

"Good, we went for a drive out to Freycinet this morning. It's such a lovely place. You'd think for someone who lives so close, I'd get out there more often!"

"Yes, you'd think so, and as things would have it, I also went out to Freycinet."

"Cool."

"Did you see your friend?" Jane asked.

"Yes, I did. Gwendolyn Ismay, do you remember her?"

"Umm…" She thought before continuing. "I'm not too sure."

"Gwen lives over on Reserve Road," she offered, trying to jog Jane's memory.

"Nah, I don't think so."

"That's okay. It's been many years, since before your mum passed," she said wistfully with a smile as she conjured up an old memory. "She had an old wattle tree in the backyard. You used to love to climb it when you were a little girl."

"Oh, I remember," Jane said eagerly as she turned in her chair, "climbing the tree, but I always thought her name was Jen. I haven't seen her since Mum died. I guess I thought that she must have died, as well, or moved away." Her tone became more sombre as she continued, "Is she okay? I should drop around and see her sometime."

"Yes, I'm sure she'd love that. What are you girls up to this afternoon?

"I've got to go out with the family tonight. Nothing special, my little sister Stacey has a music recital at the school, so that will be lots of fun," she said sarcastically with cheeky smile.

Jane laughed.

"It's good to see that you're supporting your family, Sophie. It's important, and she'll thank you for it—maybe not in words, but in her eyes, you'll see," Claire said with a motherly tone.

"Yeah, I guess so. Can I get you to drop me home soon, Jane? I don't want to upset my Mum," Sophie asked as she looked at the clock, which marked the hour at four in the afternoon.

"No probs. I'll get the keys."

"Any requests for dinner?" Claire asked as Jane left the kitchen.

"No, whatever," she replied.

Twelve minutes later, Claire found herself standing at the bay window, watching Blue Belle reverse down the driveway onto Delta Road. Jane put the car into gear and beeped the horn. The car disappeared from sight, and Claire was alone in the kitchen with the charm bag still in her hands. She looked down and sighed at the string-tied calico bag, sensing the light aroma of fire wafting up from the cloth.

It had been a long and tiring day, and Claire didn't feel like cooking, but she looked in the pantry and decided on a simple dish. She retrieved a packet of chicken curry flavoured rice and a frozen chicken breast from the freezer. She placed the chicken in the microwave and left the rice packet on the bench as she walked into the lounge room.

She turned on the tele, placing the charm bag in a dark brown wooden bowl that sat atop the entertainment unit.

Half an hour later, the hum of the V-Dub announced Jane's return to Avalon. Moments later, the music stopped mid-chorus, and silence returned. Claire waited for Jane in the kitchen, listening as she heard the car door close, footsteps on the gravel, and the turning of the screen-door handle.

"I expected you to stay at Sophie's a little longer."

"No, didn't stay long at all as she had to get ready. It's a bit of a battle over there when the family goes out as there's only one bathroom."

"Oh, I see."

"I might have a shower, as well, on that note. Was there anything that I could do to help with dinner?" she asked as she placed her car keys on the table.

"No, love. I've seared some chicken and only have to do the rice, and it's done. Will you be back in five minutes?"

"Yep, sure will," she replied as she walked towards her room.

Claire turned her attention back to the stovetop, where she had a pot with water waiting. She turned on the knob of the electric hob, and an orange light illuminated from the bottom edge closest to her. She felt distant, though. The business at Freya, casting the spell, and the clear and present danger that Jane was in all but consumed her thoughts. The weight of such concerns made her feel lethargic and tired. She yearned to just fall asleep in front of a good movie or curl up under the doona in her bed.

When the water began to boil, Claire ripped the top off the rice packet and poured its contents into the water, stirring it with a wooden spoon. She returned the seared chicken to the heat and looked in the fridge for an open bottle of wine.

"Jane, did you want a glass of wine?" she yelled from the entrance to the kitchen, but she did realize that if Jane had the stereo going, which was most likely, she wouldn't hear her.

She stood still, listening, but there was no response. So she poured herself a glass of Moscato, returned the bottle to the fridge when she was done, and went back to the hob.

Claire was putting the two dishes onto the oak table when Jane walked back in, running her fingers through her hair.

"Mmm, smells good."

"I called out to see if you wanted a wine, but you didn't hear me. The bottle's in the fridge. Help yourself if you'd like some," she said, pulling the chair out from the table.

"Okay, sounds good. I might join you," she replied joyfully.

They both sat quietly consuming dinner, the volume of the television in the lounge room the only audible distraction as they ate.

"You look tired," Jane said as she got up to clear the table.

"Yes, I was at Freya today. I've got something to give to you, but it's in the lounge room at the moment. I'll get it when we go in to watch tele."

"Okay, is it a surprise?"

"Yes and no. You'll find out soon enough."

"I want to go out in the garden again tonight for a while."

"How's the book going? Stephen King, isn't it?"

"Yeah not too bad, although, I haven't read a great deal in the last two days."

Claire got up from the table. "I'm going to get in the shower and wash the day off me. Leave the dishes," she said with a wave of her hand. "I'll get them cleaned up later."

"Sure, I might go out to the garden for a while. I'll see you in the lounge room shortly."

Claire left the room and went straight to the bathroom. She turned on the hot water faucet, allowing the water to run for a couple of minutes until the shower was steaming. She then mixed the cold water to reach the right temperature before getting in.

Claire felt refreshed after her shower; she dressed in her robe and slippers, brushed her teeth while checking her complexion in the mirror then made her way out to the lounge room, where she sank into the armchair. Channel surfing, she searched for anything that would be interesting. There was nothing on, but before she knew it, the remote had fallen from her hand, and all before her was black.

∞

Jane walked to the far side of the pond and sat on the rock wall that faced the Winesap. She opened her book to where she'd previously left the ear of the page folded down. She stared at the page. Black on white swirled mixing in a psychedelic whirlpool. The more she looked and tried to concentrate, the more the words on the page distorted.

"What's wrong with me?" She closed the book and set it aside. "Just caught up in some strange shit, but why me?" she questioned, shaking her head. "I may be a little strange. Not everyone likes me, but I've hurt no one, so why am I in danger?" she interrogated the tree as she stood. Raising her right hand to meet her forehead, she spun around—then she saw it. She slowed down. She saw it again. Stopping, she stepped aimlessly for a moment while regaining her balance. She moved closer to inspect the tree—there it was again. But what was it?

Sitting in the lower fork of the tree, it looked long and had a sparkle. Watching it, she tried to figure out what it could be. It didn't move, and she knew it couldn't be a snake.

"There it is again. Sparkles like a diamond."

Then it dawned on her. "Could it be? I haven't seen it since yesterday, but I thought I took it up to my room."

She moved towards the tree, cautiously at first. It sparkled again. The brief reflection of light allowed Jane to recognise the object that sat in the fork of the tree.

"The silver bough, it *is* you," she said jubilantly as she reached up into the tree to retrieve the magickal talisman. She held it in the palms of both hands, looking at it as she tried to recall if she had taken it to her room when she'd returned from Emain Albach. Then it sparkled again. It started at one end and travelled to the other—a hundred or more little lights ran in succession along the length of the bough, lighting up one at a time. Jane then had an idea.

"What if I travel back to see to Aedán and the others? It'll only be for an hour or so," she said, trying to convince herself as she looked from the bough to the tree, the book, to the house, and back to the bough. "Oh, I don't know— Aunt Claire wanted to have a talk." Jane walked around the base of the Winesap, debating with herself.

She decided that it would best to go back inside and see if Aunt Claire wanted to chat. She could maybe have a quick visit after that. The thought of going back gave Jane a little swagger in her step as she anticipated seeing her friends again. The door to the sunroom closed behind her as she walked through to the lounge room. The theme song to *Law & Order: SVU* filled the room. Jane found Claire asleep in the recliner, the remote on the floor beside her, legs outstretched in her dressing gown, and slippers looking quite warm and snug.

"Oh," she whispered when she saw her. "I'll leave her where she is." She retreated into the secret garden.

Not wanting to waste another minute, Jane scampered up the tree to the first fork in the trunk. She held the silver bough in her hand and pointed it downwards to touch the bark of the trunk.

"The Red Man is here in Delta, so surely I would be safe back in Emain Albach," she said, still trying to convince herself she was doing the right thing.

She looked over the pond back towards the house and around the garden, agonising over the fact that Avalon had been her sanctuary for so many years. Has it now been compromised? She'd left the novel atop the rock wall. *It should be safe there*, she thought, as the night was still and there were no visible signs of precipitation. She took a deep breath and pushed the bough against the trunk of the tree. "Reconnect the bough to the mystic tree and seek safe passage to Emain Albach.

This, I request of thee."

Instantly, the trunk began to move as a chain reaction launched with the fork breaching to reveal a gaping hole beneath her. She could feel the pull of the vortex on her body. Every loose item, her hair, and her clothing were drawn towards the hole as if the power switch on a vacuum had been switched on. She tested its resolve and tried to turn away, but the pull was too great. She lost her grip on the branch above her head. Flashes of light like bolts of lightning coursed through the walls of the hole in the direction of which she was about to be sucked through. A thunderclap resonated through her head. She felt the pressure on her grip intensify as the pull became stronger. The skin on her fingers wore on the bark as they slowly slid down the branch. She closed her eyes, turning her back towards the vortex, the bough in her right hand. She released her grip and gave in to the unrelenting force. The tree swallowed her, followed by a gush of wind and leaves.

19

Pushed by wind or sucked in a vacuum, Jane wasn't sure as she tumbled over and over as if she were being dumped by a wave. The tunnel was dark, except for the electric flashes that occurred every other moment along the walls of the hole. The intense flash lit up the shaft, allowing her to catch a glimpse of what lay ahead, although it all looked the same. Then she saw a faint glow as small as a pinhead in the distance—then it was gone. She tumbled. *Flash!* There it was again, larger and brighter, twisting in darkness. The blinding light burst again in front of her. It was coming towards her at high speed. The glow strengthened like a star being born before her eyes. It stretched out around her, pulling her limp body through it, then it collapsed in on itself as she was at its core. All sides of the energy folded in on her, creating an explosive sound that rocked her off her orbit as she tumbled through the wormhole.

Crack!

The explosion of white light was immediately replaced by colour—greys, blacks, browns, dark greens, and smears of white. The temperature suddenly dropped as a chill travelled down her spine. She tumbled then hit the ground heavily atop her shoulders at the base of neck. Jane rolled, her head tucked into her chest, as her torso and legs followed. One, two, three rolls—she found herself lying on her back. *Thank Christ for that!* she thought as she took the Christian God's name in vain, which she did regularly.

She wasn't going to hell for it, so she figured why not.

Jane blinked, stretched her jaw, and exercised her fingers and toes as the image of a large tree canopy came into focus above her head.

"I'm here," Jane said enthusiastically, ignoring a dull pain around her rib cage as she pushed herself up, taking her weight on her right arm. She surveyed the landscape around her. A biting wind that felt as if it were attacking the extremities of her body swept swirling clouds across the dark skies. She rose to her feet; the tree above her looked like the same apple tree that Aedán showed to her the previous day. Red apples lay strewn all over the ground around her. Something was different—something was wrong. She quickly ran a few yards away from the tree, dodging apples and trying to recognise where she was. Winded from the fall, Jane could feel her angst rise. Her breathing became a little laboured as she stopped and spun around.

The mounds… where are the mounds? Panting, she tried to convince herself to keep calm.

This isn't happening. Aedán, Rhoswen, and the others are supposed to be here. "This isn't supposed to have happened," she puffed.

"What wasn't supposed to have happened, lassie?" a voice said.

She spun around, jarring her neck.

"Who said that?" she asked of the shadows behind her. "Come out and show yourself!"

"Aye, I would, but I'm feeling a wee bit parched. You wouldn't happen to have any mead on you, lassie?"

"Oh, um…" She hesitated. "No, I don't have anything to drink," Jane replied as she backed away from the voice.

"There's no need to be afraid, child. I will cause you no harm. Please… please come sit with me. Let us natter for a while," the strange voice said as a hand escaped the shadows, motioning to her to come forward. "You look like a stranger to this land. Is that why you scream? Is something wrong? I may be able to help."

"Why would I approach or even trust someone who is not willing to show their face?" *Don't trust strangers. Thanks, Mum*, she thought as slogans of 'Stranger Danger' from her school days ran through her mind.

"Aye, you are right. I am a stranger—to you, lassie, but not of this land. Now, would it not be prudent to lay a little trust in someone who could point you in the right direction rather than traverse these dangerous parts on your own?"

"Not until you show your face."

"In good time, lassie, in good time. But first, tell me how a human has come to travel between the realms and on their own, as well. Not a wise choice, my dear."

"I was coming to see some friends, and um…" Jane paused. *What am I doing?* "Don't worry about it. It doesn't matter anyway."

"Oh, but it does matter, lassie. You see, you get all types around here, not just your garden-variety fairies, you know. Some can be quite mean when they want, and the likes of you should not be out on your own after dark. Besides, it does not look like your friends are showing up any time soon, anyway. So would you indulge me in a little natter, and who knows? Your friends may just be running a little late."

Jane turned to survey her surrounds one last time to weigh up her options. It looked like the same tree, but there were no mounds or village, only a forest to the east, rolling hills to the west and south, and a sweeping valley to the north. "Wait there, over there," she said pointing. "There, down the valley. There's a fire"

"Half a day's walk, at best, lassie. You better get a move on if you want the cover of darkness, but let me wish you the luck of a thousand genies "because you're going to need it." He laughed.

"Why? Why am I going to need luck?" Jane shouted back.

"Join me, we can find some mead and regale over new friendships and journeys yet to be trod."

"You're kidding, right?"

"And why would I do that, lassie?"

"Why would you think that we are friends?"

"And why should we not?"

"Argh." She grunted in frustration. "Stop it. Just stop it!"

"Stop what, lassie?"

"Just that!"

"What?"

"Being passive-aggressive!"

"Am I?"

Cernunnos and Cerridwen, oh gracious Gods, where are you when I need you most?

The shadowy veils of the night slowly parted as the moon escaped the grasp of the clouds to provide enough light for Jane to make out the figure of a man. He was small in stature, perhaps only four foot tall but definitely not over five, and a little plump around the edges.

Merry Meet, my Goddess.

"I don't have time for this," Jane said as she turned away from the stranger, "Maybe the owners of the fire will prove to be better characters than yourself."

"Aye, nor do I. I'm sure there are many butteries ripe for the plundering. Would you care to join me?" he asked as he stepped into the light of the moon.

Jane turned to see her pseudo-host in the honesty of the full light. Time had not been kind to him. His extra weight was accentuated by his short height. His skin was weathered with age and covered with warts. In particular, her attention was drawn to his oversized facial features: his nose, chin, and ears. His attire, however, seemed quite normal. He wore brown leather boots, green trousers, a dirty bone-coloured shirt, and to complete the ensemble— a brown leather hat.

"Now you can see why I live in the shadows," he said, as if ashamed of his appearance.

"Do I seem like someone who would care about appearances? Where I'm from, I'm treated like an outcast by some, not just by the way I dress and the pentagram that hangs around my neck, but because I'm a witch."

"A witch, you say? Mmm, It's been many turns of the wheel since we've had a witch roaming the lands of Emain Albach," he said curiously.

"Yes, I know. That's what Kaelan said, as well." "Kaelan... the elder of Fionghan," he stated.

"I don't know. He was the leader of the village, so I suppose he would be an elder, although he didn't look old. What is Fionghan?"

"Fionghan means "fair born." It's the name of a village that lays less than a day's walk from here. Is that who you are waiting for?"

"Yes, he and his wife, Rhoswen and Oren and Aedán."

"The shapeshifter... you have some powerful friends in Emain Albach. I would like to offer my assistance to repatriate you with your friends, if you'd allow," he said with a bow and dip of his hat.

"Yeah, sure. I guess," she said hesitantly.

"Is something wrong, lassie?"

"We haven't made proper introductions. What's your name?"

"My apologies, lassie. Hóra, my name is Taog."

"And I'm Jane. Merry Meet!"

"Jane the witch, pleased to make your acquaintance."

"Are you a dwarf?"

"A dwarf? What is a dwarf? I have never heard of such a thing. I am a clurichaun."

"A what?"

"A clurichaun. We're easiest described as a surly type of *leprechaun*, renowned for getting into mischief… and butteries." He chuckled then continued, "Stealing the wines and ales that they hold within."

"So you're a thief and a drunk," Jane replied with a smile. "No offence intended," she added.

"That's quite all right. I know who I am, and besides, it makes me happy."

"I'm glad."

"Shall we make a start?"

"Which direction do we travel? Down the valley towards the fire?" she asked.

"No, we have to travel east through the Black Alder Forest, lassie," Taog answered, his right index finger pointing the way.

Jane turned towards the dense forest that consisted mainly of black alder trees ranging in heights up to a hundred feet with smaller rowan trees growing underneath. It was dark and uninviting, not her direction of choice. They kept to a leaf-covered dirt track that round its way towards a large moss-covered stone archway that marked the entrance to the forest. Sounds of crickets, movement of the trees, and calls of the native fauna, along with the wind chill of their eerie location, sent shudders up Jane's spine.

"Are you sure that this is the best way?"

"This is the only way," he replied, "but we have to be quick. It's not wise to out in the open or drawing attention to yourself in these parts."

Jane was in quiet awe of the enormity of the carved stone blocks in the arch. "Is there any meaning to the archway?" she asked as she pirouetted underneath the structure that towered thirty-five feet into the air, absorbing the beauty and sheer feat of its construction.

"It's centuries old, built by the original Tuatha Dé Danann inhabitants of the area after they were exiled by the Milesians," he said so quietly his voice was nearly a whisper.

"Sounds like there's a history lesson in there somewhere," Jane joked as they walked deeper into the dark reaches of the forest. "Should we have a torch going, so we can see the way?"

"It's not necessary. I live in the shadows of the night. My eyes are well accustomed to such circumstances. If you cannot see, take hold of my belt and follow closely," he ordered.

You are kidding, right? I don't think so. "It's okay. I can manage," Jane replied.

They walked along a dark narrowing track. Leaves crunched underfoot as they went, revealing their presence to anyone who was keen of ear. All that Jane could see were dark silhouettes of the trees around her and the occasional fallen log or branch that lay on the track.

However, the forest was alive with sound, even in the dead of night: frogs croaking from nearby waterholes, the buzz of a passing insect, and a hoot from an owl perched overhead. But the loudest of all in Jane's mind was her heartbeat and breathing. Her heart was the constant bass in her head while her lungs played a sweeping rhythm, but as time went on, they were turning against her, playing with her mind and slowly testing her sanity as she tried to keep reason from eluding her judgement.

"Are we there—" she asked, stopping herself before she finished her question.

What are you saying? This is not a road trip with the family, and this is certainly not the backseat that you have so many fond memories of from Mum's car. "How much further now, Taog?"

Now that sounded more civilized. Jane smiled.

"If we keep a good pace throughout the night, we should be there when the sun is between the horizon and the high point of the day," he replied.

"Good," she lied as she pondered whether her body was up to such a trek. "Are there many portals in Emain Albach?"

"Portals, lassie?" Taog repeated with a puzzled tone.

"Vortexes, wormholes—you know, apple trees where you can travel between realms!"

"Aye, there are five that I know of."

"Can one pick which one they want to travel to?

"Aye."

"Are you going to tell me?"

"No, not tonight. Some other time—wait," Taog cautioned as he turned to Jane, grabbing her by the upper arm.

"Ouch, that hurts!" Jane winced in agony as Taog pulled her to the ground.

"Would you pipe down, lassie," he whispered towards her ear.

"What is it?"

"Someone or something is out there, travelling, searching. I sense their presence."

They both crouched still. Seconds turned into minutes.

Jane's right upper leg started to go numb.

"Are they still out there?" she whispered as she tried to stretch her neck to get a better look, but all she saw was black.

Taog responded by raising his hand to her face to tell her to be silent. They waited, Taog's hand still firmly clasped onto Jane's arm.

"They're here," he whispered. "Keep still, lassie."

"Who?" she asked, but Taog did not answer. *I have nothing, no charms, no tools, my BOS. It's all back at Avalon. Just my pentagram and faith, but this is not looking good. The Red Man is back at Delta, so what is out there?*

Jane pressed into Taog's side as they waited, staring into the darkness that cloaked the forest. A rush of cold wind suddenly passed them, but Jane could not see where or whence it came.

"What's that?"

"Stay still," Taog urged.

Then another burst of chilled wind pushed against her, but this time, she felt the unmistakable sensation of something touching her skin. She bit her lip and held her tongue. Jane looked towards the top of the trees, scanning for anything that might explain what was going on, then her heart stopped. She saw two glowing white lights close together, hovering up in the branches of the closest alder. They held their position for ten seconds then moved a couple of yards to the right, the distance between the lights remaining constant.

"What are those lights up there in the trees?"

Taog searched the trees. "*Cac*," Taog cursed. "They're not lights—they're eyes."

"Of what?" Jane asked, forgetting to keep her volume to a whisper.

"The Tainted Ones," Taog said, no longer bothering to keep their position discreet as he rose to his feet. "Come on, there's no point hiding here any longer. They know we're here. Run! Run as fast as you can and don't look back!" Taog yelled as he yanked Jane to her feet and pushed her in the direction of the track.

"What's a Tainted One?" Jane shouted over her shoulder as she ran blindly forward, hoping that there were no objects on the path or sharp turns.

"Just keep running, lassie," Taog barked.

Taog was beside Jane within two steps. "Follow me," he ordered as he passed her, taking the vanguard position on the track.

Shit! There's nothing between me and whatever that Tainted thing is. Why didn't I stay at home?

She kept pace with Taog, focusing on his cream coloured shirt so she would know when to turn, when to jump.

"There's two of them coming behind us fast. Keep your head down and keep running, lassie," Taog hollered as they both navigated a sharp right turn on the path.

Jane trod on a dead rowan branch that snapped underfoot, testing her balance. Moments later, she was hit in the back of the neck, thrusting her upper body forward. Her arms flailed helplessly as she felt herself missile headfirst, her legs following as she hit the ground hard and slid on the layer of debris that covered the forest floor. Her body jolted to a stop facedown and spreadeagle on the ground. Pain coursed from her chest as she tried to breathe. Her attempt was hampered by leaves that forced their way into her mouth. She lifted her head, spitting leaves. She could hear distance footsteps running away from the scene, and she realised she was alone.

"Taog?" Jane called in the direction of the footsteps, but there was no response. The sound of the footsteps become fainter and fainter. She lay there in the debris, not moving, resigned to the fact that she soon would meet her end.

Cernunnos and Cerridwen, oh gracious God and Goddess, I fear that I will be with you sooner than I imagined. Send me guiding light so my spirit may make safe passage to you.

Jane lay still, her head turned to the side as she continued to spit small pieces of flora from her mouth. Her fingers dug into moist dirt, tensioning into closed fists. She waited for that flash—the expected moment that her life would be stubbed out like a cigarette—but nothing happened. Seconds turned to minutes, and still, nothing happened. She couldn't hear anything, and by that time, she could breathe freely again. She lifted her head, searching to both sides and in front of her, but she saw only black. She wiggled her torso slowly to get movement back, working out the creeks and pains.

Feeling alone and abandoned, Jane contemplated what to do next. *I can't lay here all night. Those things may come back. I guess all I can do is try to follow the path and hope that I find my way to Aedán.*

Feeling some form of ease and safety return to her, Jane rolled onto her back and froze. They were there. They had never left. Two black silhouettes hovered just above her like ghosts with eerily deep white eyes that looked right through her. She quickly shuffled backwards on her hands and feet but found her back pressed against the trunk of a tree. She had no escape.

"What do you want?" she screamed as she threw a fistful of leaves that floated gently back to earth without finding their mark.

One figure looked to the other then ducked its head and swooped down towards her like a bird pulling up to float only three feet above her. It nodded towards the other shadow as Jane sensed that her time had nearly arrived. She closed her eyes, held her pentagram in her right hand, and waited. She sensed a flash of light through her closed lids. She opened her eyes in time to see the Tainted Ones vanish into a grey swirling mass that looked like the funnel of a tornado as the wind picked up a blanket of leaves off the forest floor. It swirled about furiously then settled atop of her. Jane brushed away at the mountain of debris as the light got closer and closer.

"I'm not going to make it," she said, realising that her best strategy would have been to keep the leaves on top of her to remain hidden. She lay still as the massive light approached, accompanied by a soft hum. Fifteen feet, ten feet, five feet—the noise grew louder. It was on top of her but kept moving. Jane waited a minute then sat up. The remainder of the leaves fell away, and she sighed, releasing the burden of her impending doom.

"Fireflies, a swarm of fireflies." She laughed. "Merry Meet to all of you and gratitude to you both, Cernunnos and Cerridwen, for looking out for me yet again.

20

The Red Man tossed and rolled in the large bed. New plans, failed attempts, and imagined successful outcomes all contributed to his sleep deprivation, and the harder he tried to sleep, the more restless he became. Adding to his woes were the injuries He'd sustained to his upper back and neck from the attack of the *ulchabhán*. Hours passed slowly as he stared at the ceiling, watching the moonlight shining into the room through the large window, frustrated that his quarry was so close yet far from reach.

He'd kicked away the quilt, which was bunched at the end of the bed, as he yearned for news from Emain Albach and the arrival of the *dullahan* to assist him in capturing the girl that He'd ached to have for so long. Annoyed, he pushed himself up to a sitting position, reached for the glass of water from the side table, and hydrated his parched throat. He sat there, and fifteen minutes passed before he decided to get up from the bed. He walked to the window and pulled open the drape far enough to see Avalon across the road, bathed in moonlight, asleep and protected by witchcraft.

A noise, anomalous for the house and the late hour, behind him drew his attention away from the window. A dark greyish cloud began to materialise, spinning in the bedroom before him. The sheets, drapes, and bottom of his red nightgown flapped ferociously in the wind generated by the funnel. Knowing that he was about to receive word from Emain Albach, he approached the funnel to await his visitors.

Two sets of crystal-white eyes appeared on the edge of the funnel. The first of the Tainted Ones glided effortlessly from the spinning cloud while the second remained within the funnel. Only parts of its dark form appeared and disappeared as the funnel spun. The first drifted towards the Red Man then stopped in front of its superior.

"I must say that I was expecting the *dullahan*," the Red Man said as he walked around the Tainted One, who hovered, motionless three feet above the floor. "That being said, however, I trust that you have arrived with good news for me."

The Tainted One replied with two nods of its head.

"Well, don't keep me in suspense, my dark friend. What news of the *dullahan* do you have for me?" he demanded.

The Tainted One communicated using a raw but effective version of sign language to convey its message. It shook its head initially at the Red Man's question. Then gestured the removal of its head, held it at waist height, and shook its head again.

"No *dullahan*?" he queried.

The Tainted One shook its head again as it glided past the Red Man towards the window with an outstretched arm pointing towards the house across the road.

"Avalon!"

Turning, the dark figure nodded, and then its shape transformed fluidly into a female with accentuated hips and breasts as it used its hands to draw attention to its heart and pointed back at the Red Man.

"The girl?" he asked enthusiastically. "Is it the girl?"

The reply was a simple nod followed by a sweeping motion of the hands that created an elongated shape that represented the Isle of Apples.

"Emain Albach, the girl is at Emain Albach! Are you sure? Are you positive that it is her?" he demanded.

The Tainted One nodded once more and drew the outline of a pentagram with its hand as confirmation.

"So she's learnt to travel between the realms. Maybe she deserves more credit than I've afforded her so far. Nonetheless—and I do not care for detail on how she came to be in Emain Albach—she is there, out of Avalon, and out of the reach of the protection spell. Enlighten me as to who she is with," he asked as he paced the bedroom, grinning unashamedly, "for they may unfortunately become collateral damage!"

The dark one shook its head and held up only one digit.

The Red Man burst into a raucous fit of laughter. "She is in my realm, unprotected and alone? I think it's time to break the lease and go home. Afford me a few minutes to get dressed and gather my possessions, and we'll leave to pay her a visit."

The Red Man retrieved his bags and cane, changed into his clothes, and turned to face the Tainted Ones once more. "Shall we go home?" he said as he put the red Paris Beau atop his head and pointed towards the funnel. The dark one outside the spinning cloud glided back to the grey mass, allowing itself to be consumed. The Red Man was two strides behind, following his subject into the funnel, and as he did, the second dark one that was holding the cone in this realm fell back into the eye of the climatic phenomenon. Amidst thunder and lightning, the vortex spun faster and faster. Suddenly, a flash of brilliant white light exploded, forming an expanded diamond shape that closed in on itself to the size of a pinhead then vanished.

21

Fatigue was setting in as Jane blindly navigated her way through the Black Alder Forest. Taog was long gone, and Jane's calves and hamstrings were beginning to ache, as each step on the uneven surface was a challenge in the dim light. Alone but unafraid, she was determined to make it to Fionghan. Hours seemed to have passed since the Tainted Ones" attack. In hindsight, Jane wasn't certain it had been an attack—if it had, it was very poorly thought out on their behalf. She was never one to be too cocky. However, in that moment, she was confident she would make it, despite the dangers that Taog talked about. She had faith that both Cernunnos and Cerridwen were protecting her. She knew that the Gods had thwarted the Tainted Ones by sending the fireflies. With this confidence, she boldly ventured forth into the unknown.

Jane endeavoured to split her concentration between looking forward to navigate the path—its twisted and turned then rose in little peaks and dropped to valleys—and concentrating on each footstep, making sure she made solid purchase on the ground.

The farther she travelled, the easier it became to see the bends and ground underfoot. At first, she thought that it must be nearing five in the morning and the sun was about to come up, but as she took a moment to stop and rest her aching muscles, she noticed that she could see stars. The sky was as black as it normally was; however, the fact that she could see stars meant that the trees were starting to thin. She was getting close to the edge of the forest.

It can't be too much farther. One more bend, one more rise—you can do this. Jane tried to convince herself, and with that motivation, she rose to her feet, dusted herself off, and marched on, determined to see the other side of the forest, to make it to Fionghan and see her friends.

She rounded a bend in the track, and she could see it— the end of the forest. There was no stone archway, but she did see a tree-lined archway that opened up to vast plain lands beyond.

Jane stopped where the forest and the plain were juxtaposed perfectly as if a line separated the two. She had a distinct feeling that she was about to tread into another world once she strode out of the forest, though she knew that it was still Emain Albach, but that first step was like closing the chapter of a forest adventure in a novel and commencing another one. *What will happen now?*

She raised her right foot and moved forward. The crunch of leaves and tree debris was gone; in fact, there wasn't much sound at all. The track was easier to follow in the plain lands, and the Goddess above provided ample light to assist Jane in navigating her way. She was probably only ten minutes past the last tree of the Black Alder Forest when she could hear the faint sound of someone calling, singing, and yelling? She wasn't sure what she heard, but the path lead towards the sound. It got louder and louder the farther she walked. She recognised another sound, as well. This one was more familiar—running water. It wasn't rushing like a river or rapids but gentle like a slow-running stream or babbling brook. The ground was starting to change, as well, becoming more uneven. Jane stopped and crouched to examine the earth beneath her by running her flat palm across the ground. She could feel the rounded edges of stones and knew that she wasn't too far from fresh water. The very thought of it made her yearn for a large drink.

Rising to her feet, she continued on. The strain on her calves as they stretched sent her pain receptors into a spin as the path started a long incline. *I need a rest and a drink. The sound of that water is so inviting, but what the hell is that wailing?*

"Wailing, that's it," she said as she stopped and listened intently for the sound again. Then she heard it again.

Sounds like someone is in pain. Don't know if I want to go any closer now, but I could really use that water.

"Could be crying. Is that the same thing?" she asked herself as she reached the top of the rise. Down in the ravine below was the silvery shimmer of the Goddess reflecting off the water. Jane was so overjoyed with emotion and thirst that she nearly ran down the hill to dive into the narrow stream. Then she was immobilised by the howls of a woman. She hit the dirt like a frightened cadet, scanning the reaches of the stream, searching for the source of the high-pitched crying. Nothing. Then the long screech sounded along the gully again. She quickly traced the stream back to the left again, where the image of a woman came into focus. She sat on a rock at the stream's edge, where the body of water was wider than the rest of the stream.

Jane watched her with keen interest. The woman didn't seem to be hurt. She was, however, washing clothes, which flummoxed Jane somewhat. She sat on the side of her hip, her two legs pulled in close on her left side. She was wearing a white undergarment with a cut and sleeves that reminded Jane of a peasant top underneath a scarlet French toast dress. She was barefoot and had black hair pulled to one side so that it sat upon her left shoulder and fell over her breast. Resting on her right leg was a washboard. The woman howled again as she pressed the clothes against the board.

The picture before her looked innocent enough, except for the howling—that part gave Jane the creeps. She opted not to go down there but to follow the stream for a bit and get a drink where she felt more at ease. She stood and began to walk away from the howling woman, taking one last look over her shoulder as she departed. Her gaze was caught as the howling woman saw Jane get to her feet. Her eyes were dark and empty like a mineshaft to a soulless body, yet the eyes held her captive. She stopped and stared right back at her, rendering her oblivious to an approaching rider from the north.

The woman howled again. Jane's concentration broke when hot breath washed over her right shoulder.. She jumped, shocked by the intruder into her personal space. She turned quickly to see a black horse rear on its hind legs, shrieking a vile bray at her while the front hooves were striking over her head. She retreated backwards five paces, but the shock and uneven ground made her lose balance. She seemed to spin as she fell; her arms flailed as she tried to reach out to catch her fall. A scream escaped her mouth as she hit the ground, the back of her head connecting with a rock.

∞

Running as fast as his legs could carry him, Taog navigated the harsh trail that led to Fionghan. It had been a while since He'd fled the forest, but he knew within himself that he could not have fought the Tainted Ones unaided. He stopped to catch his breath when the village came into sight. However, his thoughts were still with Jane. Was she all right? Was she even alive? He didn't know, but he did know that it was his duty to advise Kaelan the Elder of the terrible news of his friend.

Taog stood at the top of a rolling hill that looked down upon Fionghan. He was, at best, only a thousand paces away. The village looked peaceful. The only movement was the smoke that escaped the chimneys of each of the *sidhe* in the village. He proceeded down the hill at a brisk walking pace as the winds that swept through those parts welcomed him back by sending chills up his legs and arms to the core of his body.

"Aye, this is why I do not call these parts of the island my home," he said with a shiver while crossing his arms and decreasing his pace to conserve energy. "Looking forward to thawing my feet in front of a warm hearth."

He hadn't been to the village in probably five or six turns of the wheel, but he was sure that his old friends would welcome him. He wasn't sure which *sidhe* Kaelan would be in, so he took a gamble that he would be in the *sidhe* with the highest aspect on the hill so he could look over the village and the *Crann úll* in the village square.

It was a large *sidhe* befitting of an elder. Taog knew the night was long and that the inhabitants would be fast asleep. He didn't think it would be wise to wake them at such a time. However, this was no ordinary time. Taog marched to the door and knocked three times. The door was old but solid. The thud of each blow of his fist echoed throughout the *sidhe*.

"Who is it?" someone answered from deep within the walls.

Taog swallowed nervously, awaiting his reception. He heard the clatter of sword and buckle on the other side of the entrance.

"It's a—" He swallowed again. "It's, ah, Taog of Taraghlan," he announced so as not to meet his untimely demise when the door opened.

"Who?"

"Taog of Taraghlan. I'm a…" he hesitated. "I'm here about Jane the witch," Taog enunciated as clearly as he could.

The bolt slid back, and the door opened with a grinding drone as a rush of wind blew leaves onto and past the figure at the door.

"Come in, come in," the figure said, ushering Taog in and closing the door behind him. "Welcome. You know Jane?" Oren asked.

"Yes, yes. Is Kaelan the Elder here?" he asked as he stepped in, scanning the inside of the *sidhe* for other occupants.

"He is, but first, what business do you have with Jane?" He stepped in front of Taog, preventing him from entering the *sidhe* any farther.

"Forgive me, master, if I seem rude, but I've only just met her, and I fear that she is in great danger."

Oren allowed him past and showed him to a seat at the long table near the hearth.

"No, you must be mistaken. She can't be in danger. We know that she is safe. We saw to it ourselves."

"I make no mistake. I was just with her."

"And what is a clurichaun doing travelling between the realms?" He laughed.

"Travelling between realms," he repeated, perplexed. "No, no, you don't understand. I was just with her—she is here, in Emain Albach."

"No," Oren said, extending the word in disbelief. "This can't be. Wait here. I will wake Kaelan."

Oren went to the room closest to the front door and knocked quietly before opening the door. He disappeared for a short time, yet Taog was pleased as the time allowed him to bathe in the heat radiating from hearth.

Oren emerged from the room with another *Aes Sidhe* male behind him. He was taller than the first, and Taog assumed that he must be the elder of Fionghan. Taog pushed himself up from the seat to face his hosts.

"Taog of Taraghlan," he announced as the pair reached the long table.

"Taog of Taraghlan, Oren tells me that you have just been in the company of Jane the witch, as you called her. In her company here in Emain Albach?" he queried with great interest as he sat at the head of the table, reaching for a chalice of stagnant mead.

"Yes, master. She appeared from the *Crann úll* at Taraghlan. At first, I was afraid of her, as was she of me since I was in the shadows, but she was a curious one, I thought, and when she said that she was looking for you, I offered to chaperone her and see her safely arrive in Fionghan."

"Where is she?" Kaelan asked. "Oren said that you believed that she was in danger—so what happened?"

A heavy wooden door swung open from the second bedroom behind them, drawing their attention away from their conversation, and a horse waltzed out, stretching his neck.

"You stable your horses inside the *sidhe*? This is definitely the elder's *sidhe*, and you must be Kaelan," Taog said, turning back to the two he was conversing with at the table.

"Mind your tongue, clurichaun, for I am no ordinary horse and will sooner strike you down for such an insult," Aedán barked as he approached the table.

"Oh my, a *púca*! My apologies, Taog said as he lowered his head in an attempt to convey his remorse. "I did not mean any disrespect. This is definitely a powerful house full of powerful Fey."

"Clurichaun," Kaelan roared as both fists thumped the table. "Jane—what danger is she in?"

"We were walking along the road to come see you through the Black Alder Forest," Taog explained, "and we were almost through it when we were attacked—oh, there must have been at least five of them, maybe six. There were a lot."

"What attacked you?"

"The shadow people—you know, with the big white eyes," he explained.

"Aye, the Tainted Ones," Oren quickly yelled at the group.

Everyone looked at Oren, seeming surprised that He'd spoken up.

"I was just saying what they were!"

"Clurichaun, I'm just going to ask one last time—what happened to Jane?" Kaelan demanded.

"I don't know exactly."

"What do you mean you don't know?" Aedán asked calmly, apparently distrustful of Taog. The clurichaun was used to such distrust.

"I'm ashamed to say, Master, but I must let you know. They attacked from above. Jane hid behind some rocks, and I…"

"You what?"

"I ran. I thought that it was best to come for your aid. There were too many of them. Really, there were, and I'm not a fighter," he pleaded as he looked at each one of them in turn.

"Aye, a fighter you're not. *Cac* would be more fitting, don't you think?" Aedán said as he looked away from Taog to Kaelan. "I'm going out there, to the edge of the Alder forest to search for her."

"I think it's best if we all go."

"No, Kaelan," Aedán bellowed. "This time, I'm going alone. I'm much faster, and we have to act now if there's any chance of finding her."

"Agreed. You can get there a lot faster, but do not take any chances. The Tainted Ones are most likely the sycophants of the Red Man, so they are not going to harm her but merely detain her for his arrival or take her to him."

"Aye, so there's still a chance that she could be there. I'll be off then," Aedán called out as he galloped towards the door.

"Remember—no heroics. Come back to us, and we will react as a group! Agreed? Aedán! Aedán!" No sooner had Kaelan given the instructions than Aedán was out the door.

"So we'll just wait here then?" Taog asked, hoping he wasn't about to be forced back out in the cold of the night.

"Aye, that's right, so we might as well get comfortable," Kaelan said as he took his seat at the long table again.

They had waited just long enough to drink a chalice of mead before the door unlatched and swung open.

"It's Aedán," Oren rejoiced as he held his chalice aloft.

"What's the report?" Kaelan stood from his chair.

Aedán shook his head. "She's not there. I went at least five hundred paces into the forest, and no trace of her." "She's dead," Taog said, shocked.

"No, taken prisoner somewhere," Kaelan suggested.

"Aye, there were no signs of death anywhere. I did note that there was a running brook about a quarter of a mile from the entrance to the forest. It's inhabited by a *bean sidhe*—"

"An alluring but deadly prospect, at best," Kaelan added.

"If we can get a group together to search for Jane, I was thinking that we should use the brook as a starting point, and maybe, just maybe, with a little persuasion, the *bean* could assist us with some information."

"Do you think she'll help?" Taog asked between sips of his mead. "I mean, I did my best to stay clear of her when

I was finding you lot. I didn't want her wailing on my behalf, you know."

"We'll find that out when we get there," Aedán replied.

"We'll need some time to get a detail together," Kaelan said.

"I'm going to get some extra help, as well," Aedán said.

"What do you mean "extra help"? Who are you going to get?" Kaelan asked as he turned to Aedán.

"I'm crossing the realms. I wish to speak to the one that Jane calls Aunt Claire. She is a powerful witch in her world, and I'm sure we could use her help," he said, sounding confident.

"Are you sure It's the right thing to do?" Kaelan asked.

"As far as she's concerned, the worst thing she can do is say no, but when she realises that Jane is not there and that I am offering her an avenue to see her safe return— well, I'm positive she"ll come back with me."

"Okay, meet us near the forest's edge, but be quick. We are running out of time!"

As the last word parted Kaelan's lips, the cold air of the night rushed in through the door of the *sidhe*.

"Oren, take the clurichaun and spread the word. I'll wake Rhoswen and get the weapons ready. Meet back here when you've consulted the village." Kaelan turned to gather the weapons hung on the wall near the entry to the sidhe.

22

Claire stirred from her slumber, awoken early the next morning by the voice of a strange man in her lounge room.

"Hurry, this won't last!"

She turned to her side, stretching, and felt a sharp pain shoot through the lumbar region of her lower back. "Huh, what? Who's there?" she asked as she sat up, startled and confused.

"Pay by credit card with three easy monthly instalments, plus postage and handling."

As the haze of sleep cleared, Claire realised her situation. "Great, another night on the lounge in front of the television." She cussed as she pushed the foot rest back into position and sat bolt upright with her arms pointing to the ceiling while she stretched away the aches from her tired body.

Why did Jane not wake me when she went to bed last night?

"I wonder sometimes," she murmured as she stood up from the chair. A yawn took control of her body for a brief moment, then she twisted around, searching for the remote to put the news on while she prepared breakfast. The voice from the television changed to that of the familiar newsreader from the local morning bulletin. She tossed the remote back onto the chair then went into the kitchen, where she switched on the kettle and put bread in the toaster.

It was very cold in the house for that time of year. Claire cupped her hands around her mug of coffee to keep them warm. Moments later, the toast popped. She spread each slice with margarine and orange marmalade then took two plates to an empty table.

Where is that girl?

Claire put down her mug and marched from the kitchen to find her niece. She stopped in the hall as she heard the announcer cross to the weatherman. *Perhaps he can explain why it is so cold.* But the forecast was an expected top of twenty-two and sunny, which was normal.

"Hmm," she grunted as she turned and continued to Jane's room.

The door was ajar a couple of inches. Claire thought that was odd. Like most young people her age, Jane always kept her door closed.

"Jane, are you up, dear?" she called as she approached the door. She called again while drumming her knuckles against the wall of the hallway, but there was no reply.

"Jane, breakfast is ready," Claire announced as she pushed open the door to reveal an empty bedroom.

Claire's jaw dropped. "Oh, no," she gasped as she realised Jane's bed was still made. She had not been to bed the previous night. She turned and ran down the hall, frantic as she could feel her world crumbling around her.

"Jane!" she shrieked as she caught the wall at the end of the hallway in her right hand to assist her turning the corner towards the sunroom while her feet slid underneath her.

"Jane!" she screamed again, panic stricken that something untoward had happened to her niece. She ran into the sunroom pulling to a halt to avoid catapulting herself over the coffee table. The room was very cold, and Jane was nowhere to be seen. The screen door was shut, but the wooden door was wide open and hooked against the wall.

"Oh my Gods." Claire gulped as she raised her hand to her mouth, recognising in that instant that Jane must have gone out to the garden and not come back in.

"Please be asleep under the tree. Please, Gods," Tears began to stream down her cheeks as she pushed aside the screen door and ran along the path to the edge of the pond wall. Her intrusion had an immediate effect—the frogs ceased their chorus of croaking, and dragonflies hid, clinging to the underside of the closest leaves they could seize. She scanned the other side of the pond to the base of the tree and beyond, but there were no signs of anyone.

"Jane!" she screamed as she turned, crumpling to sit on the pond's edge. The weight of anticipation and subsequent failure of finding her niece in the garden was too great for Claire. She cursed the Red Man and burst into wailing and tears once more.

Minutes passed slowly as Claire sat on the wall, sniffling and trying to control herself. She knew she was no good to Jane if she let her emotions get the better of her.

"This can't be happening," she spluttered as she put her left hand down to support her weight while leaning sideways to retrieve a tissue from her right pocket. She felt something under her palm and looked down to see Jane's book.

"Oh, my Gods, she was here. This is her book." A flicker of hope touched her, only to fade quickly when the realisation dawned upon her that Jane was definitely gone.

Claire picked up the book and held it against her chest.

She heard a vehicle pull into the driveway, and with renewed hope, she sprang to her feet, imagining that it was Jane in the car. Thoughts of taking her in both arms flashed through her mind as she ran towards the house. She had just opened the screen door to the sunroom when she heard a knock at the door. Her heart sank—Jane wouldn't knock.

"Won't be a moment," she responded apathetically, feeling as if a hundred knives had been driven into her heart. She didn't want to answer the door, and she didn't want company. Still, she had to do something to find her niece, and maybe the person at the door could help.

"That's okay," a voice spoke back through the door.

Claire walked into the kitchen and stopped at the table as she saw the breakfast that she'd prepared for them both earlier. She grabbed the backrest of the closest chair and looked up towards the ceiling as she could feel tears welling in her eyes again.

"Oh, stop it," she told herself. She took a deep breath and exhaled while she fanned her face with her hand.

"Coming," she called as she finished lightly dabbing the corners of her eyes. She took a deep breath and walked to the door.

"Hi, Claire. How are you going?" Sophie asked, her face beaming with the widest of smiles. "Is Jane about? I thought I'd surprise her early today, so I borrowed Mum's car. I was going to see if she wanted to come for a drive over to Swansea to do some shopping. I can't live in these leggings and T-shirts my whole life!"

Claire stood there for a moment. She did not reply or meet Sophie's eyes. She was feeling despondent and empty and didn't know what to say.

"Are you okay, Claire? You don't look so well."

"Sorry, come in." She held open the door for Sophie.

"Thanks." Sophie walked in and placed her bag on the table as she looked into the lounge room. "Oh, have I interrupted breakfast?" she asked, turning back to Claire.

Claire pulled the door shut and stood on the mat. Staring out through the flyscreen at Blue Belle, she felt her emotions beginning to swell again.

"Claire?"

"She used to love driving that car. I wasn't comfortable with it at first, but it was a part of her," she said, her attention still fixated on the vehicle.

"What do you mean "used to"?" Sophie asked as she stepped closer to Claire.

"She's gone." Claire broke into tears.

"Claire, you're not making sense," Sophie said as she placed her hands on the tops of Claire's arms. "What do you mean 'she's gone'?"

"Jane's gone," she wept.

"When did you last see her?" Sophie asked as she led Claire to take a seat at the table.

"Last night, before I fell asleep on the lounge. She said that she was going to go out to the garden. I found her book out there this morning, but she wasn't there. I checked her bedroom, and the car is still here. She's been taken." She burst into tears again, her head dropping to rest in the crook of her arm on the table.

"By who? Who's taken her?" Sophie demanded, leaning closer to Claire.

"The Red Man."

"You're not thinking straight! Claire, Claire," Sophie barked. "Are you listening to me? Look, your emotions are clouding your judgement. It is not him—it cannot be him. No one has taken her, I assure you. I can't feel that happening. You said she was going out to read in the garden, and if that's the case, then I think I might know where she is."

Sniffling, Claire lifted her head and looked at Sophie. "What do you mean you know where she may be?"

"If she was in the garden, then it is possible that she may be with the faerie!"

"You mean this person Aedán that she spoke of is real?"

"I guess so." She paused. "I mean, I haven't seen him, but she also told me about him and said she was in the garden when he appeared," she said, her demeanour becoming more exuberant as she spoke.

"But there was no one out there when I looked earlier," Claire replied doubtfully.

"Some things can't or don't want to be seen, and that is my area of expertise," Sophie said with a smile. "Now get up, and let's go and see what we can find."

Claire followed Sophie through the sunroom and along the path of the garden to the pond.

"What exactly is your area of expertise, Sophie?" A new flicker of hope lifted her spirits.

"I'm surprised that Jane didn't tell you!"

"Tell me what?"

"That I have a gift." She laughed.

"What sort of gift?"

"I can connect and converse spiritually to other beings."

"Really, I didn't know, and Jane never said anything, either." Claire sat on the pond wall, surprised to find out this secret after knowing Sophie for many years. "Have you known long? Jane hasn't asked you to contact Grace, has she? Sorry, this news just raises so many questions."

"That's okay. Not many people know, but I've known for at least ten years. I think I get it from my mum's side of the family, but it's odd, though…" Sophie cocked her head to one side.

"What's that?"

"My siblings don't have my gift, but I'm getting side tracked—sorry."

"That's okay, dear. Do you really think we can find her?" Claire asked.

"I think so, though I won't be finding her. In fact, I hope to find Aedán so he'll be able to tell us if he knows where she is and that she is safe."

"Oh, okay. Well, that's a good start, I guess."

"I'll make a start at the base of the apple tree." Sophie walked around the edge of the pond before stopping.

"Claire, can I tell you a secret?"

"Yes, dear."

"Jane hasn't asked me to contact Grace, but I have already. Jane doesn't know, though. I thought I'd do it as a surprise, you know, maybe get her some answers. I hope that's okay," she asked timidly.

"No, that's okay. I wish I had known—I would have joined you. Has it been long since you talked to her?"

"Maybe a couple of months, but I've spoken to her more than once," she said cautiously.

"Is everything okay, dear? You seem a bit on edge. Were you scared to tell me about Grace?"

"I must admit, I was a little apprehensive about telling you, but I'm glad I did. I feel like I've been carrying this burden with me for a long time." She grimaced. "There is one thing that has been bothering me, though."

"What's that, dear?"

"Grace told me of her death, and it's not how it was reported in the news or how Jane knows of it. That's why I've kept my contact with her a secret."

"Oh, really," Claire managed, shocked by the revelation. "You must tell me all about it, but now is not the time. First, we need to find out about Jane."

"Yeah, you're right. She did say that she looks over and loves you both very much, though."

"Thank you, Sophie," Claire replied with a smile. "I'd like to think that she is."

Sophie walked around to the base of tree, her back facing the pond and Claire, who was still seated on the stone wall. Clasping her hands in front of her, she began to chant quietly. She watched Sophie walk deosil around the tree, and her eyes took on a different, fuller shape like black saucers that vanquished all the sclera in both eyes. After three rotations of the tree, Sophie finished in the same position as she had started. She spent a few minutes in silent meditation then re-joined Claire at the stone wall.

"Very interesting watching you do your thing," Claire said as Sophie sat down beside her. "I like what you do with your eyes—very lost soul-possessed kind of stuff."

"Thanks, I guess. Jane mentioned my eyes, as well. I don't get to see them, so I wasn't aware."

"So what did you find out?" Claire asked eagerly.

"This area is a hotbed of activity at the moment. I sense that other Fey are present now or have recently been present, which could suggest that Jane has gone with them.

I didn't actually speak to any of them, unfortunately. It would be great if there was a way to call them."

"Actually, I think there is!" Claire sprang to her feet. "Wait here. I need to get something from the house. Back in a jiffy." She ran towards the house.

Claire hurried to the kitchen and retrieved supplies. Her arms full, she returned to Sophie. "Okay, this is something that we can try to get the faerie to come out and face us." Claire exhaled loudly as she placed the clattering bundle of goods down on the stone wall.

"What have you got there?"

"Ah, this is an old fabled method of attracting faerie to your garden. I'm hoping the same principles will work in this case. Now, the theory is that we mix these ingredients and place it near a plant or tree," Claire continued with a smile of expectation. "The smell and alluring taste is said to be irresistible to them."

"Sounds like a plan! What do you have?"

Claire took an empty jam jar and filled the glass half full with hot water.

"Okay, what we do now is crush seven ginger flowers and place them into the hot water. This will release the aroma of the ginger—they love ginger, apparently," she said enthusiastically. "Now we're going to add two spoons of sugar and a couple drops of honey. Stir this for ten seconds or so." She used a spoon to stir the liquid.

"Don't burn your hand," Sophie cautioned.

"I won't, ten seconds is about enough to mix the ingredients and make sure that you don't burn yourself, as well," she joked. "Okay, now all we have to do is place the jar under the apple tree, sit back, and wait."

"Excellent, I hope it works." Sophie sat at the pond's edge while Claire placed the jar under the tree before joining her.

∞

He sat in the tree for a long time, watching the two women fuss about underneath him, walking around, saying odd little ditties, talking to each other, and then creating the concoction as they sat under the tree. The smell wafted up the tree and danced around his nostrils, nearly driving him wild, calling him to come down out of his hiding place and partake in its sweetness.

"They say"—Claire turned to Sophie—"that when the mix cools, you can apply it to the outside of your eyelids. This will aid you to see the faerie, to see through their hiding spots or to see them in your dreams."

"*Cac*, dearie, *cac*," Aedán bellowed, his voice stealing the quiet tranquillity of the garden as he launched himself from the branches above to land on all four hooves at the base of the tree. Both Claire and Sophie jumped back in shock, screaming as if they had just seen the Red Man himself. Sophie tumbled backwards into the pond.

"Argh," she moaned as she stood in the knee-deep water, Koi rushing past her legs, seeking safety in the chaos that had been thrust into the pond. "What the fuck was that?"

"Are you Aedán?" Claire asked calmly after her initial shock had subsided.

"Aye, that I am," He took the jar in his mouth and swallowed its sweet contents. "That was good. My compliments. But a bit of advice, dearie—irresistible it is; alluring it is not. I'm sure this mead you've created would attract some interesting creatures, especially in an environment such as this, but call Fey out of a hiding spot, it wouldn't. You see, I am not here by chance. I've been watching you both for some time. I was intrigued by your little performance under the tree. The things you did with your eyes—that was great. Remind me to show you what I can change into later. Nice dive, too, dearie, but you don't have to stand on my account," Aedán said.

"You're quite rude, aren't you, faerie?" Claire replied.

"When it suits, dearie, but I am not here to bicker or debate. I arrive with grave news—"

"Is it about Jane?" Claire interrupted.

"Aye, that it is, and it is not good news that I am burdened with."

"Is… is she dead?" Sophie asked hesitantly as she dragged herself back to the top of the stone wall.

"Not dead but a terrible fate, all the same. We believe that she has been captured by the minions of the darkness of the Red Man, and it's rumoured that he intends on taking her life, although we do not know to what end," he replied grimly.

"Jane is in your realm?" Claire asked.

"Aye."

"How did she get there?"

Aedán nodded at the Winesap.

"What? In the tree?" Sophie asked.

"Aye, dearie, and that is why I am here. I've come to find Aunt Claire, the witch. We believe that you may have the power to get her back."

"Yes, that's me." Claire rose to her feet. Relief washed over her, and she felt as though they were making progress towards getting Jane back.

"Well, time to saddle up. We can't waste time making acquaintances, as Jane's life could depend on it." Aedán turned back to the tree.

"Wait!" Sophie screamed. "You're not going without me. I'm her best friend, after all!"

"Aye, I thought you'd say that. Well, come on then!"

"Wait!" Claire implored.

"For crying out loud," Aedán said, "what now?"

"I just have to get something before we go. I won't be long—it's just in the lounge room." She turned and ran back towards the house. She returned two minutes later, puffing and out of breath, but she was holding a calico bag in her hand.

"What's that?" Sophie pointed to her hand.

"I made it yesterday for Jane. I was going to give it to her last night. It's a charm bag."

"Enchanted?"

"Yes. If only I'd given it to her last night, she may still be here now," Claire said forlornly.

"*Cac capaill!* I do not believe that to be true. Jane made her own way to Emain Albach. The Red Man did not take her away from this realm but had his cronies go after her when she arrived."

"That doesn't make me feel any better!"

"Just speaking the truth."

"Well, I foresee that the bag will become very handy in the future." Claire tucked it into her pocket. "Shall we go to wherever it is that you're from now?" She came to stand next to Aedán.

"Emain Albach!"

"That's what I said," Claire joked as Sophie joined them.

"Climb the tree to the first major fork in the trunk. I'll wait for you there, and then we'll get going," Aedán instructed. Suddenly, he was gone up the tree in a blaze of trailing light like a meteor hurtling through space.

"Well, no use standing around here." Claire bent down, holding her two hands with fingers clasped together. "Step on, Soph. I'll give you a boost."

23

Her vision was blurry when she dared to open her eyes. She could only lie still, not knowing where she was, where she was going, or what had happened to her. Every now and again, the vessel she was in hit a bump or divot, and she was thrown into the air, landing hard on her shoulders, back, or hips.

She relied on her hearing to determine what was happening. She could hear horses" hooves and heavy wheels with timber axels that groaned under the weight of a carriage.

That's it. I'm in some sort of horse-drawn wagon.

She could make out singular bright lights in squarish containers that broke through the darkness around her—lanterns, she surmised. The air was filled with other strange sounds and the clinging and clanging of metallic objects: cooking pots, utensils, or weapons. One sound drew her ear—a hollow high-pitched tapping followed by another and another after that. It reminded her of Aunt Claire's bamboo wind chimes. The inside of the wagon had a foul stench to it, which was familiar though Jane couldn't place it.

"C'mon, get up," a sonorous voice bellowed into the night air as a whip cracked above her head, piercing her ears and travelling through her body like a sonic boom.

She jumped, and her body tensed. The hairs on the nape of her neck stood on end. Slowly, her vision became clearer. *I'm in a wooden wagon.* She looked up at a cover stretched over arched ribs that held it in place. She pushed at the cover with her finger; it had some elasticity and sprang back when she pressed it. It felt similar to the skin of a drumhead. It reminded her of an old boyfriend who'd played the bongos, yet the smell was vastly different. The wagon hit another hole, throwing Jane back to the centre of the floor. Her attention shifted to an assortment of hanging paraphernalia clunking and clattering. Then she heard the chimes again, tinkling sweetly pitched notes that created random melodies. The pans, pots, knives, axes, and other weapons hanging precariously above her head were suspended from ribs holding the wagon cover. At either end of each of the ribs was a collection of strangely shaped rods tied and hanging from a leather ring. She pushed herself up to a standing position, legs slightly apart to keep her balance as she rode the bumps, absorbing each impact with her knees. She inspected the chimes, gasping in horror as she realised they were hanging bones. A cold chill washed over her.

Jane's throat constricted as she tried to swallow. She finally recognised the smell. The cover was made of skin.

If it was human, she wasn't sure.

A whip cracked overhead again. The three-beat gait of the horses" hooves resonated from the bare earth. Jane lowered herself to the floor of the wagon and turned towards the source of the eruption. Through the opening at the end of the carriage, she could see the corners guarded by candlelit lanterns. In the middle was the figure of a man driving the reins, holding a whip high above his shoulders with his right arm. He brought the whip down hard before pulling it back with twice the gusto. Its loud crack pierced the night air, announcing his presence to all. His hand returned to its high position over his right shoulder, and the length of the whip draped over his back. The flickering light illuminated of the white body of the whip, and Jane crawled closer, only two feet behind her captor, to study the whip.

A primal reaction took charge of her body. A sense of fear embodied by sound began in the pit of her stomach and raced through her. It forced itself from her mouth in the form of an ear-splitting scream as she recognised what the whip was. The man was holding the spine of an animal or Fey, human.

"Oh, my Gods!" She pushed herself up to her haunches in retreat to the rear of the wagon. "Who are you?" she screamed.

His grip on the reins tightened as he pulled back. The carriage jerked as its momentum suddenly declined. A snorting neigh exploded through the cabin.

"Whoa!"

Jane was thrown about like a ragdoll as she rolled towards the front of the wagon. The pots and weapons that hung above clanged wildly. She hit the front wall with a heavy thud. A heavy object fell upon her torso, pushing wind violently from her lungs. She lay there holding her pained hip. Jane looked up to investigate through teary eyes what was on top of her as she felt the wagon pull to a stop. The driver's horrible whip lay atop her. Chunks of rotten blackened red flesh littered with the twisting bodies of maggots were still attached to parts of the bone. Jane screamed again as the gloved hand of the driver reached into the cabin. She rolled, sending the spine whip to the wooden floor as she scrambled for safety. A boot swung into the wagon, and the deadening thud on the timber reverberated around the skin-covered dome.

"Stay away from me," Jane yelled, as a solidly built man wearing a long black cloak with high collar infiltrated the cabin. When he bent down to retrieve his whip, Jane observed the most horrific sight she could have conjured.

His head—shit, where's his head? Jane's eyes flitted around the shape of the figure before her as she tried to comprehend the creature that held her captive. A black void existed between the collars of his cloak where his head should have been. He dragged his right shoulder through the opening into the cabin. A lantern in his hand illuminated the small space, casting light and shadows that bounced off the skin membrane that encompassed her. A round head-like shape under its elbow, viced against its side, caught her eye. Then a vile putrid stench attacked her nostrils.

A deranged snort bellowed from the shape, sending a shiver of dread through her. Was she about to meet her end in the back of a wagon, at the hands of an unknown creature in an unfamiliar land, never to be found or heard of again?

A black line appeared on the creamy putrid object, which looked like cottage cheese. It stretched farther, taking the shape of a malicious sneer that stretched from one side of the cheese ball to the other. A fold above the mouth rolled in on itself, revealing two small black eyes that darted about its face, acting independently of each other. Jane gasped in disbelief as she realised the creature held its head under its arm rather than on its shoulders.

Jane pushed her back into that farthest corner as she began to chant, fear pulsing through her body. She stuttered her way through,

"Hail fair M-m-moon,

R-r-ruler of the N-n-night;

G-guard me and, um, mine,

Unt-t-til the morning l-light."

The creature stood inside the wagon, studying Jane for a moment. Then it shrieked at her as it raised its right arm, drawing the whip back. An explosion of fetid breath swept around her. Jane tried to hold her breath, but the lack of oxygen and stench made her woozy. Grasping the edges of the wagon, her knuckles white with dread, watching the spine with wide eyes. The creature brought it down towards Jane forcefully, slicing through the skin canopy. Caught in its trajectory, she watched it tearing through all before it, certain she was seconds from death. She felt a warmth down her legs and lurched forward, gulping for air. The malodourous aroma filled her lungs, her vision clouded, and dizziness swirled within her as she could felt herself fall to black.

∞

The Tainted Ones kept vigil at the entrance to a cave set inside a mountain range overlooking the plains. The entrance was halfway up the side, only accessible by foot along a narrow, sometimes dangerous track where jagged rocks and landslips gave way to a steep drop that promised certain death. They kept watch with great awareness on four lights that approached at speed along the track from the forest. One of the dark ones departed its post to alert its master.

The Red Man watched on with keen interest as his sycophant communicated its message of the approaching lights. He arose from his seat, a crudely crafted chair of alder and rowan branches amid two lines of juxtaposed flaming torches.

"The *dullahan* is true in his honour and comes bearing gifts." He laughed wickedly. "Come, my dark one. Let's see what the death bringer has brought to me!"

He walked out to the edge of the outcrop that jutted from the mountain face. He peered over the rim. Small pieces of rock crumbled away from its edge, prompting him to take a step backwards. Beneath him, the lights of the *dullahan's* wagon were stationary alongside its black steed. He scanned the visible sections of the trail that led up the incline, spotting the unseelie faerie, the body of a human draped over one shoulder.

"It won't be long, my dark ones," the Red Man gloated as he turned back towards the cave opening, rubbing his hands together. He returned to his throne. Flanked by his sycophants, he waited.

He waited long enough to hum two tunes to himself and was about to start a third when the *dullahan* slowly turned the last bend then dropped the lifeless body to his feet.

"Do not damage the *duass*," the Red Man barked as he pushed himself up from the chair to approach the *dullahan*, who stood motionless except for the small black eyes that darted about his head.

"Grrr," he grunted, holding out his hand.

"In good time, my deathly prince," he replied as he bent down to inspect Jane's body, rolling her from side to side. "You've done well and shall be duly rewarded."

The Red Man stood, waving the Tainted Ones over to his side. "Pick her up and take her to the farthest corner of the cave. Take only one torch so that she does not awake in the dark, and bind her well, but do not damage her. She must be in pristine condition for the ceremony."

"Payment." The *dullahan's* strong, deep voice echoed throughout the cavern.

"Patience, my friend. I've got just what I promised you right here. Allow me to get it for you." The Red Man bowed then turned to retrieve a crate from the depths of the cave. He returned with a small wooden packing box, which he held in the palm of his hand. A shrill yip escaped the *dullahan's* maw. Pieces of its cottage cheese flesh dripped from its mouth, pooling at its boots, in anticipation of the forthcoming reward. The Red Man freed the lid from the box, resting it to one side, and retrieved a white cube made of crystals that sparkled in the light of the torches.

"Payment," he repeated with his hand out, his black eyes darting frantically across his face.

The Red Man dropped the cube into the waiting hand, which quickly fed the drooling mouth behind it. His eyes steadied to a slower pace as they traversed his creamy head.

"Sweet Crystal," the *dullahan* said gruffly.

"You know, in the realm where it originates, they call it sugar cubes." The Red Man laughed. He could have the Fey of Emain Albach at his beck and call with a tool persuasion that was so easily obtained in the human world. "I thank you for your service, *dullahan*. You may go about your normal business, but be warned that I may call on you again. To prove my gratitude, I shall leave you with, let's say "a bond" for your services in the form of three sweet crystals."

The deliverer of death accepted payment by acknowledging the agreement with a bow then exited the cave to make the treacherous descent back to his wagon and steed. Satisfied that He'd achieved the first step of his master plan, the Red Man meandered back to his throne in the centre of the cavern, where he took his seat to contemplate the next phase of the plan. After some thought, he clapped his hands together twice, summoning the attention of a dark ones to his side.

"Set guards at the entry," he ordered as he sat slouched to one side, "and collect that stinking *dullahan* snot or whatever it is. It's time to awaken the *duass*!"

The Red Man bent down in front of Jane, the cottage cheese drool on a wooden plate in his hand as he admired her features.

"She's a pretty one," he said as he plunged a finger into the stinking white secretion and smeared it on her upper lip.

"If this doesn't awaken her, then she's as good as dead." He stood back up and waited. He counted. *One, two, three, four*. Her muscles began to twitch and spasm. *Five, six, seven*. Jane's eyes snapped open, wide and pleading as she gagged for air, choking on the creamy mucus as it ran into her mouth, tears streaming down her face.

"Aye it's a terrible agony to be woken by but very effective. It's said to bring the dead back to life," he emphasized as he stood above her.

A dark one glided into the cave to find the Red Man in the dimly lit reaches of the far end of the fissure. It beckoned for the Red Man's attention to the front of the cave.

"Can it wait? I'm busy," he yelled at the shadowy figure, who replied with a shake of its head. It motioned again for him to follow as it drifted farther away.

"This better be good." He drew a cloth from his pocket and threw it at Jane in disgust before walking away.

The Tainted One waited at the entry for the Red Man to join him. Its arm raised, it pointed out across the plain to the distance.

"What? What is so important that you disturb me from my work?"

The dark one just pointed towards the horizon.

He scanned the distant landscapes. "What am I— what's that?" He counted six small lights in the distance. "It's hard to say if they are coming this way. Keep watch and update me if they get any closer." He returned to the inside of his refuge.

24

A flurry of wind rushed around the tree, stripping leaves from the branches and flinging them onto the red-dotted ground. Immediately after, a burst of light opened and snapped shut on itself, extinguishing the illumination. Aedán, Claire, and Sophie arrived one after the other beneath the apple tree. Sophie, clinging to a branch, shook her head then looked back to witness the fork of the tree close itself, its wound fusing. It was dark, probably night time. The outline of the tree was visible, and Sophie smelt the smoke that she assumed was from a chimney.

Claire pushed herself up from all fours at the base of the tree and brushed herself down. "Where are we?" Claire asked as she scanned the horizon.

"Fionghan," Aedán replied. "This is the village where I live, the place that Jane was travelling to when the Red Man kidnapped her."

"Do you know where he would have taken her?"

"We don't know exactly, but we know where she was seen last, so we will start there and track her down. Don't worry, dearie. We will find her." He bent down, picked up an apple with his mouth, rolled it a few times, and crunched it in half.

Sophie climbed down the tree and jumped the last yard to land awkwardly on one foot. She stumbled around, bent at the waist, her left hand pressed against her waist.

"Are you all right, love?" Claire called out.

Sophie simply raised her right hand with her index finger extended as she convulsed. She coughed and gagged as she bent towards the ground, holding both sides of her hair, then vomited.

"Aye, there goes my bloody appetite." Aedán spat the remains of the apple from his mouth. "Get yourself cleaned up, dearie. We have to travel to meet the others at the rendezvous point."

"How are we getting there?" Claire asked.

"I'll give you one guess," Aedán replied sarcastically.

Sophie wiped herself down as she stood below the tree. She didn't have a drink or any mouth fresheners with her, so she picked up two apples. She took a bite from the first, chewed it for a while, swished it around her mouth, and spat it out. She did this until the first apple was gone then proceeded to eat the second apple. Claire stood waiting for her with Aedán, twenty yards from the tree.

"Come on, dearie. Time's a wasting," he barked.

"Are you always this blunt?" Claire asked as she placed a hand on his back.

"Pretty much, but being nice in most parts of Emain Albach does not get you far, so you just say what needs to be said." He seemed detached from people's feelings.

Sophie walked over to her two companions, arms crossed and still feeling rather peaky.

"All right then. Jump on, and let's make a move." "Are you okay, love?" Claire asked.

"Yes, I think so. Thank you."

"Will you be okay travelling up here?" Claire asked as she held an arm down to assist Sophie while she mounted Aedán.

"Don't be getting sick on me, dearie."

"I'll try not to, Aedán," Sophie replied as she accepted Claire's hand up.

Once both Claire and Sophie were mounted, Aedán commenced a slow trot through the village. Once they were clear of the last *sidhe* at the far end of the village, Aedán turned westward towards the brook and the Black Alder Forest.

"Dearie, hold on to my mane, and you hold on to your friend," he commanded as he turned his head to look at them.

"How long will it take to get there?" Sophie asked, peering around Claire's shoulder.

"Hold on and find out." He snickered as he reared slightly on his hind legs and sprang into a four-beat gallop.

An instant rush of wind pressed against their bodies as Sophie sensed a shift backwards, forcing both her and

Claire to tighten their grips. The scene before them was surreal, like being in a hyper-jump through space—everything along the trail had light trails as Aedán sped past, dodging and weaving through the maze of obstacles.

Moments later, Aedán slowed, and the elongated images of passing objects began to take on more familiar shapes again. Blood returned to Sophie's fingers as she relaxed her grip.

"That was awesome," Sophie shouted into the breeze behind Claire's ear.

She nodded back in agreement.

At a two-beat trot, Aedán tracked along a brook bordered on both sides by exposed grey stones weathered by centuries of flowing water and wind. The grasses of the plain were a couple of feet in height. Sophie imagined bending down to feel the grass run across the flat palm of her hand, but she didn't dare because of her fear of falling. She could feel soft flower heads of the grass pushing against her legs as the wind blew across the water. They followed the line of the bank, and around the next bend, Aedán deviated from the brook onto a small incline that led towards a dark forest that lay beyond the rise.

"Is it always this cold here?" Sophie asked, adding volume to her voice to be heard over the wind. Her warm breath produced clouds of steam, but no one seemed to hear her. "I'm not dressed for this weather," she moaned forlornly.

"Where are we going?" Claire shouted as she bent forward towards Aedán' ear.

"We're nearly there, dearie. See, it wasn't that long, was it? Over the hummock is the Black Alder Forest that Jane was travelling through when she disappeared. The others will be waiting for us there."

Sophie got the impression that their strategy to rescue Jane was going to plan so far.

"That's good… thank you." Claire turned to give Sophie a thumbs-up.

Then a piercing howl echoed down the vale. Aedán reared, and both Claire and Sophie struggled to hold on.

"Help!" Sophie screamed as she felt her body sliding over Aedán' croup.

Claire grabbed at Aedán' thick bristly mane, grasping a handful of hair while launching her left arm backwards.

"Gotcha" she exclaimed as she grabbed Sophie's wrist before she was dislodged. Aedán returned to all four legs, and Claire pulled Sophie back up to a seated position in front of his hip.

"Are you okay?" Aedán asked over the howling wind.

"Yes, we're okay," Claire replied, "but that was close. What was that noise? It was like a woman screaming in pain like she was being killed. It couldn't have been Jane, could it?"

Sophie tugged at Claire's top while shaking her head. "That couldn't have been her… that sounded evil!"

"Evil, it is, dearie," Aedán added. "It's a *bean sidhe*. She's a wailing woman, sitting at the edge of the water. It is said that the *bean sidhe* wails death is nigh." "Whose death?" Sophie asked.

"Usually, those who hear her."

"What? Can we get outta here before she comes after us?" Claire asked searching the horizon.

"She won't be doing the killing today, dearie. She merely warns of an impending demise then washes the clothes of the wretched victim while discarding his body, all the time crying for a long-lost love," he explained grimly.

"She's sick," Sophie said, disgusted that anyone would take advantage of some else's death like that.

"Not sick, she's a *bean sidhe*!"

"She's a banshee," Claire added. "I learnt about them in school but never thought the day would come when…" She shook her head.

Aedán returned to his course, and at the top of the hummock, a dark line of trees lay no more than half a mile before them.

"There they are." He nodded in the direction of flickering lights at the forest's edge. "Hold on," he cried as he sprang into a canter.

"I can handle this pace," Sophie called out. "Woohoo!"

Claire and Sophie dismounted in front of an audience of six Fey who stood with lanterns and weapons in hand and at the ready, awaiting their arrival at the entrance to the forest.

"*Hóra, upthóg*, welcome to Emain Albach. I am Kaelan the Elder." A short man announced as he stepped forward from the group to greet the new arrivals. "I wish we were meeting under better circumstances, but we have been given a task that we shall see to the bitter end for a triumphant outcome! Do you agree, *upthóg?*"

The group as a collective, with the exception of a small winged woman, began to beat their bronze caladbolg's against the face of their shields while chanting, "*Dé Danann! Dé Danann!*"

Kaelan raised his right hand over his shoulder, and his band of soldiers fell silent immediately.

"Allow me to introduce my companions," He turned and pointed at each one as he announced their names. "You've already met Aedán. This is Oren. And my wife, Rhoswen. We are *Aes sidhe*. The clurichaun with the pack is Taog—he was travelling with Jane when she was abducted—and two *air-foraire* from Fionghan. These are the flying warriors of the *Aes Sidhe*."

Kaelan turned back towards the new arrivals as if expecting them to introduce themselves.

"Oh, I'm sorry. I am Claire. I'm Jane's aunt, and this is Sophie, her best friend." Claire held out her hand to Kaelan.

"*Hóra*, friends. I trust that Aedán has treated you well on your journey here?"

"Merry Meet, Kaelan, and Merry Meet to you all," Claire said with a warm smile. "Yes, he was quite the gentlemen, albeit a little brash at times. I don't understand the term *upthóg*, though. What does that mean?"

"Unfortunately, there is not a lot of time for pleasantries, and we must get moving if we are to get Jane back safely. First, we have to ascertain where the Red Man has taken her. The only way we can do that is to seek the guidance of the *bean sidhe*."

"Are you serious?" Oren asked with surprise. "I didn't think you were serious!"

"Do you have any other suggestions, Oren? If we send out scouts, we'll divide our numbers. We can't afford to do that." Kaelan marched towards the brook, and the group turned to follow.

"I guess we go with them, Sophie." Claire fell into line behind Taog.

"*Upthóg*," Rhoswen whispered to Claire as she walked past. "It means "witch" or "charm-worker.""" Rhoswen smiled as she looked back over her shoulder towards Claire.

"Thank you. Is this *bean sidhe* as bad as I think she is?" she asked gravely.

"We'll soon see." Rhoswen turned back to watch where she was walking.

The group walked in single file until they reached the peak of the hummock, where they could look down on the vale and the brook below. The *bean sidhe* was perched on a large flat rock along the meandering brook. Her legs were folded back under her, and she wore a long flowing red dress that fell off one shoulder, almost exposing a breast. Its hem ended just below the knee. Her olive skin and long black hair was darker than the pale skin and light hair of the *Aes sidhe*. She was scratching at an old piece of clothing as if trying to clean away a stubborn stain.

"She's cleaning. Does that mean she's…" Claire turned to Aedán.

"Aye, dearie, most probably, but only time will tell," he replied with a mollified tone.

"Oren, come with me. The rest of you stay here and keep an eye out for any surprises that the Red Man may send our way."

∞

Oren followed Kaelan down to the edge of the brook. The water moved along ever so slowly and was so clear that the bottom of the brook was visible in the moonlight. The pair stood on the convex bank of the brook, some thirty feet opposite the *bean sidhe's* rock. She hadn't watched them approach, though Kaelan knew that she must have noticed their presence.

"Be on your guard, Oren," Kaelan cautioned as he crept towards the water's edge, his right hand resting loosely between the pommel and grip of the caladbolg.

"We're crossing over?" Oren whispered.

The *bean sidhe* shifted. The gaze of her black lifeless eyes found the pair on the opposite bank, treading lightly, and hands on weapons at the water's edge. She released a gargantuan screeching wail from the pits of her lungs, rippled the surface of the water as it travelled like thunder across the brook. The vibration hit the approaching Fey like a hammer that picked them up and threw back up the hummock some twenty feet.

Kaelan got to his feet first and dusted himself down. Oren was not as fortunate—he was writhing on the ground, clutching his elbow.

"Oren, can you stand?" Kaelan asked. "You need to shake the pain off."

Oren pushed himself to his feet, favouring his right arm. "It's not broken, but it's not good, all the same!"

"It's not your strongest arm, though, so we'll manage."

"It doesn't make using a caladbolg any easier!"

"With luck, we won't need to use them. Now this time, we'll approach with hands clear of our weapons," Kaelan instructed as he began to sidestep down the incline again.

The lady of the brook raised her head once more as the Fey approached again. Her stare was intensely fixated on Kaelan. He suffered her dark soulless eyes looking into him, but this time, he proceeded cautiously at a slower pace with his hands open by his side to signal that he meant no harm. The atmosphere in the vale was intense; the warmth of apprehension flowed through him, shutting out the cold. When he reached the edge of the water, he moved both arms to ninety degrees from his body, palms and fingers flat to demonstrate that he had no concealed weapons. The *bean sidhe's* eyes tracked every movement that the pair made.

"*Hóra*, Mourner of the Night, Lady of the Brook. I come in peace to seek your guidance. My name is Kaelan the Elder of Fionghan. My companion is Oren. We seek to borrow your sight, as we know that you see all. A girl not of this world who goes by the name of Jane, Jane the witch," he explained as the *bean sidhe* returned her attention to the clothes on the rock in front of her.

"Do you see a body?" Oren whispered behind Kaelan's back.

"Shh! She may not be watching us, but she most certainly is listening," Kaelan whispered over his shoulder in an annoyed tone. "Excuse my friend," he continued as he turned back to the lady. He stopped short when he saw her raise her left arm and point towards the mountain range behind her.

"She's pointing towards the Coiscthe Mountains!"

"Get back up with the others. Search the mountains for any signs. I'll thank the lady, and then we'll be on our way," Kaelan ordered.

"Yes, Kaelan!"

Oren scampered awkwardly back up the hummock, where the band waited.

"Is that where she is?" Kaelan asked of the *bean sidhe,* but she did not respond. "Lady of the Brook," he shouted, "is that where the girl has been taken?"

She stopped scrubbing and sat motionless. Then ever so slowly, she lifted her head. Her shadowy eyes drilled right into Kaelan's face. Her red lips parted in a smile, revealing decayed teeth as she lifted her left arm again, pointing towards the mountains.

Kaelan, cautious not to aggravate the *bean sidhe* any further, bowed to display his gratitude, sweeping his hand before him, and turned to run up the incline.

"Oren, did you locate anything?" he asked between breaths as he reached the top.

"Not as yet…"

"Wait, I see it," Rhoswen exclaimed enthusiastically.

"Up there, there's a light, a fire perhaps."

"Where?"

"Look to the highest peak and follow its contour to the right. Two peaks past that, look towards the centre of the mountain, halfway up," she clarified.

"Aye, I see it, too," Aedán said. "It has to be a cave!"

"There's no time to lose and no knowing what the Red Man may do. Follow me," Kaelan ordered as he assumed the vanguard position, walking towards the range at a trot.

The rest of the group fell into line behind him.

The chilled wind increased a couple of knots on the flat of the plain as it pushed against the party that trudged forth in search of the Red Man. They'd been walking for some time. The *bean sidhe's* wailing had become fainter the farther they travelled, and the mountain range loomed on the horizon. The light at the centre of the mountain directly in front of them was becoming stronger. Kaelan held up his right hand, signalling the column to halt. Oren advanced to his right shoulder, awaiting Kaelan's next order.

"Extinguish the lanterns. We can't afford to give the element of surprise away," he ordered, "and get Rhoswen and the *air-foraire* to grab some extra *brats* to cover the glow of their wings!"

Oren repeated Kaelan's orders to the others and retrieved three *brats* from the pack on Taog's back before returning to his position. Kaelan drew his sword, held it aloft before dropping the tip towards the fire on the mountain, and led the march once more.

An explosion thundered in the distance and rolled down the plain towards them.

"What was that? It sounded like gunfire," Sophie exclaimed as she put a hand on Claire's shoulder to get her attention.

"I don't know, but I'm sure that they don't have guns here. Let's just keep in line. If there's a problem, I'm sure Kaelan and the others will take care of it!"

25

The Tainted One at the entrance to the cave kept watch over the plain. Before long, it glided into the cave with a message for the Red Man, who sat on his throne, admiring his quarry. Jane's hands were tied and bound. She sat with her back against the wall, dirt and blood smeared along the left side of her body. Silent tears slowly rolled down her cheeks, and the foul stench of the *dullahan* still lingering under her nose made each breath a battle to contain her urge to dry retch.

"Oh, Gracious Goddess," Jane sobbed, gasping for air. She began a chant, seeking solace and escape from the agonising situation, but she struggled to form the words that usually gave her this comfort. She snorted as gastric reflux pushed its way into her mouth. She spat the contents onto ground beside her. Shuffling footsteps drew her attention, and the sound got closer and closer. She swallowed the acidic taste of her stomach that clung to her tongue and looked up. A blurred image, an outline of a figure obscured by her tears, approached her. What was he going to do to her? Thoughts of every sinister description raced frantically through her mind while her body was subdued by the crudely tied bindings, which wore away at her skin underneath.

"Don't try and wiggle your way free, my dear. Those bindings are tied so that they get tighter the more you struggle," the Red Man warned as he looked down on her.

"Who are you?" she screamed at her abductor, her emotions swelling up within her.

"All in good time, my dear. All in good time. Now be a good girl and lay still for me. I wouldn't want you to get all cut up about losing your freedom." He cackled loudly as one of his dark shadows glided to his side. "Every time I turn around, there one of you are," he snarled through the remains of his laugh as it caught him by surprise.

The Tainted One, after getting its master's attention, glided towards the entrance of the cave, pointing. It stopped five or six feet away from him and looked back. The Red Man was still fastened to his position near Jane.

The dark one started intently into its master's eyes.

"What are you doing? – What – What did you say?"

The shadow seemed to be speaking to him, but Jane did not hear its voice.

The Red Man turned to Jane. "You'll have to wait, my dear. My attention is required elsewhere," he said with a wry smile and beady expression, then he followed the dark one to the entrance of the cave.

"The lights have moved?" he asked his sycophants as he reached the opening to the cavern. The Tainted One pointed out towards the horizon, and the Red Man moved closer to the edge.

"So our travellers, whoever they are, have halved the distance between us, and considering there is nothing noteworthy in these mountains, I must assume that this is some sort of rescue party for my *duass!* Let them come and find that the only thing awaiting them is death." The Red Man triumphantly turned towards his cohorts. "To that end, we must go on the offensive to gain the upper hand. Gather yourselves together, find the *dullahan,* and attack. Report back to me when it's all over."

Three Tainted Ones gathered at the opening, facing the Red Man. They bowed before drifting off the edge of the mountain at speed. The Red Man watched their departure.

Jane struggled to comprehend the situation, and while the Red Man was distracted, she used the time to close her eyes to rid herself of the swirling haze that clouded her mind. She thought of the things closest to her heart. As always, after thoughts of home, Blue Belle, Aunt Claire, Sophie, and the shop, Jane always returned to the closest of all—her mum.

"I love you, Mum. I wish you were here to help me out of this mess I've found myself in."

"Merry Meet, my sweetheart. Don't you realise that I'm with always with you?" Grace replied lovingly as she stood before Jane in a long flowing emerald-green gown that matched her eyes. Her blonde hair hung in ringlets to her shoulders, which complemented the silver clutch and shoes that she also wore.

"You look beautiful, Mama. Where are you going?"

"I have a fundraiser to attend at the University for the Preservation of the Tasmanian Masked Owl."

"Wow. Can I come, Mama?"

"Maybe next time, sweetheart. By the looks of it, you need your sleep," Grace instructed as she pulled the dress up at her waist and crouched in front of Jane.

"Where am I, Mama? Who is this man?" Tears rolled down her cheeks.

"Be very careful of this man, Jane. He will harm you." She stood. "I must be going now. I can't keep them waiting. I love you, Jane. You do know that, don't you?"

"Mum, where are you going?" she shouted. "Mum— Mum, come back!"

She heard the Red Man stomp back into the cave. "She won't help you, my dear. In fact there's no one here that will help you." He laughed.

"Mum, I can't see you," Jane said.

"Save your breath, child—I am the only one here."

"Mama, where are you?" she called as she lifted her head.

When Jane called out for her mother again, the Red Man clamped a hand around her throat and lifting her into the air. He began to squeeze the life from her, and Jane's eyes sprung open. She felt as if her eyes might burst under the pressure of his vice. She struggled to breathe, wiggling like a hapless doll, pleading with her eyes.

"Never make me repeat myself again—do you hear me?" he berated her as she tried desperately to cling to life. "Never!"

"Ca-can-can't br-br-breathe," she managed as the image of her attacker blurred before her.

"Bah, you'll keep," he said as he threw her down against the granite wall of the cave, "but only until Beltane." He laughed.

Jane lay bruised on the ground in a semi-foetal position, her breathing laboured and shallow. She closed her eyes again as the edges became wet from the welling tears that sought to escape. She tried in vain to find the image of her mother again, to have her visit and comfort her, but there was only fear and loneliness.

∞

The band of rescuers trekked on in single file. The glowing light of the fire that marked their destination grew clearer and larger. The full moon hung low over the top of the mountain range towards the north of their position; it lit the ground with a muted light that was strong enough to assist them to navigate over tufts of grasses and the small potholes in the path.

"I'm feeling nervous, Claire," Sophie said as she fidgeted, her fingers not knowing what to do with themselves as she loosely held both hands together as one in front of her waist.

"Don't be," Claire replied without looking back at Sophie. "We'll be reunited with Jane soon."

"I know we will. It's not that, though. I just have a bad feeling that something terrible is about to happen."

"Don't think like that. We'll be okay." Claire turned and placed a comforting hand on Sophie's shoulder. "Besides, Aedán and the others will protect us." She smiled. "Now let's get back into line and get Jane."

"Okay, Claire." Sophie grimaced, trying to take some solace from Claire's words of encouragement.

"Keep a tight line," Kaelan ordered from the vanguard position of the group, his sword still pointing the way.

A clap of thunder sounded again in the distance, closer this time. Oren looked to the sky, where stars twinkled brightly.

"Storm?" Kaelan asked.

"Can't be. I can't see a cloud anywhere," Oren responded as he scanned the horizon once more.

"It's not a storm," Aedán interjected from behind Oren's back. "I think it's a whip, and you know what that means."

"The *dullahan* is here," Kaelan answered in an ominous tone after a small pause. "The Red Man must have employed his services,"

"You think," Oren added sarcastically, "and I've left all my gold back at the village."

"Well, he is not one that you'd have in your circle of friends," Aedán added.

Sophie listened intently to the conversation taking place between the Fey in front of her. *Are we in danger from this*

363

dullahan? "What was I thinking?" Sophie whispered under her breath. *Stay strong, Soph. Jane needs us more than ever.*

They proceeded with caution as they advanced towards the mountains. The Fey carried their swords drawn.

Sophie's faint singing broke the deathly silence.

"What are you doing?" Rhoswen whispered, tapping Sophie on the shoulder.

"Sorry…" She looked back at Rhoswen. "Nerves, I guess."

"Nerves?"

"I tend to sing to pass the time when I'm nervous. I'm sorry."

"Don't apologise, dear. It's sweet. What song were you singing? I don't seem to know that one."

"*The Killing Moon* by Echo and the Bunnymen. I saw the full moon, and it just came to me, it's one of Jane's favourite songs. She was always playing it when we went driving." Reminiscing filled her with great nostalgia, making her smile as she thought of her friend's love of music. "I wish we were back in the car now." Tears forced her to look away into the darkness so she wouldn't feel embarrassed by her moment of weakness.

"You know, Sophie, it's okay to feel sorrow in times of sadness, to feel helpless when there seems to be no hope, but never feel that you have to hide your feelings regardless of what others may think. Jane is your friend. You share a bond that will always remain true. I have faith that the two of you will be reunited, and you must have that same faith, as well," Rhoswen said. "I am a little troubled, though, "Rhoswen added.

"Why's that?" Sophie asked, sniffling as she fought back more tears.

"What is a Bunnymen?"

A laugh escaped Sophie's mouth. "Oh, maybe that's a story for another time, but thank you, Rhoswen, for the advice and the smile."

"You're welcome."

"Incoming, everyone take cover," Kaelan shouted down the line.

They all scrambled to find cover as one of the *airforaire* took a direct hit on the shoulder and was knocked to the ground.

"What's happening?" Sophie screamed.

"We're under attack! Keep your head down." Claire grabbed Sophie's arm and dragged her down with her behind a large tuft of grass.

The *brat* fell from the shoulders of the *air-foraire*, exposing his wings and revealing a shimmering silvery-blue glow as pulses of electricity pushed through the network of veins criss-crossing his upper and lower wings. He stood out like a beacon on a dark night, and soon, all three of the Tainted Ones were dive-bombing his position, but he stood fast, a dagger poised in his hand. He thrust maliciously at each of the shadowy figures as they attacked.

"It's no good," he called as he laboured to make any headway against his attackers. "Permission to take to the air?"

"No, stay grounded," Kaelan barked.

"Kaelan, he can't do all by himself," Oren interjected as he hastily looked from the *air-foraire* to Kaelan and back.

"They're toying with him—look." Kaelan pointed.

"They're pulling up just above his head!" "Why?" Oren replied.

"It's a delaying tactic. Can't you see?" Aedán retorted. "The *dullahan*!"

The clatter of the wooden wheels filled the air as they bounced along the dirt track, spitting stones. The horse's snort reverberated across the plain, sending a bursts of steam from its nostrils on every second beat as its galloping hooves struck the ground. The *dullahan* bellowed a bloodcurdling roar as he advanced on their position, his right arm raised in the air, holding a spinal cord as if it were a whip. He quickly closed the distance.

"Kaelan, the *dullahan*," Oren shouted, pointing at the incoming wagon.

Kaelan looked across just as a glowing white elongated flash stretched out from the wagon like a chameleon's tongue. It grasped the uncovered *air-foraire*, picking him up like a toy. It shook him violently before pulling him back and snapping him forward with a thunderous crack, slinging him into the air.

Sophie watched on in horror as the body, flaccid and lifeless, sailed through the sky then landed with a tremendous thud. He did not move.

"Why did he not fly away?" Sophie sobbed as the rest of the group hid in stunned silence.

"His wings were broken, dear," Rhoswen replied softy. "He was most likely dead before he hit the ground, crushed to death." She turned to Kaelan, awaiting his orders.

Meanwhile, the Tainted Ones hovered above the carnage, waiting for their next victims as the *dullahan* continued his advance on their position.

"What's the plan?" Aedán whispered

"We will take the *dullahan*. I need you to get the attention of the Tainted Ones and draw them away from the battle. Engage them elsewhere, and when you do, shapeshift. You'll know what to do," Kaelan said.

"Aye."

"Why the bloody hell do we get the *dullahan*?" Oren protested, as his whisper suddenly got a little louder.

"Keep it down," Kaelan ordered, holding his hand out while gesturing in a downwards motion. "Have faith, brother, for we can take him. We need to get close enough that he cannot use his whip. Then we pry his head away."

"You do realise that he can still kill us if we have his head," Oren stressed, not feeling at ease with Kaelan's plan.

"Aye that he can, but he needs to see us to do that," Kaelan conceded, "and to that end, we're going stuff his head into a feed bag and hang it out for the crows!" "And what about his body?" Aedán asked.

"We put it to the sword, of course," Kaelan answered with a wry smile.

"Is it wise to deplete our numbers and have Aedán leave the battle?"

"He is the key to our success," Kaelan replied as he turned to Aedán. "If you remove the dark ones from the battle and destroy them, we can take the Red Man by surprise."

"Taog, look after our two visitors. Make sure that they do not come to any harm. Any questions?"

"Kaelan, he's here," Oren interrupted as he pointed through the tuft of grass at the slowing wagon.

The wagon rolled to a stop as the bringer of death stood from the rumble seat, letting the reins fall to the wooden floor. He held his vile secreting head in his left arm, and the grotesque spine whip hung limp in his right hand. He surveyed the landscape, where Sophie shrank back in fear. The dark figures glided overhead, circling the wagon and the lifeless body of the first *air-foraire*.

His attention was drawn to his left as a black object shot off like a bullet, separating from the main group and making itself an easier acquisition for the *dullahan* and his cohorts. He released a throaty snarl as his left eye danced back and forth, tracking the black Fey. The right remained on the Tainted Ones, and his growl seemed to draw their attention. He pointed in the direction Aedan had flown, in the direction of the Black Alder Forest. He released another resounding wail while cracking the whip over the mound that lay before him.

The three Tainted Ones left in pursuit, keeping a tight line that glided effortlessly over the plain. Meanwhile, the *dullahan* scanned the land before him. Sophie suspected sunrise was a while away, and the wind finished freezing her to the bone, though the *dullahan's* appearance had already chilled her to the core.

26

Kaelan sat watching the *dullahan*, his right forearm held at shoulder height, his fist clenched. He could feel the group's tension, aware that they knew the future was uncertain for some of them. Yet, their morale had received a boost when Aedán successfully led the Tainted Ones away from the battle. They now lay in wait, preparing to attack.

The *dullahan* growled with frustration. Kaelan hoped the creature could not see them, though it must know they were there.

"Wait," Kaelan ordered, his fist still clenched in full view of the Fey party. "Wait!"

The headless rider turned away and prepared to disembark. He threw a leg over finding purchase on the highest of the three-foot pegs on the side of the wagon. He still held his head in the left arm, using the right to guide him down.

"Attack!" Kaelan shouted as he pushed himself forward on both feet to scamper over the top of the grassy tuft, his caladbolg raised as he led the charge. The others followed his lead enthusiastically as Taog, Claire, and Sophie all looked on from the safety of their own positions.

Kaelan bellowed a war cry while advancing on the *dullahan's* left flank. Oren's charge was ten feet to Kaelan's right as he ran directly at the enemy, who was stepping out of the wagon, sword drawn. Rhoswen, minus her *brat*, left the safety of cover, running five yards towards her target before she propped to draw an arrow and take aim. The remaining *air-foraire* pushed the *brat* off his wings, watching over his shoulder as he stretched each of his four iridescent glowing pinions. Slowly, he flapped them in unison before he bent his knees and pushed himself skyward, holding a javelin in both hands.

Kaelan was the first to reach the wagon; the *dullahan* seemed shocked that anything or anyone would have the audacity to attack him. Kaelan pulled himself up onto the wooden deck beside the rumble seat. Oren issued his own war cry as he rushed towards the ensuing battle. The *dullahan* clutched at his spine whip as he wheeled to his left. The blade of Kaelan's caladbolg sliced through the night air, cutting a piece of clothing as it narrowly missed its target. Rhoswen released an arrow. The ends of the arrow quivered back and forth as it carved the still air to find its target in the arm that held the *dullahan's* head.

He fell sideways and released an ear-splitting howl before hitting the ground hard. He came down heavily on his left side, his shoulder and upper arm taking the weight of the fall as he hit the ground, snapping the fletching of the arrow. Oren weaved between the tufts of grass as he closed in, his blade drawn and held high above his right shoulder while he protected his vitals with a round wooden shield. The *dullahan* struggled to find his feet. He pushed himself up on one knee and drew the whip back, his black eyes darting randomly across his face.

Rhoswen grabbed at the pelt quiver that hung over her left hip and prepared to take another shot. Above the melee, the *air-foraire* circled for the last time as he chose his moment to attack. The group currently held the upper hand, and they had to press their advantage. Gripping the javelin, he banked a hard left, rolling as he turned. His target was dead ahead as his altitude decreased. He passed Oren, who was running at the dazed *dullahan*, then extended the javelin to ready for the impact.

The *dullahan* cocked his arm and cast the whip forward towards its target, the tip extending outwards as its skin began to glow. The *air-foraire* began evasive manoeuvres, groaning as he banked into a hard roll, but it was too late— the tip of the whip pierced his chest. The wound smouldered, turning an orange-red like molten lava as it encircled the glowing bones of the whip, which pushed its way farther into his body. It found an exit point just below his tailbone, impaling the flying faerie whose determined expression dropped from his face as his body collapsed around the structure of the invading bones. The *dullahan* flicked his wrist, sending a wave along the whip. The jolt of energy burnt through the Fey's body like a hot knife in butter. The charred lifeless body peeled away from the whip into two separate pieces and fell unceremoniously to the ground.

Oren charged headlong, ignoring the strike that shot past high above his right shoulder.

"Arrrr," he cried as he reached the *dullahan*, who was retracting the whip back to his side. He did not have enough time to strike again, so he dropped his shoulders and lunged forward. Oren launched himself into the air and thrust his blade down into the *dullahan's* shoulder. The creature knocked Oren backwards. As he fell, his trailing sword cut deep into his opponent's upper back.

Rhoswen waited with her second arrow drawn as Kaelan stood above them atop the wagon, watching and waiting for his own moment to strike, his caladbolg by his side, a hessian bag in his free hand.

∞

"I'm going," Claire protested in frustration as she looked from the developing confrontation back to Sophie and Taog.

"Going where? You can't go anywhere. It's too dangerous out there. You'll get yourself killed—no, I think it's best if we all stay here," Taog advised as he watched his two companions. "And besides, if the *dullahan* didn't get us, then Kaelan would for disobeying his directive!"

"I think he's right, Claire. We should stay here, where it's safe," Sophie added as she rubbed a gold crucifix between her thumb and index finger.

"Is that gold?" Taog asked.

"What about Jane? She's up there alone with the Red Man, as we speak, being tortured for all we know." She looked up the side of the mountain, at the light being emitted from the mouth of the cave. "The headless guy is busy. The shadows are gone! We can slip past them and get up there and save Jane."

"No, no, no," Taog said. "That's not a good idea. The Red Man is dangerous. I'll take my chances down here, I think." He seemed unable to take his eyes off the trinket around Sophie's neck.

"Claire, don't go," Sophie said nervously.

Claire regarded Sophie for a moment. "I promised Grace that I'd always look after her little girl. She's all grown up, but I will always look out for her." A lump formed in her throat, and her eyes became watery. "I'm going up there, with or without you." Claire stood. "When we're back, come into the shop, and well change that charm to a talisman that matches your power." She smiled. "Now wish me luck and stay safe. I'll see you soon." Claire ran off towards the base of the mountain. She heard Sophie calling to her, but she ran as fast as she could.

She stumbled occasionally over the rise and fall of the moonlit plain. She chose a course at ninety degrees to the battle and followed the direction that Aedán had taken when he lured the Tainted Ones away from the others. When she was sure that she was safe, she slowed to a walk before stopping, her hands on her knees as she bent over to catch her breath.

"I haven't had to run that far since school," she puffed as she looked back at the ensuing skirmish before turning her attention to the light high above her.

"I'm coming, sweetheart," she promised as she began to run towards the base of the mountain with a renewed energy and determination.

Claire reached the base of the mountain and stopped to look up at the light escaping the open mouth of the cave to get her bearings. She was directly below it and knew that the path leading to the cave wouldn't be too far away, so she began to search desperately as every second that passed without her interference was possibly a second too many for Jane. She ran along the face of the cliff, trailing her hand against the granite outcrops as she investigated each and every hollow for the concealed passageway. After some twenty to twenty five yards of nothing, Claire turned and ran frantically back the way she'd come, looking above her to find her starting mark.

"Show yourself," she screamed at the gigantic formations.

She ran another ten yards then slowed to a walk, panting and frustrated. "Where are you?"

Claire stopped to compose herself as she looked at her surrounds again. She started to pace back and forth. She drew some deep breaths to clear her head—she knew that panic would only disrupt her efforts.

"A spell—there must be a spell or chant that I can use to assist me to find the way. Think, think!" She pressed both palms against her temples.

"I got it!" A renewed sense of hope came over her. "Okay, okay, here will do," she said as she looked around her feet. She knelt, shaking the tension out of her shoulders and arms while she stretched her neck from side to side and exhaled a slow, long breath.

"Okay, good. I'm ready. Let's do this." She took her pentagram between her right thumb and index finger and closed her eyes.

"O Gracious Goddess,

O Gracious God,

Grant me the gift of foresight.

Reveal the path hidden by night.

Grant me strength to scale the summit.

Give me the agility so I do not plummet.

Reveal the path that I may follow.

Grant me this for Jane's tomorrow.

O Gracious Goddess, O Gracious God, Make us three.

So mote it be."

Claire sat with her eyes closed for a moment, reflecting on the spell she had just cast, imagining the ripple effects of the words as its purpose was sent forth into the universe to do her bidding. Slowly opening her eyes, she was astonished to see a vision of gold zigzagging its way up the mountain face.

"The path to the cave," she murmured in awe as she stood and approached the spectacle in front of her, jaw ajar, her eyes reflecting the sparkle of the gold dust that coated the rocks. She pointed a finger at the glowing granite, lowering her digit to touch the dust that seemed to float around the outline of the pathway. She was ever so careful, lowering her finger gently, but the gold dust parted around it as a floating object would wash through your fingers when attempting to pick it up.

"Don't want to be touched? I can respect that," she whispered with a smile, "Thank you, Cernunnos. Thank you, Cerridwen, and blessed be, but now it is now time to rescue Jane," she declared as she brushed her hands together and begun her ascent up the mountain.

∞

Aedán's snout flared with each steaming breath as he galloped over the plain towards the Black Alder Forest. The Tainted Ones raced after him, jockeying for the lead position, to be the first to strike him down. The forest loomed as the outline of the trees before him grew larger. Aedán prepared to turn and make a stand. He hadn't fought the shadows before, but he knew what he would do— follow Kaelan's advice. He veered to his left as he found the track that led to the forest, two hundred yards and closing. He heard the wail of the *bean sidhe* coming from the brook to his right. He had to act—the time had come, but as he was about to turn and make his stand, two dark almost-black projectiles zoomed past overhead.

"What the hell was that? No one told me that these things can actually can use weapons." He huffed as he decided there was no going back. "I'll be darned if this is how it ends!" he shouted as he pulled to a stop, throwing clods of grass and earth from under his hooves as he dug his hind hips in. His pursuers launched a third dark bolt at him. Aedán yowled in pain as the missile found its mark, hitting him in the back. As he slowed, his nostrils filled with the smell of burnt hair. A pulsing throb coursed through his body, but he was not maimed to the point of conceding the battle. He turned to face the enemy head on.

The shadows were only fifty yards behind and closing fast. The closer they got, the clearer the expressions on their faces became—broad smirks on all three. They must have known that they had made the first vital blow, but was it enough to turn the battle in their favour?

Twenty-five yards.

"This better bloody work, Kaelan." Aedán grimaced as he watched the marauding pack glide in for the kill.

The lead Tainted One reached behind him, revealing a fourth bolt.

Fifteen yards.

He gripped the bolt in his right hand, his fully extended arm back beside his thigh.

"If I miss, I'm dead," he reminded himself as he raked the ground with his front left hoof. A small cloud of dust dissipated into cool air.

Ten yards.

"This is it!" he shouted as his body tensed, adrenaline pumping through his veins. "Come get it, boys!"

Five yards.

Aedán closed his eyes and willed himself to shift. His father had taught him at a young age that to shift, he had to visualise himself as the being that he wanted to change to. His decision now as the Tainted Ones closed in was an eagle. He began the metamorphic change of the shape shifter. The colour of his skin became lighter as a spiritual light from his inner being glowed through him. The light took on the shape of a ball that encircled the body. It pulsated as it grew quickly, expanding at a horrific rate, becoming blindingly brighter and brighter. The Tainted Ones tried in vain to stop, but there was no ground beneath them to create friction or apply force to. Instead, they slid towards the growing light before them. Head splitting cries were cast into the night air as arms flailed, grasping at nothing, until their only relief was to shut their eyes.

The ball expanded quickly to three or four times its original circumference before it imploded in on itself, drawing in the darkness that surrounded it. The Tainted Ones were helpless as the vacuum sucked them into the centre of the void as the light shrank to the size of a pea, encasing them like a prison. It then stretched outwards on both sides at a hundred and eighty degrees, stretching and stretching until it could go no farther. Like a rubber band, it had to give. Both sides snapped back towards the centre of its origin like two bullet trains travelling at max speed until they collided, creating an explosion of a thousand white lights like a firecracker on Guy Fawkes Night.

The thousand white twinkling lights changed to a golden shade as they fell from the sky, fading to a blackened ash before settling on the ground. Silence fell on the site of Aedán' stand as the black of night cast its cape over the scenery once again. The *bean sidhe's* wail broke the silence as she called for the corpses of the dark ones, but there were no bodies to be delivered, only the burnt ash that covered the ground of the site.

∞

As if on cue, the shot presented itself, the path was clear and the target stood hunched to one side as Oren's body hit the ground at the *dullahan's* feet. Rhoswen released the arrow, and the missile tore through the black trench coat, burying itself deep into the *dullahan's* flesh on the left side of his chest. His black eyes went crazy bouncing across his lumpy face as another piercing bellow emptied from his lungs, echoing across the plain. The impact jolted his body back into the side of the wagon. The moment they had planned for had arrived—Kaelan seized the moment and launched himself at the enemy.

He leaped from the top the carriage, a war cry of sorts dragging behind his body as it descended. He hit the shoulders of the bringer of death and toppled him to the ground with a thud. A second scream boomed into the night and bounced off the cliff face of the Coiscthe Mountains. The pain was etched on Oren's face as he lay trapped under the *dullahan's* body. Another arrow whistled through the air and pierced the *dullahan's* shoulder as Kaelan rolled to his feet. His caladbolg clanged to the ground as he dropped it to take the hessian bag in both hands.

"Rhoswen, get over here now," Kaelan barked as he scampered sideways around the tangle of bodies on ground before him. "We have to get his head now!"

Kaelan looked up to see Rhoswen's silhouette running towards him, then a brilliant white light flashed along the horizon behind her. He blinked furiously, trying to restore his vision, but all he saw were blurred shapes around him as he stumbled awkwardly towards her.

"Rhoswen!" he screamed, "Rhoswen!"

"I'm here, my love." She grabbed onto him. "What's wrong?"

"I can't see properly. My vision, It's all distorted by the bright light. Did you see it? Behind you, when you were running. It had to be Aedán." He gasped in despair. "It's up to you now. Here's the bag." He held it in the direction of Rhoswen's profile.

"He'll be okay, as will you," she replied. "Not all is lost. You can see objects in front of you. You had to have some vision to offer me this bag, and before long, the rest of your vision will return," Rhoswen said reassuringly as she took the bag from Kaelan.

The *dullahan's* body began to stir. The head was still firmly clenched under his arm, the black eyes darting across his face, watching, determining, knowing that its fate was dependant on his body being able to respond and stand.

"*Cac*," Oren screamed, "the bloody thing is starting to move. Would you stop the chatter and take that ugly excuse for a head!" He grabbed the *dullahan's* arms. "Take it! Take it now!" he shouted.

Rhoswen held the bag in both hands as she high stepped carefully between Kaelan and the *dullahan*.

"The head—get the head," Kaelan barked.

"Kick the bloody thing," Oren called to her.

"Let me concentrate. You just keep holding on!"

The *dullahan* groaned and twisted as Oren struggled to hold on to him.

"Rhoswen, quickly," he said, the strain of the scuffle evident on his face.

She pushed the *brat* off her shoulders, revealing her wings, which she stretched while stepping over Oren's body to face the *dullahan's* head. His manic eyes slowed, returning to a somewhat stationary position on his face. His stare locked onto her, and he gave an almighty final push to get to his feet.

Kaelan blindly dived on top of the tussling duo as everyone seemed to cry out in unison under the pressure of conflicting energies. Rhoswen didn't have time to use any magicks on the unseelie Fey, so she struck out at the *dullahan's* head with all her might. Her mistimed blow hit the *dullahan's* forearm and deflected up into his face, dislodging the head from his grasp. It fell hitting the ground with a thud. The *dullahan* screeched as his head rolled a couple of feet before Rhoswen scooped it up into the hessian bag.

"Got it!" Rhoswen shouted gleefully as she held the bag aloft.

"Get it as far away as you can," Kaelan ordered as the *dullahan's* headless body threw him to the ground.

"Oren, can you roll away?"

"Well, I am not hanging around here." He moved out of the way as the *dullahan* stumbled about blindly, swinging his arms.

Rhoswen flapped her wings and launched herself into the sky, the hessian bag securely in her hand. The *dullahan* howling as she flew away from the wagon.

"Strike him with your blade," Kaelan ordered, but Oren couldn't put weight on his injured leg to get to his feet.

A blue trail of light tracked Rhoswen's trajectory towards the brook and the *bean sidhe*.

Kaelan stood, his caladbolg firmly gripped in both hands as he swung the broad sword at the first dark shadow that he could make out through his blurred vision, hoping that he would connect with his intended target.

"To your right, to your right," Oren barked, as Kaelan's sword sliced nothing but air. "Four more feet!"

He adjusted his stance and swung the heavy blade across his body. He felt a small jolt on the blade as it slowed ever so slightly against resistance.

"You did it, you got him, Kaelan," Oren cheered as the headless body cloaked in a black trench coat collapsed to its knees then fell forward, crashing to the ground. It lay there motionless at Kaelan's feet, and he rested against the pommel of his sword as he caught his breath.

"We did it? He's really dead?"

"He sure is, my dear," Rhoswen replied as she landed gently beside her husband. "The beast's howling stopped as I approached the brook. I knew it—I knew you had been successful, so I dropped the bag, and here I am. Are you all okay?"

"My sight is returning, but it's slower than I'd hoped for."

"And you, Oren?"

"My leg—I think it's broke. I can't stand."

"What are we going to do? We need to get after Claire. She slipped away during the battle, to the mountain." Rhoswen turned to look at the light emanating from the cave.

"She's gone after Jane," Oren exclaimed.

"We have to go after her," Kaelan added as he looked from his comrades to the mountain above.

"But I can't move!"

"I could try to carry you up," Rhoswen offered.

"You can't," Kaelan said. "It would be too much."

"Perhaps I could be of assistance," a voice offered from behind them.

Kaelan spun around to see Aedán standing there, regarding them.

"Aedán," Rhoswen said joyfully, "you're back!"

"You were successful! May your deeds never be forgotten," Kaelan congratulated his friend.

"Aye, I was successful," he replied as began to walk towards them.

"Aedán, you're hurt!" Rhoswen moved towards him.

"It's nothing, just a flesh wound. It'll heal."

"Let's get moving then." Kaelan looked towards the mountain again. "Will you be okay to carry Oren up there?" he asked, turning back to Aedán.

"Aye!"

27

Claire approached the summit of the path. The gold dust that had revealed the path had become sparse nearer the entry of the cave, but the light spilling out from the cavern led her. Taking a deep breath, she crept forth to the last rock that would conceal her presence as she scanned the opening, looking for guards or anyone who would put up resistance. She saw none.

"This can't be right. Surely someone or something must be on lookout! What if it's a trap?" she asked herself. She looked behind her in case she'd been followed. Still there was no one.

Satisfied that she was still unnoticed, she crept across the twenty-yard expanse of the granite bluff to rest in the shadows beyond the edge of the cave mouth. Collecting her thoughts, Claire took a deep breath and peered around the corner into the Red Man's hideout. She couldn't hear anything—no talking, crying, or footsteps. So she gathered all the courage she could muster and tiptoed as quietly as she could into the cave, hugging the granite wall where the light danced with the shadows, where she would have the most protection.

The farther she ventured in, the more pronounced the wind's whistle became as it traversed the labyrinth of tunnels inside the mountain to escape over the ridge and into the valley below. Claire was cautious with each step, placing it gently, as she didn't want to alert Jane's captor of her presence. Then she heard a noise come from around the corner. As she approached, the light source got brighter. Then she heard the sound again. Someone was clearing his throat. It was deep and raspy. It had to be the Red Man. Claire, shaking with nerves, crouched down and edged her way to where she could safely peer around the corner.

A man was pacing back and forth in the centre of a huge chamber lit by open-flame torches. A large crudely constructed chair stood against the left wall of the room, and at the back of the chamber, Jane sat in a ball, her chin atop her knees, rocking. Claire wanted so desperately to call out to her, to run over, pick her up, and carry her away, but she knew it would not be that easy. The Red Man was dangerous and unpredictable, so she had to bide her time and think of a plan.

∞

"Mum, I need you." Jane sobbed as she pushed her face onto the tops of her knees as she sat alone, rocking back and forth. She struggled to see clearly through the tears that clouded her vision and the flickering light emitted by the torches, but she knew the Red Man had to be close by. He needed her for something, something to do with Beltane, which if she remembered correctly was still two days away. "Oh, Aunty Claire, I should be helping you prepare for the sabbat, and yet I'm somewhere. God, I don't even know where that is! I must still be in Emain Albach, as I do not remember porting to anywhere else. This is so confusing." She lifted her head towards the ceiling of the cave then nestled it back in the crook created by her knees. "Taog, I was with Taog." She realised he had abandoned her when the shadows—the same ones that she'd seen in the cave—tried to attack her in the forest.

"It's no use. It looks like I'm by myself," Jane said as she began to wiggle her limbs in an attempt to free herself of her bindings.

Jane looked up and watched the Red Man pace. He was preoccupied, talking to himself. He seemed in the midst of hatching a plan. He'd said earlier that she would keep until Beltane. She didn't know what He'd meant by that. Jane thought long and hard about the meaning of Beltane and how the sabbat was practised in relation to Wiccan belief.

Why wait until Beltane? It marked the beginning of summer, the celebration of renewal. *Fertility? Rebirth, rebirth, rebirth...* She looked within herself for an answer. *Rebirth... starting afresh... starting over. That has to be it— he's going to restart and be reborn.* She doubted her reasoning. "But who are you, and what do I mean to you?" "Have you figured it out yet, girl?" A stern voice intruded on her thoughts, jolting her back to reality.

She raised her head to stare directly at the Red Man, who had deviated from his pacing to draw near her.

"Who are you?" she shouted. "Why do you need me for Beltane? What's happening? Am I going to die?" She broke down into a flood of tears. "I hate you, you foul excuse for a man!"

"I've been called many things, my dear, but "a man" has never been one of them. Many refer to me as the Red Man, but that is purely because of the clothes I wear. As for the rest—well, as I said before, there will be time for that." A smirk touched the corners of his lips. "But let me reassure you that when that time comes, it will be an interesting, if not an exciting, experience"—he bent down to take Jane's chin in the palm of his right hand—"for me." He pushed her face back against the granite wall and stood.

"Why don't you tell her who you really are?" a loud voice boomed from the front of the cave.

The Red Man spun around, his face twisted with anger.

"Who's there? Step out into the light and show yourself, or I promise that your next words will be your last," he yelled back, throwing his arms in the air as he pranced about on the spot in a rage.

"I see some things have never changed, Silas." Claire stepped from the shadows.

"*Cac,*" the Red Man cursed through an involuntary snicker. "You've got some *magairles* to show your face in these parts, Claire."

They eyeballed each other while standing their ground some fifteen yards apart.

"Let's not discuss the past, Silas, nor why your delusions insist on repeating them in the future. I will not allow you to tear this family apart again, so if you know what is good for you, you'll hand Jane back to me, and we'll be getting back home!"

"Know what's good for me?" He laughed as he stole a quick glance over his shoulder towards Jane. "My dear, do you forget who you're dealing with? My days at the coven are long in the past, and my powers have grown tenfold. Do yourself a favour—turn around and go back where you came from. You have no right over this girl." He slowly took two steps towards Claire with his arms out by his side. "Her blood is thicker to mine than it is to yours."

"You have no right to lay claim on her," Claire snarled, her skin turning red in anger as the veins in her forehead began to pulsate.

"More so than you, my dear, more so than you." He chuckled.

"And her fate, will that end with your hand as Grace's did?"

While the Red Man's attention was drawn to Claire, Jane slipped the bindings from her wrists by contorting her appendages until she could pull a hand free. She gingerly ran her fingertips across the right side of her cheek, wincing when they caressed the abrasions caused when the Red Man rammed her face against the granite wall. She pushed herself up to her hands and knees, suffering the haze of what she suspected was a mild concussion, and a familiarity pushed through the grey that clouded her mind.

She pushed herself up to a standing position, using the granite wall as support.

"Grace died in a car accident, which can be seconded by my statement and the police statement, as well as the coroner's report." He chuckled. "Claire, Claire, Claire…" He took another couple of steps towards her. "After how many years—eight, nine, is it?" "Ten," she quickly replied.

"Ah, ten years… time does certainly go quick, doesn't it, Claire?" he asked with a wry smile as he leant forward towards her, rubbing his hands together.

"Cut the bullshit, Silas. The whole coven knew you were responsible. You have always been a loose cannon. Your interest in Wicca and magickal lore was minimal, at best. You eventually became powerful with time, thanks to my sister, but it is a shame that Grace did not see through it, as we did. It's a travesty we did not warn her earlier. You know, as time went on, it became more apparent that something was amiss, and to now find out that you're Fey— well, that explains a lot!"

"What are you doing here, Claire? Surely it's not to tell me that you feel guilty about Grace's death."

"I feel guilt—I feel guilt every day of my life, but I do not seek you out to find a shoulder to cry on or to reminisce about times when people thought you were a wonderful person."

"Then why?" he asked with a shrug. "If it's about the girl, then forget it. I have big plans for her, and she is not going anywhere. So unless you want to be with your sister, then I would suggest turning around and going back where you came from."

"You know I can't do that, Silas," she replied grimly as she took a wand in her right hand from the waist of her pants and pointed it towards her adversary.

"Aunty Claire, is that really you?" Jane asked. Still feeling the effects of the Red Man's malicious attack, she stumbled towards the centre of the chamber. "Oh, Aunt Claire, it *is* you!" Jane said, realising the figure closest to her was the Red Man.

"Stay where you are, girl," he snapped, stealing a glance over his shoulder.

"Yes, dear, it's me. I've come to take you back to Avalon."

"She's not going anywhere. She's mine!" He raised his *shillelagh* in the air. The grip, a large stone polished by many years of wear, began to glow and emit a bright golden-orange light.

"She's not yours, Silas," Claire bellowed. "You gave up that right many years ago when you killed Grace and abandoned your daughter. You're a pig of a man and a sad excuse for a parent," she charged vehemently as a bright light emanated from the tip of her wand. The light shot outwards before turning back on itself, separating in all directions around Claire, cocooning her behind a protective shield of energy.

"Nice trick, Claire, but can your shields protect you from this?" An orange light shot forth from Silas's staff and connected with the dome that protected Claire. The light made a hissing sound like an electrical current, and when it hit Claire's blue light, a terrible surge of power and smoke resulted as the orange light mushroomed off the surface of the shield.

"Stay back!" Claire shouted at Jane.

∞

Oren gripped Aedán' mane and gingerly pulled himself onto his back. "What about Taog and Sophie?" Rhoswen asked as she turned to Kaelan.

He sheathed his caladbolg before replying. "Probably best that they stay down here out of harm's way!"

As Aedán whistled for them, they all looked in the direction of where Sophie, Taog, and Claire had taken cover amongst the tufts of grass.

"We're coming out," Taog called. Two of them stood up to re-join the group.

"We're going up to the cave to retrieve Jane and Claire." Kaelan motioned towards the light with a nod of his head. "I need the both of you to wait here—we can't risk anyone getting hurt unnecessarily."

"I think I should go up there with you." Sophie stepped past Taog to address Kaelan directly. "I'm Jane's best friend. She'll need me when all of this is done!"

"And that's why you should stay down here with Taog," Rhoswen replied as she reached out to take Sophie's hand. "She will need you when this is all done, but it's too dangerous up there. We need bodies there that'll know what

393

to do, when to do it. You understand what I mean, don't you, dear?"

"Yes, stay out of the way and let the clurichaun babysit me. He's been doing such a great job so far," she snapped in a sarcastic tone as she pulled her hand back from Rhoswen and stomped off in the direction from whence she'd come.

"Stupid fairies," she cursed under her breath as she left.

"We heard that," both Rhoswen and Aedán said simultaneously.

"Whatever!"

They all looked at each other and back to Sophie, who disappeared over the mound closest to them.

"Come on then," Kaelan ordered as he trudged off towards the cave.

"The pathway narrows up here," Kaelan called out to the group behind him. "Keep your footing firm and your eyes front. We'll be at the summit shortly."

Kaelan was followed by Aedán, who was carrying Oren, and Rhoswen, who was on the rear-guard. They had followed the fading sparkles of a golden dust trail.

"You still with us, Oren?" Aedán asked.

"Aye, I'm all right," he replied between winces.

A bellowing shriek rang out across the plain below, piercing the lull that had settled in while the group navigated the mountain pass.

"What was that?" Rhoswen asked anxiously as she looked down upon the plain, where the *dullahan's* wagon was just visible under the light of the full moon.

"There," Oren said, his tone filled with a sense of urgency, pointing down towards the forest. "Over there, a horseman is approaching at speed."

A second bone-chilling cry boomed across the plain.

"It's another *dullahan*!" Kaelan exclaimed.

"What about Sophie and Taog. They're down there, defenceless. We have to go back," Rhoswen pleaded as she looked from the wagon to the rest of the group.

"We can't, Rhoswen. We are almost at the top. To turn around now would take us precious moments to reach them, and I am afraid the *dullahan* would achieve that before we would. We have to keep going—our priority is to get to Jane and Claire. There is nothing we can do," Kaelan insisted as he turned to keep going up the path.

"I can fly down. I'll reach them before the *dulhahan* does!"

"And do what, Rhoswen? You cannot carry them both away, and if you do arrive first, he will soon be there. You cannot fight a *dullahan* by yourself. The chances of survival are slim at best without numbers at your back. I am not going to lose you. Niamh is not going to lose you. We just have to hope that the two of them hide and remain hidden until the beast leaves. Taog will know what to do."

"Aye he's right, Rhoswen. You'd be starting a fight that you cannot win. Best that we stay together," Aedán added.

"All right then, but I hope for your sake, Kaelan of Fionghan, that the two souls down there are safe and will see the sun rise again over the mountains," Rhoswen said.

∞

"What was that?" Sophie asked timidly as she and Taog lay at the bottom of the valley amongst unruly tufts of wild grasses.

"Are you sure it was not your stomach?" Taog asked.

"Yes, I'm sure. It sounded like some wild animal or something!"

"You have an over-active imagination."

"No, I don't," Sophie argued as another shriek boomed across the plain. "There it is again." She grabbed Taog's arm. "Did you hear it?"

"Yes, I did. Wait here. I'll investigate." He recognised another familiar sound, which was getting louder and louder.

"Hooves," they said simultaneously.

"It has to be another *dullahan*," he hypothesised, trying to give the impression that he had some authority on the matter. "Do you still have that gold cross that hangs from your neck?"

"Yes. Why?"

"Give it to me," he ordered, holding an upturned hand out towards her. "Come on, girl, and give me the necklace!"

"Will it help us?" she asked, her voice trembling.

"Just shut up and give me the gold!" he shouted.

"No, you can't have it," she wailed, tears welling in her eyes.

That's not the right decision girl," Taog said angrily as he rolled over her to straddle her waist, pinning her to the ground. The necklace slid down her chest, back towards her neck, revealing itself in the moonlight as it escaped the protection of her blouse.

"What are you doing?" she screamed as she struggled to push the clurichaun off her, but he had anchored his feet under her legs, and she was not able to budge him.

He removed the *scian* from his *crios* and drew the weapon high above his right shoulder. "You *bitseach*, you are all the same. You should just learn to hold your tongue and do as I say," he preached as he thrust the dagger downwards.

"No!" Sophie screamed as she thrashed about on the ground, her eyes wide like saucers, as the bronze knife plunged in slow motion towards her chest. His steely determination to get the necklace would have him stop at nothing to achieve his goal. The knife tore through the blouse, and her firm, tight skin offered no resistance as the blade sliced through the flesh, deep into her torso. Her upper body lurched forward as the gold crucifix slid down the side of her neck to rest on the ground beside her ear. She grabbed at the blade, each attempt sapping her energy until the strength in her body diminished as her life gradually slipped away. The air from her lungs bubbled though the blood-oozing wound left by the *scian*, which remained in Taog's right hand. Sophie's chest slowly eased to the ground, her body gave one last involuntary kick of her legs, and she was gone.

"You shouldn't have made me do that, lassie," Taog said with disdain as he pulled the blade from her chest. The puncture wound spurted blood, which oozed across her blouse.

The snort of a horse above his head caught Taog's attention, and he panicked, looking skyward. The horse of another *dullahan* reared up on its hind legs, its front legs kicking high above him. Dropping the knife, Taog reached for Sophie's neck, fumbling about roughly without regard for her corpse. He tore the necklace from her neck as he pushed himself backwards, rolling towards the bottom of the gully.

The *dullahan's* shrill bellow struck Taog's ears. He recklessly threw his hands to the sides of his head to protect his ears as the persecuting cry infected his mind. He turned around to face the beast above him, its head cradled only by its left arm. One stationary eye fixated on him while the other darted about its face as it scanned for other beings out on the plain. The sight of the beast paralysed Taog. The broad figure of the cloaked body atop the black steed was daunting. His mouth was dry, but he tried to swallow anyway. Self-preservation took control, and he began to slowly back away on all fours up the other side of the gully wall as the *dullahan's* horse came back to solid ground. The unseelie Fey guided his mount down the embankment towards Taog, who remembered in his retreat the necklace was in his hand.

Do it! Try it now. It's your only chance, a voice within him said.

The *dullahan* raised his right arm, a bone whip trailed behind him as he slowly approached the hapless clurichaun.

The horse closed in—fifteen yards then ten.

Do it now!

Eight yards away, the *dullahan* adjusted his grip on the bone whip and lowered his striking arm back.

"Stay back!" Taog shouted as he sprang to his feet, holding his arm aloft, his fist clenched. "Do not come any closer," he ordered nervously. He could feel the moist warmth of each breath from the death bringer's steed.

Silence ensued as they stared each other down, waiting for the first to flinch.

Then, without warning, the *dullahan* roared with laughter. "Time for you to die, clurichaun," he said with a deep, rasping tone that almost made his words incomprehensible.

Taog dropped the crucifix from his hand. Its fall seemed to slow time as the chain extended towards the ground. Then the charm bounced back towards Taog's fist as it reached the full length of the chain.

The *dullahan's* advance halted. He pulled back on the reins as Taog extended his arm, holding the chain aloft for the beast to see. The crucifix swung from side to side. The death bringer leant forward and released another ear-piercing screech aimed right at Taog's head. He was sure he could feel the energy of the scream rush past him, beating on his skull as it flowed around him, but he stood fast.

∞

Kaelan reached the top of the pass and signalled for the others to hold their ground. He surveyed the granite outcrop, looking for the custodians that He'd expected to be protecting the mouth of the cave, but he saw no one. He drew his caladbolg and signalled for the others to follow.

Another piercing shrill rose from the plain. Rhoswen hung back while Aedán cautiously followed Kaelan's lead, crossing the crag to the edge of the cave mouth, seeking cover in the shadows of the mountain face.

"The others must have remained hidden—the *dullahan* has ridden off," Rhoswen managed between breaths as she re-joined the others.

"They must all be inside," Kaelan whispered. "Aedán, Oren, you stay here make sure nothing and no one comes in or out. Rhoswen, come with me and stay close," Kaelan ordered before sneaking inside, staying as close as possible the grey walls of the cave. Rhoswen followed closely, her *bogha* in her left hand, an arrow from her pelt quiver in her right. When they had ventured twenty-something yards into the cave, Kaelan signalled to Rhoswen to hold her ground and be vigilant.

"Can you hear that?" he asked softly as he leant towards her.

"It reminds me of a storm. Is it possible that there can be lightning inside a cave?"

"We'll soon find out. See that rock by itself, five yards from the wall at the bend up ahead?" He pointed.

"Aye."

"I'll seek the cover of the rock. You stay by the wall."

Kaelan's new position allowed him to see into the large chamber, where Claire and the Red Man faced each other in battle. He was shooting streams of orange light from the end of his staff. The light hit and ricocheted off the surface of Claire's conjured shield. Each strike sizzled and cracked, exploding into a cascade of smaller flares as it hit its target. The sound was deafening in the chamber, and the air became thicker with smoke from each strike.

"There's your storm, Rhoswen!"

"Look," she said with excitement as she reached out for Kaelan's side, but he was too far away, and she clutched at air. "Jane, its Jane at the back of the cave by the wall!"

"Is she healthy?"

"I am not sure. She looks healthy, but the cave is filling with smoke," she replied with concern.

"That may be in our favour. Draw your *bogha* and get a line of sight on the Red Man's *shillelagh*. We have to disarm him," he exclaimed as he tried to scheme a plan to overpower the Fear Dearg.

"Kaelan, it's Jane behind Claire and the Red Man," Rhoswen said, pointing.

"Yes, I see. Keep your aim steady. We can't risk injuring her."

"What's she doing?" Rhoswen asked as she took a sideways step from her cover.

"Rhoswen, wait, don't move. Let it play out for the moment. Watch and listen," Kaelan instructed.

"Who is he?" Jane shouted. "What did he do to my mother?"

However, her pleas for answers were ignored as Claire and Silas battled it out in front of her. They traded ineffective strikes on each other for a short time, each strike producing a sparks of glinting flares and small mushrooms of smoke.

"They're not listening. If there is a clear shot, take it!" Kaelan ordered.

Rhoswen released an arrow, which struck the Red Man's left side, jolting him back.

"An arrow!" Claire twisted and looked up at Kaelan and Rhoswen. Claire's protective shield of blue shimmering light dissipated as she retrieved a small calico charm bag from her pocket.

"Jane, Jane!" she called.

Slowly, Jane looked up to her aunt. "What's happening?"

"Just take the bag," Claire yelled as she threw the sack to her. It tumbled through the air before hitting Jane on the upper arm and falling to the ground.

"Hold it tight and be ready to use it when I say so." Claire turned her attention back to the Red Man, who had just snapped the end of the arrow that protruded from his arm.

Rhoswen drew a second arrow. She released the bowstring, shooting the arrow towards the Red Man's chest. Just then, Claire seized the opportunity to try to overpower him. To Kaelan's horror, Rhoswen's arrow tore through Claire's upper right arm and continued towards Jane, who had bent down to pick up the charm bag. Though the arrow narrowly missed her, she screamed then looked up from the weapon towards Claire.

Claire fell headlong towards the Red Man, clutching her right arm. He raised his *shillelagh* towards her throat as she fell, and the weight of her impact drove them to the floor of the cave. He pressed the handle of the *Shillelagh* into the fleshy base of Claire's throat below the thyroid, and the foul stench of burning skin mixed with the smoke already in the chamber.

"Quick, take another shot!" Kaelan yelled to Rhoswen.

She reached over her shoulder between her head and wing to retrieve another arrow from her quiver and hurriedly drew the bowstring.

Kaelan, sword in hand, sprinted towards the confrontation. He dropped his shoulder, preparing for the collision, as he aimed for Claire's body, hoping the impact would knock her free of the Red Man's grasp. Two yards away, Kaelan felt a rush of wind swoosh past his ear. Then the third arrow found its target, lodging into the hand that held the *shillelagh* to Claire's throat. Dropping the staff, he howled in pain.

Claire gasped after the sudden release of pressure on her throat, and her body fell on top of Silas, pinning him to the floor. Kaelan launched himself into the air just a second too late, and instead of colliding with the bodies, he sailed over them. He had only the landing to contend with.

28

Oren sat uncomfortably atop Aedán, adjusting his seat every four turns as he paced back and forth at the mouth of the cave.

"Do you think we should go?" Oren asked. "I think I can hear a fracas. Can you hear a fracas?"

He turned towards the cave, listening. "Let's go in. They may need our help!"

"Aye, that they might, but Kaelan gave us strict instruction—nobody in and nobody out."

"I don't think he was talking about us," Oren replied.

Aedán nodded as he considered the situation. "And if we go rushing in, then who will be here to stop anybody going in or coming out?"

"Aye, there is that, I suppose."

"There is what?" a voice asked from behind them as the pair wheeled around to see a familiar brown hat appear first, followed by the rest of Taog as he slowly pulled himself up the last part of the pathway.

"Taog, you're safe!" Oren said, smiling. "We heard the *dullahan*, a second one!"

"Aye, it was, but it didn't stay for long," he managed between deep breaths while bent at the haunches, hands on his hips.

"Is Sophie far behind you?" Aedán asked.

Taog briefly looked towards the moon and huffed. "I'm afraid not... the *dullahan*... it found us. It was quick—the attack, I mean. Before I knew what was happening, it struck her with its whip. I did not know what to do." He gulped for air. "I... I just laid still as if I was dead. Then he turned and galloped away across the plain."

"Sweet mother," Oren whispered. "Jane will be heartbroken."

"Aye, it's not like a *dullahan* to leave somebody alive, though," Aedán said suspiciously, as he looked Taog up and down.

"He must have thought I was dead."

"Mmm..." Aedán looked from Taog over his shoulder to Oren. "It is a big loss... a big loss." He turned back towards the mouth of the cave.

The mood outside the cave was sombre, heads were down, and chatter was minimal. Aedán tried to move to keep his mind active, but he caught himself stopping after a couple of yards, his energy and enthusiasm waning.

"I think we should go in now," Aedán announced. "I couldn't bear losing anyone else today while I stand around doing nothing when I could be doing something," he said, hearing the frustration in his own voice.

"Aye, agreed," Oren added, "though I do not have much choice, do I?"

"Right, lead the way, and I'll take up the rear." Taog pulled a *scian* from his trousers.

"Don't know if I trust him behind us with that blade," Oren whispered in Aedán' ear as he leant forward.

The three of them moved slowly, cautiously into the cave, walking down the centre of the cavern. They were about ten yards in when Aedán heard shouting up ahead.

∞

"Claire!" Jane screamed. A sudden feeling of dread came over her, making her think the worst. She pushed herself off the floor like a sprinter at the starting line, the charm bag in one hand, the arrow in the other. Claire was lying on top of the Red Man, and Kaelan hit the floor with an almighty thud, his caladbolg clanging, dragging along on the rock as he rolled. Rhoswen was running towards the pile of bodies on the ground, her *bogha* armed and drawn.

"Claire, Claire, are you okay?" Jane cried, dropping to her knees as she reached her. "Aunty Claire?"

Claire didn't respond. She lay still atop the Red Man, who was only starting to moan and stir. His *shillelagh* was by his side but out of his grasp.

"Don't pick me up," Claire said, her voice rough and husky.

Rhoswen abandoned her *bogha* and quickly dropped to Claire's side to help pin the Red Man to the floor.

"The char—" Claire coughed as she tried to speak, her face buried in the Red Man's cloak.

"Quick, turn her head to the side, Jane!"

Jane did as Kaelan suggested, and a flood of emotion overwhelmed her. She smiled when she saw Claire's eyes then fought back the tears when she saw the burn marks on her neck.

Claire swallowed, wincing. She tried to clear her throat to talk, the unseelie Fey's left arm swung across the floor, striking at Claire's side.

"Get off me, you wretched woman," he yelled, thrashing his limbs about.

"Stop it!" Jane cried as tears rolled down her cheeks. She tried to fend off the Red Man's relentless strikes, her hands and forearms taking the brunt of his unorthodox attack.

"Rhoswen, keep his arm secure," Kaelan yelled as he pinned the Red Man's left arm to the granite underneath him while the captive lay beneath them all, screaming to be released.

"I will kill you all, starting with you, Claire," he threatened as he spat on her face.

She ignored the vile fluid that slid down her cheek and looked into Jane's eyes before she attempted to talk. "Jane, the charm bag—did you get it?" she asked, her voice so hoarse that its sound and image of the staff pressing against Claire's throat sent shivers up Jane's spine.

"Yes, Aunt Claire. I have the bag right here." She glanced down to her left hand.

"Put it in his mouth, dear," Claire replied as she looked upon Jane. Her irises absorbed her pupils, and they turned as black as the night sky.

"Should I cast a circle and invoke the Gods to bless the charm?" she asked hesitantly.

Claire lifted her head, answering in rhyme.

"No circles, no chants, the spell has already been cast.

Place the bag in his mouth so his powers will fast.

Take him to the portal for his essence will see that his body will not pass, but his spirit will be,

To be free, dear, deliver the bag and take Silas to the tree."

"Okay, we can do that," Jane said.

Claire closed her eyes, inhaled deeply, and repeated the chant two more times. On the third, when she opened her eyes, the natural colour of her irises had returned.

"Hold him tight," Jane ordered as she pressed down on his chin with her palm, trying to pry open his mouth, but the harder she pushed, the more he resisted. He clamped his mouth shut, and each time Jane held the charm bag close, he shook his head ferociously, moaning as loud as he could through closed lips.

"Come on, open your mouth!" Frustrated, she tried to force the bag into his mouth, but his lips would not part.

"His weapon, Kaelan. It's at your feet. Let's see if we can use his own energies against him," Jane nodded toward the *shillelagh*. "Press it against him and see if we can make him suffer as he did Claire!"

He reached for the staff. "I do not know how to use it. I think it best if you use it on him, being that you are a witch."

Jane took the staff as the Red Man watched on intently, still refusing to yield. Jane stood beside him, rolling the staff in her hands.

"Okay, I'll use the staff on him just enough that he'll curse in pain. Rhoswen, I'll give the charm bag to you—when his mouth is open, force it in!"

"No," Claire interrupted. "The charm was made for you and can only be delivered by you. Otherwise, it will hold no power!"

"Then who will hold the staff?" Jane asked. "You're too weak…"

"Then maybe one of us can dearie," Aedán said cheerfully as he entered the chamber, with Oren and Taog in tow.

"I thought I told you to keep guard," Kaelan barked.

"We did. Then Taog found us. We heard a skirmish and thought we'd be better used in here," Aedán replied.

Rhoswen asked, "And what about—"

"There was only Taog," Oren interrupted, "but maybe we shall learn more when this night is over."

"Do any of you know how to use this staff?" Jane asked as she held it out, waiting for someone to volunteer to use it.

"Aye, that's a *shillelagh*." Taog stepped forward. "I had one when I was a wee lad, but there are better ways to pry the lips!"

"I'm surprised to see you, Taog," Jane said.

"I was only going to get help. I am here now—with help," he replied.

"Maybe so," she replied with some suspicion. "So what do you suggest?"

"You be ready with the bag." Taog smiled as he walked around to the Red Man's feet. He laid the *scian* on the ground. Taking the Red Man's right Ligonier shoe in both hands he slipped it off followed by the red sock, exposing the bottom of his foot.

"Are you ready?" He looked up at Jane. "This will be one hell of a show!"

Taog picked up the *scian* and held the tip of the blade against the skin of the Red Man's foot. He looked up again, a sly smirk on his face as he looked around the group.

The Red Man began to struggle violently. His eyes bulged, and his complexion went as red as the coat he wore. The veins in his forehead pulsed. The more he struggled, the greater the pressure his captors placed upon him. Despite his injury, Oren rushed to dismount then assisted by lying across the Red Man's legs.

Taog drove the *scian* deep into the Red Man's foot, his face furrowed with determination. The unseelie Fey arched his back under Claire weight. Jane pressed down on his chin, which he struggled to hold firm. He threw back his head, and his eyes rolled into his skull. A scream of sheer pain forced open his mouth.

"Now!" Aedán yelled.

Jane crouched over the Red Man. The sight of the gaping hole that was his mouth triggered her response automatically, and she plunged the bag deep into his throat, pushing it as far as she could. He gagged reflexively, trying to cough up the blockage and free his airways. However, Jane pushed the bag deeper into throat.

"He's turning blue," Kaelan said as he continued to fight with the arm that he pinned down.

"Quick, get some water," Jane ordered frantically. "We can't let him die—he has to swallow the bag." She continued pressing on the bag as he tried to bite down.

Aedán retrieved a buckskin water sack from the leather bag slung over his shoulder. He threw the bag to Jane, hitting the Red Man in the chest. Jane pulled the stopper with her teeth, removed her fingers, and allowed him a breath of air before she forced the spout into his mouth. He coughed, spewing water. Then the water allowed the bag to slip down into his oesophagus. He lay there, his energy spent. His surrender was evident by the expressionless void on his face.

"Get off him. Get off him," Jane said. "He'll be no harm to us anymore." She looked up towards Kaelan, who nodded in agreement. "Aunt Claire, are you all right?" she asked as she knelt beside her aunt.

"I'll be okay, darling," she replied. "Help me up, will you?"

"After three! One, two, three," she counted as Rhoswen assisted.

"Whoa, easy does it."

"Will you be okay?"

"Sure, I'll be okay, darling. It's just a flesh wound. I'll be as fit as a fiddle in a week, although I might not be much help with Beltane." Claire cupped Jane's hand in hers.

"I'm sure Gwen won't mind, given the circumstance."

"No, you're probably right, darling."

"What about the Red Man?"

"Silas? He'll be taken care of soon, and when he is, the three of us will have to travel back to our own world straight away to fulfil the spell," Claire said.

"The three of us? Who else is coming?" Jane asked.

"Why Sophie, of course." Claire grinned. "When you went missing, Aedán came to fetch me. Sophie was over at the time. She'd come looking for you. We were about to go, and she was very persistent," Claire explained as she looked around the group. "Actually, where is Sophie?"

"Sophie is here in Emain Albach?" Jane asked as she tugged at her aunt's hand.

The Red Man's body began to convulse as if he were having a fit. His only sound was a low-pitched drone, interrupted only by the vomit and foamy saliva that spilt out of his mouth like a volcanic eruption.

"What do we do?" Rhoswen asked.

"Nothing, dear. Leave him. His body will go limp soon. He is not dying, if that's your concern—well, not yet anyway."

29

The mood was quite subdued in the chamber. The Red Man lay on the ground, very still but very much alive. His eyes were open but glazed. Opinions were divided on if he was watching them or could even hear them.

"Is Sophie outside? I don't see her," Jane said as she scanned the chamber.

"Kaelan, Aedán, can you please help us get Silas back to the Apple Tree?" Claire asked as she stood over him, nursing her injured arm.

"Hello, did anyone hear me?"

"What's that, dear?"

"Sophie! Do you know where she is?" Jane scurried across the chamber, looking for her friend.

"I do not know, darling."

"Taog, we left Sophie with you. Where is she?" Rhoswen asked as she gestured with open palms.

Oren cleared his throat, and when he had Rhoswen's attention, he motioned by wiping his hand across his neck a couple of times.

"A second *dullahan* attacked…" Taog said.

"We saw it from up here, but it also left very quickly. Has she been hurt?" Rhoswen asked as she approached the clurichaun.

"What's a *dullahan*?" Claire asked.

"It's a headless rider, like the one that attacked us," Kaelan answered.

"What about Sophie? Is she okay?" Jane cried, frustrated by Taog's lack of cooperation.

"She's dead," Taog blurted, displaying no empathy or regard for Jane's emotions.

"Dead?" Jane yelled back at him as she threw her hands against the sides of her head in disbelief. "How can she be dead? She's not supposed to be here," she screamed. She turned back to Claire and the others, bursting into tears. "How… can… she… be… dead?" she stammered between tears and jerked breaths.

"It wasn't my fault," Taog said quietly under his breath.

"Rhoswen, do you mind taking Jane outside for a moment while we take care of things in here?" Aedán asked.

"Of course." She wrapped a comforting arm around Jane then led her to the mouth of the cave.

∞

"Taog, I require your assistance to get this beast onto Aedán' back," Kaelan said.

Kaelan and Taog prepared to move the Red Man's body while Claire assisted Oren down from his mount. They both grimaced with pain as Oren awkwardly fell into Claire's arms.

"Got you," Claire said, wrapping her arms around his waist as she began to pull him from Aedán' back.

"Be careful of the leg please," Oren pleaded as his body began its sideways slide toward her.

They arranged the Red Man's body facedown across Aedán' back, just below his withers, allowing enough room for Oren to mount for the journey back to Fionghan.

The group stepped into the veil of darkness beyond the cavern's light. Rhoswen and Jane stood at the edge of the rock face. Tears still streamed down Jane's face as the raw emotion of losing another person she loved.

"Why, why was she here?" Jane sobbed.

"Because she loved you," Claire said over her shoulder as she stood with the others waiting, giving her a moment to get some degree of composure before their journey down the mountain. "She will be sorely missed, my darling, by none more so than you, but we must press on back to the tree. The spell is only half-complete. If we do not get there soon, he will awake, and we'll have a big problem on our hands."

"Okay." Jane sniffled.

The group began their descent down the narrow winding path. Claire and Kaelan brought up the rear.

"You spoke of the Red Man with some knowledge. Do you know him?" Kaelan asked Claire.

She regarded him for a moment with a furrowed brow. "I have not told Jane as my intention is to protect her.

Therefore, what I tell you, you must keep to yourself. Do you agree?" she asked as she stared him in the eye.

"My word is my honour, Claire, and I will not break your trust." He bowed his head and twirled his hand.

"The Red Man, as you all call him, is known to me as Silas O'Fihelly. I believe this to be his true name. He is part human and part Fey, so Jane told me from a warning she received from Aedán." They walked a number of yards behind the shape-shifting Fey.

"Fear Dearg is his lineage, but because his blood is not true, he would have been treated like a changeling and cast out into the human world," Kaelan explained.

"Yes, he was cast out, according to the stories he told of his youth. He was a ward of the state in a place called Sydney, where he went from the orphanage to foster homes and back to the orphanage again. It was a vicious cycle, as he could not adapt to our world. He learnt many evil ways in his bid to survive. He grew up and eventually made his way down to Tasmania, where he crossed paths with my sister, Grace. They took a liking to each other, and before long, he settled down in Delta and began attending coven meetings. He became an initiated member and commenced rising through the ranks as his knowledge and adaption of the craft evolved."

"Aye, sounds like a hard life, but I've never met a changeling who was a contented child," Kaelan offered.

"No nor do I take pity on him—quite the opposite, actually. He was responsible for Grace's death, and as such, he was banished from the coven."

"Do you mind if I enquire as to how she passed?"

"She was driving in her car when a road train hit her side on, on the driver's-side door. The force split the car in two, and she was killed instantly."

"My apologies for your loss, Claire, but if I could beg your indulgence by asking what a car and a road train is?"

"I'm sorry. I shouldn't have assumed that you'd know what they are. You probably hadn't even met a human before Jane arrived here," Claire said with some embarrassment. "A car is what we travel around in, and a road train is a large truck similar to a car but a lot bigger, used to carry things from one place to another."

"I know what you are talking about. I've seen them before when I have travelled to your world on brief visits. I just was not familiar with the names. I did not interact with humans when I travelled, though I have met one a long, long time ago. She was also a witch, and she reminds me of you actually in many ways. Her name was Eerin. She had snow-white skin, blonde hair, green eyes, and a smile that would warm a cold heart. She stayed in Fionghan for one waxing cycle of the moon. She didn't say where she was from or why she was travelling through, but she did tell me that her name meant "small grey owl." I remember I was honoured by that gesture, as to know one's name is to have great power but more so when you know the meaning behind it, especially when it is given freely by a pure heart." Kaelan smiled, as if warmed by the nostalgia.

"Eerin, that's a pretty name. Do I sense a connection lost and a heavy heart as a result?"

"Aye, special! That she was," he answered as he stared off into space as if reliving the past in his mind.

"What happened, Kaelan?"

"Oh, nothing. When the moon waned, she left Fionghan and travelled north. She said she would return, but that day never came." He sighed. "But I've still got the memory, and now I have Rhoswen and wee Niamh to look after, but she will always be in my mind."

"It seems that she made quite an impact on you. I'm glad that she did, and I'd assume that she would have had great affection for you as well," Claire said cheerfully. "Why thank you, Claire. That's kind of you to say." They rounded the last turn of the granite path.

"Well, it looks like we've reached the bottom," Kaelan said.

The group ahead stepped onto the softer earth of the plain. The rest of the band gathered behind Aedán, using him as a windbreak while they waited for Claire and Kaelan to join them.

"We'll pass the *dullahan's* wagon and collect the fallen to take with us back to Fionghan," Kaelan ordered.

"Aye, let's commandeer the wagon. My back cannot carry such a load," Aedán said. "And you'll be the first to go, Oren." He laughed.

Jane walked past, staring at Aedán while he still laughed. Her eyes puffy and red, tears still rolling down her cheeks, she said nothing to him. She didn't have to.

"I'm sorry, dearie. That was very disrespectful of me."
Aedán fell into line, then Claire quick stepped past him as
she tried to catch up with her niece.

"How are you feeling, darling?" Claire asked when she'd
caught up with Jane.

"I can't believe she's gone." A new wave of tears rolled
down her cheeks. "I just want to take her home now!"

"That would be nice, darling, but unfortunately we can't.
Aedán said to us that if we die, our bodies could not return
to Delta. She knew that—she knew the risks, but she
wanted to come, to find you." She held on to Jane's arm as
they walked back towards the *dullahan's* wagon.

"Then I'm just going to be more determined to try," she
said a little more spirited than before. She pulled her arm
free and started to put some distance between herself and
Claire.

"She's taking it hard, blames herself, but in time, she will
heal," Rhoswen offered as she sided up with Claire.

"Yeah, she's suffering, the poor child,"

They walked on, over the rises and falls of the plain.

"The wagon is just up ahead," Oren called, "just over
the next rise."

The group matched on, the seemingly increasing breeze
pushing against them like a huge hand that was trying to
drive them back to the mountains.

"Here it is," Oren exclaimed as the group traversed the
final rise.

"Taog, join me in gathering the fallen. Rhoswen, check the harnessing and assist Claire with Jane," Kaelan ordered.

"Is this where Sophie was with Taog?" Jane asked, searching for signs of her friend. "Maybe he was wrong. Maybe she is hiding somewhere. We just need to find her," she said forlornly.

"Let's get into the wagon, darling."

"Kaelan is searching now. He'll find her," Rhoswen said as she secured the reins and checked the brake.

"Do you think the *dullahan*—the second one,—took the first one's body away?" Oren asked. "I don't see it anywhere. We slayed it right here beside the wagon. It should be there."

"Aye, that it should," Aedán concurred as he raised his snout to the air, as if searching for scents.

"I don't like this one bit. Rhoswen, do you mind helping me down and into the wagon?" Oren asked, still surveying the bloodied ground.

Kaelan and Taog returned to the group after scouting around for a while.

"There's nothing!"

"What do you mean?" Aedán asked.

"There are no bodies—not Sophie or any of the *airforaire*. It's like they all got up and walked away." Kaelan shrugged as the pair joined the group at the wagon.

"The *dullahan's* body is gone, as well." Aedán nodded towards the ground near his hooves. "All that remains is the blood where the body laid."

"This isn't a good sign," Taog added as he began to fidget nervously.

Oren nodding his agreement.

"I agree. Let's mount up and make way for Fionghan," Kaelan ordered.

30

"Let's move it out," Kaelan said as he picked up the reins. Rhoswen joined him on the box while the others rode in the back.

Oren lay there, trying to keep weight off his leg. He was sure it was broken. He did not say too much to his companions—he was content to lie back and observe.

"Where were the bodies, Aunt Claire?" Jane sobbed. "Do you think we'll find her to be able to take something back with us for her family?"

"I'm not too sure telling them is the best thing to do, darling."

"Why not? We have to tell them. We can't lie!"

"Nor should we have to. I didn't raise you that way, but I think this is a circumstance where the white lie's benefits far outweigh the heartache and angst created by the retelling of a story that most will not receive well. Do you know what I mean?" she asked.

"Yeah, I know that no one will believe us. I just thought…"

"You have a big heart, Jane McKinnon."

For a moment, Oren forgot his own pain. He smiled as he witnessed the interactions of the two humans across from him.

"Would you like me to ride out front, to make sure we're not travelling into any traps?" Aedán asked Kaelan.

"No need. You can walk alongside if you wish." Kaelan flicked the reins, prompting the steed to walk. The wagon lurched forward a couple of inches and rolled back one before it sprang forward again. It rolled at a steady pace, bumping across the uneven ground of the plain.

"Very well," responded Aedán as he also got underway.

The heads of the passengers in the back of the covered wagon bobbed with every bump of the trail. Jane watched the mountains through a split in the hide.

"Are you okay, sweetheart?" Claire asked. "You're awfully quiet." She leaned closer to the girl. "Jane!"

She turned back to Claire. She sniffled as she turned, managing a contrived smile as she made eye contact her with aunt.

"We'll get through this," Claire reassured her as she raised her left arm to offer a warm side and cuddle for comfort.

A long high-pitched cry broke the rhythm of the wagon wheels as they approached the summit of a rolling hill, where the trail forked.

"What was that?" Taog asked anxiously, his body tensing as he sat bolt upright.

"The *bean sidhe*. We're approaching the brook," Kaelan replied.

The wailing woman cried out again. The shrill howl sent goose bumps up Oren's arms as he manoeuvred closer to the side of the wagon to peer out of the canopy where the stitching between two pieces of skin had separated.

Oren knew the path to the left led back through the Black Alder Forest towards the distant villages of Taraghlan, where Taog hailed from, and Artagan, a town known for its stonemasonry. The band would take the path to the right, which followed the brook towards Fionghan.

They came to the same stretch where Kaelan and Oren had made acquaintances with the *bean sidhe* earlier that night.

"There she is," Kaelan said as he gestured towards her with his head, "over there on the rock."

"What's she doing?" Rhoswen asked.

"Washing, by the looks of it. I've heard the stories, but I've never seen…" He paused for a moment. "Try not to look. We'll be around that hillock soon," he said as the wagon rattled around the path.

Despite toiling at her task, the *bean sidhe* turned to scrutinise the wagon as it descended the knoll before her. Releasing another spine-tingling wail, she continued to push down on her washboard. Her long, gaunt fingers gripped the blood-stained apparel that she rubbed up and down the carved-bone washboard. Blood pooled on the rock under her legs, and she hummed an eerie uninviting tune as she laboured.

Jane peered through the tear in the canopy, and screamed out to Kaelan, "Stop! Stop the cart!" She scrambled to her feet, holding onto the ribs of the carriage. Kaelan pulled back on the reins hard, and a stifled neigh blurted from the horse's mouth.

"What is it, Jane? What's wrong?" Claire asked as she leant towards Jane.

"That woman"—she pointed towards the brook— "knows where Sophie is!"

"How do you know, dearie?" Aedán enquired from outside the wagon.

"She has her clothes. I just saw her hold up a pair of jeans!"

"Are you sure? It could have been anything. She's not exactly close," Claire asked as the others watched silently.

"Of course I'm sure. Who else would be wearing jeans in Emain Albach?" she asked condescendingly. "A faerie? I don't think so!" She pushed past Rhoswen and jumped from the carriage. She landed on her feet and took flight towards the *bean sidhe*.

"Quick, stop her," Claire called desperately as grabbed for Jane.

"*Cac!*" Aedán exclaimed. "I'll get her!"

"I'm right behind you," Kaelan added as he vaulted from the carriage.

∞

Kaelan and Aedán sprinted as fast as their legs would carry them. However, Jane's head start was too great.

"You!" she yelled at the *bean sidhe*, but the Fey kept on washing, paying the young human no mind. "Look at me when I talk to you! What are you doing with Sophie's clothes?" Jane's features were red with anger; her veins in her temples pulsated. She could feel the hairs on the nape of her neck standing on end as a raw, unadulterated flood of emotions surged through her.

"What have you done with Sophie, you bitch?" she screamed as she stood over her in a rage.

The *bean sidhe* just sat facing the brook, strumming the washboard with Sophie's jeans.

"What's wrong with you?" she screamed hysterically. "I will hurt you." Jane raised a fist to the women, tears again streaming down her face. She struggled to comprehend the emotion of the moment.

The *bean sidhe's* twisted her head at incredible speed to face Jane, her black soulless eyes staring past Jane towards her raised fist.

"Give me her clothes, bitch, or I will take them myself!"

"Try, witch," the *bean sidhe* replied. Her deep, raspy voice sent shivers through Jane's body as she gulped a mouthful of fear.

What the hell am I doing? Well, I cannot turn back now.

The *bean sidhe's* eyes bored into Jane's face. With her hands clenched around the jeans that sat stagnant against the washboard, she did not move. She seemed lifeless, except for the daggers that she threw from the black depths of her eyes.

Jane sensed her erratic breathing as she gathered her courage. She closed her eyes then drove her fist downwards, imagining the woman's face—her olive complexion, beautiful lines, gorgeous long black hair. She visualised her fist connecting between her nose and cheekbone as the *bean sidhe* wailed in pain, blood splattered over her face.

Jane's forearm hit something solid much earlier than she'd expected. A dull pain coursed up toward her shoulder. She pushed harder, but the resistance was too great.

"That will do, Jane," a male voice said from behind her.

She opened her eyes and focussed on the creature sitting before her. The *bean sidhe's* black eyes still bored into her—and her face was still perfect, no injuries or blood.

"What do you think you're doing, dearie?" a more familiar voice asked as an instant clarity came over her. She looked up to see a hand gripping her arm. Turning, she found Kaelan and Aedán regarding her.

"Well, dearie, do you have some sort of death wish or something?"

Jane tried to smile, yet all she could achieve was the quiver in the corner of her lip as she fought back the overpowering urge to break into tears.

Kaelan pulled her arm, and she fell into his chest. He squeezed her tight.

"I now see what jeans are," he said as he pushed Jane towards Aedán. "Hand over the girl," he commanded as he stepped toward the Fey, unsheathing his sword a number of inches so the moonlight bounced off the polished bronze.

Still, her only response was a persistent, eerie stare.

"Tell me where she is or so help me, I will run you through," he barked as he drew the full length of his caladbolg from its scabbard.

The *bean sidhe* remained fixated on Kaelan as he raised the blade, his eyes brimming with contempt.

Without warning, she broke into a curdling laugh. Her stare fractured as her head bobbled. She raised her right arm and pointed a long index finger towards the calm body of water in front of her. Both Jane and Aedán closed in behind Kaelan, curious to see what the crone was pointing at.

"What are you pointing at, woman?" Kaelan asked.

Jane saw only the black surface of the water.

Her laughter ceased, and she waved her palm over the water. The water released the secrets hidden deep beneath its surface. A shroud of blackened silver rippled outwards, unveiling water so crystal clear that the rocky bottom beneath was visible in the moonlight. After an upward gesture of the Fey's hand and an unexpected shrill, bodies began to rise from under the rock bed of the brook.

"*Cac*, do you see that?" Kaelan asked, obviously stunned.

"Aye, we see it," Aedán said.

Several naked bodies rose but did not break the surface of the brook. They hung suspended in lifeless form, moving only as the current flowed past their corpses.

"There's one, two, three bodies," Jane counted. "Two faerie and a headless beast," she exclaimed, not believing what her eyes registered.

"And there's a fourth." Kaelan pointed. "A female."

"It's Sophie," Jane screamed as she tried to push past her two companions, thinking she could retrieve her friend, but they blocked her passage.

"Jane, there's nothing you can do. She's gone."

"He's right, dearie. She's gone—you can't take her back home with you. I made that clear to her and Claire before they travelled across, and they accepted that risk," Aedán explained.

Tears began to swell in Jane's eyes again as she turned, stamping her foot in frustration. "But her family—they'll want to have a funeral. *I* want to have a funeral!"

"But the tree will only accept the living, Jane. There is really no way of getting her body back to Avalon."

Jane broke down into uncontrollable tears. Gasping for air, she threw her arms around Aedán' neck.

"Can we bury her here, give her a proper send off?" she managed between gasps, snorts, and unladylike explosions of saliva.

"I'm afraid not," Kaelan answered. "The *bean sidhe* owns them now. If we entered the water, she'd order the floor of the brook to consume the bodies once more. We can take her clothes back. They will travel across the realms with you."

Kaelan turned back to the crone and pointed the tip of the caladbolg at her. "You have her body to wail over. Relinquish her clothes to us, and we'll leave you in peace," he commanded.

Still pointing towards the brook, she looked up at Kaelan. A smirk developed, separating her lips to reveal rotten, chipped teeth. She nodded her agreement and released her grip on the clothes in her left hand. Jane pushed forward and retrieved the garments before retreating to Aedán' side.

"We'd better leave," Kaelan nodded to the *bean sidhe* and lowered his sword.

"Let me look upon her one last time," Jane pleaded as she stepped back to water's edge.

"Don't do anything silly!"

Jane looked down upon the body of her best friend floating under the water's surface. Jane studied her, fighting back the urge to cry. She convinced herself to remain strong, to capture this moment so she would never forget; she owed Sophie that much at the very least. The extremities of her body swayed with the undercurrent as her body was secured by a toe to the bed of the brook. The light refracting through the water made her skin appear whiter than normal. Her arms and her blonde hair drifted in the current above her head. The skin around eyes was red, as were the whites of her blue eyes as blood vessels had burst, presumably at the time of her death. *It must have been a terrible death.* Then she saw the gash that had killed Sophie: a puncture wound between her breasts, still seeping a little stream of blood. *A knife? A sword?* Jane's attention was drawn back to Sophie's face, which held an expression like a plea for help. The image slowly burnt its way into her memory.

"Okay, time to go." Kaelan placed a hand on Jane's shoulder. "We must go," he whispered. He and Aedán turned to trek back to the wagon.

"I'm coming," Jane replied. "I love you," she whispered to Sophie as she kissed her middle and index fingers then blew the kiss towards Sophie's body. Jane dragged her gaze away then joined the others.

"You made it back! Are you okay, darling?" Claire asked as she embraced her niece. "What were you thinking?"

"I had to try, Aunt Claire. Sophie's dead—it was so terrible," she exclaimed as she hugged Claire tight.

"I'm so sorry, sweetheart."

"Come on. We have to go," Kaelan ordered.

31

The wagon bumped its way into Fionghan, its passengers bruised and battered. Still, the expedition was not quite finished.

"Do you think Niamh is all right?" Rhoswen asked as she burrowed into her husband's arm when the wagon continued past their *sidhe*.

"I'm sure she is. The minder from the village will be taking good care of her, and I'm sure she's still sound asleep, the same as when we left," he replied, full of pride for his family.

They drove the wagon through the centre of the village while the rest of the *Aes Sidhe* were still tucked away in their beds. Before long, the sun would once again grace the land with its warmth and glow and wake all living things from their slumber. Life would continue into the next day for those willing to grasp and reap the rewards of life's simple pleasures. Jane had been quiet for the remainder of the trip, her head down, staring at the jeans lying across her lap. Claire, Taog, and Oren had not conversed much, either.

"Whoa," Kaelan commanded, slowing the carriage to a complete stop near the apple tree on the far side of the village. The wagon's passenger disembarked, with the exception of Oren. He said his goodbyes to Jane and Claire, wished them well, and vowed to see them again when they next visited Fionghan. Kaelan and Taog carried the Red Man's limp body to the tree then dropped him unceremoniously at the base of the trunk.

"What do we do with him now?" Kaelan asked.

"The full effects of the black locust will soon be complete."

"And what's that? He isn't in any condition to port to Avalon at the moment," Kaelan observed as he looked from the Red Man back to Claire.

"The poison from the bark will take his life eventually. Two hours, normally, if that means anything here of course. My aim is to port at the moment he expires."

"And what will be gained by this action?" Kaelan questioned as he began to doubt Claire's plan.

"The aim is to pull his spirit through the tree back to Avalon to fulfil the spell that was cast on the charm that's in his stomach. The timing is critical—as Aedán has mentioned, the dead cannot port. Therefore, we need to go precisely when his spirit departs his body."

"Interesting. Is there a fall-back plan in case if this does not work?" Kaelan asked as he looked back to the body at his feet.

"Plan B? No, there's no plan B, because this is going to work. It has to," Claire said confidently.

"Let's hope so. Will you excuse me while I check in on Oren?"

"I'd prefer that you don't, if you don't mind. I mean, I'll need your help with him." Claire nodded towards the Red Man. "Please?"

"If you wish, Claire," Kaelan replied as he watched Jane step towards the centre of the informal gathering.

"I want to express my thanks and gratitude to you all for risking your own lives to save mine tonight. It's reassuring to know that I have such great friends—and family." Jane managed a little laughter for the first time in a while as she looked towards Claire. "It also reminds me of how precious life is and how we should all love and appreciate the ones closest to us every day. Sophie was my best friend, the closest person I had to a soul mate. I will miss her every day for the rest of my life." She sniffled. "That's enough of that," She shook her head and gave a half-hearted smile. "I don't want to cry… not now. I'm sure there'll be plenty of tears in the future. What I do not understand, though, is why the Red Man hunted me down. He said he was saving me until Beltane, but when I was captive, I had a lot of time to unravel his plans. Then it struck me!"

"What was that, dearie?" Aedán asked.

"It was what you told me, Aedán, in Kaelan's *sidhe*. You told me the Red Man was dying, the human part, you know. He needed a young girl who was pure, right?"

"Aye, that's right."

"Okay, so I fit the bill, but so do lots of girls, who would have been easier to kidnap. Why did he come after me?"

She looked from one person to the next. "Does anyone know?"

"Because you're a powerful witch," Rhoswen offered.

"That's flattering, but I'm not that powerful, not yet at least. I've only been practising for five turns of the wheel, and I have so much still to learn."

"Maybe he knew that you'd be powerful then."

"I don't think so. There has to be another reason."

"Rhoswen is right." Claire stepped towards Jane. "He knows who you are. That's why he sought you out. His name is Silas O'Fihelly, and we knew each other well a long, long time ago. I met him via your mother, actually. He was a very nice man at first. He and your mother fell in love, and then—"

"What!" Jane screamed as she turned away.

"Jane, this is needs to be told." She reached out for her niece.

"What, now after what happened to us all tonight?" Jane looked at her aunt furiously. "I think there are better times to tell me that my mother was having an affair, don't you?"

"No, Jane—no, she wasn't. She was very single at the time when she met your father, as she was when she met Silas."

"Are you saying that man there"—she pointed—"is my father?" Jane asked as she paced back and forth, a hand on her hip and a stunned expression on her face.

"Yes, dear. That man is your father." Claire pulled Jane into a tight embrace.

"But Mum said that Dad died in an accident at work... just after I was born."

"Yes, she did say that, but only to protect you—for many reasons. I promise to tell you all of them in the future, but for now, all you need to know is that he was banished from the coven, and Grace sent him away. We thought that was the last we'd ever see of him, but he returned when you were nine years old—" "When Mum died." Jane interrupted.

"Yes, dear."

"Did... did he do something to her?" she asked despondently.

"According to the authorities, it was a car accident, but we all suspected that he cast a hex that led to her death."

Jane broke down in her arms. Tragedy after tragedy seemed to have manifested in a space of twenty four hours.

"So he was going to kill me?" Jane wept.

"Based on Aedán' reckoning, yes—to replenish his body. The fact that you are a blood relative would make the bond stronger, and the effects would last longer. Rhoswen, do you mind?" Claire asked, gesturing to her to take Jane for a moment. Then she turned back to Kaelan.

"You have a long history with this *Fear Dearg*," he observed as both he and Aedán stood beside the Red Man.

"Yes, unfortunately, we do," she replied with a half-hearted smile as she surveyed the distance between the Red Man and the first fork of the tree. "Do we have to get him up there?"

"Not necessarily, but he does need to be connected to you when you cross over," Aedán answered. "You could prop him up against the trunk and hold his arm. That will work."

"Okay, let's give it a go." Claire turned back to Jane and Rhoswen. "Ready to go, sweetheart?"

"Yes." Jane sniffled as she turned to thank Rhoswen, manoeuvring to hug her carefully so as not to hurt her wings.

Claire and Jane shuffled between the other members of the band, saying their goodbyes and wishing the others well. Finally, Jane turned to Aedán and threw her arms around his neck. "Thank you for coming after me," she said as she squeezed him tight. "I'll never forget you!"

"You're welcome, dearie, but I don't recall anyone saying that we won't see each other again."

"I'd like that!"

"Claire, his breathing is laboured. I think the time to depart is near," Kaelan warned as he ushered Jane and Claire towards the portal. They quickly climbed the tree and positioned themselves above the first fork. Claire held Sophie's clothes as Jane pulled the silver bough from her back pocket.

"Ready?"

"Wait a tic." Claire shoved the clothes into the front of her own pants then reached for the Red Man's hand, which Kaelan offered up to her. "Thanks, and, Kaelan…"

"Aye."

"Thank you for rescuing my niece. I'll be forever in your debt." She briefly squeezed his hand before grasping the flaccid limb of the Red Man.

"We look after our friends, Claire, and friends you shall always be," he said warmly as he looked up at her, smiling.

With her free hand, Claire took hold of Jane's arm. "Okay, I'm ready when you are."

Jane extended her arm, pointing the silver branch at the fork of the apple tree.

"Reconnect the bough to the mystic tree and seek safe passage to Avalon. This I request of thee."

∞

A flash of white light erupted around them, sucking them into the depths of the tree. Overwhelmed by a sensation of weightlessness, Claire spun helplessly, buffeted by rushing winds that channelled a myriad of bluish-silver lines that passed around and between her and the others as they fell. Suddenly, a burst of light blinded her again as the tunnel transformed, giving way to a wide space filled with blues and greens. Then her body collided with the hard earth below.

They rolled unceremoniously like ten pins down the knoll, away from the tree, coming to a stop before they would have hit the rock wall of the pond.

Claire sat up gingerly, trying to shaking off the symptoms of vertigo. She belched the contents of her stomach into her mouth and swallowed it again.

"Aunt Claire," Jane whispered loudly, "Claire… look." She was pointing towards the tree.

Claire's eyes rolled about in their sockets as she tried to hold herself upwards in a seated position. She finally focused on an object rising from the apple tree. A shimmering translucent silhouette of a masculine body, it wore no clothes and had no visible genitalia. The figure hovered on the same spot, about eight feet off the ground, for a moment…

Then the spectre hurtled into the distance as if it had programmed a jump into hyperspace.

"Well, did you see it?" Jane asked eagerly.

"Yeah, I saw…" Claire paused, raising a hand to her mouth as she burped. "A glimpse… the spell! It is in the process of being finalised."

"Okay, you'll have to tell me what the spell was when you're feeling better. Are you okay, though? You're not looking the best. Perhaps we should go inside so you can lay down or have a shower?" Jane helped Claire to her feet. "I wouldn't mind a shower myself or something to eat— breakfast! That would be good. I wonder what time it is. Are you hungry? Oh, of course you're not, silly me," Jane rambled as she led Claire to the sunroom.

"Maybe later," Claire replied, "but a shower does sound good. Do you mind getting it ready for me, sweetheart? I need to make a call first. Oh, and I have Sophie's clothes here, as well."

"Thanks, Aunt Claire. I'll put them in my room," Jane replied, "then I'll put the kettle on for a cuppa!"

As Jane proceeded to the bathroom, Claire stood adjacent to the side table that the phone sat upon, waiting for her niece to exit the room. She picked up the handset and dialled a number.

"Gwen, its Claire. Sorry about no pleasantries, but I have an emergency that I need the coven's help with," Claire said in a low rushed tone.

"Merry Meet, Claire. What's wrong?"

"We're back. The spell has been cast and seems to have worked, but Jane's friend Sophie—she came with me, and unfortunately… well, she was killed."

"Oh my, Claire! What happened?"

"I'll tell you some other time, but I need help to get rid of a few things."

"The body?" Gwendolyn asked hesitantly.

"No, no body. Only living creatures can cross the realm. It's the car—she drove her car here. Is there anyone in the coven that could come and take it far away?"

"Realm?" Gwen exclaimed, sounding confused. "I don't understand. I thought you said Silas was in Delta. Where did you go, and why was Sophie with you?"

"Gwen, I'm sorry, but I don't have time to explain—I really don't. You'll have to trust me on this one. Do you have anyone who could help? Jack maybe?" she pleaded. "I'll tell you everything later. I promise!"

"Okay, okay. I'll see what I can work out, but why do you need the car removed?"

"Because Sophie is dead, and before long, questions will be asked as to where she is. I know it sounds callous, but how do I explain her car and no Sophie when the investigation starts?" Claire's exhaustion after such a long ordeal boiled to the surface.

"Okay, I'll see what we can do, but I must make myself clear, Claire, that we cannot afford to bring unwarranted attention onto the coven. I'll make some calls and send someone around, but just know this, Jack or whomever else may come to assist will be doing it as a favour to you, not the coven. We are not to be involved if something goes wrong! Can you give me your word, Claire?"

"Yes, Gwen. You have my word and gratitude."

"Very well. Leave the keys in the car, okay?" Gwen instructed.

"Oh, the keys. Bugger!" She felt her hips for side pockets. "No, no that's okay. I remember she left them here in the kitchen when she arrived. I think her purse is here, as well. I'll get Jane to put them both in the car. Thanks again, Gwen. I'll owe you one!"

"I think that is two you owe, now, isn't it?" Gwen replied. "Talk to you soon, Claire. Blessed be."

"Blessed be, Gwen."

Claire pressed the disconnect button and returned the phone to its cradle. A feeling that she was being watched overcame her. Twisting, Claire discovered Jane standing in the doorway, waiting.

"The shower is ready for you."

"Thanks, darling. I'll be there in a moment,"

"Who was that?" Jane asked, pointing towards the phone.

"Oh, um, that was Gwen. I called her about Sophie's car," Claire replied as she regarded her niece, studying her body language.

"Sophie drove here? Her mother will be looking for the car. She doesn't normally let Soph take it." Jane said. "Not that she wouldn't look for her own daughter first. You know what I mean, don't you?" she asked sombrely.

"I do, dear. I asked Gwen to get someone from the coven—I was thinking Jack—to come around and get rid of it. Somewhere like Swansea would be good."

"But why would… oh, I see," Jane replied. "Um, don't forget that the water is going."

"Thank you, darling."

The pair kept to themselves for the remainder of the day. Jane confined herself to her bedroom, and Claire heard the Cure playing on loop. She imagined Jane had turned to her beloved music as solace since she could no longer turn to her friend.

Claire tried to keep herself busy to get through the day. After her shower, she took Sophie's keys and purse out to the car and left them on the front seat. She trifled around the house until dinner, checking in on Jane from time to time.

At six o'clock, Claire called out to Jane for dinner.

"Sorry about dinner, love. I just threw it together. I hope you don't mind."

"No, it's okay. Thank you," Jane replied lethargically, making no attempt to hide the fact that she had been crying.

"Are you okay, darling. Did you want to have a talk?" Claire reached out to stroke Jane's hand.

"No, I'm okay, Aunt Claire. I miss her, you know. I've had her clothes that you gave to me on my bed since we got back, but it's not the same. Sometimes I think I can smell her on them, but I know that it's in my mind." She looked away towards the ceiling as her eyes swelled with tears again.

"It's hard, but it will get better with time. Jack took the car this afternoon, but you'll also have to hide her clothes, as well, until the time is right to do something with them, to remember her by, I mean. It might help you heal quicker, as well, if they're out of sight for a while."

"Okay I'll do that after we eat."

They sat in silence for the remainder of the meal. Then Jane disappeared back into her room with a glass of cola. Claire retired to the lounge room, where she relaxed in the recliner, shuffling through the stations on television. When she was ready for bed, she tuned in to the local news. She thought she recognised the woman being interviewed. The caption reel at the bottom of the screen identified her as Rachel Ison.

"Please, if anyone knows anything about Carla's death, please contact the police straight away." She bawled, holding a handkerchief to her face as she addressed the camera.

"Thank you, Rachel, and condolences for your loss. Let us pray that the perpetrator of this heinous crime is caught and brought to justice sooner rather than later. I'm Aaron Bailey, reporting live from the sleepy town of Delta. Back to you in the studio."

"Oh my, Carla Ison is dead?" Claire said to herself in shock. "Her car! We saw it across the road yesterday." *Murdered. Could it have been him?*

Claire stood from the chair and walked to the stairs outside Jane's room. She could still hear the same Cure album from earlier playing on the other side of the door as she walked up to the attic. Carefully she navigated her way through the room, lit only by the moonlight that entered via the large window before her. Standing to the side of the open drape, Claire could see the lights on in the house opposite and the red and blue flash of police vehicles still at the scene. *It must have been him. He had to have been watching us. It scares me to think that he was so close, so close to Jane, and yet Carla's life was taken unnecessarily.* "Such a waste," Claire sighed as she closed the drapes.

32

Three months later...

Jane felt exhilarated when she woke. The January sun streamed into her room, filling her with a zest for life, which had been missing for some months. She had been preparing for this day for some time and was playing it out in her mind while she sat on the edge of her bed, getting dressed.

She stood, dressed in her jeans and a loose white cotton blouse. She pulled her long brunette hair out of the collar of the top and adjusted the pentagram hanging around her neck.

"Right, I think I'm ready." She gave herself a once-over then picked up her purse and keys and bounded out of the room.

She found Claire in the kitchen, brewing a pot of ginger-and-honey tea.

"Merry Meet, sweetheart!"

"Merry Meet, Aunt Claire. Beautiful day, isn't it." She smiled broadly.

"Yes it is, dear, isn't it? You seem rather upbeat this morning. Did you have a good sleep last night?"

"I did actually, but I've decided that today is the day. I am not going to mourn anymore. I lost my best friend, and I've cried a river, but she wouldn't want me to be this way. She'd want me to remember and celebrate the good times that we had, and I want to honour her for that." Jane tilted her head.

"I'm glad, dear. It would mean a lot to Sophie, and I think it'll be good for you to have some closure, as well."

"Mmm." Jane was lost in thought as she stared at the wall behind Claire.

"Well, you'll need some energy for the day to keep you going–Jane!"

"Huh? Sorry, I was distracted. What did you say?"

"Breakfast?"

"Oh, yes. Any toast on?"

"I'll put some on now. One or two slices?"

"Two please!"

"That's great that you're feeling that way. It's been hard watching the amount of pain that you've had to deal with, but it's like you've turned over a new leaf. You look so fresh, like the weight has been lifted. Are you going to do anything special to honour Sophie's memory?" Claire turned to sip from her cup. "I'm sorry, dear, did you want a tea?"

"No it's okay. I'll just make a cup myself." Jane went to the sink to fill the kettle. "I've even been thinking about going back to visit Aedán and the others in the next couple of weeks," Jane added.

Claire didn't respond, and Jane suspected her aunt didn't approve.

"I'm going to bury her clothes today," Jane said with a hint of gravity after a protracted silence.

"Really? That's a big step. Are you sure you're ready?"

"Yes, I'm sure. As I said, it's time to move on and remember the good times," Jane said as reassurance, probably more for herself rather than her aunt.

"That's great! I am so proud of you. Did you want company?"

"No, it's okay. I think I need to do this myself, but thank you. I do appreciate the offer," Jane said sincerely as she walked back to the table with her breakfast.

"Do you have everything ready?" Claire asked.

"Yes, I've actually had it ready for some time, stowed behind the battery under the backseat of Blue Belle!"

"That's great, sweetheart. I'd love to chat more, but I have to get ready to go into the shop… I'll see you later?" Claire asked as she stood from her chair.

"You sure will." Jane said as Claire bent down to kiss her on the cheek.

"Blessed be," Claire said as she exited the kitchen.

∞

Sophie had been listed as missing the day after Jane and Claire returned to Delta. Her picture was plastered on missing person's posters all over town within days, and her family gave a television interview, pleading for information on her whereabouts. The police questioned Claire and Jane, but any suspicion they had dissipated when Sophie's car was found abandoned in a ditch off an old forest service road on the way to Swansea. Although she was still officially listed as a missing person, it was widely suspected that she'd fallen victim to Carla Ison's killer.

Jane sat a while longer, sipping her peppermint tea and eating toast while contemplating the day. She was apprehensive yet enthusiastic, hoping the process would help her move forward instead of just reopening old wounds.

Jane started the car, and the beat of Blue Belle's engine was the sweetest tune to Jane's ear. Although The Cure ran a close second. Jane turned down the volume as she cruised out to Freycinet so she could contemplate what she was about to do. She did have Joy Division's *Live in Amsterdam* album in the player. Jane had both the vent and main window down. Her elbow rested on the doorframe, and the wind blew through her hair as she drove past the tourist information centre at the entrance to the park.

Jane eased to a stop in the car park then looked around to gauge the activities of other patrons. A family had set up a picnic table beside a motor home at the other end of the parking bays, and a few other cars were scattered between her and them. Confident that she was able to continue, she turned and killed the motor and reached into the glove box to retrieve her purse. She pulled the knob that allowed the seat to slide forward, permitting her access to the rear seat.

She pried loose the bottom half of the bench seat to reveal two white plastic bags. After retrieving them, she returning the seats back to their original positions and locked the car.

Surveying the car park, she was satisfied that she had not drawn any attention to herself. She marched purposefully along the trail to the sacred ground of Freya, the white bags bouncing along.

At the fallen log marked with the cross, Jane hesitated. A rush of tingles spread over her back—she was being watched. She looked up and down the track—and saw no one. She stepped off the path two paces then stopped. *Maybe it's not someone but something.* She froze, listening. But she heard nothing. Necessity pushed her forward to the fallen she-oak. She looked behind her one last time then dropped to her hands and knees to scurry under.

Jane crawled past the white kunzeas and banksias, where the ground was damp with rotting leaves and moss. The soft warm air changed to fresh wafts smelling of Huon pines and eucalypts blended with smells of auguring rain that cooled the skin. Jane blinked her eyes, adjusting to the darker light. Standing once again in the beautiful surrounds of Freya, she breathed in deeply through her nose and held the crisp air in her lungs, drawing in its purity. She slowly exhaled.

"Merry Meet, Freya," she said, greeting the sacred ground that felt like a home to her.

"I come here today to perform a very special task for very special person. You met her last time I was here." Jane paused to collect herself as tears began to well. Placing the bags on the ground, she fanned her eyes with her hand. "I promised myself I wouldn't cry… not today! It's been three months now, and my eyes have been dry for the last one." She spoke to Freya as if she were a close friend or relative. The emotion of the occasion quickly got the better of her. However, her streaming tears and runny nose did not distract her from the task at hand.

She walked around the large pentagram on the ground towards the altar between it and the black locust. Then a sudden movement in her peripheral vision gave her a fright. She turned to face the tree, but nothing was there. She looked at each of the corners of the clearing and couldn't see anything. Then a flash moved quickly in and out of sight. The movement was gone by the time Jane had twisted to catch a glimpse of whatever was in the clearing with her. She stood still, facing the space that lay between the altar and the tree. Her body tensed as the need for self-preservation kicked in. The tears remained, but they were shed in fear.

"Is somebody there?" she called out into the wall of trees. She turned, scanning for any signs of life. "Hello?" she called. "I know somebody is there… show yourself."

Only noises, probably animals, from beyond the tree line responded. Jane's anxiety levels climbed the longer she waited. *I couldn't be dreaming, could I?*

The presence did not feel the same as the feeling she'd experienced on the path. She tried to reassure herself, but the unknown was daunting. She was here to lay a part of

Sophie to rest, and that played some part in heightening her senses, as well.

Jane tiptoed towards the altar. The plastic bags crinkled as they brushed against her leg with each step. Searching the landscape through tearful eyes, Jane held her breath, trying not to make a sound as she got closer to where she thought the mystery thing was hiding. Jane reached the stone altar and placed the bags on the ground. She slowly turned to face the tree.

"I know you're behind there," Jane said nervously as she watched both sides of the trunk intently. "There's no point hiding. Come out!" She swallowed hard, but nothing responded. She waited a little longer then gingerly took a step towards the tree, still holding her breath.

"I know you're there. Come out!"

She took another step towards the tree, and her foot came down on a twig, which cracked underfoot. Her heart stopped as she heard a rustle. Then a spray of leaves mushroomed from the base of the tree, and a possum crawled up the trunk, circling the shaft as it went.

She released a long, slow, moaning sigh. The tension evaporated from her neck and shoulders, and she shook her arms, trying to relax. Taking two more steps, she looked up, watching the possum climb to the highest reaches of the twisted branches. A smile touched the corners of her lips as a smothered chuckle pushed through her nose. She realised as she sniffled that her tears were gone, her anxiety had departed, and she had nothing to be fearful of. A smile stretched across her face.

She bid the marsupial farewell then turned back to the black locust.

"What… what's that?" she screamed as she backpedalled. "What are you?" she demanded at the image of a face that appeared in the bark of the tree. Then she tripped, releasing a blood-curdling scream as she fell backwards. She hit the ground hard. Despite narrowly missing a rock that used to be part of the pentagram behind her, her head sustained a hard impact on the forest floor. She lay sprawled on her back, moaning, but still conscious.

"What happened?" she muttered. "What was that?"

A couple of minutes later, the haze surrounding Jane's head started to clear. Clarity replaced her confusion, but something was different. Something had happened, but she wasn't sure what. She remained on her back in a submissive position should she be in danger. She convinced herself she wasn't feeling the same sensation she had on the path. Then it dawned on her—she was alone, truly alone. Complete silence reigned over the forest, as everything was still—no birds, insects, or animals.

The face! she thought. *I have to be dreaming right!* She stared up at the tree towering high above her, and there it was. A human face in the bark of the tree stared back at her. She blinked furiously for a couple of seconds to make sure that the haze from her tears and the knock to her head wasn't making her see things. She refocused; the face was still there, staring straight at her. It had a predominant forehead and cheekbones and a defined nose, mouth and chin, but there were no signs of hair, teeth, or ears. The face seemed pressed against the bark as if it were looking from the inside out. Jane froze, and she knew she had not imagined being watched. Then, to either side of the face the bark, small mounds began to grow—five on each side. A larger U shape spread underneath them. *Hands!* she realised. *They're hands, five fingers and the bottom of the palm!*

The face, still pressed against the bark, pushed itself at great speed diagonally up and around the trunk, out of sight.

"What in the Gods' names was that?" Jane asked herself in disbelief as she looked up the trunk of the tree, trying to catch another glimpse of the face. Sensing some urgency to complete her memoriam, Jane convinced herself that the face was gone, albeit she was very nervous about its possible return. She rolled to her feet, retrieved the plastic bags, stepped over the lines imbedded in the earth that outlined the pentagram, and emptied the contents in the centre of the five-pointed star. Facing the altar, Jane arranged circle of white candles around her, ensuring that there was still enough earth in front of her to dig a hole. She laid Sophie's clothes out in front of her then rose to her feet, a box of matches in one hand and a white candle in the other. She stepped over the rocks once more to place the candle atop the altar table; she waited until there was no breeze before striking a match. The flint sparked, but as she was about to light the wick, Jane paused. The face in the tree was back, suspended a metre above the ground on the ritual side of the tree, watching her. Fear crept back as Jane studied the face, but the longer she did, a new emotion began to swell within her: an intensifying feeling of anger and resentment towards the face that had interrupted her ritual.

Jane stormed towards the tree, her finger pointing at the face, as its features stretched the outer layer of bark. "Who are you, and what do you want?" she yelled at it. "I will…" Her voice then trailed off as a realisation came over her. She stepped to the side of the towering guardian, watching the man in the tree. "Hello?"

The face continued to look straight ahead towards the altar. Jane moved closer and waved her hand in front it— nothing. She walked across its line of sight to the other side of the tree—still nothing.

"He can't see or hear me," she said curiously. She repositioned herself back in front of him, crouching down on her haunches to be at eye level. "I recognise you," she said softly.

The face pushed against the bark, the tips of its fingers gouging at the inside of the tree.

"You are trapped, and there you will always stay," she said as if she were passing her own judgement on the face. "You will never find a weakness!"

Jane stood, shrugging off the anger that almost consumed her. She returned to the altar, where she struck another match. She held the flame over the wick until it engulfed the braided cotton, creating another flame.

"Merry Meet," she said, stepping back into the pentagram and her circle of candles. She lit each candle. Each candle was then lit in turn, preparing her mind for she had to say.

"Sophie, I am here for you. To take these worldly belongings of yours and commit them to the earth as a symbolic burial so that you may renew and move on, as I know you will." Jane sat back on her heels, her emotions stirring, swelling inside her as she prepared to say goodbye.

Jane carefully unfolded the clothes, which had been wrapped tight for the last three months. A scent of mildew wafted into her nose, yet the stench did not deter her from holding the garments close to her heart.

"I love you, Sophie Bainbridge, and I'll miss you terribly." Jane sobbed as tears rolled, falling onto the clothes in her hands.

"You shall be in my thoughts daily," she cried as she looked from the jeans in her lap to the black locust tree, where the face and hands still moved around, pressing on the inside of the tree like a mime trapped in a box.

She sighed. "Remember when we spoke of growing up together? You'd be my maid of honour at my hand-fasting ceremony, and I, yours at your wedding. We'd have kids at the same time so that they grew up to be the best of friends like you and I. You know… you know, I always pictured us coming down to the Esplanade, grabbing a coffee at Froth n Stuff and taking the kids to Civic Park to watch them play while we would chat. We used to have the best chats, don't you think?" Jane wept through a pained laugh.

"I'm not sure if we'll see each other again. I hope so. You were not Wiccan, but I pray that your soul will journey to the Summerland to find peace. Just like a plant that buds, flowers, drops its seed, withers, and creates a new plant in its image, I hope that your spirit finds reincarnation. A beautiful soul such as yours truly deserves to live on. I return these clothes to the earth so that one day you may find them when you're in need," she said as she carefully placed the garments into the hole. "I also have a photo of us together so that when you're lonely, you'll be able to remember the great times we shared. And lastly, a flower, an orange tulip. Your favourite, the last of season," Jane said as she took them from the bag beside her and laid them on top of Sophie's clothes.

"I must admit, though, I grew this one myself. I got some bulbs from the nursery many months ago. I found them at the back of the fridge, and although late in the season, I nurtured it for this very occasion—just for you." She wept as she picked up a handful of dirt. Cupping it, she finished by reciting a chant that she had created for the occasion.

"O Gracious God,

O Gracious Goddess,

Cast upon Sophie's soul a light of protection.

Give her warmth, clarity and a sense of direction. May her new path be virtuous and filled with love, Given opportunities and challenges to rise above.

Bless her new life with many a child,

A family renowned, that to all is beguiled.

O Gracious God,

O Gracious Goddess,

I commit to the earth these trinkets of hers.

Listen to my plea.

So mote it be!"

Jane cast the dirt into the hole as she finished the chant. Then she pushed the pile of dug earth into it and pressed it flat. Tears escaped her closed eyes as she sat in quiet contemplation, reflecting on Sophie's life and the good times they had spent together. Five minutes had past when she opened her eyes and sighed. She took the pentagram that hung around her neck and kissed it to comfort herself, but she was strong. She would heal and carry on. Sophie would be with her every step of the way.

Everyone had someone looking over them.

She gathered her belongings and packed them back in the bags. She retrieved the final candle from the altar table, extinguished the flame between two wet fingers, and took one last look at the black locust. The face in the tree still searched for a way out.

"I'll be seeing you, Father," she said under her breath as she turned towards the tunnel that would take her back to the path.

She rose to her feet. The sun directly above her was bright, and she shielded her eyes, which were sore from the day's roller coaster of emotions. She thought she couldn't possibly shed another tear. However, as she stood there, shielding her eyes and getting her bearings, a familiar feeling of being watched came over her again.

"This is getting too creepy," she said to herself softly as she looked around.

Following the gravel path, she ran towards the car park, her hair flowing in the breeze, the bags slapping furiously against her hip and upper leg. She looked behind her to see if she'd been followed.

Lunging for the handle on the driver's door, she fumbled for the right key. Her heart racing, she finally got inside and locked the door behind her. Drawing deep breaths to calm herself, she turned the key in the ignition. Blue Belle rattled to life as the player cued the next song: *Love Will Tear Us Apart*. The haunting melody and sometimes eerily grey lyrics sung by Ian Curtis a month before his own death seemed unusually upbeat yet apt for the moment, although Jane's mind was elsewhere. She sped off towards Delta Road.

∞

I waited until Jane was out of sight from my vantage point high in the She-Oak. I knew where she was going. That is my purpose—to know her whereabouts, to look over her, and to protect her as I've done since she was born. I pushed forward, spreading my wings to catch the closest updraft, which lifted me high above the trees of Freycinet and followed the little blue Beetle back to Avalon.